Sapphires in the Rubble

& *A Collection of Vignettes*

J.L. Caban

ISBN: 979-8-9869855-0-3

Rare Jewels Literary Works

Dedication

For my father, Jose Luis "Joe" Caban, III

Whom I know is looking down upon me from heaven, forever my guide in this convoluted world.

For my youngest son, Julian Lincoln Caban

Through his eyes I see the brightest of stars. Reach for them, my baby boy… don't stop until you have taken hold of them all.

For my wife, Cecilia Cruz

Thank you for being an amazing wife and mother to our boy. Also, thank you for your twenty years of Service as a first responder, especially during the 9/11 attacks… the city of New York owes to you its incalculable gratitude.

For my brother, Ivan Caban

Thank you for your Service as a soldier in the United States Army, securing our way of life, so that we may be free in our pursuit of happiness.

CONTENTS

NOTE FROM THE AUTHOR

This novelist believes, without a single shadow of doubt, that one inordinately crucial piece of information needs to be made abundantly clear, lest someone believe a thing to be true that is, by every and all means, not. Put into simpler terms, this entire work, *Sapphires in the Rubble*, is completely fictitious in nature, a fabrication of the imagination, a libretto for the daydreaming mind; and, if you pardon and allow just one more bit of elucidation for the layman: there are no parts of this diegesis that contain any concrete facts… not really, not as a whole. That being said, let us take a small step back (or perhaps a mighty redound, depending on one's particular retreating stride), to delve into the not-so-simpler terms of the thing: the tale in which you are about to embark is not *entirely* false. There are segments of the story that, I am certain, bear *some* truth; that is to say – analogous to the axiom, 'even a broken clock is right twice a day' – surely these scenarios in which your frontal lobe will momentarily make acquaintance happened to someone, somewhere, at some point in time! Furthermore, when and if these events did, in fact, occur, they have now been conveniently and thoughtfully mixed and mashed into this modest little novel before you; therefore, as a consequence of this action of coalescence, would be quite unrecognizable and indistinguishable, even to the subjects of which these occurrences transpired, you see. Are you thoroughly confused, yet? If so, dear reader, think of it as you would a delicious smoothie, wherein you have, perhaps, a banana or two, some berries, maybe throw in a bit of kale or spinach, topped off with a dollop of peanut butter… you depress the 'on' button to allow the amalgamation to meld into the delightfully healthy liquid that you will unquestionably savor; but – henceforth driving home the crux - it is no longer simply just a banana or just a handful of kale… it is now a fusion of several things all blended into one. *That* is precisely what makes up '*Sapphires*'… a collection of moments and ideas that have been commixed to create that lovely fruity beverage provided in my analogy above; except, I must warn you, sir or madame, there is somewhat of a bitter tang to *this* particular potation, here and there… more akin to a concoction of sour cream, blue cheese, with a punch (yes, punch… as opposed to the more palatable pinch) of cayenne pepper. Not quite the delightfully flavorful libation described in the former illustration, I'm sorry to say.

In '*Sapphires in the Rubble*,' the reader will accompany our protagonist, James Cardona, on his journey from a child to a young man, eventually witnessing his becoming a member of a Police Department located in New York. James allows you to experience all of that which leads him to the point of this momentous, life altering decision, including his father's incessant inveighing of the very idea, which weighs heavily on his thought process and decision making, as well as his heart and soul; the reasons for which will be revealed in his tale. All of the *Job's* twists, turns, ups, and downs – and how Officer Cardona deals with it all - will be explored, giving one a glimpse into the involute… sometimes even serpentine… world of the Police Department, whose men and women are tasked each and every day with keeping the citizens of New York safe from those that wish to cause nothing but harm and destruction. In the end, with any good fortune, the reader will emerge on the other side of this allegory slightly more enlightened to the plights of all the Officers out there that risk life and limb, day in and day out… in the dealings with not only the average citizen, but the grueling hardships of the inner workings of their particular *cosa nostra* – a concept most of us simply never bother to consider, the very thing that Mr. Cardona will exploit in his forthcoming testimony. On the other hand, there is a more than perfervid potentiality that you may simply reach the conclusion of the yarn owning little more knowledge as was had at the commencement of the confounded thing; possessing confusion equivalent to that of whence the journey began; this time, however, with raised questions, wishing – demanding - to be answered… questions that would never have been conjectured had one been deprived of James' journey (*'seek and ye shall find; ask, and it shall be answered'* and all of that sort of thing).

At the conclusion of *'Sapphires in the Rubble,'* I have gratuitously thrown in, as it were, a few short stories of which I affectionately call *'Vignettes;'* their brief synopses I shall provide to you *tout de suite*. The first of these little anecdotes, entitled *'Obsessions and Crossroads'* – a tale which actually features two characters who made their inaugural appearance in my previous book, *'Butterflies in Production; Five Short Stories,'* Jasper and Greta – will explore the intricacies of a relationship that has unfortunately reached its nadir, in contention with a thing that, much like Socrates' Cave of illusion – so eloquently presented Plato - no more real than the shadows on a wall, but seemingly so attainably realistic that Jasper cannot resist in pursuing this new flame. In the first installment (just to provide thee with a bit of context), these two star crossed lovers, so it goes, make their acquaintance in a bar in which Greta is the server and Jasper the patron; their meeting being somewhat a saving grace for the young man, having experienced bouts of depression and thoughts of taking his life. In this sequel of sorts, we now find the two at odds, separated from one another, Jasper now a modestly successful novelist, having developed a fancy for another woman, an international singing sensation, whom he wishes, most desperately, to court, but is hesitant to take the plunge, so the saying goes. Where will Jasper's heart take him? Will he choose love or desire? One shall only discover these answers subsequent to one's continuing to read on! The second narrative is a play, featuring a young man, Jonathan, who has committed the atrocity of infidelity against his partner, Eleanor… a venial sin that leads to one of cardinal proportions, choosing to take his life as a means of terminating his anguish; the twist here being that he has, apparently, undergone this 'process' of death (due to his perpetually inauspicious conclusion concerning one of the iniquities) on several occasions. How in the world is this possible? the reader might inquire. It is the Afterlife, you see, which grants him numerous opportunities to make amends, to set things right, to atone for his actions. The reader shall bear witness to one of these loops in time in '*It All Happens Below Heaven.*' The Third of the vignettes, '*The Librarian; from the Diary of Miss Leah Elisabeth,*' is a poem of the unorthodox variety – free verse I believe it is officially labeled – wherein one will espy a diary entry penned in the year 1964 by a young, emotionally and physically distraught young girl of twelve, who happens upon a library, and, in it, a Librarian who captures the child's mind and spirit, transporting the young maiden to a world far and away from her doleful existence. This particular piece is somewhat unique in that it was co-written and inspired by my mother, Lisa Calladine, and I wanted very much to share its powerfully heartfelt message of how one person, like the supporting protagonist, the Librarian, can change a person's outlook on life… how mightily a human can turn the tide of emotions within another being's world. With any great fortuity, there is such a soul in all of our lives, especially for those who find themselves spiritually destitute, wanting nothing more than hope for something better… something more. Finally, the last of the installments, '*An Excerpt from an Untitled Work; The Woodlawn Incident Chapter*,' is precisely as the title suggests, a slice of a larger pie, as it were, whereabout this author serves to you but an appetizer in contrast to the larger work in progress; which, in a proverbial nutshell, flirts with the apocalyptic future, imagining a world – tattered and torn, obliterated by pestilence and disease – wherein the police, of what was once the United States of America (now a rogue, ragtag independent entity), roam the wastelands to serve and protect… that is, for the right price. The particular segment provided to you in this excerpt focuses on one of the established settlements, Woodlawn, having had a singularly important individual removed without permission or authority, under the noses of their would-be protectors, a thing which must now be met with the most severe of consequences; if not expeditiously dealt with would, most assuredly, lead to the breakdown of an already convoluted, prophetic society.

It was a pleasure, my dearest friends in the bond of creative writing and reading, to scribe these stories for you; therefore, I wish only that you enjoy reading them half as much. The world can be a lonely and cruel place; but, with creativity – whether it be the written word, an exquisite painting, or a wonderfully performed melody – we find, with any hope, an outlet, an escape, from the madness of reality… if only but for a shimmering evanescent moment in time. And for the dreamers of the world, never cease to stretch as far as your heart's desire… listen not to the naysaying little voice that urges you to capitulate to the enemy of expressiveness… to pack it in… to throw in the towel… &c; instead, give it all you've got! Scribe, blot, blow that horn! If you love a thing, do it until you reach its equivalent of the tallest mountain; and, when you have done with that, find an even taller one, and have at it once more. Until we meet again, lover of the written word, be well and enjoy my '*Sapphires in the Rubble & A Collection of Vignettes.*'

"It was the best of times, it was the worst of times, it was the age of wisdom, it was the age of foolishness, it was the epoch of belief, it was the epoch of incredulity, it was the season of Light, it was the season of Darkness, it was the spring of hope, it was the winter of despair..."

-   A Tale of Two Cities, Charles Dickens

I

There's some shit I need to get off my chest – some things that you all need to know about before I get to where I'm going, because once I get there, I ain't never going to talk about it again… ever – and I'm pretty damn sure a lot of people aren't going to like all the stuff I'm going to share. What I mean is, if you're asking me to be more specific, the organization that hired me – the ones whom I've been employed by for a little over twenty years – are going to have a serious hemorrhage (perhaps two) concerning the story about to be divulged. The thing of it is, they – *the Job* – don't like it too hot when one of their own spills their proverbial guts all over the goddamn place; airing one's dirty bloomers for all to bear witness, 'tis not a sight pleasing to the powers that be and all of that shit; which, to be honest, I sort of understand. I mean, if *the Job* knew a bunch of crumby stuff about me – stuff that I didn't want the rest of the entire miserable world to know, I sure as shit would be a little put out myself. But a guy has to be honest when he's telling a particular story… he shouldn't be censored, leaving a ton of details out (the best, goriest details), or else how could that guy expect anyone to take him seriously? His entire audience would probably end up walking clear out of the room, right in the middle of the spiel if that were the case, if he were going to start out by being dishonest, I mean. So let's just understand the following point straight right out of the ol' gate: I'm a miserable, no good, low-life, piece of dog crap for spilling the ol' beans about what *really* goes on in the Police Department, right here in the great big city that never slumbers.

For those of you that live under a rock and don't know, New York is a major city of about 8.8 million people; consisting of about 468,484 square miles; inhabited by approximately thirty-two percent White, twenty-six percent Hispanic or Latino, twenty-two percent African American, thirteen percent Asian, and, finally, around four percent American Indian/Alaska Native; and its Police Force – one of the largest in the world (rivaling that of a small army in some countries, totaling around forty thousand – give or take) overseeing it all; and, for as long as I can recall, it has not been the most pleasant of relationships between the beloved Department and their antagonists, *the mob* as it was affectionately coined by the Caesars of the Empire. I mean, look, there are tons of people who love the *Boys in Blue*; but, there are just as many who wish we'd all die a fiery death… and this particular group of people, the latter, are inordinately good at promoting that feeling. I'm getting ahead of myself, though. The point of this whole rant is to tell you about a bunch of stuff that happened to me while I was employed by the mighty enforcers of the law – about all the crap I went through and all, during the twenty years of my life that I will never get back.

To understand, completely, the tale that I'm about to tell, you kind of have to know a little about me and my experiences growing up prior to linking up with the men and women of the Department. What I mean to say is, perhaps we should become a little more acquainted before I spill the entirety of my internal organs all over the cutting board… maybe chew the ol' fat for a little bit before diving into bed and pillow talking about all of my personal particulars is the point I'm driving at. I was born and raised in the aforementioned City; the aggregate of my forty-one years as a subject of the rules and laws of the most famous metropolis in the entire world; at least, the most infamous, to be sure. Back in the days of my youth, things seemed so simple. Bad guys were bad guys, good guys – if there exists such a thing – were true to their kind, and the police? well, they were superior, above us all. I mean, sure they had their detractors: anti-cop and anti-establishment organizations, gangs, and low-life freebooters to name a few; but, they were all outcasts who weren't taken seriously by any red-blooded American, not in those days. The detractors were a nuisance who had to be *dealt with*, and the good, law-abiding citizens wouldn't be caught dead supporting or associating with these kinds of cretins. Not to mention, if you recall (those of you out there old enough to do so), there did not exist any kind of pesky social media outlets to keep the flame of that sort of a movement alive; just regular ol' newspapers and magazines, which only remained current until being replaced by the next morning's chronicle, or the next big, juicy *page six* story… what with people's less-than-scant attention spans and all. Man, social media today can really keep an idea alive, can't it? You get a bunch of people together on '*Face*' this and '*Gram*' that… well, you can certainly do some damage to an ideology is all I'm saying.

Anyway, I got into a whole boatload of trouble when I was younger, and had plenty of run-ins with the ol' *Flatfoots* (a moniker given, by the way, to the old *beat* cops who would walk foot patrols for their entire shifts; those poor fellas would trek the streets for so long, they'd develop these flattened out feet, hence the aforesaid nickname. Seriously, that's a real thing… you can totally fact check it). There was this one time I was perambulating along the tracks of the Amtrak train… as a matter of fact, now that I mentioned it, I was actually with my father that day (he grew up a bit of a rebel in his time – being raised in a real seedy area and all, a very unsavory part of the city). He thought it'd be a great idea to walk along the tracks, as a short-cut, to get across to where we lived, seeing as how it shaved a good ten minutes off the trip. "Pop, why are we walking along the tracks? Isn't it kind of dangerous?" I inquired, looking up at him as though he were the largest of mountains, at that particular moment in time towering above me; although, in actuality, he stood barely at five feet tall. I was about ten years old at the time, and – although filled with dubiety about the decision making of my creator on Earth at that precise juncture in time – continued to follow him unhesitatingly.

"Is it dangerous? Life is dangerous, kiddo." he replied, without looking down at me. His focus, undoubtedly, on the impending arrival of the large, metal conveyance, with the prospect of its bearing down upon us at speeds upwards of one hundred miles an hour, to be sure.

"Then why don't we just take the foot bridge? Isn't it safer?" I rebutted, whilst simultaneously focusing my attention down upon the rocks that were spread all about between and around the tracks, bending over to pick one up.

"Jimmy, don't be stopping in the middle of tracks;" my father scolded, frantically snapping his fingers to gain my compliance, "this isn't the time and place to be stopping and smelling the flowers… and, for your information, this way shaves about a good ten minutes off of the arrival time. And it's the scenic route… you get to enjoy the ambiance." My father had this unique way of putting things that, although not necessarily incorrect, never quite hit the ol' nail squarely on the head; I referred to these linguistic quirks of my father's as "Pop-*isms*," sort of like Yogi-*isms*… you know, as in Yogi Berra, the famous New York Yankees baseball player who always worded things in a way that made you scratch the hell out of your head. Look him up when you get a chance, the Yankee guy…

it's pretty funny stuff.

"Sorry, I just wanted to get one of these rocks. Why are there so many of them here? Won't they mess up the train?" I inquired, taking the retrieved stone and holding it close to my face, as though I were examining a rare, precious, find.

"It's to hold the wooden cross ties in place;" he answered abruptly, annoyed at having not only to prevent the tragic, and most painful, demise of his son, as well as himself, but also to provide, I'm sure, the most cumbersome of explanations of railroad anatomy, "which in turn," he continued, "hold the rails in place. Keep moving, Jimmy… I don't know why I have to keep telling you that."

I accepted this explanation as gospel for three simple facts: first, in those days of yore, a parent's explanation to any given inquiry was always more than sufficient, not needing to be seconded by any sources of alternate reference; second, not having the intelligence devices possessed by the brats of today's generation, there was no way to contradict and fact check every goddamn statement made out of a human being's mouth, let alone my father's who would, most certainly, have sent me into a high altitudinal orbit had I the balls to attempt such a thing; and third, he – my dear old dad – watched a helluvalot of factually based television… there wasn't a thing on this entire planet in which he didn't have some odd bit of knowledge. This all being stated, these especially indisputable facts did not stop me from maintaining my original opinion that, perhaps, the bridge would've been the safest method of travel. "Pop, I wouldn't have to keep moving if we had taken the bri-"

"Don't piss me off, James…" he interrupted. "I just finished explaining that crap to you. Right now, you need to pay attention to what we're doing. It's not *talkie-talkie* time, it's *walkie-walkie* time. Stop going off on tangents and pay attention to the situation at hand." he concluded, with a countenance indicating an imminent lashing-out of epic proportions. That's one thing you never wanted to do, you never wanted to get my dad to *that* point, the point of no return… the point wherein one moment you were mouthing off, the next instance your face was on the opposite side of the room. It's like being in the Situation Room at the goddamn White House or some crazy thing like that, turning the ol' keys and pressing the *red button*, launching a few hundred nuclear missiles all over the goddamn place; there's no coming back from it. As I mentioned, he was minuscule in size, but not in heart. As vertically challenged individuals go, my father was of the upper echelon in physical fitness; he had a bit of mass to him is what I mean to say. He was always working out in the gym or playing some sport to keep himself looking like a kind of pit bull or really buffed chihuahua. Not a bad looking fella overall, if you pinned me down and threatened to never let me up unless I divulged that bit of information. In addition to his muscular physique, he was always stylishly dressed, well groomed, and had one of those killer, especially sociable, personalities… always getting on with members of his community and all; like, he could've run for mayor; or, at the very least, become the tenant president at our apartment building or some insanity like that. He really could've.

"I'm not trying to piss you off, Pop. I'm just saying, it would've been easier to just go across the bridge." I carefully replied, looking up at him, gauging just exactly how much slack I had to work with. Seeing no real threat of annihilation, I continued. "When is the train coming? is it coming soon?" I asked, glancing at our rear, extending my neck to espy any oncoming iron horses barreling down upon our position.

"These Amtrak trains come about every hour or so… the next one shouldn't be here for another five minutes. That gives us plenty of time to get to that cutout in the fence over there; that is, if you don't continue your dilly dallying." said he, pointing to a hole in the previously mentioned fence, about a hundred or so feet away, separating decent law abiding citizens from criminalistic encroachers. "And anyway, see the rails there?" he continued, pointing down at the metal railing of the tracks, "You'll hear a ping if there's a train close by. The 'pinging' sound gets closer and closer as the train gets closer and closer. It'll sound like this: *ping…*" Here he paused to indicate a lapse of time. "*Ping… ping…*" he added after a few seconds. "*Ping… ping… ping!*" he crescendoed after a few seconds more. "That's when you know you better get your ass moving; after that *ping, ping, ping.*"

I don't know why, but that bit of information fascinated me. I was amazed at his in-depth, locomotive certitude, an enlightenment that was, for certain, attributed to some kind of first hand experience, perhaps some near death escapade during the time of his youth; therefore, I made an inquest to learn what was sure to be a nail-biting, edge of your seat, adventurous tale. "Did you and your friends almost get plowed by an oncoming train, Pop? Did you guys have to dive out of the way to save your lives? Did you push one of your friends out of the way at the very last moment to save his life? Were you the hero? and did they carry you on their shoulders and shout your name?"

"Huh? What in the hell are you talking about? Hero? Save

lives? No, I saw it on an episode of Raw Hide."

We finally reached our destination, seemingly avoiding peril, having to climb up, initially, from the area wherein the tracks lay, through the aforementioned hole in the fence (where, no doubt, other outlaws committing similar felonious acts once traversed), and onto the public street, when suddenly we were unceremoniously halted by the long arm of the law (literally, as the Officer that stopped us extended his pretty lengthy arm, taking hold of the collar on my t-shirt with a vice-like, Herculean, grip). "Well, well, well… what do we have here? a couple of little field mice, huh?" said the Officer, Officer McNamara - according to the name tag that rested about half an inch below his shield - a larger than life figure, standing at, what seemed to be, ten feet tall (but in all reality about six foot three). "Just what in the hell do you two think you're doing on the train tracks? Apparently the *no trespassing* sign doesn't apply to you little brown boys, eh?" He was referring to, unbeknownst to me at the time, our ethnicity… we being of Hispanic descent; although, to be honest, as a naïve young bairn, I could never understand how people had the ability to distinguish that sort of a thing… our race… due to the distinctly perceptible fact that our epidermis was more akin to that of a typical European Spaniard - as opposed to the Caribbean variety - being on the lighter shade of the ol' spectrum.

More importantly, for me at that very moment, was the fact that, as I remained in the clutches of the exceptionally colossal Irish patrolman, my father – my protector – continued walking on ahead in a disturbingly plodding manner, away from the crime scene, as though he had not a clue as to the current situation at hand… something that the Officer, apparently, was very well aware of. "Hey, little man!" he addressed my birth-giver, "Where do you think you're going? Don't let me have to chase you… if I run, you and your tiny friend here get hurt, see?"

My dad, for a brief moment, seemed not to have any regard for the Officer's foreboding, continuing to take a few additional steps toward freedom; however, he ultimately stopped – though still not turning to face my captor and I – most likely, I can only assume (and much to my dismay), considering all of his options, including that of a clean getaway. Finally, turning around slowly and facing Officer McNamara and I, he uttered, head held high, with all the cockiness of the great Emperor Napoleon Bonaparte, "I'm right here, I ain't going nowhere, man."

"Doesn't look that way to me, big guy… looks to me you're trying to beat it out of Dodge, leaving your buddy here behind."

"I'm not his *'buddy;'*" I interjected, having heard the fallacious reference once too many times. "I'm his *son*… he's my *dad*."

"Oh! is that so?" McNamara said, now ogling my father with a look of utter disdain. "Is that right? *dad*? This here is your son?"

"That's right." answered my father, knowing exactly where Sherlock Holmes' good ol' brain was headed. He, my dad, knew that the Officer was going to make a federal case about him not staying put after me getting pinched by the fuzz and all, the singularly despondent expression of this notion spread across Pop's countenance like a deflated balloon the morning after a child's birthday party.

"So let me get this straight, and correct me if I'm wrong,

you was just gonna up and leave your little bundle of joy over here to fend for himself? Even knowing that I yoked him up and he had no way out, you was just gonna go on your merry way? Does that about sum it up?" There being no response from the patriarch of the Cardona clan, McNamara continued his homily, "Listen, *Pops*, far be it from me to question your apparently impeccable parenting skills, but you may wanna keep *junior* over here away from train tracks and things like that. While you're at it, seeing as how you obviously missed *parenting 101*, you may want to stay away from walking on highways, airport runways, over snake pits and... well, I'm sure you get the idea. Is that clear? *papa bear*? Do I have to bring you in or anything like that? or do you think you can manage to handle this on your own?"

"I hear you. I got it, Officer." answered James Cardona, Sr., realizing all too well that this slap on the proverbial wrist was, incidentally, an act of mercy, having experienced vastly different outcomes not too many moons ago, during the years of his juvenile delinquency.

Not to veer too far off the point, but a brief synopsis concerning the aforementioned James Cardona, *the elder*, and the men charged with keeping the citizens of our great City safe, comes to the ol' noggin... once upon a time (about five or ten years prior to the day of the train track fiasco), he ran with some pretty shady characters of the felonious sort. There was this particular time that comes to mind, when James Senior was dealing a particular illegal pharmaceutical to an individual in need of his product, when members of the 53rd Precinct made an unexpected appearance at the point of exchange. With the speed of Iris flying out of Olympia to join the Titans, my dear old dad made a run for it, bolting down the street, zig zagging in betwixt pedestrians and dodging oncoming cars to flee the scene, all the while the *Coppers* in close pursuit. Well, as you can probably imagine, this didn't bode too well for the future paterfamilias of yours truly; as the fugitive, whose spermatozoa contributed to my existence, was quickly apprehended halfway into an alleyway that excluded any on-lookers from bearing witness to the punitive events forthcoming.

"You like to run, huh? you little fucking *spic!*" exclaimed the gentleman garbed in a uniform azure and indigo in color, responsible for Mr. Cardona's seizure.

"You got it, Officer… you got it!" my father answered, in an attempt to conciliate the now infuriated Officer: although he knew, without any doubt whatsoever, this white flag plea for mercy was a futile endeavor. The unwritten rule – you must comprehend, my dear reader - understood by both parties (the criminals and lawmen, alike), was that if you had the unmitigated audacity to make any member of the constabulary break into an advanced trot, you had better make certain you weren't caught, because the fare – the going rate, as it were - for an out of breath cop was a cudgeling of the worst magnitude; and, after the thrashing, you were henceforth taken to the *House*, where the gaoler provided you with several surplus lumps and bruises to the entirety of your body. That's just the way it was; and, it was also well known that the alternative to the *beat down* was going through *the System* and ending up with a record that would, with no uncertainty, follow you to the end of time; so, my dad, prostrate upon the pavement, with Officer Smith's knee squarely upon his back, readily braced for his licking in that alley.

"You think you were actually gonna get away from us, you

little punk?" shouted the enraged and out of breath Officer.

"I'm sorry… I'm sorry, sir!" pleaded my dad, not necessarily wanting the looming beat down, but preferring prison much less.

"You're sorry, huh? Yeah, I'll bet you're *real* sorry… sorry you got *caught*!" was the Officer's reply, pushing the face of a young Mr. Cardona into the filth of the city pavement.

"I didn't mean to… I didn't want… look, I'm just real sorry, sir! I didn't mean to make you upset… I was just scared!" my father adduced, his muffled voice barely audible due to his entire face being planted into the concrete.

"Trust me, you need to be scared… *real* scared!" the Officer said, turning the prisoner over onto his back, raising his substantially sized, closed fist into the air, poised to begin the dreaded corporal battering, before offering the dreadful ultimatum, "Listen, you little nigger, spic, punk… you got two choices: you either take your beating like a man or your ass comes with me to the slammer. Up to you, little shit… choose before I make the choice *for* you."

"The beating… the beating, sir." my father chose, a deluge of tears now flowing from his ducts.

Taking James Cardona, Senior by the lapels of his white, guayabera style shirt, propping him up the way a child would a stuffed animal, the Officer began issuing a surfeit amount of back and forth slaps across the face with brute force until tiny trickles of blood began cascading down from his nostrils, consciousness commencing to escape him; all the while the Police Officer spewing (in addition to choice racial epithets) a riot act of sorts about how never, ever, to make a Cop utilize his legs for the purposes of a pursuit again.

It was due to this particularly memorable event in his life that James Cardona, my old man, humbled himself before Police Officer McNamara that day, now returning to the present time, near the Amtrak train tracks. I'm sure his gruesome encounter with Officer Smith weighed heavily in his decision not to make any regrettable choices by leaving me behind to fend for myself. I can almost guarantee that. And for what it's worth, I sure am glad Pop decided not to beat it the hell out of there, leaving me holding the proverbial bag by myself and all… because, if you happened not to know this particular little fun fact, the corroborator of a crime – innocent or not - usually makes for a great consolation prize for a scorned enforcer of the law. Just saying.

II

I had a few more run-ins with the *protectors of life and property* a few years later that I want to tell you about before I get to the ol' meat and potatoes of my story, if the reader will so patiently indulge me. One of those particular moments being when I was about thirteen or fourteen years of age, around the time I was dating my very first girlfriend, Ellison… a cute little number of about thirteen years with dirty blonde hair and these really beautiful blue eyes – a kind of blue that seemed to retain the ability to hypnotize anyone, like the tepid waters of the Caribbean that ever so gently kiss the white sands of some uninhabited island, when you looked directly into them and all of that sort of jazz. Really captivating, if you want to know the truth. Anyway, I was dating Ellison around that time and she had this insane argument with her parents… something about not letting her go to a Madonna concert (Madonna was on tour – the *Like a Virgin* tour or some craziness like that – and just happened to be making a grand appearance at Radio City Music Hall; an event which, if you could not attend, was of such fantastical import that you were supposed to head directly on over to the tallest building you could find and throw yourself right off the penthouse. Real weighty stuff), so she – Ellison – figured she'd run away from home and skip on over to my place (my dad's place) for some good old fashioned harboring. The thing of it was, my dad wasn't too keen on the idea of that sort of thing… providing shelter for refugees and all; ergo, at the threshold of the apartment door, her entire body drenched from the tempestuous storm currently raging outside, I had to sort of tell her to get lost… to scram, you know what I mean?

"I can't let you stay here, Elli." I called her Elli for short, on account of the fact that her name was Ellison, a name in which she wasn't insanely fond of, for whatever reason. I thought it was a pretty cute name, if you asked me… she just didn't care for it, so everyone just called her Elli to avoid being castigated and whatnot. "My dad would *kill* me if I let you… seriously, he'd put his hands around my throat and squeeze the life outta me if I did… that's no joke, you *know* him, Elli… you *know* he would."

"What am I supposed to do, James? Am I supposed to sleep out on the street? Is *that* what you want? you want your girlfriend to sleep out on the *street*?" she lamented, with the worst kind of crocodile tears. She possessed the most God-awful cry one would ever have the great misfortune to see or hear. I mean, I don't know what kind of sobs *you're* accustomed to dealing with; but, I'm willing to bet all the loose change and gnurr in my pocket that this abhorrent, thespian-like, Shakespearean Tragedy-esque performance topped them all. Ellison had this kind of weeping face that utilized all of the muscles that make up the human facial structure, somehow arranging them in such a way that portrayed an indescribable agony of the worst kind. It's as if her body were being torn to shreds by some kind of butcher's meat grinder, her ghastly countenance expressing every twist and turn of the machine as it mangles her body apart into a million and one pieces. Not a pleasant sight… not at all.

"No, of course that's not what I *want*." I reasoned. "It's just that… jeez, you know my dad… he's really a hard-ass about people coming over in *general*, let alone *hiding out* here. I don't know, Elli, I think -"

"I can *NOT* believe you are just gonna… you *do* know that it's raining outside, don't you? I mean, it's fucking *raining* outside! You're really not gonna let me stay here? What kind of a boyfriend *are* you, anyway?!" Her voice echoed throughout the entire hallway of the apartment building, reaching, I'm certain, the ears of the probing neighbors throughout the floor… neighbors that were exceptionally meteoric in bringing to my dad's attention the goings on of my current bailiwick.

"I'm really sorry… I *really* am! It's just -"

"Yeah, yeah, yeah… your daddy won't like it… got it. Jesus, what a fucking little daddy's boy you are! You know what? just forget it! I'll figure it out by myself. Fucking useless, I swear!" she pouted, folding her arms across her chest and stomping her foot to the ground in child-like, temper tantrum fashion.

"Listen… Elli, would you *listen* to me for a goddamn minute, please?" I pleaded in between her incessant bawling before going on. "I have a plan." Now, against my better judgment, the ol' lightbulb flashed above my head, giving me the bright idea of bringing my loving girlfriend to my best friend Juan's place. This aforementioned best friend and I lived in the same building (he just seven floors below); a suggestion that she gladly, with uncommonly little hesitation, accepted. To be honest, I wasn't too hot about the proposed scheme because Juan was somewhat of a ladies man of sorts… as a matter of fact, his goddamn nickname throughout the neighborhood was *Don* Juan, the epithet given to the man who happened to make a living out of sexually slaying all types of women (although, for those of you that don't know, the actual character in the poem *Don Juan*, written by a fella named Lord Byron, was about a guy who is, incidentally, the one that *gets* easily seduced by woman, no matter how hard he so desperately tries to stop the madness… seriously, no matter how hard he tries, females can't keep their filthy hands off of him); which, come to think of it, ironically, was the potential situation at hand with Ellison. What I'm getting at is, Elli was sort of a nymphomaniac and it was *she* that I really worried about. I mean, Juan was a pretty decent looking guy – *more* than decent, actually – if I'm being completely transparent. And for the record, I'm not a homosexual, by any means; but, if I *were* going to hop on over to that side of the axiomatic fence, hypothetically speaking, I wouldn't mind going a few rounds with good ol' Juan… again, if I'm being entirely forthcoming.

She and I zipped on down the staircase to his floor and rapped on the entrance to his apartment until he opened it, shirtless, abdominal muscles protruding ubiquitously to the apparent pleasure of my better half, her eyes extruding from their accursed sockets, with only a pair of especially short boxer briefs to complete the ensemble. "Hey, guys… what's up?" he stated, thereafter grabbing from the chair beside his door, and thankfully adorning, a very form fitting wife-beater style T-shirt.

"Ask your *best friend*." she uttered in a, I must say, sardonically haughty manner, to which his eyes shifted in my direction awaiting, no doubt in suspense, for my riposte.

"Well," I began, shooting, initially, a look toward my loving girlfriend before providing the reply to Juan's state of quandary, "*material girl* over here…" (material girl referring to the hit song by the musical artist whom Ellison Vanetti was supposed to have seen on that particular night, which was the catalyst of the conundrum at hand… I thought that was pretty clever, incorporating Madonna's moniker to Ellie, if I do say so myself) "… decided to run away from home because her parents didn't let her go to a concert; she thought the best thing to do was to run away to *my* house, knowing full well that my dad would have about three conniptions if he found her there."

"I mean, most guys would have the decency to let me at least dry off before sending me away… I'm pretty sure *most* guys would do that." Ellison – still possessing quite a bit of moisture about herself - exclaimed, handing to me a look that would make the emperor of the underworld blush.

"Yeah, girl, you are dripping wet over here… come in, let's get you all dried up before you catch cold." he said, taking her into his arms and leading her into the apartment. Man, he really was smooth. I mean, I hadn't even thought of that, her still being a sopping mess. I could honestly see why this guy was a hit with the signorinas.

"Thank you! Ugh, what a gentleman you are." Ellison commented, laying it on insanely thick by settling into his arms as they headed towards the living room, he making a sprightly detour to the linen closet for a towel, before she finished her verbal assault upon me: "A *real* man."

"Listen, why don't we do this;" Juan began, "why don't we just keep Ellison here with me. My parents are out of town for a couple of weeks. She can totally stay here and hide out until things cool down with her folks. I think that'd be a great idea… what do you think Elli?" he concluded, as the lecher gently patted her dry with the towel. Much to my great chagrin, she responded to the idea by diving into his chest, wrapping her arms around his insanely muscular body, and planting the largest, juiciest kiss upon his mien. I have to share with you my particular sentiment to this ruination of the relationship between Ms. Vanetti and myself: the whole confounded scene of her being dried off, coupled with the indescribably disturbing sight of the two of them intertwined in each other's arms, like a deuced laugenbrezel, was an extremely unsettling business, just in case any previously stated implication wasn't made abundantly clear to you.

As they stood there, right in front of me, entangled in what seemed an extremely amatory embrace, I cleared my throat to remind the two philanderers that I was still in the room; they, in turn, responded by quickly disentangling themselves from one another, exchanging the most vile and discomfiting smile, both subsequently fixing their eyes downward towards the floor. I broke the proverbial iceberg, simultaneously attempting to abort this ridiculous plan (*my* plan) of my fair maiden stowing away with this Lothario, saying to Ellison, "Listen, maybe you should just go back home and take the punishment. I mean, you already missed the concert, so why don't you just go home, take the punishment and let things cool off. I think it'd be a thousand times worse this way – you staying here. I really do. You should just go home, take a nice hot shower, jump into bed and just let things cool off. It's the best thing… it really is."

"You don't get it, *do* you, James? You just do *not* get it!" answered Ellison, now draping herself onto the sofa, making herself extremely comfortable.

"What? what don't I get? Explain it to me Ellie… *Ellison*," I corrected myself, no longer wishing to refer to her nickname, thereby passive-aggressively expressing my unfettered anguish. "Explain to me what exactly I don't get." I was beginning to lose my cool, especially catching a glimpse of good ol' *Don* Juan obnoxiously shaking his perfectly squared head – complete with full eyebrows, sitting above a pair of iridescent brown eyes, aquiline nose, and plump, pouty, lips – gazing disapprovingly at me... at what I *didn't* get... as if *he* actually fathomed what in God's name she was rambling on about.

"You don't get that I won't go back. I *can't* go back. It's not just about the stupid concert -"

"Then what? what *is* it about? Please tell me, I'd love to know!"

"Hello! that's what I'm trying to tell you! It's *everything*! Every single thing!"

"What do you mean? '*everything*?'"

"Exactly what it sounds like... *everything.* They try to control every part of my life; I can't do anything without hearing their mouths about it. They don't let me go anywhere, do anything... it's like fucking prison!" she exclaimed, beginning to literally cry; not the usual crocodile tears, but actual liquid excreting from her ducts.

"It can't be *that* bad... I mean, I know they give you a hard time, but what parent doesn't? What parent isn't a pain in the ass once in awhile?"

"Once in awhile? You just... you know what, James? you *do* realize that they don't even want me seeing *you*, don't you? Yeah, that's right, they don't want me seeing a, how do they put it?

'a brown boy who will probably grow up to be what brown boys usually become… drug dealer? janitor?' Does *that* change your tune a little bit? Well? *does* it?" She was screaming now, and the *Don* began to comfort her by way of another embrace. Damn, he was such a pro at the whole coquettish thing, you really have to give him that.

"Listen, dude," he interjected. "maybe you should just take off… whattaya say there champ? maybe that's a good idea for now. Let her cool down and we can all talk about this another time. That's a good idea, I think."

"Oh, you think so, huh? You think that's a good idea? Well, I think you're trying to move in on my girl… that's what *I* think!" I finally lost my temper, letting that particular locution fly out of my mouth, knowing that not only was I the instigator in this whole wretched affair to begin with, but, more importantly, it played right into his hands. At this point, I was the evil, unsympathetic boyfriend and he was the strapping hero who comes to the rescue of the damsel in distress. Hostile takeover 101.

"I'm… huh?" Juan stammered, in classic, '*who? me?* denial mode.' "Dude, I don't even know what you're saying… what the f -"

"Are you out of your mind, James?" Ellison flew in to provide succor to her new beau, "Why would you say something like that? Juan is only trying to help me… something *you* failed to do!"

"*Really*?!" I exclaimed, my voice now trembling from the fury raging in my chest, my heart racing a million beats per second. "You're *really* gonna defend him over me? I didn't *fail* anything… I already explained a thousand times why I couldn't do it. I told you my dad -"

"For the love of God! I know, I know! your *daddy* will kick your ass… how many times are we gonna hear the same sorry shit? You know what? maybe you *should* just go. I think *Juan* can handle it from here."

"Wow… yeah… okay. Maybe that's best." I said, standing there like a complete moron, the *coup d'etat* now being complete.

"Yeah, it is!" she concluded, burying her face, once again, into his burly chest, this time capping it off with the return of the ghastly phony cry. And with that, I exited *stage left*, with my tail pretty much tucked between my legs like a battered and bruised *beta* who, after making a run at the throne, has lost the battle for supremacy of the pack.

Later on that night, as I lay in my bed, stewing in a huge pot of my inexorable defeat, humiliated by what had transpired earlier on in Juan's apartment, images of God only knows what going on between the two quislings, I heard a thunderous pounding at the front door, the sound of it so dynamic that it resonated throughout my entire bedroom. Before I got a chance to even raise my head off of the bed, I could hear that my dad had made his way down the hallway to answer, followed by the sonorous voices of two members of the Police Department's Detective Squad.

"What's up, bro?" the first of the voices stated. "My name is Detective Warren and this is Detective Mora. We're looking for a girl… Ellison Vanetti… she's missing and we have reason to believe she's here."

"Would you know anything about that, bro?" Detective Mora chimed in. "If she's here, you had better tell us now… we don't wanna have to do things the hard way."

"Ellison? my son's girlfriend?" my dad answered, the sound of his voice extremely perplexed. "You think Ellison is *here*? Why would she be here? it's after ten o'clock in the evening."

"Bro, we're well aware of what time it is; we don't need a time check from you, got it? What we need is for you to tell us the whereabouts of little Miss Vanetti… like I said, we have *strong* reason to believe she's here!" snapped Detective Mora.

Afraid of even batting an eye lash, I continued to eavesdrop, having at this point ejected out of the bed, with my ear practically plastered onto the closed door of my room; the beat of my heart pounding ever so vigorously, I was sure it would be discerned by ol' Dick Tracey and Colombo out there; although, for the time being, a good fifty feet separated us. At some point my older sister, Gracie (whom I will go into more detail about later on – so as not to impinge upon this portion of the account) sneaked into my room – the opening of the door nearly decapitating me - with a countenance expressing a melange of fear, satisfaction, and indignation… frightened that the Police were at the threshold of our home, and thrilled that it was I who was the subject of the cataclysm, feigning outrage when, in fact, she was, I'm most certain, quite pleased at the opportunity to condescend me all to *Avernus*. "Oh my God, Jimmy, what in the hell have you done now?" she exclaimed, her faced scrunched up as if she ingested a few gallons of lemon juice.

"What do you mean, '*what have I done*?' I didn't do any

damned thing?"

"Well you did some *damned* thing because the freaking Police are at our door and they're asking about your little lover girl. What have you gotten yourself into with that little floozy?" Gracie said, with an almost taunting grin across her face, whilst simultaneously shaking her head.

"She isn't a floozy." I started, before making a slight modification to my statement, in light of earlier happenings and all. "Well, she's a floozy *now*, but she wasn't before today."

"Holy crap, what in the world hap -"

"Would you pipe down? I'm trying to hear what in the hell they're saying out there." I exclaimed, once again pressing my ear up against the door to get a load of what was going on with the Detectives and my dad.

"Like I said, Officers -" my father continued, before being verbally muscled in on by one of the sleuths.

"We're *Detectives*, little guy… *not* 'Officers'…" interjected Warren, "and we already heard what you said. What we want is to talk to your son; where is he? is he here? Bring him out here, we need to talk to 'em."

"Don't make this difficult, big man;" added Mora, "if we want, we can just find out if he's home ourselves… we're tryin' to be nice here, see?"

My father's precipitating footsteps could be heard headed in my direction, and – from the mere sound of it – I could tell that they were pretty goddamn apoplectic steps; therefore, I dove onto my bed and grabbed my copy of 'Franny and Zooey,' a book written by my all time favorite author, J.D. Salinger, and feigned as though I were smack dab in the middle of an intense read, Gracie running to the window pretending to take in the view of absolute darkness, the sun having set over three hours antecedent of the events now occurring, as the door flew open with no courteous preamble or knock, forsaking all forms of accepted etiquette in a civilized society upon entering another person's room, I may add. "James! why in the fuck are there Police Officers at my door?"

"I think they're actually *Detectives*, Pop." I uttered, looking up from the book with widened eyes, instantly regretting the correction in vernacular, as this emendation not only was ill timed, but clearly revealed my awareness to the present state of affairs at our front door, thereby negating the false pretense of laying around, nonchalantly reading Salinger.

"Seriously, Jimmy?" instigated Gracie, "I highly doubt Daddy gives a rat's ass about their stupid rank!"

"Seriously, Gracie?" I shot back. "Why are you even in my room right now? pretending to look out the window when, meanwhile, it's pitch black outside." I concluded, receiving only a snarling countenance in return, followed by the protruding of her tongue.

"Don't mess with me, Jimmy… this ain't the time, this ain't the time at all! Why are they here, James? Where is Ellison? Do you know what time of night it is? Do you know what these cops are talking about?" He belted me with this barrage of questions;

however, not waiting around for the answers, grabbed a hold of my arm – pretty damn hard I must say - and lead me down the hallway towards the front door where the inquisitors awaited.

"You know where Ellison Vanetti is? squirt? If you do, you had better come clean, and fast… we don't wanna have to run you down to the station." started Mora, who I could see now was a very thin, older gentleman of about forty years of age, sporting an inordinately large mustache, a medium sized afro-style hairdo, attired in a dark gray suit and tawny colored overcoat.

"She ain't here? is she? But I'll bet my left nut you know *exactly* where she is." Warren added, weighing in on the portlier side, appearing much older than his crony… maybe in his mid-fifties… with hair existing only on the sides and rear of his dome, donning nearly the same outfit as Mora, with the exception of his trench style coat being gray in color.

Hesitating, only briefly, I answered, "No, she's not here." I volunteered no further information, noticing, from my peripheral, Gracie's head poking out from my room and, after offering a quick glance in her direction, beheld her distinctly disapproving leer, I suspect to express her displeasure at my not divulging more unambiguous intelligence in regards to Ellison's whereabouts.

"Well? do you know where she is?" responded a vexed Warren, the plethora of worry lines on his forehead becoming ever more prominent. "Are you gonna seriously make us drag your ass to the precinct? you little shit."

"Listen, tiny fella, why don't ya make it easy on all of us?" interpolated Mora, shaking his head with querulous disapproval.

"We know that you know *very well* where she is… don't make our lives a living hell, would ya, kid?"

I have not a clue as to why, precisely, I didn't just go on ahead and sing, forthwith, like Frank Sinatra at the Sands, divulging all in which I was privy to knowing about the duet, located a mere seven floors below. I just had this sort of natural inclination not to be a stinking rat; but, I suddenly realized that I had absolutely no loyalty to the two turn-coats that were probably going at it like a couple of horny toads; and, knowing precisely how the *Don* operates, he was most incontestably getting his *sexy* on to the tune of '*Don't Disturb this Groove,*' brilliantly performed by *The System*, by the by, right there on his bed, his lava lamp illuminating the room providing, parenthetically, a most sensual milieu for love making. The thought sickened me; therefore, I suddenly squealed like a farm pig in heat. "She's at my friend's… my *ex-friend's*… house, downstairs… apartment 7T." this particular revelation leading to a rather resounding gasp emanating from Gracie (still positioned halfway down the hall), similar to the reaction one offers after a season ending plot twist on some popular as all hell television series.

I'd like to think I held onto that particular bit of information socially acceptable in length, so as not to qualify me as a proverbial *dime dropper…* that the Dicks pulled a few of my teeth, so to speak, in the process of obtaining the esoteric details… before I spilled the beans, even though you and I know that not to be the case. Revenge was my motive. And if we're being completely on the level with one another, then it's safe, I believe, to say that the explicit circumstances at hand (that of the interlopers) should, without question, have absolved me of that especially mortal sin. I'm certain it would have. Anyway, the Detectives showed their approval and appreciation for this shred of intelligence by patting me on the top of my cranium, as if I were an obedient canine who narrowly escaped a *correction*. Just for good measure, Mora added, "Good job, sport… glad we didn't have to run you down to the station and kick the living snot outta you. That wouldn't have been pretty."

Warren provided a little sadistic chuckle, simply following up with, "Oh, yeah, not pretty at all," before they both sauntered off towards the elevator to, with any luck, give the ol' hard business to the swains down below. As for what *exactly* happened, I couldn't tell you… I wasn't there, and I never spoke to the two Benedict Arnolds, Ellison and Juan, ever again. I mean, I saw them once and awhile holding hands and shit like that; but, the lot of us never spoke actual words for the rest of our lives; which is completely fine by me. There's no sense in beating the good ol' dead horse… it serves absolutely no purpose, you know what I'm saying? You just end up looking like a complete psychopath who can't accept the fact that you've been dumped, thrown to the trash like yesterday's Wall Street Journal, and I certainly didn't want that. Would you?

***

A year or two later, on my way home from really painting the ol' town red down in the nightclub district of the city with a bunch of my buddies and a few real interesting females we picked up in one of the establishments, the lot of us ended up jumping on a locomotive - the number Four train - to head on back home. My cohorts and I were all in competition, making a play to be one of the lucky fellas to snag these lovely gifts from the heavens above, the 'XX' chromosomes outnumbering the 'XYs' five to three. It was a real hardcore display of Darwinism on that train, the weakest of us ending up alone in our rooms, having to care for our own needs sensual in variety, the odds of which, I have to admit, were not exactly in my favor. I mean, I'm no hobgoblin, if that's what you're thinking. What I'm saying is, I'm not scaring away children on Halloween upon answering the door without a mask or any crazy thing like that… not by any stretch of the imagination. The point being, I was attractive *enough*, having what society considers a handsome physiognomy, all of the important features equidistant to one another and appropriately proportioned in relation to the conformed and accepted vision of an agreeably looking human being. I also possessed, if I may say, a decently shaped body, seeing as how I was on the football team – as a running back - at my high school, my core and arms being the real deal sealer… they were pretty chiseled. The problem, the only downfall, of my situation was always my height, or lack thereof. I was what one referred to as *pint sized*, often hit, ad nauseam, with the entirely overused idiom, "good things come in small packages" by those that made the inefficacious attempt to redress my encumbrance, my standing at a disappointing five feet and seven inches tall; therefore, I did not always score the proverbial touchdown in the game of *boy meets girl*. This shortcoming (pun categorically intended) was what always prevented me from contributing to most conversations with the fairer sex, especially if – as in the case at hand – the chances of my going home with any of these girls was about the same as being struck by lightning twice in the same night. I chose, instead, to be a mere spectator, as the train made its way back uptown.

"Hey, that last place was the shit!" Eric, a decent looking fellow of about five feet and eleven inches, medium complexion, with dark eyes and strong jaw line, said to the group.

"Oh my God! so dope! Really! The light show was to die for,

and the DJ was really killin' it!" one of the girls, a really sexy dame, wearing a very mini dress, along with a pair of fishnet stockings, agreed. She had a short bob haircut and a very cute, rounded, face, but wore entirely too much makeup… especially the lipstick, which ended up smeared all about her front teeth.

"For sure! the DJ was seriously Dope… what was his name again?" her friend, a taller girl with red hair and tons of cute little freckles all about her nose and cheeks, rejoined. Her outfit was only slightly less reveling, but no less attractive. Her black, low cut, v-neck tube top shirt was accompanied by these very form fitting blue jeans that accentuated every single one of her assets. Very sexy.

"Oh, the DJ?" the third girl responded. "Joey Jamm… he's tight, for sure… I have all of his mixed tapes. The guy is on point. Flawless. He has a bunch of girls from different schools selling his tapes and promoting his gigs… genius if you ask *me*. I mean, who's gonna say no to a girl selling his tapes? Selling *anything* for that matter. All the silly boys always end up buying two or three of them, just to get in good with the females. So predictable, these guys!" she concluded with a light chuckle, her particular facial features not being quite as attractive as the other two, but towered about ten stories above me; therefore, not within my field of play.

"What can you say? the man is a regular Bill Gates!" Mark, one of the members of my crew commented.

"Bill Gates? What in the fuck are you saying? What does Bill goddamn Gates have to do with what in the hell we're talking about?" Eric lamented, everyone joining in on a laugh at Mark's expense, much to his displeasure, he being the supercilious sort.

At that moment, as the train's doors opened to allow passengers in from the station, a group of singularly unsavory individuals entered, immediately fixing their leering glances upon our group; something not noticed instanter by anyone but myself at the onset. One item, chiefly, that seemed to catch the attention of the seedy bunch was Mark's phenomenally large gold, rope-style, chain, with an equally gaudy medallion in the image of the Lord Jesus Christ, distastefully dangling from the neck piece which, incidentally, included two especially shiny rubies situated inside of His orbs. Seeing the would be ne'er-do-wellers advancing upon our position, I immediately sat erect and tried, unsuccessfully, to grab the attention of my unheeding clique with a series of throat clearing sound effects, achieving positively no desired outcome. Before anyone else could ascertain the gravity of the current condition, the consociation of seven were therewithal among us, cracking their knuckles and ogling the way a famished lion would an especially delectable looking antelope, the train now having departed once again leaving us trapped within the car with our new pals.

"Yo, bee-boy, that's a nice chain." one of the fellows commented, simultaneously licking his lips, while the rest of his posse simply stood by, bearing the most intimidating grins upon their dastardly faces.

The girls instinctively closed up, as if shrinking within themselves, the way a turtle retracts into its shell when startled; the boys, their reaction not too dissimilar in regards to intent of engagement, all glanced at one another as if, quite like John M. Darley and Bib Latane's *bystander effect*, the expectation to do something about this unfortunate circumstance lay with the other man to his left and right, as opposed to themselves. Mark, the subject of whom the comment was addressed, simply replied, "Th-, thank you," avoiding eye contact with the villain at every cost.

"Yeah… no doubt," said the apparent leader of the obtruders, relentlessly moistening his lips after every spoken word, "check this out, homey… let me see that shit."

Offering, at the onset, a haplessly feeble, and quite pointless, glance toward us (we responding with a somewhat comparably disquieted visage), Mark returned his attention to his interlocutor, responding, "Um… my dad doesn't let me take it off… to… to show strangers."

This drew a collection of laughs from the alpha and his pack of hyenas, before the leader – incessantly and profusely continuing to licking his lips in a much more rapid and intemperate manner – rebutted, "Word? papa won't let you show strangers, huh? Is that right?"

Mark provided a silent and unquestionably pusillanimous nod to what was undoubtedly a rhetorical question, as his dialogist simply reached over, pilfered the piece of jewelry with no resistance whatsoever, handed it to one of his associates, and finally, altogether nonchalantly, reached into his rear pants pocket, removing and brandishing a large cutting instrument, commencing, at that point, to menacingly wave it in our direction as he provided to us his disclosure: "Now, if any of you pretty little boys and girls think of doing anything stupid, like yelling for help or calling the Cops, let me tell you that we run these trains; so we *will* find you and carve you up like a Thanksgiving turkey… you feel me?"

We all obediently acknowledged his commination with silent

nods (although I had some serious doubts about his ever having come even remotely close to whittling a gobbler on the day of giving thanks), watching as they retreated from the now, once again, stationed train, Mark's chain pendulously swaying from side to side around the neck of its new owner and figurehead of the retreating clan, he and his band of raiders breaking into a run, disappearing up the stairs of the terminal and into the darkness of the night.

Contrary to the thief's explicit wishes, Mark – once at our home terminus – flagged down a couple of Transit Cops that were leaning up against the posts on the platform. "Five-O! Yo! Five O!" he frantically hailed, much to the dissatisfaction of the Officers, who exchanged looks of indignation toward one another upon my friend's approach, not verbally responding to the cries of the robbery victim, but keeping a steady eye on him just the same. Mark, once close enough to plead his case, continued, "Yo, Officers, I got jacked on the train, son! A bunch of guys ran my chain, yo!"

Reciprocating disapproving looks to each other once more, one of them finally said, most indifferently, "What'd they take?"

Remaining in a fit hysteria, Mark answered, "I just told you… my chain!"

"Uh huh, and where did it happen?" the Officer inquired, lethargically taking out his pad and pen, all the while continuing to offer an air of disinterest across his face.

"Yo, ya'll are not listening to me, son! I already told you all of that… I got jacked on the train, son!"

The Officer looked up from his pad, placing his writing

instrument within centimeters of Mark's face, and scolded, "Look here, you little shit, I ain't your *son*, you understand?" Mark responded with a roll of his eyes, to which the Officer countered, returning his pad and pen to their initial resting place within his shirt pocket, "Listen, I don't have time to deal with your *yo, yo, yo* nonsense. How's about you go home and sell some more of your weed and get yourself another chain?"

"So you ain't gonna do anything? You ain't gonna try to catch these mother fuckers, man?"

"Hey!" the other Officer shouted in a stentorian tone of voice, "watch your mouth, you cock sucker! You want me to run you in for disorderly conduct?"

"Disorderly con-… oh, man, this is whack, son… fuck this, I'm outta here!" announced a dejected Mark, as we all exited the train station, making our way back home, minus three females and one gold chain… we clearly not members of Mr. Darwin's idea of the fittest of denizens.

***

A few weeks later, on a cloudless, warm, June afternoon – way too magnificent a day to waste attending the mundane classes of high school, especially since it was almost summer break, the teachers having long given up the good fight for the year – I, along with the same companions as the night of the chain snatching – minus the feminine variety - wound up hanging out around a park in which all the degenerates congregated, upon committing similar infractions vagrant in nature, inhaling some of the planet Earth's finest mind altering vegetation and philosophizing about the great wonders of the universe. In short, we were getting stoned.

"Man, this is some good shit, my brothers." declared Albert, one of the aforementioned associates, with a countenance that indicated he was somewhere up in the outer reaches of the Milky Way, en route to some neighboring solar system, after taking a rather long drag of the previously mentioned chronic, before passing it on to the next participant.

"Yeah, I got it from that spot on Cauldwell Avenue… they always have the best blaze over there." replied Eric, taking in his portion of the intoxicating smoke. "I was worried when they pinched my guy; thought I'd have to find me another dealer… thank *God* he wasn't in the joint for too long and went right back out to work." I'm pretty damn sure *God* had nothing to do with this particular entrepreneur's speedy release; but I decided to withhold my opinion on the matter, as the marijuana cigarette finally made its way to me.

Taking hold of the pleasure stick, I placed it gently between my lips and inhaled, allowing the vapor to enter my mouth, glide down into the depths of my esophagus, and settle into my lungs for but a brief moment before, ever so gingerly, releasing it from whence it came. I repeated this process once more – as per *weed smoking* procedural law – afterwards stating, "This is what life is all about, boys… nothing better than this," before handing it off to my left, where Mark waited ever so patiently.

"You said it." agreed Mark, ingesting his first pull of the pot, his eyelids shut in pure ecstasy. "Bro, I don't ever want to grow up… have to get a job… be responsible. I just wanna be young and smoke herb all day long. That is pretty much all I want outta life."

"Ambitious!" teased Eric, patiently awaiting his turn. "This man will definitely go far in the world!"

"Fuck you, Eric… like your life plan is so fucking extensive!" lashed Mark, always ready to solemnly defend any position he took, even ones expressing little to no aspiration.

"Easy, bro… *easy*!" Eric countered. "I'm just messin' with you, man… jeez! you know, weed is supposed to relax you, dude; not amp you up. You need a fucking chill pill!"

"Boys, boys… what's with all of the strife?" I broke in with an air of tranquility, my words undulating along with the haze that surrounded us. "You're killing the buzz over here."

"Talk to your boy over here!" groaned Mark. "He's poppin' all kind of static up in here, dissin' me… trying to make me feel type small."

"What are you even saying? You're just too sensitive, bro; that's your problem." returned Eric, swiping the joint from Mark's clutches.

"Imma show you *sensitive*, dog… just keep playin' me!" shouted Mark, now beginning to stand up with intentions of posturing above Eric.

"Alright! Enough! What the fuck?!" I ejaculated, taking control of the powder keg situation. "You dudes are drawing attention to us over here… you got people looking at us and, might I remind you, that's a bad thing; I mean, we are here very illegitimately, if you all don't recall that very essential fact."

"Yeah, Mark, sit your ass down and relax, man." Eric concurred. "If any of these *narcs* call the *Po Po* on us, our asses are grass."

"Aw, man, what are the *pigs* gonna do to us? Honestly." replied Mark, returning to a seated position atop a large rock.

"Plenty! Namely, tell my dad… which, in turn, will lead to the kicking of my ass." I riposted.

"Ditto!" supplemented a singularly distressed Eric. "My dad will rearrange my face if he ever found out I was cutting school and smoking grass… and I'm too pretty for my face to be rearranged!" he concluded, running his fingers through his John F. Kennedy style hair.

"Man, it ain't your *dad* you should be worried will lump you up… it's the Cops you should be afraid of. Those mother fuckers will do more than rearrange your face; they'll put an end to your ass, real fast. I don't mess around with those guys, no way." Albert, who had been voiceless up until now, exclaimed.

"Let those porkers try to put their hands on me… I'll -" Mark began, before Albert interjected.

"You'll *what*? Man, you ain't gonna do nothing."

"Oh yeah? what do think about this, then? Maybe *this'll* change your tune." Mark rebuffed, pulling out from his waistband a small, rusted, .22 caliber handgun, waving it around as if he were merely displaying a trinket of no significance perchance purchased at the local novelty store.

"Oh, shit! are you fucking crazy? put that away! there's a bunch of people right over there!" I exclaimed in a panic.

"Relax, bro… they ain't even looking over here." he casually replied, taking a half glance over at the bystanders. "Besides, it ain't loaded, so untwist your panties, why don't ya?"

"If it ain't loaded, why do you have it?" Eric argued. "Like, what's the point of the damn thing?"

"Oh, so I suppose you don't remember me getting' jacked on the train? I suppose that just up and slipped your memory?" Mark reminded.

"No," answered Eric, "it did not slip my memory, but are you saying that you would've shot the fool who took your chain? Is that what you're saying?"

"Yeah, that's what I'm saying."

"With an unloaded gat… real nice!" chortled Albert.

"Obviously not, pinhead… I got bullets. It just ain't loaded right *now*."

"So this dude takes your chain, and you figure you'll commit murder to make it all better. That's the logic you're going with, huh?" said a disgusted Eric.

"Better than having my shit taken from me, like I'm some kind of little bitch or something like that. I ain't no little bitch, you feel me?"

"We got it, Mark, we got it… you're not a bitch." stated I. "No one ever said or thought you were. I mean, maybe a little metrosexual from time to time; what, with the perfectly gelled hair and three hundred earrings on your lobes… but no one here thinks you're a bitch at all."

Pondering upon my comment, I suppose to determine whether or not to be offended, Mark finally chuckled, replacing the gun into his waistband, saying, along with a chuckle, "Man, ya'll ain't shit… '*metrosexual*'… what the fuck does that even mean?"

Some moments sauntered by as we continued our powwow when, before we all knew it, appearing out of thin air, about ten of the city's Finest had come from all directions, surrounding us, leaving no room for an expeditious escape. We all threw our hands to the sky and subsequently froze, with the exception of Mark who had the bright idea of reaching into his waistband for the deadly object mentioned beforehand. I noticed this particularly suicidal act of unquestionable stupidity and, without moving an inch of my body, with stiffened lips and eyes extended to their limit in his direction, I said, "Mark, what the fuck are you doing? Just keep your hands in the air, man."

"I'm just gonna get rid of the *jammy*. I'm just gonna toss it!" he answered, determined to be rid of the weapon.

"Man, no!" Eric interjected. Just leave it, bro! Tell 'em it's in your waistband, but don't touch it… yo, man, don't –"

At that point, quite instantaneously I should say, all of Tophet was unleashed in the direction of the poor young man. What sounded like front row seats at a fireworks display, a thunderous barrage of nine millimeter and .38 caliber rounds ejected from the commingling of Smith & Wesson and Glock 19 Police Department standard issue firearms, making their way into, and some clean through, the body of Mark Santino, killing him in a matter of seconds; his body now riddled with lead, laying bloodied and lifeless on the ground before us. My first instinct, in my initial disbelief, was to bend down to grab the corpse and shake it back to life. I motioned toward the body, my hands extended and reaching outward; but, before I could fully complete the act, I was taken hold of from behind - by whom, at that precise moment, I had absolutely no idea. My reaction, hence, was one of resistance, desperately, and with all of my might, attempting to push outward to break free from my captor; the force of his grasp, coupled with his forward momentum, however, was all too overpowering, he taking me immediately down to the floor with my face now embedded into the grass. The strange thing about it was that the pressure and weight of the subduer, upon our reaching the earth, alleviated just enough to continue keeping me down, but not quite so much as to hurt me… it was almost a comforting sensation of shelter and protection, as though the gaoler only wished to keep me out of harm's way. Continuing to hold me to the ground, he said, "Just stay down, big guy… just stay down."

My reflexive response to that was another slight jerking motion upward… and I remember myself shouting something to the effect of, "I just wanna help my friend… they shot him! They shot him!"

"I know, kid, I know…" he replied. "just stay down right now… there's nothing you can do for your friend… just stay down. There's a lot of Officers with guns out right now and the last thing they need is for anybody to be moving around. We don't need no one else shot, you know what I mean?"

After things settled down, the Cops realizing that Mark was the sole gun-toting individual amongst us, I heard them call for an ambulance; but, to be honest, they should've just called a hertz… maybe it was just procedure or something, who knows. We ended up being transported to the Police Station, where we were questioned about the knowledge of Mark's *piece* for a couple hundred hours. I think they must've realized and believed that we were all pretty much clueless to the ol' *who, what, when, where, and how's* of the thing. As for the *why*, we all told the story of the train robbery, and how Mark tried to explain it all to the Transit Cops that day. I suppose our story all added up in their brains because they put us into a waiting room and said we'd be getting the hell out of there and going home soon. Officer Whitney, the one who tackled me like a lineman does an opposing quarterback, came over and made sure we were all okay; something none of his other comrades went out of their way to do. He was an older man, I would say in his late fifties; a full head of salt and pepper colored hair; some wrinkles, but not too many… sort of the amount that makes a guy look distinguished, I guess; and a kind, gentle, face – as if he hadn't the ability to even harm a pesky bug flying around in his face. "How are you guys holding up?" he inquired, with an earnest inflection upon his countenance. "We notified your parents and they're all coming here to pick you up, but I just wanted to make sure everyone here was okay."

After initially moaning and groaning in agony at the thought of my father being privy to this situation, he becoming aware that my friend was shot right in front of me due to his possessing a gun; discovering that I was in the park and smoking herb when I was supposed to be receiving my brilliant education; and having to come to the Police Station to retrieve my sorry ass (all being enough to have said ass thoroughly handed to me), I inquired, "Why are you being so nice to us? I mean, no one else cares how we feel. Every other Cop here is just looking at us like we're a bunch of no-good hooligans."

After taking a brief glance over at the other Officers in the Station House, who were all crème deep in an assortment of doughnuts, washing them down with stale coffee housed in boxed containers, he returned to me and replied, "I'm an old dinosaur around here, kid… I come from a whole different time than a lot of these young bucks around here, and I'm from a tough neighborhood where I saw a lot of real crappy stuff. You guys kind of remind me of the crew I used to run around with when I was about your age; and, believe me, we got into a bunch of crap… much of it because we were in the wrong place at the wrong time. What you need to do, before it's too late, is make yourself a plan. You gotta figure out what you wanna do with your life now, before time runs out on you; and, trust me, the time is gonna go by very fast. Before you know it, you'll be an old guy like me, and you're definitely gonna want to have your shit together, or else you'll be on the other end of those steel bars over there." he concluded, pointing to the cells that, incidentally, were filled with a couple of significantly unwholesome looking gentlemen… most assuredly not a place I wanted to be.

"I appreciate it, sir," I said, "and I'm going to do better. I really am. I'm going to figure out what I want to do with my life and start working towards that goal." I meant it, too. I truly did. I knew right then, this was a kind of turning point in my life; I was going to make a concerted effort, a life altering change, for the betterment of my currently meaningless life.

"Good, I'm glad to hear it. And if you ever need anything, any help with your goal, you just swing on over here and ask for me. Understand?"

"Yes, sir… thank you, sir… I will."

My father showed up at the Police Station shortly after me having the talk with Officer Whitney, the look upon his face spelling certain doom for the likes of me, complete with a laser-like stare that had the ability to penetrate the inner workings of a person's molecular makeup. Fortunately, Whitney met with my dad briefly before handing me over, which might have saved me from a horrific pounding, let me tell you. To my surprise, after thanking Whitney, he enclasped me in a warm embrace and said, "My son, are you okay? The Officer told me what happened… I'm sorry about your friend… it's an awful thing. I'm just happy that you're good. That's the most important thing to me. That's all that matters."

If you know my dad, you know that he is terrifically far from being the emotional type; so this display of affection was out of his wheelhouse, as it were. It was for that reason that I didn't utter a single word; I only wrapped my arms around him and returned his hug; which, I'm not too embarrassed to admit, felt pretty damn good after what I witnessed on that fateful day. It's amazing how a person can totally revert into their younger selves when faced with adversity or strife; it's like some kind of light switch that gets flicked, turning a cocky young punk into the three year old version of himself, snuggling under the protective wing of their patriarch to insulate them from the evil realties of the world. Pretty interesting stuff.

Well, for your information – in case you were wondering whether or not I actually did allow the wise words of Police Officer Whitney to penetrate through, and adhere within, my brain – I ended up deciding what I wanted to do with my life, after all. It struck me that the one thing I desired to do was to be like him… to be in such a powerful position, yet have the ability to connect with a lowly nobody kid like myself and make a difference in that person's life. It was truly fascinating to me, and I wanted to possess that very same adroitness, to maybe pay forward the kindness and compassion that I was given, whilst at the same time, having the awesome capability to take the bad guys, like the ones that victimized us on the train that day, and eradicate them from the face of the planet. That's pretty much what I wanted to do.

III

The day I told my old man that I had taken, and passed with flying colors, the Police exam, he was less than thrilled, to put it mildly. Remember, I told you about his tumultuous experiences with them, the Law, throughout his vexatious adolescence; so, you can kind of get a pretty decent idea as to the feeling of dissension that was swirling around inside of him upon receiving the – according to his point of view – exceptionally disquieting news. With the force of an extraordinarily active volcano, James Cardona, Sr., my dear old dad, quite dynamically exclaimed, "Are you fucking serious, Jimmy?" his eyes transitioning to a color similar to that of the Martian surface. "Why the fuck would you want to be a part of that? huh? Please… please explain that one to me. I mean, what in the mother fuck would possess you to want to have *anything* to do with those pieces of shit?" he asked without waiting for a response. "Explain why you'd wanna be a part of it, because I'm having a really tough time sitting here trying to figure it all out right now… I'm really racking my brain over here."

"Pop, I explained all of this to you before… remember?" I replied as calmly as I possibly could, so as not to further his state of sheer exasperation. "I told you that the benefits were good, the retirement package, all the perks… there are a lot of good reasons."

"Yeah, you told me about all of that nonsense, but you never told me you were taking the test... you never told me anything of the like. And I know the *reason* that you didn't tell me is because you know damn well that I would have told you to forget about it… not to even *think* about it. Those guys are a bunch of crooked animals with no souls… they have absolutely no souls, Jimmy, you *know* that… you *know* what I've been through with those barbarians. That's what they are, you know. Barbarians."

"Pop, first of all, I know what you've been through… I know it. But… you know… how is anything supposed to change if we don't get in there and change it ourselves? Like, from the inside. That's the only way things get better; we have to make changes from within. And secondly, I *did* tell you about it way before the exam… I *did*… one hundred percent, I know I did. I told you the test date and everything."

"Okay, yeah, you told me the test date… I thought you were just letting me know when they were offering the test. What does that have to do with you actually *taking* it? And changes within? The only way that can happen is if you rank up so high that you'd be the damn Police Commissioner. Nothing is gonna change, Jimmy; nothing at all."

I screwed my face as though I had the greatest of gas bubbles in my belly, as I responded, "You don't need to be the Police Commissioner to make changes; anyone can make a difference. A Police Officer walking the beat can make a difference with just a smile and kind word to the people in the neighborhood. And why would I tell you the test date if I wasn't gonna take the exam?"

"Listen, man," he said, his tone drastically reduced all of a sudden – not because he was less angry, but because he was *so* infuriated that his comportment morphed into what I called '*white hot*,' which is to say that it transcended mere ocular and auditory emotion… it was sort of more spiritual in nature and, let me tell you, it was eerie as all hell, if you can envision what I mean. "It seems like you have an answer to everything I say;" he dispassionately continued, "so, how about this: you do whatever the hell you want. You wanna go join that corrupt, no good, organization, that's on you. I got nothing else to say about it. I don't like the Cops and I don't ever *want* to like the Cops… I don't want anything to do with this garbage of you being one of *them*, so you just go your way about it and I'll go mine. And don't even daydream of coming to me for anything ever again… you got your boys in blue now; go to them for food and shelter, or whatever the fuck else you always take from me."

"Why are you being that way? Why can't you support me and my decision?"

"Why do you need *my* support?" he replied, sustaining his blasé, carefree tone of voice. "You don't need anything from me, it seems like you can make your own decisions without needing my help. You were man enough to put this into the works, so now you can be man enough to deal with it without support from me. Look to your new little blue buddies for support."

"Alright, Pop… I understand. I guess I just have to do it without your back."

"I guess so."

I ended up leaving the apartment shortly after that conversation and headed over to my very good friend, Rose's place – someone I had been hanging out with since I can remember, getting into all kinds of mischief as children, things that best friends effectuate, that sort of bonded us together. Now, as young adults, we tend to one another's emotional needs here and there… nothing romantic or anything like that… not *always*; just somebody I could call up, or go see, and chew the ol' fat with. She was really good at listening to all of my problems, and – most importantly - not afraid to give me the business if she felt I was in the wrong about this thing or that. I didn't have to worry about her being fake or telling me solely what I wanted to hear… ol' Rosie had no problem bending me over and giving me the proverbial wooden paddle if I deserved it. In between all of that, if we felt like it, we'd sort of kiss and stuff… one of the little perks of the friendship, I suppose; but certainly not something that defined it. What I mean is, she had her amatory relationships and I… well, I had my, mostly, nugatory flings; none of which ever trammeled our *affaire de cœur*. I knocked on her door and she answered with the grandest smile anyone ever saw, I'm pretty sure of that fact. I guess she had just gotten out of the shower or something because she was wearing this really short, gray, robe that accentuated her long, toned and tanned legs… she was somewhat of a fitness buff, so the muscles in her walking sticks were terrifically pronounced. You could tell she was wearing absolutely nothing under that robe, too, because the cleavage from her size D's – to my pleasure - was, in sooth, protruding, demanding all my attention.

"Hey, beautiful, you just caught me coming out of the shower." she said, with teeth that could illuminate the gloomiest of caves. "Come in! come in!"

"Sorry about that… I guessed I should've called first; although, I'm kind of glad I didn't." I said, giving her the once over from top to bottom, something that was not lost on her, she offering a little coquettish giggle, motioning for me to enter the apartment with a slight nod of her head. She really was gorgeous, I have to say. Her parents were from Belize, this country located in South America; her features consisted of a pleasant mix of Mayan and Spaniard, giving her a pair of terrifically sexy high cheek bones; staggeringly captivating almond shaped eyes, and the typical long, stunning, jet black hair belonging to the indigenous peoples of the land, blended with the fairer shade of skin from their Spanish counterparts… very scrumptious, if you care to know.

"Take a seat on the sofa;" she said, motioning to the beige, wrap around sectional piece that enveloped the living room. "I'll be right out, just give me a sec to throw something on."

"Don't go through any trouble on my account… I'm perfectly fine with what you have on." I flirtatiously replied. She giggled, but offered no rejoinder; instead, heading into her room to cover up that amazing body of hers, much to my disenchantment. "Hey, do you mind if I grab myself a drink?"

"Of course not! help yourself… you know where everything is." she shouted from the other room.

I swung on over to the kitchen to pour myself a tall glass of Coke, throwing a few cubes of ice in it, and by the time I got back she was sitting on the sofa. She patted the spot next to her, indicating for me to have a seat, so I plopped down and took a long, deep breath. It was nice to be there, relaxing at peace, no one around but us; although, she could tell that something wasn't quite right with me… my goddamn *chi* was off, or some insanity like that. Rose was really good at that, telling when I was bent out shape about a thing; it was like she had this sort of ability to see right through me… kind of creepy if you really think about it. It's the kind of thing that got gals burned alive up in ol' Salem a couple of hundred years ago. Honestly, it did. One didn't want to go around reading people's minds back then, is what I'm saying. They'd tie you right up to a pole and burn the living hell out of you while the entire village watched. It was like their damn night out or something. Folks back then, back in those primitive days, didn't have streaming networks and internet, so the next best thing was engulfing a few witches up into flaming embers, you know? Anyway, she turned to me, reaching out to gingerly push back a few of the rouge, long, bangs from my full head of hair, placing them behind my ears, and said, "What's up, beautiful? there's something on your mind… I can tell, you know."

"Yes," I chuckled, "I know you have that *gift*. I still think you're some kind of a witch or something. You should look into that… to see if you're a bonafide sister of the underworld. You really should. I bet there's a real calling for that sort of thing… somewhere out there. You could read palms, turn people into frogs… pretty much anything you want!"

"Ha, ha, very funny… seriously, though; what's up? You know you can talk to me about anything. You know that, right? Anything at all." she said, in the most sincere and loving way. She really did have an amorous way about her… as if she were everyone's mother. What I mean is, she was so genuinely affectionate towards me, that I felt as though she popped me out of her ol' uterus and nurtured me from birth. She was always concerned for my well being and all. I think that's why I gravitated towards her in times of need; when I felt down and out, requiring someone to lift my crummy spirits.

"I know, I know. I just wanted to sit here and look at you for a little… I just wanna sit here and look into those sea-green eyes of yours before I start blabbing all over the entire place. Is that okay? Can I just look into the ol' windows of your soul and hold your hand just for a bit?" I was feeling kind of emotional, I have to admit. Sometimes when a person feels out of sorts, they just want to seek comfort, enclasped in the warmth of another human.

"Yes! of course you can." she said, with the most soothingly melodic tone, bringing me to her chest and stroking the sides of my head. In that moment of time, I felt safe with her… I felt secure; as if nothing in the entire world could hurt me… again, very maternal.

"This is nice… thank you, Rosie. I really appreciate you." I said, my eyes closed in euphoric bliss, lost in her touch, the weight of the world cascading from my body with every brush of her finger.

"You're welcome, love." she replied, placing upon my forehead a most tender, but galvanizing kiss, sending my heart into erratic sputters, causing my lungs to require an extra helping of oxygen.

"No," I said, sitting up again, taking her eyes into mine. "I mean it, Rose; I *really do* appreciate you. You're always here when I need you, and I can't say that about pretty much any other human being on the face of this crummy planet."

"What is this all about, James? You're starting to worry me. Honestly, you are."

"It's nothing, really. Well, the thing of it is… do you remember when I went to go take the Police exam? You know, to become a Police Officer and all of that?"

"Yes, of course I remember." she replied, pulling away a little, giving me a kind of vexatious glare. "I also remember telling you how I hated that you were doing it. I don't like the idea of you becoming a Cop. It's too dangerous. There are people out there who don't care if you're an Officer or not and they'll try to hurt you."

"Believe me, I know. I mean, I know what you think about the whole thing. And trust me, there's a part of me that thinks about that, too… you'd have to be some sort of a nut not to have those kinds of thoughts; so I don't *blame* you or anything crazy like that." I paused before continuing… to sort of gather my thoughts about the next installment of my soliloquy. "Well, so… the thing of it is… I passed… I passed and I've been going to these appointments with my Investigator for the past few months – this guy whose job it is to make sure I'm not some kind of a lunatic before they completely hire me and all." I desisted for a moment to gauge the severity of the stunned look across her mug (the whites of her eyes completely visible, mouth agape) before continuing, "Anyway, I guess he thinks I'm normal or whatever, so I'm gonna begin the Academy in the next couple of weeks. My dad is absolutely losing his shit about the whole thing; I mean, *really* losing his shit. You know how he feels about the Police." Rose's countenance reflected that of a person who knew precisely what my father felt by raising her eyebrows and scrunching her lips. I didn't have to explain to her the… *animosity*… that was felt by the man – to put it lightly – about the particular profession in question. She knew about all of his run-ins with them, about all of the beatings he had been handed, when reeking havoc back in the days of his youth. "Anyway," I continued, "I sort of stormed outta my house because he was being a real asshole about it. He basically said that he wants nothing to do with me if I take the job. Can you believe that? He's actually threatening to practically disown me or some craziness like that. Just because they tuned him up a few times when he was a kid… doing fucked up shit, mind you. I mean, it's not like he was out there walking old ladies across the street or heading to choir practice, you know. It's not like he was coming home from reading Shakespeare all day at the library. You know what I'm saying?"

"I… I don't know what to say. I mean, you said you were taking the test… to be honest, I never really put much thought to it afterwards. I guess I didn't consider what would happen next. You never even told me you passed… I guess I'm kind of disappointed you didn't say anything about that."

"I know." I responded with my head held low in contrition. I knew I should've mentioned it to her and I felt like a complete piece of manure for the omission. I mean, here I just finished explaining to all of you that she was basically my best friend in the entire confounded world, but then I go ahead and keep a huge thing like this from her. "I suppose I just didn't want to disappoint you, you know? I knew how you felt about the whole thing and I didn't want to cause you any grief. As it is, I already expected all of Satan's wrath to envelop me, in terms of my dad and everything. I just couldn't bear the weight of how you'd react as well. It was wrong, Rose, I know it… I'm not making any pathetic excuses about it; I'm just telling you the reason why. That's all."

Rosie just kind of took hold of my hand again, placing it into hers, not saying a word, giving me the kind of look that you'd give someone whose pet goldfish had gone to meet its maker. I mean, I don't blame her or anything like that. What was she supposed to say?

I think, hand to Bible – which is to say that I swear on everything that is Holy and pure - taking my hand spoke volumes, anyway. I didn't want to hear any goddamn homily at that moment, to be honest. Sometimes when a person has a lot on their mind, really heavyweight sort of stuff that makes them feel as though everything is entirely too fuzzy, too dark, to get a hold of, they only want to be able to vent it out, like piping hot steam from a radiator. Look, let's get something crystal clear here: I completely understand where James, Sr. was coming from, I'm not some sociopath, having not the ability to empathize with the feelings of others; I especially wouldn't have such a callous attitude towards the guy who raised me all by himself, without any help from anyone in the entire world, lacking a legitimate, valid, reason. I'm not some kind of a goddamn cyborg who can't comprehend the exceedingly important fact that his jadedness stemmed from a plethora of deeply disturbing episodes with *The Man*, as the moniker goes; but, I also can't ignore the feelings and wants for what I desire in my own life. In this entire world, in every walk of life, there are good and bad people, no absolutes; therefore, to judge something – an entire entity – based solely off of one's personal experiences (the experiences of, lets be completely forthcoming, a juvenile delinquent) would be insanely unreasonable. Insanely.

"Look," she finally said, some time in between my introspection, "your dad loves you; he's just concerned for you and -"

"He's concerned for his own personal feelings on the matter." I abruptly broke in.

Screwing her entire face to one side, she stated, "I was *about* to say: *and* I'm sure there are some personal feelings, *his* personal feelings, involved; but, believe it or not, that just might be a kind of smoke screen to mask his real concern… a very warrantable concern that his son is about to embark on something that could, quite possibly, put him in harms way." She paused to assess my reaction; but, at this point, I sat transfixed, with my eyes down towards the floor because, truth be told, I knew what she was saying made a whole helluva lot of sense; there was nothing I could say to refute it. I suppose, at that point, she realized I was sort of stalemated, so she continued, "Just give him some time to wrap his head around this whole thing. I'm sure, once he's had some time to settle into the idea, he'll come around. Just give him some time, love." She paused a bit before asking, "What does Gracie think about the whole thing? Is she team James Senior or team James Junior?" As I already stated earlier on, Gracie is my sister. I mentioned her in the beginning, and said that I'd tell you a little about her; so, I guess now is as good a time as any.

Dr. Gracie Cardona, born approximately a half generation before yours truly, has always been the sworn protector and true chip off of the old block, so to speak, of our dear old dad. There was pretty much nothing on the face of the entire planet Earth in which she wasn't in accordance, in terms of my father's entire ideological outlook on things. It was quite annoying, if you must know the truth. Anytime I so much as discussed the goddamn weather with my elder sibling, rest assured, her feelings on the matter were a sentiment that was an exact reflection of our birth-giver's. Gracie, nowadays, makes her living as the Dean of Undergraduate Student Life, and English Professor, at Columbia University; where she, incidentally, received her Doctorate in the subject of English Literature about a year ago. Really big deal, especially for Pop who practically did about a few dozen somersaults upon receipt of the news, announcing her acceptance at the Institution; not to mention her graduating and landing the singularly impressive dual gigs at said hamlet of education. A lot of back breaking hours, working two jobs for a major portion of his life, went into all of that edification she received… an investment that proved its worth with all of her accomplishments. She pays it all forward, too, let me tell you. She sends him tons of money and all of that shit; so you can imagine what a shining star my big sister is in his eyes… a goddamn constellation worth. Really. In the spirit of being completely open and honest, we – Gracie and I – are not that close, due to the aforementioned philippic that I just shared. Don't get me wrong, we speak here and there… I do keep in fairly regular contact, at the most stringent behest of my old man and all; we're simply just not meeting up for tea and crumpets on a regular basis, discussing daily current events or matters of the heart and crap like that. To be altogether certain, in response to Rosie's inquiry about what 'team' my sister would support, with regard to my joining the Police Department, that was a given… I stood no chance of gaining any type of succor from my sibling – and Rose most assuredly should have known this; therefore, I had zero interest in entertaining that question, but replied nevertheless, "I guess team *anyone but me*." I acquiesced, sarcastically; again, not wanting to delve into the morbid world of the relationship with Grace. "Listen, can we just watch some television or something. I honestly don't wanna think about this anymore today. I'm kind of spent, to be honest, and I just want to do something that requires absolutely no thought. Is that okay with you? Do you mind, terribly?"

"Of course, love…" she consented, grabbing the remote

control, turning on the *boob tube*, flipping it to MTV where the latest episode of some reality show was currently airing; which, incidentally, I hadn't the slightest interest in. You see, I wasn't exactly being completely sincere when I told her that I didn't want to think about it anymore... the truth of it was, it was *all* that was floating around my noodle; the TV just sort of provided a little cover for me to be silent and work it all out in my head. We spent the rest of that day cuddled up on the couch in her apartment, just being silent and enjoying each other's presence; we could just do that kind of thing - ol' Rosie and I - and be completely content, not needing a whole lot to be at peace. Those kinds of moments are truly the best, if you ask me. You don't need a lot of pomp and circumstance or people jumping through fiery hoops to find happiness; just two individuals, sitting around and watching mindless programs, will do the trick just fine.

IV

"On September 11, 2001, 19 militants associated with the Islamic extremist group al Qaeda hijacked four airplanes and carried out suicide attacks against targets in the United States. Two of the planes were flown into the twin towers of the World Trade Center in New York City, a third plane hit the Pentagon in Arlington, Virginia, just outside Washington, D.C., and the fourth plane crashed in a field in Shanksville, Pennsylvania. Almost 3,000 people were killed during the 9/11 terrorist attacks, which triggered major U.S. initiatives to combat terrorism..."

-    *September 11 Attacks, History.com Editors*

Everyone remembers where exactly they were on that fateful day, the day of the attacks on the Continental United States, which took place on an otherwise bright and sunny Tuesday morning in September. I recall clearly seeing, in the distance, the skyline pluming with smoke from the large windows of the office building where I worked as a clerical assistant (still awaiting the call from the Police Department to come on over and join them). In the midst of the chaos, not certain of pretty much anything at that point in time – seeing as how our world appeared to be undergoing the most terrifying verses of Revelations, from the Last Testament in the Bible - people dropped whatever they were doing to try and head home to their families. My boss, the senior vice president of the company, came barreling out of his office to tell us all to beat it the hell out of there; they were closing down due to the impending end of all things. The employees frantically tried giving their respective loved ones a call on their cell phones; but, almost of them had zero luck accomplishing this goal for the simple fact that, I suppose, millions of other people going bonkers were attempting to accomplish a similar task, so the lines were, essentially, scrambled eggs. As for myself, I made my exeunt pretty damn calmly; I suppose, if you asked me the reason for that seemingly callous reaction, it was for lack of completely grasping the enormity of the devastating state of affairs befalling us. I mean, I knew it was a pretty serious thing; but, I simply didn't realize the extent of it as a whole… in its entirety. I just dealt with it in this sort of apathetic, cool as all hell, manner; to such that, any Tom, Dick, and Harry who happened to rest their gaze upon me would most probably utter, 'Now what in the blazing hot hell is wrong with *that* guy?' Very zen-like. There was even a point when, as I passed by this pizza stand – with the perilous calamity of the city doused in flames in perfect view – I stopped to grab a pepperoni slice. Now, I don't want you to think I'm some kind of certifiable screwball who has no feelings, someone who should be locked away in a padded room, an individual whose lobotomist struck a few centimeters too deep… because I'm not. It's just that, growing up, one of my father's most inestimable life lessons was, in times of crisis, the first order of business is survival (eating encompassing the majority of this survival dictum). No matter what was going on, irrespective of the nightmarish biblical misadventure being unleashed upon God's children, you had to grab yourself a bite to eat. Forty day flood? Eat. Rain of fire torrentially descending upon Sodom and Gomorrah? Eat. The Four Horsemen of the Apocalypse galloping down the street? you guessed it… grab yourself a bacon cheeseburger and fries because nothing is more important than keeping your wits about you; and, the only way to do that is to make sure you have sustenance in your ol' belly. It's honestly a singularly simplistic ideology, so I don't see the big deal about me downing the goddamn slice… I really don't.

I finally got home about an hour or so later; luckily, I lived pretty close to my job, and – more importantly – far from *Ground Zero*; so, unlike most people who were not as geographically fortunate, I had very little trouble getting to my humble abode. Upon flipping on the TV, the devastation hit me in the face like an uppercut, followed by a left hook, from Mike Tyson. What I bore witness to sent my stomach into directions I didn't know were possible, and something I could never even attempt to convey to you… if you didn't see it for yourself, with your own eyes, no words could possibly paint the appropriate picture, accurately describing the heinous reality that lay surrounded by the inferno of the nether region during that day. What I *can* tell you, what I can – unequivocally – make you aware, was at that precise moment, right while those buildings crumbled to dust and ruin, with all of the bodies of those poor souls tragically perishing, I wanted nothing more than to be a member of the Police Department… to be on the proverbial front-lines, heading toward danger rather than running away from it. I took a long, deep breath, peering helplessly at the television set, wishing I were there to help hoist the American flag proudly above the wreckage, the way in which those brave firemen did later that day.

***

Standing there on that dark, cloudy Monday morning, garbed in a cheap, standard dark blue business suit from a local variety store, inside the auditorium of some Brooklyn high school with the rest of the recruits was insanely surreal, as the tune, *'Where My Heart Will Take Me,'* by Russell Watson, subtly played on a loop, all the while the stragglers filing in, attempting to find their way to the seats that were assigned in alphabetical order; which seemed an impossible task, the neophytes bumping into each other and doing 360 degree turns like those antique wind-up dolls you find in a *grandma's attic* store, apparently unable to complete the very menial task given to them. It was quite comical, if you want to know the truth; considering that – in about six month's time – these would be the very people you'd call to solve the most intricate of quandaries, presently unable to crack the enigma of order chronological in nature. Outside and apart of the song, continuing its maniacally incessant loop over a loud speaker, one could hear the proverbial pin dropping onto the floor; there seemed to be some sort of understanding that, although no one had given such a command, all twenty-one hundred of us were to remain voiceless. It was for this reason that I was startled out of my American Eagle underwear when a rather gangling young man of about twenty-five or so leaned over, practically placing his severely chapped lips upon my ear and whispered, "Hey, bro, what's up? My name's Sam, Sam Herzog. What's yours, bro?"

Retracting slightly in the opposite direction, away from his clear violation of personal space, and possible laceration of my earlobe in what appeared to be a perspicuous indication of dehydration judging from the fissure around his kisser, I replied, "James, James Cardona."

"Nice to meet you, James." he said, reconnoitering the entire place for any lurking sentries who may be seeking to cease all communication between us greenhorns, before continuing, "This is something else, huh? Kind of crazy; there must be thousands of people in here. You'd think, after what happened to the Towers… you know… the Twin Towers… you'd think nobody would want this job."

"I can't imagine who wouldn't." I whispered. "What's not to want about being a part of showing these cowardly terrorists who's really boss? Plus the whole chasing bad guys in the police car at insane speeds down the highway; getting into shoot-outs with bank robbers, bullets flying all over the place; diving and sliding over the hood of cars as you run after them… what's not to like about any of that?"

"Bro, what in the hell are you talking about?" he replied, his voice slightly elevated causing us both to take a quick gander around before he returned his attention to me with a look on his face that implied I had a few screws loose up in the ol' cranium. "None of that happens on this job. I mean, maybe the car chase thing; that is, until the *Duty Captain* comes over the radio and calls it all off. They kind of frown upon car pursuits in the middle of the city, you know what I mean? Too much liability. People get kind of bent out of shape when you plow into 'em at high rates of speed, even though you're going after the Son of Sam reincarnate… they sort of don't want you to do it while mowing a bunch of families down in the process. You feel me?"

"Really? are you sure about that?" I responded with slight vexation. "I mean, how would *you* know that for sure? You're new here, just the same as me."

"Simple, I used to be a Cadet for this job; that is, until I passed the Police Exam… now I'll finally be a Cop!" he answered, holding his unusually colossal sized dome up high, with an air of pride.

"Wait a minute… you *used* to be a Cadet?" I quickly replied with some confusion. "What in the hell are you now? Aren't we all Cadets here in this auditorium?"

"Huh? no, man, we're not Cadets; we're *Recruits*. Big difference, bro. *Cadets* are college kids who work, like, part-time doin' administrative stuff inside Police Stations; you know, filing; copying; typing… administrative shit. *Recruits* are us; probationary Police Officers with no guns going through the Academy. Big difference, bro. And I can tell you with all certainty, there'll most likely be none of that shit you just said, about shoot-outs with bank robbers and sliding on hoods of cars… do you have any clue whatsoever the law suit you'll catch if you go ahead and dent somebody's BMW doin' some crazy shit like that? Jeez."

"You're actually blowing my mind right now. I had this whole… wow, I… it's not what I expected."

I almost got right up off of that wooden auditorium seat and beat it the hell out of there, coming to the grim realization that my fantasy of essentially emulating the action heroes of the silver screen, capturing the villain after being hot on his heels, rescuing the girl, then capping off the night with said damsel in the boudoir, was essentially null and void. What a let down of epic proportions, I'll tell you. I didn't leave, though; I decided, instead, to stay put and go through the whole swearing-in ceremony. For one thing, I was in the middle of the aisle, so it would have been pretty goddamn obvious – not to mention awfully embarrassing – to have to squeeze by a bunch of people, apologizing all over the place as I attempted to make the getaway; secondly, I had already quit my employment at the office, so it would've been ill advised for me to go back home jobless, seeing as how I had to pay my dad rent and all (we worked it out wherein I'd pay all of the rent in exchange for my treachery of joining the Department)… and that's not something you ever wanted to do: explain to my dad that you didn't have his eight hundred confounded bucks at the beginning of the month. It was officially, at that point, a capital offense in his household, punishable by death at the guillotine, I'll have you know. Trust me on that one.

The actual 'swearing-in,' if you want to call it that, was pretty much a let-down, to be deathly honest. What I mean is, it wasn't as intimate as you might consider something of that magnitude to be. Essentially, it consisted of all two thousand one hundred of us raising our stinking hands all at once, swearing that we'd uphold the law and all of that shit… *all at once*! as in, the *same exact* time. I stood there wondering, with my right arm held up high, reciting the vows, how in the world anyone could possibly know if the entirety of the auditorium was truly participating? I'm sure they weren't… not *every* single person; certainly not the guy who, minutes after we were dismissed, went around the corner of the building, in front of some poor family's private house, whipping out his *membrum verile,* relieving an entire pint of his egesta onto their rose bushes. Certainly not *that* guy (who, incidentally, was expeditiously terminated – having been positively identified through the homeowner's fully functioning security cameras - bringing the manifest of our class to a grand total of two thousand ninety nine… one hour subsequent to all of us swearing to God we'd hold our crummy selves to a higher standard). In any event, I was officially, after that ceremony, a member of the City's Police Department, due to commence the six month Police Academy training the following day.

To merely say that the first day at the Academy was chaotic would be like saying a baking pan just *might be* a bit tepid subsequent to a few hours of five hundred degree heat in the oven. Anyone going through their initiation nowadays wouldn't understand the sheer bedlam that existed back during the time of my coming through; and I say this with every single bit of confidence. First of all, the locale is completely different; when I was wearing the gray recruit shirt, with the blue ice cream-man hat, pledging into the mighty Blue fraternity, we were down at 20th Street, between 2nd and 3rd Avenue… very minuscule compared to the newer, much larger, facility they have the kids going through now. And, believe me, the actual physical structure isn't the only difference between what *was* and what *is*… not by a freaking long shot. Let us begin with the most significant difference between the *then and now*, which is the actual quality of the product the Department was putting out. Analogous to the Hostess cakes they have the unmitigated gall to put on the shelves today, which are most definitely wanting compared to their more desirable counterparts from the wonder years of yesterday (most assuredly contributed to the shortcuts taken by a less caring manufacturer), the rookies in which the present day Academy – over at the brand new compound in Queens; which, incidentally, has the look and feel of a community college campus – are currently puking up are an embarrassment, to say the absolute least; but I'll get more into the specifics of that later on.

Right now, I'm just giving you all a sort of pellicle description of the thing, so you can get an idea of what I'm trying to convey, which is that there exists a tremendous difference between the two localities, is all. Take the gymnasium… if you were to waltz into the

Academy gym now, you'd think the kids therein are earning their associates degree in yoga meditation or some crazy thing like that. I mean, there's no yelling, no screaming, no crying, no expressions of enervation upon the dejected countenances of the Recruits; it's sickening, quite honestly. At the Old Academy, they worked us until our skin oozed off of our bones, like fine, tender, smoked ribs. They'd have us running around the gym, a room the size of a broom closet, with practically no ventilation, temperatures soaring in the hundreds, with about a dozen Instructors yelling obscenities in our faces, making us feel tantamount to the size of semi-digested peanuts that dwell deep inside a few dozen large chunks of excrement (another thing, incidentally, that isn't done anymore – the shouting of indelicacies; the reason for this being that it is no longer acceptable to degrade or demean the poor feelings of the new and improved valetudinarian Recruit. Unreal). Give me the old days, anytime; there's nothing more germinating, nothing that puts more hair on your chest, than having another human being, inches from your dirty, sweaty, face, as you gasp for what little breathable air exists within that torture chamber of a gymnasium, telling you what a complete waste of life you are. A real character builder.

"Goddamn it, Recruit! What in the fuck do you think you're doing? you miserable fuck. Do you realize your entire Company is running past you?!" one of the Instructors, jog-trotting side by side with us, yelled into the ear canal of the girl directly in front of me – Cunningham, her name (this I could tell from the back of the gym shirt that we all adorned, an article of clothing which bore our last names and the designated Company number to which we belonged) - spittle ejaculating from his mouth and onto her face, and the faces of those unfortunate enough to hold positions to both their immediate rear.

"Yes… sir… I'm… sorry… sir." replied the calorically challenged young woman, gasping for dear life, her lungs searching, in vain, for any remaining bit of oxygen within Satan's sauna room.

"You're sorry?! You're *sorry*?! Are you fucking kidding me right now?! *Recruit*, get your ass out of this run! Do you hear me? get your fat ass right out of this goddamn run right now!" the Instructor bellowed; a guy who – while only standing at about five foot three, at best – soared about seven feet above the portly Recruit (this being implied by the sheer boisterousness of his aura, as he bleated these pejoratives at the top of his lungs).

Cunningham fell out of the run, off to the side, and leaned over placing her hands upon her knees, continuing her quest for finding whatever H2O remained in that dank dungeon. This clear sign of what could very well have been an impending heart attack won no sympathy from the Instructor, as he continued the relentless attack upon his now demoralized prey. "Holy shit, what in the fuck are you doing *now*? Are you taking a *break*? Is it *break* time? Is that what it is? nappy time?"

"No… sir." Cunningham gasped.

"Goddamn it, Recruit! straighten up and walk your lazy ass in the opposite direction of the run. I want everyone who is busting their ass - everyone else in this entire Godforsaken place who is running like proud brothers and sisters of the Department - to see your pathetic face as you leisurely stroll on by! Do it! do it now!"

Cunningham complied, inchmeal – at a rate of speed

comparable to that of a Galapagos giant tortoise – plodding in the opposite direction of the entire gym block, so that every single runner could see the dejection upon her mien. I felt kind of sorry for her; the humiliation was infectious, as we all knew – deep down within our beleaguered souls (what was left of them) – that this could be any one of us at any given moment, the prospect of which was especially horrifying, to say the least. The maligning didn't cease there, though. The Instructor, all the while Cunningham was being emotionally hazed *on the yard* like a lowly initiate in a sorority, continued to berate the Recruit. "Look, everyone! Look at this lazy, out of shape, disgrace of a human being! Go on, take a hard, long, look at her! This is the one – when you're in an apartment, fighting a perp… desperately fighting for your life and calling for help on the radio… this is the one – with a goddamn jelly donut in her hand, the residue of which most definitely will be plastered all over her uniform shirt – this is the one that will slowly be squeezing her morbidly obese sack of shit body out the patrol car… this is the one that won't make it to help you! *This* is what's on the way to save your life, ladies and gentlemen! This horrendous excuse for a human being will probably even wait for the damn elevator, I bet! That's right! she'll wait ever so patiently for it to come down to her, then roll on in, and even let a bunch of tenants slide on in to get to *their* floors, leaning her corpulent goddamn self on the wall, patiently waiting to get to the apartment that you're dying in, instead of running up the fucking steps to assist to you. Take a goddamn look!"

Silent tears started to flow from the ducts of Cunningham's eyes, as she continued to saunter, counter clockwise, around the platoon, desperately trying to avoid eye contact with any of us. Although a crude and insensitive tactic, I thought then, and still believe now, that this is a necessary method of training people who are going out to fight a war; and make no mistake about it, that's exactly what it was out there... war. After the attacks of 911, the streets sort of went to the shitter, so to speak. The thing of it is, people thought it was the end of God's creation, so the street pirates all took advantage and went to work, raping and pillaging like mad. And anyway, I don't know when in the hell we started to believe that being kind, and all *Kumbaya*, in police academies and military boot camps was a good strategy, in terms of breeding our keepers of the peace and soldiers. When in the hell did that become an accepted mode of preparing people whose sole job it is to protect us from the evils of the planet? These heroes, charged with keeping us all out of harms way from predators who will – without hesitation – flay us all alive and suck every bit of meat off of our bones, need to be as strong minded and willed as the criminals who are out there killing, robbing, burglarizing and violating all other prohibited acts set forth by the Commandments, constitutions, rules, and regulations all around the globe. Personally, I prefer my Law Enforcers to think and act like absolute beasts, untamed animals, Roman Colosseum gladiators... only they'd fight for my team. The demons of the world should fear St. Michael's soldiers, fear the very thought of them, if you ask me. That's the silly part of the whole debate in regards to the use of force; everyone wants to feel safe, and everyone wants the police and military to provide that safety, wanting to leave their front doors open in their neighborhoods, wishing to walk through dark and desolate alleys unscathed, ride the subway at any hour of the night or day without having their gold chain pilfered; but they want these saviors to do it with a kind heart and a smile upon their face... and they don't ever want to be the subject of a possibly negative interaction with Enforcers, either; as if there's some sort of bad guy detector that allows one to distinguish an evil person from others. Unreal. In order to keep a society safe, we all need to do our part, and if that means my father had to get thrown against a wall and slapped around when he got caught selling drugs or walking around with pocket knives to shank some rival gang member, then we're all the better for it at the end of the day. It's all so ridiculous.

Not to veer too far off the ol' yellow brick road; but, I once had this insane conversation with Mark, before he got filled up with brass and died that day in the park, where he commented, "Man, I hate the fuckin' Police. I mean, I fuckin' *really* hate them."

"You don't say." I replied with uninspired enthusiasm. This was a topic discussed repetitively, long windedly, and I had very little interest whenever it was brought up; however, you never wanted to make the guy feel as though you weren't giving him your undivided attention because he was, as previously alluded to, a bit of a narcissistic sociopath and all.

"Yeah, I do say. Not only are they fucking useless as all fucking hell, but they're fucking physically abusive on top of it all. Fucking Police brutality… We should just do away with the mother fuckers… be done with the whole institution. You feel me?" he stated, his eyes focused on rolling his joint.

'That's ridiculous. Do away with the Police?"

"That's right. Fucking eradicate them from the planet." Mark replied, licking the stem of the cigarette.

"So, let me get this right: no more Police. They're gone and now we have to fend for ourselves. No one around to keep anyone from robbing or stealing… raping and murdering."

"We don't need them to protect us from a goddamn thing." he said, coolly, now lighting the marijuana.

"Okay, soooo… how exactly do you propose we stop the evil people out there from doing evil things? Even better still: what would you do if you came home and saw your mom tied up and gagged while the robber was standing right there about to cut her up into tiny little pieces?"

The thought of this caused him to immediately prop his head straight up, erect, his eyes to widen, and to remove the weed stick from his lips. Contemplating on this thought for a brief moment, he then responded, "Bro, I'd put a cap right between that mother fucker's eyes."

"Wow, sounds pretty *brutal*." I reposted with a sarcastic smirk, playing on his previous 'Police brutality' comment. Something which was absolutely not lost on him as he paused for a few seconds before squinting his eyelids and saying, "Man, shut the fuck up;" thereafter passing the marijuana to me.

As good ol' Cunningham trodded along – now returning to my story subsequent to that brief digression - in an apparent agony of the worst variety, the Instructor would, just to remind everyone of her failure, have all of us dive down upon the deck once in awhile to do push-ups or, what was worse, these confounded things called *bear crawls*, which was a diabolical business of bending down in this sort of hunched position, placing one's hands on the slippery floors, deluged with perspiration, whilst one's feet were simultaneously grounded, essentially crawling all over the place until our entire bodies collapsed, face first, onto the bacteria filled marshiness of the gym mats where, I am positively certain, a brand new form of microbe – not yet known to man – had begun to form. Not a fun time. Centuries from now, when the scientists seek to discover the origins of the three eyed, fifteen fingered, three legged mutant species on the planet, they'll come to find that it all began inside of the old Police Academy gym, right there on that feculent floor. Anyway, if you're lounging there, really beating yourself over the noggin about the plight of dear old Cunningham, you'll be thrilled to know that she ended up whipping herself into phenomenal shape because of all the verbal abuse and mortifying shame the Instructors put her through. She really did. If memory serves me correctly, I believe she ended up having some kind of record breaking time in the final run, at the end of the six month program. Go figure. To top it all off, I'll tell you something to really make your heart warm and fuzzy inside: I heard from the proverbial grapevine that she wound up becoming a goddamn one star Chief and shit, which is pretty darn high up on the Department's food chain. Good for her.

Anyhow, moving right along, the conclusion of gym period was always a treat; that's when a couple hundred Recruits squeezed into a locker room the size of a tuna can (with the smell of aforesaid can swirling around and entering our nostrils and lungs, to boot). What made it that much more undesirable was the fact that – after waiting, in the suit that you flew out of your mother's womb with, on a *cheese-line* with your intermittent organ dangling approximately a centimeter from the ass crack of the guy in front of you - there was one very small shower room to be shared by all of the male members of the platoon, open concept, mind you (no private stalls), with only about five or six shower heads, not all of which were always in proper working order, as was the case for practically the entire six month training. This is another severely dissimilar aspect of today's academy. Today, they have this tremendous locker room, a plethora of shower stalls… *private* shower stalls… complete with a mini changing area where you can leave your belongings whilst you indulge in a hot, steaming, wind-down from your *light* jog in the state of the art, air conditioned gymnasium, complete with a ½ mile, cushioned track. Unreal.

Attempting to complete my shower (unmolested and not wishing for my *little trooper* - my male member - to be seen, lest they all realize that it was, by far, subpar according to any and all measurements known to man), a fortuitous conversation began taking place in the tiny paddock. "Hey, man… anybody take any good notes from the behavioral science class today? That dude talks way too fast, man… and it's all that psycho-babble bullshit that I don't understand." said one very naked, and extremely well endowed, African American Recruit – Tyrell - who happened to be lathering (damned thoroughly, I might add) his essential areas to the right of my position.

"I know, bro… I don't understand why they teach us that shit anyway." answered a voice from behind - Vicente. "It's this whole new thing they're doing, trying to teach us empathy and shit… it's such bullshit. My brother came out like seven years ago, in ninety-five, and I told him about this class… he said it's a crock of shit and they came up with it because they got this new thing called CCRB that lets regular people – civilians - like, interview cops to find out why they tell people to fuck off sometimes. He said it's a bunch of horseshit. No one takes them seriously when they get sent for; but, they still have to go downtown to see these fools if they get notified and all."

"Yeah, I heard about that – CCRB… Civilian Complaint Review Board… what a mess, huh?" yet another voice – Abrams - sounded amongst the soaking wet, bare skinned, bodies in the stall. "Like, how in the fuck do you have the nerve to call a Cop down to explain his actions to some college grad, fresh outta school, who has never, in his life, been on the street fighting crime? That absolutely boggles my goddamn mind, you know? I mean, you don't see *us* calling *them* down to the precinct to find out why they used the *Times New Roman* font instead of *Bookman Old Style* on their fucking reports."

"Bro, who's '*us*?' you're still in the Academy, you ain't on the job!" Vicente argued.

"Man, you know what I mean."

"Listen, bros, none of that matters at this point." I exclaimed, finally breaking into the conversation, in a desperate attempt to put an end to the blasted colloquy. "Right now, we need to just concentrate on passing these classes, graduating, and getting the fuck outta this building. This shit is straight up nasty, bro. We need to get back to life!"

This, my attempt, failed miserably; instead, prompting Vicente to break out into song: "*Back to life, back to reality, back to the here and now, yeah; show me how, decide what you want from me; tell me, maybe I could be there for you!*" he belted from his diaphragm, offering a significantly horrific rendition of Soul II Soul's hit track, 'Back to Life.'

"Oh, shit n—! that's my jam!" Tyrell exclaimed, breaking out into a dance, lifting his hands up into the air, spinning around towards the middle of the shower room, gyrating his hips left and right, causing his abnormally large male member – similar in all aspects to a woolly mammoth's trunk - to become extremely visible, swaying back and forth like Big Ben's mighty pendulum… not an especially welcoming sight; unless, of course, that sort of thing tickles your ol' fancy. I'm no one to judge.

Utterly mortified, the sight of this particularly gruesome pantomime not being what floats my ol' boat, I washed the remaining bit of my body as rapidly as any human being possibly could, beating it the hell out of there, subsequently heading up to the classroom, where I'd spend the next couple of hours being enlightened by a burnt out *five year wonder* Cop who, by means of a hook – a favor given to him by someone of influence - landed a teaching spot in the Academy, where he had the opportunity to share with his students all of his specious as hell war stories… stories that, had he the balls to spew to the *real* Officers in his old Command, would have had him laughed out of the building. Lucky us. When I arrived upstairs, there were a handful of Recruits already *standing-by* outside of the classroom, awaiting the arrival of the aforementioned Classroom Instructor. The thing was, you couldn't go into the room until everyone was mustered up in perfect rows of three, and even then we had to wait for the Instructor to grace us with his presence, so that he could inspect us before we entered. It was all very showy, but I didn't mind it all that much; I always wanted to join the military, but never got around to it, so all of this hullabaloo made me feel as though I was in actual basic training for the Army and all that crap. While standing there, giving myself the once over to make sure I looked 'the part,' I caught a glimpse of this super cute chic who was in my Company, named Victoria… and man, was she a dime piece… a real looker. She had this whole exotic thing going on, sort of like she was from the Amazon or something like that, not too dissimilar from Rose, now that I think of it. Very homogeneous features, both Rose and Victoria, if I'm being completely forthcoming… maybe I've got a *type*, who knows?

Anyway, I was right in the middle of checking Victoria out from top to bottom when, before I knew it, and before I had a chance to look away like a cowardly second grader, our eyes met, pupil to pupil. I thought, for sure, that she was going to give me the screw face for gawking at her (it's kind of what usually happens when I end up ogling the fairer sex); but, to my great astonishment, she gave me this sort of coy smile, which I immediately returned; although mine, I must say, was more of the philandering variety, being the sexual deviant that I am… in my mind, at least. I decided to follow it up with a salutation. I figured, what the hell? what did I have to lose? "Hello." I said, still wearing this insanely kittenish grin across my face.

"Hi." she answered, with a well-nigh diffident air in her reply, extremely bashful I must say. It was pretty damn cute, though. I mean, some girls – especially the ridiculously hot ones – come off as though they believe their feces to possess the aroma akin to a field of gardenias. Not her. Here was a bewitchingly gorgeous belle, who could've swatted me away with looks of disdain in a fit of pique; but, instead, she throws me the most charming little smile. Very high class.

"I'm James… James Cardona."

"I know." she responded with a modest giggle. "We're in the same Company, so I kind of hear it every day at roll call."

"Right." I said, possessing a hint of embarrassment. "And you're Victoria… Victoria Almonte."

"Yep, that's me." she replied, smirking just enough to express interest, but not showing any teeth, almost as if she were holding herself back from an ejaculation of everything that is ravishingly exquisite in this world.

"Nice to meet you, Victoria. So how are you liking it all, so far? Is it everything you hoped, wished, and dreamed?" I asked, providing a little facetious humor to shake off the proverbial cobwebs of my flirting game. Sometimes humor has this necromantic ability to stimulate a situation when stupid nerves prevent a fella from talking to young ladies of the nubile sort, you know what I mean? Not to mention that it had been a great while since having the opportunity to break the proverbial ice with someone whose acquaintance was not made. I was a bit rusty, to be honest.

"Hoped, wished, and dreamed?" she mimicked, this time offering a hearty laugh, the force of which caused her head to fall slightly to the rear. "That's a little extreme! I mean, I wouldn't quite say it in those *exact* words."

"Yes, there was a small hint of sarcasm in the question, I admit." I replied, also with a slight chortle. "I'll tell you what, it's definitely not at all what *I* expected. I mean, I recently found out that, when we get out of here and onto the streets, there'll be no high speed car chases, shoot-outs with bank robbers, or any sliding across hoods of cars. My dreams have pretty much been crushed."

"Oh my, I'm so sorry to hear that; although I'm sure it taught you a valuable lesson; never allow yourself to dream so big… you shot way too high up into the stars on that one, I'm afraid!" she replied, with a raised eyebrow and laugh that, this time, showed a set of brilliant, sparkling white teeth.

I laughed at her jest, appreciating the return of some good, dry, humor, seeing as how I kind of have this proclivity to offer a similar brand of jocularity, arid in nature, from time to time. "Listen," I began, feeling positive about my chances of furthering this conversation, outside of the prying eyes and ears of our fellow scholars in the enforcement of law. "I was wondering… would you want to maybe meet up after class? Maybe grab a drink or something? If you can't, it's okay… I mean, if you're busy or whatever, I -"

"Yes," she interrupted, all the while maintaining that magnanimous grin of hers, "I'd love to."

"Oh… great! That's great. Okay!" I stammered, exceedingly grateful for not getting rejected all over the goddamn place; but, simultaneously, ill prepared for the favorable response.

Just then, after all of the other guys and gals had made their way up from the gym, now all lined up in perfect formation, the Instructor appeared before us as though he were the Almighty atop Mt. Sinai, with his usual air of superiority, ignoring all but one of us, which happened to be the Company Sergeant (not a *real* Sergeant, mind you; just some bum – a Recruit, like us – who happened to have some kind of military background, so they threw him a couple of brass chevrons for the collars of his uniform shirt; which, incidentally, filled this *wanna-be's* head up with more gas than a squadron of hot air balloons). "Company!" the makeshift Sergeant squealed at the top of his stupid lungs, "Aaaatennnnnntion!" This prompting us to snap to a position of attention, which is, essentially, standing tall with your hands straight down along your sides, thereafter not moving one single muscle in your body. I mean it, not a single one. No matter what, you were supposed to stand as still as one of Medusa's wretched victims; and, in the event that you just happened to have the itches at the edge of your schnozzola... well, that's just too bad for you; you were simply going to have to stand there and suffer... perform some sort of powerfully majestic, Tibetan monk-type, trick to fool your mind into believing there *is* no itch; otherwise, you were sure to catch all of hell's fury and fire. Seriously.

"At ease." said the Instructor in a suave as hell manner, feeling pretty damn high and mighty, I'm sure. It's a helluva mind sweller to have a bunch of people snap their spines upright when you come waltzing around the corner. Real empowering stuff.

"Company! paaaaaraaaade resssst!" the fake sergeant replied aloud, which meant we could relax our stance just a bit by placing our hands behind our backs, one hand over the other, and widening our stance.

Facing the delusional sergeant – within a gnat's reach of one another's noses – the Instructor, continuing the daily ritual, before we were permitted to enter the classroom, barked, "Company Sergeant! report!"

"Sir! the Company is accounted for and awaiting your orders."

"Very well, Company Sergeant, you may post your squad."

"Company! fall in!" which, at long last, meant the torturously protracted charade was over, the lot of us finally being able to enter the room and take our goddamn seats.

VI

Victoria and I met up a few days later at a swanky little spot downtown called The Red Velvet, wherein we both got just a tad sloshy after pounding down a few dozen boilermakers each. I must confess, she and I were a hot mess after only a couple of hours consuming our libation, spewing some pretty outlandish dialogue to one another. If I remember correctly - which is to say, I barely remember at all – the scripts of the *exact* conversation, it was singularly insufferable in nature. I shall do the best I can… my very best… to recall the libretto, because I'm sure you're hanging on the edge of your Lazy Boy, shoveling a buttery bowl of popcorn down your throat, awaiting the juicy details. The place, The Red Velvet, was a fairly decent joint; the atmosphere being on the trendy side, having the whole *undone* look about it - a most popular spectacle in those days, what with exposed pipes running along the entire ceiling, making it appear as though you were inside of some sort of an industrial basement or maybe a kind of warehouse. Who knows? It really was the new look; every place was doing it. As a matter of fact, if the spot you went to *didn't* have that particular design, you and everybody else were supposed to turn right around, *tout de suite*, beat it out of there, and scour the entire metropolis to try and find someplace that *did* sport that distinct look. They also had these black and white photos of real slick actors and singers hanging from the walls, people like Madonna during her *Vogue* phase of life, striking *une pose elegante*; James Dean lounging on a deck by the water, scowling at the photographer in a way that only the great Mr. Dean could do; Johnny Depp in some old-as-all-hell vintage kitchen – right out of the 1950s - perched upon an old fashioned stove with a cigarette dangling out of his mouth; and other pretty cool rustic artifacts scattered all about the beanery… insanely appealing.

The music selection was wanting… at least to me. I'm not too much into popular music; like, I don't go crazy for the latest jams that are playing, ad nauseam, on the radio; I'm more of a *plug in your device and listen to your mixed tape* kind of a guy, so I didn't share her enthusiasm for the song, 'If I Could Go,' by Angie Martinez, that was currently emanating from the speakers. "Ooo, this is my song!" she said, closing her eyes; lowering her head; puckering her lips; lifting her arms up in a ninety degree angle; and snapping her fingers in unison to the beat. "Isn't it so hot? the song? I totally love her… I mean it, I *love* her! Don't you?"

"So hot." I parroted with lackluster enthusiasm.

She opened her eyes with an astounded look painted all across the entirety of her countenance. "You don't like Angie Martinez? But this song is so dope right now… like, *everyone* loves it. It's *so* dope."

"Oh, it's cool." I said, not wanting to spoil the mood with some kind of debate about the bullshit song. "I mean, I'm sure it's really popular. I'm just not a pop-song kinda guy. I sort of keep to the beat of my own drum… uh, no pun intended."

"Well I think it's dope." she rehashed, shutting her eyes once again, retreating back into her trance, undulating to the rhythm.

At this point, I wanted very much to get up and walk out on her. It was clear there would be absolutely no future whatsoever with this girl… no way that this division of artistic taste could be tolerated. I could not bear to spend the rest of my life with a person that, every time some ridiculous song came on the radio – a song she'd already heard ten times in a matter of hours on the goddamn radio – would subject me to this outrageous, overly theatrical, performance. Luckily, just before I went ahead and pulled a Harry Houdini-style escape, she snapped out of her musical reverie and said, with a somewhat vampish look upon her mug, "Do you wanna get outta here? to my place?"

"Absolutely."

What? Was I supposed to have said '*no*?' You look me straight in the ol' peepers and tell me you would've refused that request. If you insist on saying that you, my dear reader, would have declined the invitation, we may as well part ways now… this relationship can only continue if we're being completely genuine with one another. I won't have any of that '*holier than thou*' crap going on while I'm here spilling the entirety of my offals all over the hardwood, telling this story… I just won't. I have cut the ol' umbilical cord with other human beings for lesser reasons than that, just so you are aware. Anyway, we ended up leaving that place and swinging on over to her digs; a very cozy little apartment in Park Slope, Brooklyn… an especially posh looking pad, I must say; although most of her nicknacks were of the TJ Max variety. Not to say that this particular brand of fashion isn't *a la mode* – it was actually all quite elegant looking and very tactfully placed; it's just that, had any of that exceedingly fancy stuff been authentic, she'd have some serious explaining to do in terms of the ability to afford said appurtenances, is all. For instance, take the two marble end tables that rested on either side of the grey, pleather, couch: I'm most certain that if I, on an occasion where sheer boredom had set in - with nothing on this planet to do but mindlessly fidget - went to scraping the edges of the aforementioned tables, we would – no doubt – find the material to be of a *fictus omnium gatherum*. We would discover it not to be the crystalline metamorphic form of limestone that it purported to be, is all I'm trying to get at. Not a big deal. Not at all.

Now listen, in regards to she (Victoria) and I, the specifics of the thing – the play by play, if you will – going on in her bedchamber will be left to your wonderfully vivid imaginations (because, frankly, any man who would discuss the goings on of such a thing should have his reproductive seed-conduit removed with a dull, rusty, butter knife as far as I'm concerned); but whatever we *did* do continued to be done for about a month, or so, subsequent to our first rendezvous. That is, until Instructor Dong – both his real surname as well as the underlying reason for our parting of ways, his *da ganzi* being far superior to my poor excuse for a provider of pleasure - our law teacher at the Academy, cudgeled his way into the picture.

He, Dong, was good for two things: teaching the New York State Penal Law by day and laying down the *penile law* with his female students at night. The guy was a *class A* womanizer, but he was also a pretty damn good looking gentleman, so he could sort of get away with whatever he damn well wanted. It was for this reason, this haughty confidence, that he felt the gratuitous desire to feed us a bunch of horse manure every single day, in between actually educating us on more relevant topics, i.e., the subsections of Criminal Sexual Act in the first degree, in addition to the parlous violation of walking around New York City with an ice cream cone in your pocket (which is a real thing… look it up) to name a few. "You guys," so his soliloquy began, "have absolutely no idea what it's like out there… you really don't. All you little knuckleheads who think you got what it takes to be an Officer in this city, like it's no big deal… like you got it all under control… man, let's just fuckin' say that I wish I could be the fly on your shit riddled boots when they finally – God help us all – release your candy asses from the sanctity of this place and put your pathetic asses on the street." Many of us, at this point of the sermon, inconspicuously looked around the room at one another, rolling our eyes and screwing our faces unbeknownst to, and out of sight of, the preacher.

One of the Recruits, Lawrence, was battling (and apparently losing) the compulsion to enter REM sleep, his head bobbling back and forth as though a screw had come loose in his neck; only the whites of his eyes visible; his lids fluttering like the wings of a hummingbird, which – unfortunately for Lawrence – caught the attention of the big bad Dong. "Recruit!" he trumpeted, simultaneously banging his closed fist down upon the table of the noctambulist, alarming and awakening every other comatose soul in the classroom. "Wake the fuck up, you goddamn loser! Is this what you're gonna do out on patrol? Are you gonna fall asleep and leave yourself open to some kind of ambush? Is that it? Is that what you're gonna do?"

"No, sir." answered Lawrence, meekly, whilst attempting to regain his bearings as to where, precisely, he was at that moment.

"You could've fooled me! Next time, if I ever so much as see any portion of your fuckin' eyelids, I'm gonna take the pen that Libardi is chewing on over there," here the Instructor pointed to Libardi, an innocent victim in this tirade, who just so happened to be devouring his pen cap, before continuing, "and shove it so far up your ass, you're gonna be able to take notes by clutching his pen through your teeth."

Libardi, the nosher of said writing instrument, immediately spat the object out onto the table in front of him, with a look of sheer repugnance upon his countenance; Lawrence, the intended recipient, along with the rest of us lot raised Libardi's repugnance with utter incertitude, trying desperately to shed the odious vision from our brains.

He, Dong, then went on to resume the rest of his pleonastic disquisition; which, for me, had begun to fall upon deaf ears, not so much due to the fact that it, in and of itself, became a kind of white background noise after about three minutes or so, but – much more importantly – as I continued to reconnoiter the room, I espied my *amoureuse,* Victoria, much to my chagrin, totally undressing the orator with her caramel colored eyes. At one point, right as the two of them locked irises with one another, she languidly swirled her tongue three hundred and sixty degrees around her mouth, concluding with the biting of her bottom lip; to which he responded with a slight pause in his dissertation to deliver a very obvious wink of the eye, accompanied by a slight pucker of his lips… a grotesquely obscene gesture that everyone, including the formerly zombified Lawrence, discerned, all who now faced me with a look of astonishment upon their countenances, my love affair with the Jezebel having been well known during those days. It was honestly one of the most humiliating moments of my life… clearly the subject of some reprehensible, double-dealing, treachery.

I'd love to have confronted good ol' Vic right after that Law class to give her a piece of my mind… to read her the goddamn riot act and explain to her just how much of a dirty vixen I thought she was, as well as to wish her and her new beau, that no-good home-wrecker, a healthy and happy life together; but I couldn't on account of the fact that we had Gym right after. If you were late for Gym, the Instructors (who were, as was previously mentioned, akin to military drill sergeants) would essentially tear you a brand new asshole by PT'ing you until your muscles disintegrated into dust, so I sort of refrained.

It was boxing day down in the sweat box, which was perfectly apropos for the way in which I was feeling... like, I had a great yearning to send someone's cranium soaring away from their framework, to be insanely honest. Leather pugilist gloves were passed out to the Platoon, and we all were partnered up with someone in which to fight. I got paired up with this Russian kid who I thought I could take pretty easily; he was about my height, not much going on by way of mass, and this sort of goofy hairdo that looked similar to a fully used ear swab... the kind of fella that you could seemingly mop the floor with, as it were. "Heh, my main man," he said to me right before the bout, in a thick Russian accent, not too dissimilar from Drago, the terrifying antagonist in the feature film Rocky IV, "mehbee you no heet de face? yes? Ezzpecially mehbee you no heet de nose and de mouth, heh buckaroo? Donna try to be cowboy, vat do you say? heh? vee haf deeel?"

"No promises, bro." I said with an indignant timbre; the pugnacious feelings, obviously, not intended for him; but, nevertheless, receiving the collateral damage of my discontent... and, in a matter of seconds, the balls of my fists.

"Now listen up, you wastes of life," an Instructor bellowed, interrupting the parlay between my co-combatant and I, "the point of this exercise is to give you an opportunity to hone your fighting skills... which I'm very sure are practically nil. I don't want to see any pussyfooting in here… if I do, I'm gonna put *my* gloves on and take over for your partner, and you don't want *that*, trust me. Got it? dirtbags?"

"Yes, sir!" The gym block shouted in unison, at which point I looked at my fellow pugilist and shrugged my shoulders, communicating to him an implication of, *'you heard what the man said, it's out of my hands.'*

The Moscow Marauder simply leered back at me with a countenance that expressed his great disappointment in regards to the apparent breakdown in diplomatic relations between us. Just then, emanating from the Instructor's cell phone speaker into the megaphone being held in his alternate mitt, the sound of a ringside bell was heard, sending all of the participants into a gallimaufry of flailing hands and closed eyes, not a single one knowing what, in the name of all that is holy and pure, they were doing. There was no skill, whatsoever, amongst the lot of us… myself included; merely a conglomeration of internecine warfare. A pitiful sight. It was by sheer chance, just a simple matter of the *law of averages* in full effect, that one of the agrestal swings offered by my dancing partner found its way to the medial portion of my left temple, sending me, instantly, into a stage three nap; the begrimed floor, muddied from the combination of sweat and God knows whatever soiled the bottoms of everyone's shoes, befouling the entirety of my face.

I guess it served me right. I mean, whatever I was feeling about Victoria and Instructor Dong didn't give me the right to take it out on poor Ivan Drago, who apparently had more in common with Rocky Balboa's foe than I had anticipated. Good for him. I deserved it… a good ol' knock across my bow… it's precisely what

I needed to put some sense into my brain. To be quite forthcoming, those who let unrelated situations dictate their actions and emotions, taking out their anger and frustrations on innocent folks, ought to be sent to the mud splattered floors of moisture laden gymnasiums… and much worse, if you want to know the truth of it all. So, upon regaining consciousness, now being helped to a *fowler's position* by the Instructors – in addition to becoming surrounded and gawked at by the entire student body (including Victoria) – I got up and immediately shook hands with ol' Drago and said, "Nice shot, brother." What else can one do?

Quite honestly, there isn't much more to tell about the Police Academy… it was a lot more of those humdrum lectures, note taking, saluting, and all that jazz. The only other thing I can tell you about was graduation; which was, I have to admit, a pretty decent affair that took place over at Madison Square Garden, this huge arena in New York City where the Knicks basketball team and Rangers hockey team play. It was kind of neat to see all of us newbies in our dress uniforms, shiny eight point caps, patten leather shoes, and white gloves all gathered together in that proclaimed Mecca of sports. The Police Commissioner hurled an exceedingly motivating speech at us about being the greatest Police Department on the face of the Earth and all that good shit, which sort of made the hairs on my arms get up and stretch, to be honest. The only thing that spoiled it for me, the thing that ruined my entire stinking day, was seeing the two star crossed lovers, Victoria and Instructor Dong, leaving together hand in hand, heading off into the sunset. It was a pretty miserable sight. There was no time to dwell on my fractured romance, though. I was officially a newly appointed probationary Police Officer of the Big Apple, and it was time to take a nice, juicy, mouth watering bite… although, sometimes, when you sink your teeth into the fruit whose consumption caused the inaugural and most tragically epic banishment in human history, you end up on the wrong side of Eden.

VII

It was a glacial, but otherwise bright and sunny day in January when I arrived at my brand new Command in the sultry borough of the *boogie down* Bronx. About fifteen freshly graduated Rookies were sent to this particular Precinct, all of us ushered into the Muster Room (where, for the reader's informational purposes, every day before the start of the *tour* Cops stand and receive their assignments for the day). I'm not afraid to admit – not one single, solitary, bit – that I was practically soiling my bloomers at the thought of actually *being* a Police Officer; I mean, I realized that I had just spent the last six months training for every possible scenario which could arise out on the street; but I had no clue - no *real* clue - as to what was in store for me… did these guys *actually* expect me to go out there and uphold the law? Couldn't I just explain to them that this was all a terrible mistake? Like, 'Sorry, fellas… sorry to waste your time; this has all been one big, very big, misunderstanding. Here's your gun, your shield… here, take it all. Be well and thanks for the laughs. It's been real!'

Before I could really allow that singularly tempting idea – at the time - to sink in and make a bee line out of there, a Sergeant, a *real* Sergeant (not the fake Company Sergeant, like in the Academy) walked through the door with an Officer. We all jumped to our feet and snapped to attention like well trained circus animals, until the Sergeant, Sergeant Portico - while bursting out into a fit of laughter - said, "Holy shit! You little mother fuckers scared the shit outta me!" He was referring to the fact that, when we bolted out of our seats like someone shoved a stick up our rectums, all the chairs sort of slid back causing some very minor clashing and clattering… certainly not enough racket to draw such an overwrought reaction as his, though. Very dramatic. "Holy shit! Jesus. Did that scare *you*, Haas?" he inquired of the Officer who entered with him.

"Very scary, Sarge." was Haas' curt and obediently sycophantic reply.

"Jesus! sit the fuck down, all o' yooze." Portico continued. "This ain't the Academy… don't ever do that again; that is, unless a *DI* or above happens to waltz on in here… otherwise, cut that shit out" he exclaimed, referring to someone in the rank of Deputy Inspector or above, which is a rank above a Captain, whose entrance you must acknowledge by leaping as high in the air as you possibly can before snapping to attention, as if Queen Mary of Scots had just graced our presence by waltzing in the goddamn room or something.

We all took our seats, looking at each other like a bunch of lost souls in *purgatorium*. I mean, we had just spent the last six months in a hell hole that drilled into us the all important rule of showing courtesies, jumping to our feet a thousand and seven times a day, saluting anyone that *wasn't* us; but now, conversely, we were being told to never do it again. We were lost. And this would not be the last time we lot would feel this way… all of us were going to learn that, in spite of everything that was taught, the whole of the lessons that were painfully ingrained into our crazy heads through a surfeit amount of cruel and unusual corporal punishment were basically all for naught. We were going to learn the stinking reality of it all. At this point, once we returned the seats to their damned upright positions, Sergeant Portico, along with his penumbra, took a seat in front of the probationers and continued, "Now listen up: my name is Sergeant Portico and I'm gonna be your Field Training Sergeant. This here is Officer Haas -"

"Andy… call me Andy." interjected the Officer.

"There you go," Portico continued, "this is Andy; and he'll be your Field Training Officer. Our job, Lord help us, is to take the last six months of your life and wipe them clean outta your impressionable little domes. Whatever those burnt out *five year wonders,* who couldn't hack it out there in the streets, poisoned your brains with… well, we're gonna try our best to lobotomize outta yooze..." He paused at this point, apparently becoming aware of the absolute look of trepidation on our countenances, Andy and he exchanging a surreptitious glance at one another before Sergeant Portico continued, "… now, uh, listen here, we're not telling yooze to forget *every single* thing… that's not *exactly* what I'm saying. There's just a huge difference between what you read in a bunch of books and what actually happens out there in the real world, you understand? Those Instructors… well, they're mostly kids who had hooks and only possess a handful of years doing *actual* police work, you get me?"

The look of terror remained upon our miens.

Andy broke in, probably realizing that it would take a bit of time before our white-washed brains could accept that this was not some sort of ruse; that, perhaps, it was best to start slow – maybe ol' Andy, a peer (somewhat), would have a better chance at reaching us, as opposed to a Sergeant who, in the Academy, equates to the rank of viscount in aristocracy. "Listen, guys, we're gonna jump in the van and take a ride around the Precinct, so you all can get a lay of the land. We'll stop at a deli or something beforehand, so you can get your bacon, egg, and cheeses, or whatever; then, we'll take a few spins around the 'hood'… how does that sound?"

We all, in unison, nodded our heads in the affirmative, but remained seated, waiting for permission to be told to exist otherwise. This was most definitely going to take some getting used to. The Academy had broken us down to our studs, like wild mustangs on a farm, tirelessly and relentlessly breaking us for saddle and harness; now, it was time to build ourselves back up and tear from the reins of our equestrians. This, as you could possibly envisage whilst you read this story from your wrap-around sectional sofa, cocktail in hand, with Mozart Sonatas playing in the background, would prove easier said than done.

***

About a week or so after that maiden encounter with Sergeant Poritco and Andy, we – myself and the rest of the Rookies - were already ankle deep in reality; the fantasy land of the Police Academy already a lifetime in the past, as I found myself, on a daily basis, walking a solitary foot post – no other Officer in sight – in one of the worst neighborhoods within the Precinct… on a midnight tour, no less. Back then, as contrasted with the way it's done in today's zeitgeist, it was not a requirement to walk a post with a partner. A few grisly assassinations in the years subsequent to this time period changed that, I suppose. On most nights, I'd end up – to remain warm, fed, and dry - taking shelter in grocery stores, Chinese food restaurants, or pizza shops. Remaining safe from any possible ambushes by bandits who didn't appreciate a Cop hanging around their zone of influence was a welcomed little variable to taking positions in these aforementioned places of refuge, by the goddamn way.

My dad, who drove a cab for a living at that time, to my

pleasant surprise, just happened to, serendipitously – according to his account of things – be in the neighborhood of my foot post. Personally, I think he showed up because he didn't like it so hot that I was walking around by myself in that shitty area; but, he'd never admit a thing like that, not to me anyway. I wasn't complaining, though; it was the middle of winter and my phalanges felt like they were about to break off of my hands and feet. There wasn't a single member of the human race in sight, and very few cars on the road; so, when I saw a bright red 1983 *Reliant K,* with one faulty headlight, approaching, making a perfusion of backfiring sound effects as it rolled down the street, I sort of knew it was my old man. He pulled over to my post, leaned over to manually roll the passenger side window down, and said, in his insanely desiccated, but whimsical, way – typical of every dad in the entire world, dry humor seemingly a necessary prerequisite for fatherhood - "Excuse me, Officer, I'm lost, you know where I can score some cheeba?" He meant marijuana, which was actually pretty funny at that moment in time. Take it from me, whenever you find yourself alone in the middle of a crappy neighborhood, wondering if you're going to make it out alive, and your dad pulls up telling platitudinous 'dad jokes,' you tend to expand the range of your sense of humor. All jesting aside, I was pretty goddamn happy to see him.

"Pop! What are you doing around these parts?" I said, walking over to his car and leaning into the passenger side window.

"Oh, man, I just dropped off a fare not too far from here." he replied, gesticulating his thumb backwards, to indicate that the aforesaid fare was to his rear. "How's the night going?"

"It's going… I don't know what direction, but it's going."

I replied, picking myself up from the window for a brief second to conduct a 360 degree recon of the area. You never want to lean into a car too long without giving an ol' *once over* to the neighborhood every few seconds or so. It's sort of tactically sound and all of that shit.

"Mm hm." he replied. "You hungry? Want to go grab a slice?"

"You read my mind, sir."

We ended up heading to this pizza shop that was, technically, still within the confines of my post, so I wouldn't find myself in *extremely* terrible trouble if I were to get pinched by the good Sergeant. Some of the local miscreants were dining in the establishment when we entered, and I could feel the burn of their laser beam-like stares upon my dad and I, wondering, I'm sure, why some old guy was walking into the place with a Cop at his side. "Such welcoming glances we're getting." I said, with a tinge of concern, not fully prepared to come face to face with the antagonistic fury of the masses.

"Fuck 'em." he countered. "You just gotta stare at 'em right back. Look 'em right in the eye and stare right though them. You're the *Po*-lice, dude, what else is being *the fuzz* good for? if not to impose your will upon the meek and innocent people with a good old fashioned venomous stare." he concluded, placing some sort of strange emphasis on the word 'police,' strictly – I'm sure – for the purposes of aggravating me.

"Yeah," I laughed, "that's what we do all day long, imposing our will by leering at people as they down their pepperoni calzones."

"Got news for you, my son… that's *exactly* what they do… right before they place an open hand slap across your face at a hundred miles an hour." he countered, matter of factly. "Oh yeah, shit, I almost forgot… so busy talking about *Po*-lice bullshit." he said, reaching into his coat pocket and pulling out an object that I couldn't quite make out at first, due to the fact that it was in some kind of casing. "Gracie told me to give this to you. It's a belated graduation present. She wanted to give it to you in person, but you got these crazy hours, so I figured I'd bring it to you myself."

"What is it?" I inquired, while peeling apart the covering, which was held together by some kind of Velcro.

"Open it and see."

"I am… oh wow, it's a tourniquet." I said with vapid enthusiasm. I wasn't a practical gadget sort of guy; like, I wasn't one of those fellas that get all out of control excited about tools and other masculine items… I'm more of a cologne and leisurely electronics guy. Get me a bottle of sweet and sexy smelling Joop, or a sick pair of Sony headphones, and now we're talking… *that's* what really floats my ol' boat, in case you were wondering what to get me for the next special occasion and whatnot.

"Well, you never know when you're going to need the thing, so tuck it away in your back pocket. And show some goddamn appreciation… you can't be so ungrateful, James. Your sister thought of you and that should be enough for some gratitude."

"I'm not ungrateful. I *do* appreciate it. I'm gonna call Gracie tomorrow, I promise." I said, now riddled with overwhelming guilt. I have this confounded self-condemnation thing going on whenever someone tells me I don't appreciate something; like, I get all dispirited and crestfallen about crap like that. It's this weird sensation I feel in the depths of my chest and stomach, something that's been a part of my insides for as long as I can remember… like an overwhelming sense of regret about my personal decisions… and I hate it. I'd love to sit down with a shrink and have her excavate the cause of that from my soul one of these days. I really would. Maybe one day I'll get around to doing just that, sitting down on a nice, comfy sofa and having a psychoanalyst mince my subconscious into little fragments to figure it all out. It's on my *to do* list, for sure.

"Mm hm. Listen, speaking a little about everything, how are you doing with this… the whole Cop thing. I see they're putting you out here all by yourself; not too bright, your *Po*-lice Department friends. A lot can go wrong out here and you ain't got nobody to have your back." he said, taking a bite of his slice, whilst simultaneously gulping his Diet Coke.

"I *do* have a radio, you know." I contended, picking the pepperonis off of my pizza… I enjoy eating them separate and apart from the bread, sauce and cheese, don't judge. "I can call for backup anytime I'm in trouble."

"A lot can happen in between all of that nonsense, real fast, kiddo." he argued. "That little radio of yours is only gonna help them find your cold, dead, body."

"Jeez, Pop, that's real nice."

"Hey, you gotta have thicker skin now, Mr. *Po*-lice;" he added, "what I'm saying shouldn't be hurting your feelings."

"It's not hurting my feelings, it's… anyway, so I have a radio; and I have a bunch of stuff on my gun belt that can keep me alive while backup is heading my way. That's all I'm trying to say… *jeez-us*."

"Oh yeah? okay… well, if you got everything figured out…"

"I'm not saying I have everything figured out; I'm just saying it's not as grim and hopeless as you're making it sound. That's all I'm saying."

"Okay." he said, taking another a bite of his pizza, looking around the shop, now avoiding eye contact with me in disquieted silence… his way of passive-aggressively sending me a message of displeasure, a precursor to the 'white-hot' thing I told you about earlier.

"Listen, Pop… I know you're just looking out for me." I began, not only wanting to avoid sending him into the abyss of no return, but also suddenly remembering the words of Rose, the friend I told you about right before I went into the tirade about the Department. "You're just concerned for my well being, I see that and I appreciate it. I *really* do. And I know you don't have the greatest love for this job; but it's what I am… who I am… now, and I've got to give it a chance to work… I'm hoping - *really* hoping - that you can give it a chance, too. I know you've had some very shitty experiences with Cops; but I'm not them… and there's a bunch of guys and gals just like me, who are also *not* like them… trust me, I've personally met these individuals. You just have to give it a chance… give *me* a chance."

"Okay, kiddo." he replied, after some moments of silence,

with an inkling of disinclination remaining in his tone. "We'll see how it goes. Eat your pizza, it's getting cold."

We sat together in that pizza shop for a couple of hours and I must admit – apart from the slight hiccup of our difference of opinion - it was something I'll never forget. All these years later it dawned on me – I mean, it *really* dawned on me – the significance of his little sojourn on my post that wintry evening in the middle of the night. There are no existing bounds between a loving, caring, father and his son. Not even the turbulent history with an entity that represents, to him, all that is evil, with echos of a beleaguered past sauntering around in his hippocampus, can bifurcate the divinely numinous relationship of a patriarch and his offspring. I would, without any hesitancy or apprehension, spend a thousand more nights such as that one with my dad.

VIII

Sometime in the sweltering summer month of July, our Field Training – which essentially consisted of excruciatingly monotonous days, standing those lonesome foot posts - had come to a much welcomed conclusion, and we were all, subsequently, sent to various platoons and squads. I ended up on the four by twelve tour, which is to say that I worked from about three in the afternoon until somewhere around eleven thirty at night; incidentally, the busiest shift there was, not just in my Precinct, but, pretty much, Department wide. That was just fine with me because I was beyond uber ready to get into a Police car (something we had all yet to see the inside of) and do some real Police work. The thing of it is, they – the powers that be – still didn't trust us to gallivant around in vehicles on our own. It was one thing to throw us out to the wolves by ourselves, essentially putting *our* lives in danger, it was an entirely other thing to place their precious cars at risk… the Department won't stand for such blatant disregard for these valuable assets; therefore, we had to ride around with Senior Officers at the onset of our new assignment. It was either this or *use and abuse* us for little odds and ends (undesirable jobs) that Rookies, derelicts, and dinosaur Cops got stuck with. From the above mentioned list, the latter two actually *preferred*, and *thoroughly enjoyed*, those sort of dead-beat assignments because it bore very little responsibility and, more importantly, meant that they didn't have to run around, *chasing the radio*, answering jobs, and responding to all kinds of outlandish situations that either got them in trouble or put them in danger of being hurt.

On this particular Friday afternoon, the temperature practically soaring in the mid thousands, I walked into the muster room, which was, you should know, just about double the temperature outside. That's one thing about every single Command in the entire city, whatever the weather might be outside of the building, you can rest assured that it can be multiplied by two within its walls in the summer and, conversely, divided by the same factor in the winter. Anyway, so I walked into the muster room to prepare for Roll Call, sitting off in a corner by myself (this was due to the fact that I was a foreign entity and didn't really know anybody… and I had enough sense to realize: there's not a single Cop in the room that would make random conversation with a spanking new Rookie). The thing of it is, there *was* an unwritten system which, incidentally, does *not* exist today – a hierarchy if you will – which determines, depending on the time you have on the job, who and who will not give you the time of day. It's quite simple, really. If you are fresh out of the box new – which commences at the moment of your arrival to approximately eleven months subsequent to this time - or are a transfer from another Command who is not known and is not vouched for, you are, ipso facto, less than a baboon's bowel movement. Outside of anything job related, you have the worst of the plagues known to man, therefore will be quarantined and ostracized, living in the world of the non-existent; if you have between one to four years *on*, you live in an incestuous pool of other one to four year Cops. Basically, you only talk to one another about personal shit, even though, if you need help, the Officers with five to nine years will guide you with any work stuff; the ten to fourteen year guys are in this weird, adolescent stage of the job, wherein they sort of *think* they have a ton of time on, but are reminded of their lesser station by the *true* Senior Cops, which are the ones with fifteen years and above in Service. That's the way it was in our *thing*, and the sooner you accepted it, the better off you'd be; either you dealt with the reality of it, or you learned your lesson by retrieving your locker from the nearest (or sometimes furthest) subway train car.

Anyway, like I was saying, before I went off into outer space with my drawn out explanation of things, I was sitting in the muster room when someone shouted, as was the custom, "They're coming!" referring to the Patrol Sergeant and the Platoon Commander (the Platoon Commander being the Lieutenant in charge of any given shift), both of whom could be seen through the muster room's door window, now stepping down from the main desk and making a beeline towards us. What occurred next was another time honored tradition which is not always observed in these modern times… the Cops jumped up and scurried to the center of the room, filing into commensurate rows of three, placing their eight point caps upon their domes, and ceasing all conversation, leaving the proverbial pin drop to be the sole surviving sound. By the time the Sergeant and Lieutenant walked in, the room bore resemblance to the workshop in 'March of the Wooden Soldiers,' the old Christmas movie staring Laurel and Hardy, wherein all the toy soldiers stood proud and tall, in perfect rows, quietly awaiting their instructions. My chest surged with a sense of pride, seeing what was clearly a display of the gleaming professionalism that was the Police Department.

"Alright, fuck-o's, attention to roll call!" barked the Sergeant (McMahon, I could see on his nameplate) deflating, instantly, the whole *'gleaming professionalism'* thing I just mentioned feeling in my chest… the sensation was probably an effect attributed to the copious amount of garlic powder that I added to my lunch, anyway. At this point, he spewed out the names on his Roll Call Sheet, containing the assignments for the day, with spiritless effort; that is, until he got to my name. "Cardona? who in the fuck is *Cardona?*"

I raised my hand like a well trained, obedient, six year old in first grade; but, seeing as how I was situated all the way to the rear, it went unseen. Thankfully, before any of it registered into McMahon's ol' cerebral cortex, avoiding, I'm certain, a cataclysm of embarrassment with my hamburger holder standing with the erectness of a *blue pill* consumer, the Lieutenant broke in, leaning into the Sergeant's ear, and mumbled, "New guy;" along with a giggle and some gratuitous eye rolling before continuing, "we got one of those new jacks that just came off of Field Training… these guys are supposed to be *heroes* because they took the job when the Towers fell."

"Oh, right… great." concluded the Sergeant. "Well, *new guy*, wherever the fuck you are in there, you're with Jones and Alvarez, in Sector Adam."

He still hadn't spotted me, but I shouted, nevertheless, "10-4, sir!"

"Lord… *my* hero." he responded under his breath, drawing yet another chuckle from the Lieutenant, as well as a few snickers from the Platoon. "Anyway… Alrighty, you filthy cock bags, prepare for inspection… you know the drill, come on now, that's it, open ranks. Let's go, let's go, I don't have all day, move your asses." The first row of the platoon responded by taking a step forward to allow Sergeant McMahon to methodically inspect them up and down, front to rear. When he was done with the first row, he then barked the same order to the second row and, finally, to my row… where things were about to go terribly wrong. "What in the fuck is this?" he yawped, standing directly in front of me, looking down at something that was, apparently, out of sorts with my uniform shirt.

What exactly? a clue I had not; furthermore, I had not the proverbial balls to move a singular muscle to find out. "What in the mother fuck is *this*?" he roared again.

At this point, due to the fact that he inquired yet a second time, I tilted my skull to take a peek at what was causing his conniption fit. I realized, then, the catalyst of his fury was an unfastened button - more specifically, the 4th button from the top – which must have come loose when I took the seat just moments prior. I began to correct the error, whilst simultaneously conveying my most sincere apology. "I'm sorry, sir, I'll -"

He cut me off, slapped my hand away from the shirt, as a mother would the hand of the cookie jar bandit before dinner, and shouted, "Shut your fucking mouth and fall the hell outta my Roll Call. Get your ass outta here and get your shit together, fucking Rookie! And don't come back until you do."

I left the muster room, as ordered, to the sounds of chuckles and whistles, wanting desperately to continue walking right out of the front door of the Command. I had never been so mortified in my entire life; I wished, at that moment, I could just disappear from existence, to transport my body to another, far distant, world to escape the humiliation and embarrassment of what had moments ago transpired. All for a button. I couldn't fathom how such a minor oversight lead to the overwhelming calamity of which I had just endured; especially when, for the last six months in Field Training, at the behest of Sergeant Portico, practically every single day was spent convincing us that similar days - such as what we experienced in the Academy - were long over and done with. It just made no sense. I attempted to make my way, after addressing *the issue*, back into the muster room, but, by that time, Roll Call was completed, the platoon already falling out and going about their business of the day.

Jones and Alvarez, the guys that I had been assigned with, spotted and approached me. "Hey *Buttons*," Jones called out to me, apparently as a consequence of the aforementioned debacle, baptizing me with the most quaint of sobriquets, "grab a radio from the radio room and let's hit it… I need my coffee and Alvarez needs his Cubano sandwich." And just like that, it was business as usual… as if nothing had occurred at all. I could see, at this point, that being a member of the Police Department would, indeed, prove to be an inordinately convoluted ride.

* * *

Sitting in the rear of a Police Car – where the prisoners and other vermin are placed – equipped with a cage that divides the free from those in captivity was, if you hadn't ventured to wonder, *not* fun. Not only does one feel as though their knees are burrowing into the particularly hard plastic border below the glass partition, but the controls for the windows are disabled, so there's no hope for any fresh air. Emanations of vomit; the putrid smell of the worst kind of body odor; stale blood from *back seat corrections*; and all other unimaginable excretions make up the especially tart amalgamation of a scent that can be singularly best labeled – if one had occasion to bottle and brand such a fragrance - *Ode de Back Seat a la Police Car*. For the life of me, I could not comprehend – now being done with Field Training – why I couldn't simply be assigned to one Senior Cop, thereby allowing me to sit in the front like a normal human being. I suppose they just didn't trust us new kids or something like that, and it just wasn't fair. I wasn't a child; I was a grown-ass man who had been driving a car since the tender age of ten. Seriously, my old man had me behind the wheel of that Reliant K before I grew one single hair on my Mike and Ike sized pecker. By the time I was fourteen, I was joyriding the hell out of the damned thing (unbeknownst to my dear old dad who, once becoming aware of the crime, *unauthorized use of a vehicle* to be specific, voiced only one concern, one request, "Next time you steal my car, make sure you put some fucking gas in it;" a supplication I most certainly obliged); so, I didn't understand, nor appreciate, the lack of trust by way of my new Employers. I mean, that's what I thought back then; now, of course, it's as clear as the morning sky in the spring time. There's no way in hell that I'd hop in the car by myself with a gleaming spick-and-span kid with only six months on the job. No way. They're still civilians in my now tenured eyes, continuing to transition into the *life*, probably thinking that sliding across the hood of cars is a viable and realistic option. Of course, however, this was not part of my reasoning twenty years ago, thus the indignation running rampant inside my head.

"You alright back there, Buttons?" Jones called back from the front of the car, adjourning my especially invidious rumination.

"All good." I uttered, with a thumbs up, while trying not to inhale the aforesaid noxious fumes. There was no way in hell I could tell these guys what I really thought about the whole sitting in the back situation… they'd rip my head clear off my body. Remember, I — at my stage of the previously laid out rubric – was nothing more than a minuscule grain of sand in the vastness of the Antarctic Desert within their subculture.

"Good," he replied. "we're stopping here to grab a cup of joe and this guy's sandwich. You coming?"

We stepped into this cuchifrito place because my *au-pairs* raved of the best Spanish coffee this side of the planet apparently offered at the establishment; not to mention that the Cuban sandwich Alvarez craved was apparently so succulent that one had to end their life upon its consumption, due to the fact that everything else in the world would mean nothing. I ended up ordering one of those coffees and, when it was time to pay, began reaching into my pocket for some dough when Jones leaned into me and said, "Hey, Buttons… uh, keep your allowance money, it's *on the arm* in this place; they *do the right thing*." He could see by the look of incertitude on my countenance that I hadn't a clue as to what he had just postulated to me. "We don't pay." he clarified.

"Oh, no, it's okay… I have it, its not a big deal." I naïvely responded, not understanding the importance, the significance, of the most rigid observance of the unwritten, timeless, aphorisms, '*do the right thing*' and '*on the arm.*'

Jones and Alvarez shot a look of malaise to each other, unsure, I'm all too certain, of just how to proceed with me. Was I some kind of rat? An Internal Affairs mole or some discomposing business such as that? That's what *I'd* think, if the ol' roles were reversed, that's for damn sure. It's why, at that point, no doubt, they both ceased communication, allowing me to hand the money over to the register girl who, in turn, offered the identical, bewildered, facial expression on her phizog; the very one that was given by my compatriots, whilst meekly uttering, "Ees okay… no pay."

"Oh, no thank you, it's fine… *really*." I insisted. What a

complete narc I was being, honestly. If there were some way to get my paws on Mr. Wells' infamous time machine, I'd return to that cringe-worthy moment in time, go right up to *past me* and give myself a good ol' *Will Smith to Chris Rock at the Academy Awards* slap across the face, then return to my seat, much in the same fashion as the movie star, and howl, "Keep your fucking money in your fucking pocket!" Honestly.

The register girl, completely at a loss as to what to do, gaped at the two Officers adjacent to me, as if to obtain their approval to accept my payment; they, in turn, shrugged their shoulders to indicate their lack of understanding or control for my implausible actions, saying not a word, for fear, I can only conjecture, of a hidden electronic device taped onto unseen parts of my body, transmitting every syllable uttered, awaiting the precise moment when the high crime of failing to compensate an establishment for refreshment and comestible was committed. It was for this reason, this deplorable act of inconformity in the eyes of my cohorts, that I was not assigned to ride with anyone else for a long while. The word had gotten out that I was a possible *cheese eater*, a rat – in the appropriate vernacular – who had infiltrated the Command. Instead, for about two grueling months, they stuck me with the worst, bottom of the barrel, assignments they could find. Things like babysitting corpses of all kinds; which, to be honest, wasn't the worst... so long as they were the fresh ones that just recently expired. It was the creatures that had long departed the Earth, dead so long that they had begun to fossilize into the floor of their hot, ill-ventilated apartments, giving off an especially rancid aroma that would singe one's nostril hairs clean off, that disturbed me the most. Not a lovely experience.

Just when I thought I'd spend the rest of my time on this job amongst the lamented, ready to take a long walk off of a short pier somewhere, they assigned me to this dinosaur, Brentwood – much to his chagrin, I'm certain - who had about three hundred and fifty years on the job. He was old enough to have patrolled the Land of Nod, possessing all the rustic accessories of a bygone era of policing: old hickory night stick; nickel colored Smith and Wesson revolver that rested inside of a swivel holster, attached to a worn-out gun belt that dangled below his hip, resting upon the top of his waist like the cowboys of the Wild West, tumbleweed rolling by, saloon to the right, sheriff's office to the left, whore-house three doors down; and a heavily discolored and stained uniform shirt, smattered with every single morsel he ever attempted to consume over the course of his interminable career. A true relic. Museum worthy, I'm certain of it.

After Roll Call let out, I sauntered over to grab a radio from the radio room, subsequently heading over to meet up with Brentwood; however, he was nowhere to be found… he just basically vanished into thin air. I foraged the Earth looking everywhere for him, yowling his name – "Brentwood? Brentwood?" - like a stark raving lunatic, but there was no sign of him at all. Most guys who worked together didn't just take off like a bat out of hell, leaving a partner clueless as to their whereabouts, giving them no choice but to go on a goddamn manhunt… it's just not something that anyone ever did; so, you could imagine my discontent to find good ol' Brentwood already in the Police Car, parked somewhere off in the farthest corner at the rear of the Command, stoically facing forward, not showing any indication of wondering where *I* might possibly be. Like, if I never showed up at all, he wouldn't have cared less, not one single miserable bit; and, there's not a shred of doubt that the primordial bastard would have gone about his day just fine had I not ever made an appearance.

After the ten mile trek to the car, I opened the passenger side door and passively-aggressively commented, "Hey, I didn't see you all the way over here," to which he responded by grasping the gear shifter and placing it into the 'drive' position. I practically dove into the car as he began to slowly lift his foot off of the brake, bringing the vehicle into a slow forward crawl. "Oops," I said, facetiously, "almost didn't make it in," which were the last words uttered for the entirety of the eight and a half hour tour, compounded, incidentally, by the fact that, because he was a full fledged member of the Jurassic period, we were given the piddling assignment of guarding an elementary school. Essentially, we had to make sure that the little ruffians – ages six through twelve – didn't go terrorizing each other upon dismissal, and even after the kiddies made their way home we had to remain there, at the school, to guard with our lives the empty playground; which, if you haven't already figured it out, is to say that Brentwood and I did absolutely nothing from the beginning to the end of our day. Gouging one's eyes out with a rubber spoon would have been a much more preferable pastime, by far.

To my boundless vexation, he and I were paired together every single day for the next few weeks and, whether you can believe this or not, we said not a single, solitary word to one another for the duration of that time. Seriously, not a word. Well, I mean, it's not like we didn't say *any* words to each other… just nothing that was not directly in relation with our assignments; which was, much akin to our initial day together, a lot of nothing. Like something right out of the movie, '*Groundhog Day*,' with Bill Murray, the tour always began the same way: I'd go on that peregrination from the Command to the Police Car, where I'd find him sitting, looking straight ahead in a trance-like state, offering no sign of intelligent life as I settled into the vehicle; we'd drive on over to the deli to grab his usual roast beef on rye with a little mustard, lettuce – hold the tomatoes – and coffee (black, no sugar); swing on over to the nearest newspaper stand to retrieve every single New York City tabloid available (none of which I was at liberty to indulge, lest I create crinkling noises, thereby disturbing his harmonious placidity), along with a few packs of cigarettes, he having a penchant for Pall Mall's; and finally, after a few hundred years gone by, we'd arrive at our nugatory post… never a Sector, where we'd have the opportunity to respond to radio runs (which, I'm sure you aren't aware, are 911 assignments given to Sector Cars). For hours upon hours, days upon days, we would merely sit there, ingesting plumes of smoke, with nothing to do… nowhere to go. Terrifically mind numbing. Many brain cells went by the wayside during that period of my life, many brain cells, indeed.

All of that changed in a matter of microseconds when - somewhere in between the crossword puzzle and the article about the Yankees facing the Red Sox in the playoffs (I could only conjecture from peeking over, once in awhile, at the chronicles he very penuriously kept all to himself) - over the Department radio blared the most shrilling call for help I had ever, in my *whole entire* first year on the Job, heard. "Sector King! Sector King! 10-13! Shots fired! Shots fired!" At this point, the first thing that came flying from the depths of my amygdala was that the Officer in peril did not provide to his helpless manumitters *where* exactly this horrific situation was taking place. One of the precious jewels that the Academy jackhammered into our good ol' encephalons, perseverating it by way of this crazy kind of shock tactic, was to always remember our location. The thing of it is, they had these street signs, *real* street signs, like the ones you espy out in the actual world, all around the institution; every floor, every left and right turn throughout the hallways, had a street sign that bore the name of some avenue or some boulevard or some road… and the classroom numbers on the entrance doors represented what would be the building number on an actual tenement. For instance, if you so happened to be traversing down the hallway of the third floor, on any given side of the Academy, you'd look up to see a sign that read something like, "Maple Street," and if your classroom happened to be 'room 307,' you knew, unless you had no brain floating around in your dome, that you were located at '307 Maple Street.' Pretty simple stuff, except for the fact that – every single day – they switched the signs around, so you couldn't just simply store it into your trusty short term memory bank. You had to actually look up everyday to find out where in the God forsaken hell you were. Once in awhile (actually, now that I think about it, pretty goddamn often) you'd have one of the Instructors appear out of thin air, like some deranged maniac, from a cut-out in the wall that you didn't happen to notice, and he'd shout, "BANG! you're shot! Where are you?! What's your location?!" You'd have to reach down to your waist and *pretend* to grab your radio (we didn't have real radios, yet, on account of we weren't *really* on the streets) and yell what your location in the building was at the top of your stupid lungs. If you didn't know it, if you happened not to look up at those confounded signs before you were essentially ambushed and didn't know where on the planet you were, they'd make you do a million push-ups; and, on the last one – the last push-up - you'd have to maintain a hold at the top position until your arms burst into a flesh melting combustion… so you sort of made sure you knew where you were at all times. It kind of behooved you, you know what I mean? I have to say, to this day, even though I'm long departed from the Job, I still look up at all the street signs wherever I go… just in case one of those bat shit crazy Instructors – if any of them are still amongst the living – jump out from behind the goddamn bushes to ask me where I am. You never know.

Anyway, I was telling you about the Cop that was screaming on the radio: so, he bellowed out that he needed help, but no one knew where in the world he was. Lamentations from anxiously awaiting Officers of, "Location?!" and "Where are you?!" went eerily unanswered. I shot a glance over at Brentwood to sort of gauge where his *mentis statum* lay - what his intentions were - about the singularly disturbing scourge unfolding before us, searching for any indication that he would be taking some semblance of action to provide succor to our helpless brother in arms; but, outside of the fact that I espied his chest cavity barely rising and collapsing in its usual quotidian manner (thereby ruling out the possibility of his demise at this point during the harangue), he was, essentially, immutable.

Central, the faceless voice responsible for disseminating information over the radio, including the aforesaid *radio runs* – someone most of us never lay eyes on due to the fact that this particular unit (the Communications Unit) is located in a fortress far from the majority of the Precincts in which they conduct their communique, desperately cried out, "Sector King? where are you? What's your location? You need to tell me where you are, so I can send help!"

"Central, this is the Patrol Sergeant… where was Sector King's *last* location?" interjected the Patrol Supervisor, in an attempt to deduce where exactly to send the support needed for Sector King.

"Sergeant, they're not on any jobs." Central replied. "I show them unassigned and available."

"Central! get me some units over here! we need help!" Sector King cried out again - the sounds of a struggle clearly discernible, the voice of the distressed Officer muffled and shaken… again, leaving their whereabouts an innominate mystery.

"Where are you, Brother? what's your location?!" pleaded an unknown voice over the air.

Unable to withstand the anticipation a second longer, what happened next was what could best be described as a demonic possession of sorts: something, some unseen kinetic force, took hold of my hand, placed it onto the switch that activates the spinning red turret lights above the Police Car, and — Lord help me - depressed the button that triggers the insanely raucous wails of the siren. I must tell you, to this day, I haven't the slightest goddamn clue what cacodemon was responsible for such contumaciousness as that - I honestly wish I knew… just another one of those cringe-worthy, *needing a time machine*, moments, I guess; and, you can bet your last penny that Brentwood was not a happy camper about it… not at all. As I withdrew my hand from the device, he, with speeds rivaling that of Achilles' death-blow upon Hector at the gates of Troy, slapped my wrist, like a singularly vexed catholic school nun correcting a disobedient novitiate. "Don't you *ever!!* touch my lights and sirens again!" he groaned, undoing what I had the unmitigated nerve to have done, turning the lights off and deadening the yelp of the siren.

"Are we just gonna sit here while King is screaming for

help? We cant just sit here and do nothing! Can we?" I wined like an insensible child who clearly does not understand the sum total of a particular situation in which the adults are engaged.

"We ain't sittin' here doin' nothin', ya dumb fuck. We're waitn' for Sector King to give us their location… where exactly in the fuck would you like me to start headin' to? huh? You want I should drive around in big ol' circles or somethin'?"

That simple logic rendered me mute as we continued to sit and wait, in between more pleas over the radio for King to reveal their *locus arcanum*. It's a pretty sickening feeling, just so you're aware… in case you can't bring yourself to conjure up the acrimoniousness of the thing, whilst laying on your beach chair, doing some light reading by the ocean, or snuggled up with your throw blanket and chamomile tea, listening to the '*Barefoot Acoustic*' playlist undulating the sweet sounds of warm, gentle, and earthy melodies… the ability to do absolutely nothing while, simultaneously, Sector King is possibly getting their ass handed to them, not to mention the morbid fact that there was mention of shots being fired, the identities belonging to the subject and victim also in ambiguity. Were the poor souls shot? bloodied and unconscious, unable to respond to the shouts for their compliance? or were they engaged in a gun battle, fiercely fighting off the enemy, hanging on for an opportunity to transmit the missing piece of vital information needed to get us to the location where they were making their last stand?

Just then, as hope was taking a winding descent into the abyss, Sector King blurted out, "2121 Gable Street! third floor!" to which Brentwood responded by thrusting the gear shifter to 'drive' whilst simultaneously depressing the gas pedal, causing the tires of the Police Car to caterwaul, sending anyone in the way of the conveyance diving for their dear lives onto the sidewalk, away from its proximity. The old man whom I thought, just moments ago, had one foot in the proverbial grave was now whipping in and out of traffic with Dale Earnhardt precision and velocity. On the radio, transmissions of, "Hang on, brother! we're coming!" and "Keep fighting, bro! Don't quit fighting, we'll be there soon!" and "One minute out! Almost there!" could be heard one after another. My heart thumped against my bullet proof vest so hard that, after awhile, I could hear nothing else but its reverberations within myself… the rest of the voices over the air became like a heavy fog draping over all things auditory.

Pulling up to the particularly frenzied scene, one could see nothing but a sea of Police Cars parked in every which direction like abandoned, unmoored boats after a tempestuous storm, Officers running toward the sound of gun fire while all others not employed as enforcers of the law scattering away from the cataclysmic affair. Everything appearing and existing around me – all of my peripheral vision – began to inwardly collapse, having the ability to see only directly ahead, as I entered the building, feeling like an apprehensive child who is about to enter a blood-curdling haunted house at a carnival; which, based on the sanguinary residue splattered all about the walls of the lobby, made the aforementioned analogy pretty damn apropos. The bloody gore on the walls and floor belonging to one of the Cops engaged in the gruesome gun battle – he now slumped over in the lobby where all of us were currently making our advent - left a trail that led up a narrow set of stairs to the second floor wherein the daunting affray continued to ensue. The downed Officer, Smithson, one half of Sector King, was fatally struck by one of the bullets unleashed by the ArmaLite-15 rifle, now pinning down the second half of Sector King inside of the apartment, in the kitchen – to be precise – located adjacent to the landing above.

Following the arterial spray up to the next flight, and right up to the apartment door, Officer Nicholson was found crouched down below the serving window that separated himself from the shooter who, incidentally, nestled himself behind the sofa, now flipped over onto its side to provide the bandit with enough concealment so as not to have given the aforesaid Officer a clear shot. "Nicholson! Where's he at? where's the shooter?" one of the responding Cops, directly in front of us, inquired.

Gesticulating with his hand, Nicholson pointed in the direction of the knave, shouting, "Behind the sofa! Behind the sofa!" letting all of his fellow gendarmes know exactly where to direct their course of fire; however, intercepting this bit of dialogue, the brigand released a barrage of leadened projectiles in the general vicinity of where we were planted, one of the rounds abruptly striking Brentwood, causing him to fall backward, right on top of yours truly.

"Fuck! kid, I'm hit!" he cried out in agony. "I'm fucking hit… goddamn it, bro!"

Not knowing, at that point in time, if I had also been shot – having never had that particular experience – I conducted a lightning quick assessment of my life functions, which took all of mere seconds, before lifting myself from underneath my partner, who had passed out, now drenched in a pool of vivid cerise fluid, subsequently dragging him out of harms way, all before scanning his body for holes not naturally belonging to him. What I found were a few entry wounds, two in his right shoulder and one, more unfortunately located in his right arm, just above the bicep. "Fuck, bro," I shouted to no one in particular, Brentwood remaining in a state of extreme torpor, "I think it's the brachial artery." After about seven seconds of sheer hysteria, the ol' proverbial lightbulb went off and I reached for my tourniquet, remembering the one that my father gave to me that day in the pizza shop; actually, the one that my sister bought me (whom I never got around to thanking leading to that moment in time, by the way… I'm less than zero; save your breath, I already know). Anyway, I reached for it, strapping it as close to the armpit as I could, applying it tighter than the anus of a straight guy in a Pride Parade, which is pretty damn tight, let me tell you.

Within seconds of my wrapping that thing around his arm, one of the Cops – about the size of a Yeti (seriously, this guy was huge… like, whoever is looking for Bigfoot can cease the search, he's got a job with the goddamn New York City Police Department) had come up the stairs and spotted us, wasting no time at all lifting Brentwood, throwing the old man over his shoulders like a rolled up area rug, jettisoning down the stairs and out the building, straight into his Police Car, speeding off directly to the nearest hospital, where he underwent hours of surgery and spent nearly a month in the ICU. He survived, ol' Brentwood did. It was touch and go, as it were, for awhile; but, the geezer pulled through and, eventually, recovered swimmingly, you'll be delighted, I'm sure, to know. As for the villain – for those of you that care at all… for those singularly special individuals who fancy that *all life is precious* – the bastard went to Dante's Inferno. He'd now have to plead his case to the Centaurs in the Outer Ring of Alighieri's underworld; for, he was riddled with bullets too numerous in quantity to tell for certain, putting an end, thank the Old Testament God, to his sojourn in this world of the corporeal.

I went to visit Brentwood at the hospital a bunch of times, and we got pretty close, I have to say. We'd sort of chew the fat and spend time… not doing anything too mind blowing; I'd just kick back and watch him break the nurse's balls all day, winking at me the whole time he was doing it. Hilarious stuff. I'd bring to him his coveted periodicals and, once in awhile, a roast beef on rye with a little mustard, lettuce – hold the tomatoes – and coffee, *real* coffee – not that hospital crap (black, no sugar). But the best part of going to see him was when he'd tell me all of his *war stories* from way back when he was a *young-buck* and all. He told me how much things had changed since the 1980s and 1990s… his generation… how kids (new Cops) didn't have any respect nowadays and how people, civilians, were starting to lose respect for Officers out on the street. It was pretty damn sad to hear him go on about that stuff because you could really tell how much he was hurt by it and all… about the people thinking poorly of the Police. In the time of yore, Brentwood would actually sit with the citizenry, in front of bakeries and shit like that, to have a quiet cup of java and discuss regular things like sports, politics, or whatever else normal people talked about; he'd walk his beat and wave at all the folks in the neighborhood, and they'd smile and return the gesture. It was certainly a whole other world from what goes on in these times, that's for sure. In this alternate reality, scowls and whispers of, *'fucking pig'* and *'bitch-ass cops'* make up the entirety of the relationship between the Department and the community. A crying shame, if you ask me. He mentioned how he was just biding his time until retirement (which, truth be told, should have been about ten years ago, except he got into some sort of budgetary hiccup in his personal life and wound up staying), but now, with this injury, he could finally get the hell out. I was happy about that… not about him getting hurt, but about him finally getting out. I couldn't even imagine what it might be like to figuratively walk in his combat boots; but, I did get to literally walk in his uniform jacket, seeing as how he passed it (along with some other random little accessories) down to me… there was a catch, though: in order for me to have it, his jacket, I had to swear on all that was holy and pure that I'd never wash the decrepit thing… ever. That was the deal, and I kept my word. I never even *thought* about cleaning it. That ol' thing certainly ended up with a lot of miles on it by the time both of us were done; I ended up wearing his jacket until my final day – something he never got a chance to see, on account of his passing about seven years later from the cancer… lung cancer. I'll tell you what, though, I truly think he came down from heaven to check on it every once in awhile; because, from the moment I put that old, grimy thing on, up until my final tour of duty, the eminently robust fragrance of Pall Mall continued to drape over it like the wings of some sort of angelic aura from above.

IX

A bunch of years went on by, about five if I had to take a stab in the ol' dark at it, since that day of the shooting, and my situation at work had become very different. For one thing, I ended up partnering with this kid, Officer Kevin Harper, who had graduated the Academy with me; we didn't get together right way, though… it took about a full year for that to happen. Brentwood never returned to full duty after getting out of the hospital; spending most of his days at rehab until he was discharged with a *three-quarters* retirement status (which means you get to keep three-quarters of your salary, as opposed to the half that the rest of us get when it's all said and done) on account of the fact that the nerves in his shooting arm never fully recovered, which was fantastic for him. For me, not so much; I spent that initial rotation around the Sun as a *floater*, which means I was doing a lot of that whole watching rotted corpses thing again; this, and *sitting on*, guarding, prisoners at the hospital (those requiring medical attention subsequent to their arrest) or answering phones in the Command. Not fun. But, over time – after that year – I ended up being steady partners with Harper for a good long while.

Seeing as how we, at the onset, were still Rookies in the eyes of our peers, the two of us were perennially assigned to the worst Sector in the entire Precinct, which was Sector Adam – a shitty area that bordered our singularly most diabolical sister Command's outer reaches, inundated with all sorts of the lowest types of scum… from drug peddlers and users, to prostitutes, gang bangers, and countless other vermin that one might see in some kind of superhero action movie, wherein the city has been overrun by scores of villainous foes; seriously, I think *Joker, Riddler, and Penguin* from DC Comics all sprouted from this Godforsaken area. These heathens, as fortune would have it, were our daily clientele… all of whom, on any given day, could either be the perpetrators or, conversely, the victims of the incessant crime that took place in this particular area patrolled by Kevin and I. The fact of the matter was, they'd switch roles depending on the situations; like, for instance, on one day we would respond to an assault in progress, with the prostitute calling to proclaim that one of her *johns* had given her a fat lip, and on another completely different day, we'd have to arrest the same chic for *working* the goddamn corners. It was just one humongous cesspool of endless *mopery*, trust me on that one.

One of the jobs during those five years on patrol with Harper that has been burned, *animus revertendi*, in my good ol' hippocampus, was the *jumper* in which we were called to handle, on a rather blustery and bone penetratingly frigid afternoon in February… not an especially pleasant day for such a call, I must say. It actually all started out just swell, the day; not much going on – the radio barely buzzing and the weather being especially unwelcoming, which is always a good thing in terms of the majority of the city cozily hibernating in the warmth of their homes. We, Harper and I, were goofing off with some of the other guys assigned to the adjoining Sectors at a local *cooping prone location* (which basically means, in layman's terms, we were somewhere that we were not supposed to be – according to, for whatever God only knows reason, the powers that be) when Central interjected by putting over a job which happened to be, *lucky us*, in our geographic area of assignment. The job, as fortune would have it (and I mean this in the most facetious of ways), ended up being a female who apparently decided she no longer wished to be part of the human race; therefore, she headed on up to the roof of her residence with the intentions of taking a twenty-one story dive to the concrete below.

"Damn, bro… that sounds legit." began one of the Officers, Morgan, we were hanging out with. "I'll bet she's *ground* meat before you get there… no pun intended."

"Trust me, brother, it's better that way;" added another Cop, Dannon. "So long as she's up on the ledge, it's a whole freaking production."

"Yeah, I know… you gotta call the *boss* and ESU… what a mess. I got plans today, bros! I don't have time for all of this bullshit!" exclaimed my partner, Harper, with much trepidation (ESU, by the by, initials belonging to the Emergency Service Unit, our Department's version of SWAT… we one of the few law enforcement organizations not to use that pseudonym because, well because we're so damned special, that's why).

"I guess we should start making our way over there… like you said, Morgan, she's probably a pancake by now. Let me check." I commented, while grabbing my radio, all of us now making our way to the Police cars. "Sector Adam to Central," I said, transmitting into the radio, "what's the status of my jumper? Is she down or up?"

"Standby, Sector Adam, let me check the call-back." Central responded, she now placing a call to whomever initiated reaching out to 911.

"Please let her be down, please let her be down!" desperately pleaded Harper aloud.

I half threw him a look of aversion, but understood where he was coming from, being that we had all been though these types of jobs a million and seven times before, and it was always the same: the diver would spend hours contemplating the choice between life and death, considering all of the pros and cons, I suppose, of the fateful decision, whilst the rest of us waited around yanking our wieners the entire time. Once they did it… once they made the plunge… then all one had to do was have the medical examiner scrape them off the pavement and complete the Complaint Report and Aided Card. Done deal. So you see, it really was much easier to have them just go on ahead and catapult off the ledge.

"What? Don't look at me like that! I have plans bro… *really* important plans!" he justified in response to the look of discontent I had just given him.

"Sector Adam?" Central's voice emanated over the air.

"Adam, go." I responded.

"Adam, be advised that the jumper is still on the roof… female caller states she's currently on the roof with her sister and she's trying to get her to step down from the edge."

"Let's go, partner… time to save a life." I asserted.

When we finally pulled up to the building, a twenty-one story Housing Authority Development, we could, upon peering skyward, clearly espy our potential skydiver hanging onto the wrong side of the gate (a structure, ironically, that was probably placed there to prevent such tribulations from occurring in the first place), leaning outwards, seemingly on the brink of an imminent plunge. "Fuck, there she goes, goddamn it." said Harper.

"Shit! she's dangling from the edge… she's gonna go any minute now!" declared I.

"I should be so lucky!" exclaimed my partner, receiving yet another dissatisfying glance from my direction.

Within minutes of reaching the roof landing we could see the jumper's sister was, indeed, making every attempt to change the mind of her troubled sibling. "Maggie! please, please don't do this! You know we all love you! You know that! You're not alone!"

"I *am* alone… I'm *very* alone!" Maggie earnestly contradicted. "You don't know… you got no idea what I'm going through. You got your family, you got your life."

"You *are* my family… you *are* my -"

"Oh, *please*!" Maggie broke in, with a resigned simper. "You know what the fuck I mean… you got Mike and the kids… you got people to love, people to care for and shit."

"So, you're saying that you don't have me and your nieces to care for? You don't care for *us*? What about *us?*" Maggie's sister squawked.

"Come on, Galinda, you know what I'm talking about right now… you exactly know what I mean… you know what? fuck this shit…" Galinda's disconcerted elder sister wailed, beginning to loosen her grip from the railing.

"Maggie, wait!" I impetuously called out, not having any idea what in the world I was doing, or what I would possibly utter next. Yelling out her name was a reflex which bore no conscious thought;

henceforth, when Galinda and Harper swiveled their skulls in my direction, my guess was as good as theirs in regards to what would transpire next. I continued my discourse out of sheer situational pressure at that point, hoping like hell that whatever spewed out of my pie hole wouldn't make matters worse than what they already happened to be. "Maggie, listen… you don't want to do this, you really don't." I said, while creeping towards her ever so slowly.

"How the fuck you know what I want, *Cop*? You don't even know me!" the distraught woman declared.

"You're right, Maggie, I don't know you; but, trust me, I know about troubles. I know about a person not having anyone in their life." said I, getting closer and closer to the fence, sliding a half step between each word.

"You think you could connect with me, Cop?" Maggie replied. "You is five-O. You got a good job, and I know you got some honey who you be going home to! so don't play yourself… don't try to be acting like you know what I'm about."

"I *don't* know, I'm not trying to say I know *exactly* what you're about… but I *do* know problems, Maggie. I do know about them and I know it fucking hurts like hell… *that*, I do know." Closer and closer still.

"Yeah? what you know, *Cop?*"

"My mom… my mom…" I stammered, not entirely ready to reveal my goddamn personal strifes with the dangling damsel in distress, operating on sheer instinct alone. "… she left me and my sister, Grace, when we were kids… when I was only seven years old. She left me, my dad, and Gracie to run off with some guy. That crushed me, Maggie… it crushed me and I grew up wondering if there was something wrong with me… if I had done something wrong to make her go away. That was huge, you know?" Within reaching distance now… meager steps away.

"That *is* fucked up. She shouldn't have left you… you was too little to do that. A little boy needs his mama at that age. That's why some niggas out here be not knowing how to treat a woman; because they don't be having a female role model in they lives… but, check this out, you need to back up, Officer, or we gonna have a problem up in here."

I quickly drew back so as not to cause further alarm, failing to realize she was apparently keeping tabs on my progression towards her. "Okay, Maggie, okay… I'm stepping back."

"Yeah, don't play me, Five-O. Anyway, that's real sad what happened with your mom and shit… I feel bad for you; but, you a grown ass man now, and I know you got some little shorty at home who cares about you or whatever, so you ain't all that miserable… you ain't like me."

"Oh man, Maggie, no, that's where you're wrong… you see, I never could grasp the hang of the whole relationship thing. Maybe it's like you said – the thing you said about the way guys are out here - maybe I never learned to fully understand how to be with a woman; but, whatever it is, whatever the reason is, I am alone, so I do get it, Maggie… I do get what it's like to be on my own. As a matter of fact, my ass got left for another guy, not too long ago… this girl I was seeing for awhile, in the Academy… someone I really liked - *a lot* – she went ahead and dumped me for our teacher. Now that's some fucked up shit, isn't it? isn't it, Maggie?" I took two very small steps toward her; this time with my hands extended in a pleading manner, before continuing, "Maggie, do me a favor: come off that ledge, huh? Let's finish talking about it on this side of the fence. Can we do that? can we talk on this side?"

"Why? Why you wanna talk about this? What's the point? There ain't none… there ain't no reason for me to live, Cop."

"Believe me, Maggie, there is… there is a reason; and it's not for any guy or any gal or anything else but you! *You're* the reason for you to live. That's the thing you gotta understand. The thing that you have to get into your head. Life isn't about living for others, it's about living for, and loving, yourself. Life's about loving yourself… seeing and doing as much as you can before our time… our real time… is up; and that's not for us to decide, that's up to the Big Guy in the Sky to say." As soon as I uttered these final words, unbeknownst to her, or myself for that matter, I managed to take one lengthy stride in her direction, grabbing hold of her by wrapping my arms under her armpits and around her back, interlocking my fingers, as though I were giving her an enormous embrace, and squeezed for dear life. She attempted to break free; but, by that point, the entirety of a 911 activated system (about a hundred Cops, fire department and ambulance personnel) swarmed us and secured Maggie, pulling her up and over the fence, subsequently rushing her from the roof of the building to the ambulance that awaited her below.

Within seconds of good old Maggie being carted off, I found myself collapsed onto the ground, mentally, physically, and spiritually drained. Nothing left in the proverbial tank. If not for

Harper lifting me up off of the asphalt, I'd have stayed there for at least a few weeks, all of my energy and will to do otherwise depleted. "Let's go, buddy… up you go." he said, as I ascended back to my feet.

"Holy shit, did that really happen?" I asked, the feelings of what had just transpired being all too surreal.

"Sure did… you're a regular freakin super hero!" he replied. "Come on, bud, we gotta escort the *bus* to the hospital. I'm sure she's already packed up and ready to go."

While driving behind the ambulance (the aforementioned '*bus*'), following it to the psychiatric hospital, I tried wrapping my head around all of that crap, but I just couldn't do it. Things like that, traumatic events, need time to settle inside the cranium; you can't just expect your brain to process it instantaneously. We're not cyborgs, you know what I mean? The goddamn brain and body have to go through the whole *fight or flight* process before a fella can sit and meditate on the thing. Anyhow, halfway to our destination, Harper broke the silence of my pensive cerebration by inquiring, "Was all of that stuff true?"

"Huh? what stuff?" I answered, still in a state of astonishment.

"The stuff you were telling the jumper… about your mom and the Academy chic; was all of that true?"

"You think I could make that kind of stuff up? What am I? an award winning Broadway actor or some crazy thing like that?"

"Hey, I'm just saying, you were really good up there… like,

kind of amazing, bro. That was like watching some kind of thrilling TV show or something. Amazing, bro." he declared in earnest.

He was being terribly serious, I could tell from the look plastered across his countenance, which was pretty neat. Usually, people on my Job are breaking your stones all over the place, especially when you've done something out of the ordinary. No one simply congratulates you or pays you philanthropic encomiums in those kinds of situations; instead, they make a person feel like a bag of smelly testicles by *ralphing* insanely inappropriate remarks, or coming up with some *round the twist* thing that essentially spoils everything you've done in the first place. Cops are God-awful that way, they really are. If you've ever been in the third grade – more specifically, been around a shit load of third graders with no teacher in the classroom - you can just go on ahead and compare the Department to that… matter of fact, proceed to multiply that number by a few thousand. It's pretty goddamn similar, let me tell you. Terrifically immature. You can imagine my cynicism, then, when he paid me the compliment, and why I answered, "Well, at least it was entertaining."

"I don't mean it like that… I'm just saying: it was a good thing. It was real good what you did."

"I just hope she can get the help she needs." I rejoined. "I sort of felt her pain; I can kind of identify with her, just a little bit." Harper shot me a quick look as if to say, '*do I have to worry about this guy*,' thinking – I'm sure – that'd I'd be scouring the city for a plank atop a ledge in which to dive; so, I clarified by adding, "Not the jumping off the roof part… just the other stuff. The feeling lonely stuff. I get that."

"Yeah, I suppose." he remarked, subsequently remaining silent. That's another thing about my little sodality that I can tell you for sure: Cops don't like to talk about feelings lachrymose in nature, theirs or anyone else's; it's sort of taboo. We'd just as soon head on over to the local bar to drown our metaphysical worries away than to open up and expose our inner workings, our weaknesses, to the outside world and, more especially, *our own* world. I suppose that's why a lot of us end up blowing our brains out. You can't keep the weight of a bunch of baggage all cooped up in your attic for too long of a time; after awhile, the cellar door gives way and all that crap comes tumbling out all over the goddamn place. Once that happens, it's pretty damn cumbersome to have to pick it all up… all those pieces. Better to torch the damn things, take a match and burn the entire thing to Kingdom Come, and hope for a better situation in the next life. I mean, listen, I'm not saying I'd actually go ahead and *do* it – blow my thinking sponge into pieces - what I'm saying, if I'm saying any damn thing, is that I get it. That's all.

Anyway, we arrived at the hospital and, shortly after, Maggie was carted out of her transport and into the facility to see the doctor where she, with any good fortune, could begin the journey back to mental health. After filling out some paperwork at the intake area, I could see from my peripheral that someone was approaching me; it was Galinda. "Excuse me, Officer?" she called in a sort of timorous manner, as if she weren't sure whether or not I'd bite her entire head clean off her shoulders. What I mean to say is, the Police aren't known for their *rolling out the red carpet* dispositions, if I'm putting all my cards on the ol' table. We're not the welcoming committee, waiting with open arms with a bouquet of goddamn daffodils in hand for the general public to saunter on over to us, you know?

Approaching a Cop out in the streets is like someone moseying on over to an alligator who is hovering, mouth wide open, minding its own business, not wanting to be meddled with, in the marsh… it's just not a thing that we thoroughly enjoy. I mean, listen, if you've got a legitimate thing that needs handling, that's one thing; however, if the reason you're slithering over to us is for some crazy, out of this world ridiculousness, then you have to expect the alligator to take a couple of your essential appendages off your person, that's all I'm trying to convey. Pretty elementary concept, I think. What people don't know, what people fail to understand – because I can totally see the look of disparity in your eyes, not truly understanding the essence of why we are this way - is that crazy nut jobs approach Officers all of the time trying (and sometimes succeeding) to hurt us and all of that insane shit. These psychopaths will walk right up to a Cop and shoot them, stab them, club them with pipes… you name it… for absolutely no other reason than to cause harm and havoc. And if you're sitting there, sipping and dunking your crumpets into your hot cocoa, mumbling to yourself, 'that's not true… that can't *possibly* be true,' then you ought to put down this work of historical fiction, run straight down to the nearest library and hit the ol' microfiche machine, so you can read the thing in black and white for yourself. Honestly, go on ahead; shove a bookmark here and do some goddamn research… I'll wait. Anyway, so I was telling you about Galinda coming up to me at the hospital: she approached me and said, in that distinctively apprehensive tone of voice, "Excuse me, Officer? Can I speak to you for a moment?"

Once I realized who it was, I put down what I was doing, turned to her and replied, "Of course… it's Galinda, right? I heard your sister say your name up on the roof."

"Yes, Galinda, that's right. Listen, I just wanted to say… well, I wanted to say thank you; thank you for saving my sister. I… I can't even imagine what would've happened if she… if she… I'm just glad you stopped her. You saved her. You saved her life. There are no words."

"That's not necessary, I was just doing my job. There's no need to -"

"No, Officer, really… not many Cops would've done what you did. A lot of them would've just stood back and not went all-out like that. My sister is alive because of you, and I will never forget it." she concluded, a single tear emanating from her duct, cascading down her cheek.

"Well, Galinda, thank you for your kind words; they mean a whole lot to me. They really do."

At this point, after a brief moment of hesitancy, most likely contemplating on whether she should or should not do whatever was dancing around in her mind, Galinda reached over and enveloped me with a warm and loving embrace, supplementing it with a small, but beholden, peck on my cheek before taking off into the waiting area. I have to admit, that's one of the nicest things anyone has ever done. We don't get much appreciation for the things that we do out on the streets, but sometimes, just once in an ol' while, someone says or does something that really makes our day, reminding us why in the hell we're out here in the first place.

***

It is with incalculable vacillation that I am about to share this succeeding installment, my dear reader, because it will appear to have no validity, no semblance of verisimilitude whatsoever, as though I am telling a delusory tale of sensational fiction; but I assure you, it is, as a matter of fact, quite veracious. In layman's goddamn terms, I give you my word, this shit really happened**. We were just about to head on in to the Command after an insanely busy day, filled with every imaginable scenario one could possibly fathom, or not; including numerous assaults of the worst kind; robberies, some with weapons and some of the strong armed variety; vehicle accidents involving multiple conveyances leading to the loss of lives; shots fired… you name it. Harper and I were making our way back to the Command after this particularly frenetic day seeing, finally, the proverbial light at the end of the tunnel, when he exclaimed, "Man, what a fucking day. Dude, seriously, what the mother fuck? Is it a full fucking moon or something?"

*** see Note from the Author (still a work of fiction here… not real, my readers)*

"Pure insanity. I can't wait to get outta this monkey suit and into a hot shower." responded I. "My bones feel as though a jack hammer had at them."

"You ain't kidding, bro. I got me a date with *you know who.*" he commented, flipping the visor down to glance at the mirror, now giving his mug a once over, licking the tips of his fingers, applying to them some fresh saliva, subsequently using the moistened phalange to flatten out his wild, bushy, eyebrows.

"No way! The German chic? The one with the huge -"

"That's right, the very one… and she's DTF, for sure… she told me to bring the Magnums." he said, now inspecting the rogue hairs spilling out of his nose, which, incidentally, looked like a million tentacles emanating from two miniature caves.

"First of all… *Magnums*? What? she want you to cover your entire body in prophylactic? because there is no fucking way you're even close to a Magnum sized condom. And second, what in the hell is DTF?"

"I *do* fit a Magnum, for your information… maybe I'll whip it out right now and verify it for you; would you like that?" he said, reaching down at his zipper, unlatching its first few teeth.

"Whoa, whoa, whoa! No, thank you! I'll take your word for it, Jesus!" I screeched, nearly losing control of the wheel, sending us full throttle into a bunch of senior citizens crossing the street directly in front of us. "And *DTF*? what in the hell is that?"

"Seriously, bro? You have *got* to stop reading those fancy novels and start watching some quality TV… it's from *Jersey Shore*! They say it all the time when they're talking about some girl they're gonna smash. It stands for *Down To F -*"

"Got it." I said, holding up my hand to discontinue the tutorial.

Laughing, he rejoined, "What about you? Got any plans? besides your steam spa bath with scented candles, lavender oils, and pink champagne? you freakin queer."

"You, sir, are an uncivilized barbarian with absolutely zero appreciation for the finer things in life. I am not ashamed, not even one single bit, to say that, yes, I will most likely surround myself with said items."

We both chuckled at what I thought a singularly marvelous end to such a maddening work day, when the dreaded voice of Central squawked over the radio, "We're receiving a signal 10-31, burglary in progress, at 3737 Jacob Street. Sector Adam?" she called to us.

"No fucking way… no fucking way, dude!" My extremely distraught partner ejaculated, pounding his fist into the dashboard in front of him.

"Fuck, we have to answer her, bro. The Sergeant is definitely listening, especially since, just the other day, he bitched about guys not picking up jobs close to the end of tour. You *know* he'll drill two new assholes into us if we don't pick this job up." I reasoned.

"Bro, the midnights are just about to come out… let's let *them* pick it up."

"Dude, they're still in Roll Call, they won't fall out for another ten minutes… we can't hold off that long, it's a 31! Do you actually *want* to shit out of two separate assholes, dude? I know *I* don't."

"FUUUCK!" he howled, now directing his fists, with unspeakable fury, upon the roof above him.

Grabbing the radio, I acknowledged Central's transmission. 'Sector Adam read on that last transmission, show us responding."

Central replied, "Ten-four, Adam… Female caller states that three males entered her private house and tied up her entire family, but she managed to flee the location. She was hiding in the closet when it was happening, so the suspects did not see her leave the house. She further states the male perps and her family are all still in the house. The family is tied up in the living room, but she does not know exactly where the suspects are."

In a great show of camaraderie, the other Sector Cars began to transmit their intentions to back us up, which is always an especially welcoming prospect. "Show Sector Boy on the back." said Sector Boy over the radio.

"10-4, Boy." Central acknowledged.

"Show Sector Charlie backing as well."

"10-4, Charlie."

"Sector David is going."

"Got you, David."

"Eddie going."

"Sector Eddie, 10-4… Sergeant? you read on this job?" she inquired of our Supervisor.

"Affirmative, I read direct, show me responding." Sergeant Walsh replied. "Advise the approaching units to cut the lights and sirens when they get close to the scene." This, turning off the emergency lights and sirens on the Police Cars, done to prevent the home invaders from being prematurely alerted to our arrival, causing them to flee, or something even more alarming, like bringing harm to one of the family members in some act of desperation; so, in situations such as this, we all attempt to arrive at the scene of the crime like children on Christmas Eve tiptoeing down the stairs, hoping to espy and catch good old Saint Nicholas red handed in the act of his annual breaking and entering ritual.

Being minutes from our 'end of tour' for the day – although it would most assuredly be met with an especially depreciating sentiment by way of the higher-ups - any one of us could have disregarded the call; however, all units available went over the air to back us up… and as I already mentioned, it's a pretty damn special kind of feeling to hear the voices of your peers sending out their intentions to head on over to your location, when they could, instead, be at the Command, washing their sweaty balls and feet, preparing to get the hell out of Hades. It's a pretty empowering thing to hear. Within minutes, the Police Cars could be seen creeping silently towards the house, all of our lights – including headlights – off, exiting the cars and huddling close together with whispered voices, like a football team that is strategizing together at the goal line, the dwindling seconds of the fourth quarter diminishing to nothing, with merely one down remaining. "Alright, listen up," the Sergeant said, "Thomas and Vortman, you guys hang out here and cover the front; Alexander and Hernandez, take the right side of the house; Simmons and Gerardi, you take the left side; Feliz and Almonte, you guys got the rear… watch the windows on the first and second floor, make sure no one tries escaping through any of them; Cardona and Harper, we're going in the house, but we'll enter through the back. Turn your radios down and keep your eyes open."

The huddle was broken up and everyone flew to their

assigned places on the 'field of play;' Harper and I following Sergeant Walsh and his driver, Conroy, into the fray as directed. Just before arriving, the female caller, a girl of thirteen, informed the 911 operator that there was a hideaway key underneath a garden gnome, just before the rear door of the house, which we used to make our ingress, incidentally, as tacitly as ever possible, lest we apprise the demoniacal muggers of our presence. Upon entering, with our firearms drawn and at the ready, we made our way, clearing all open doors as we passed them, making certain that there were no human beings in occupancy; and, seeing that there were none thus far, we continued traversing towards the front of the house where we, at last, descried the mother, father, and brother, all of whom were bound and gagged on the living room floor, precisely as the young lady – the escapee and reporter – described, now patiently awaiting the extrication of her bloodline a few yards from her home.

Expeditiously removing a pocket knife from my gun belt, I holstered my gun – not wanting to accidentally put any leadened projectiles into the bodies of the detainees – and began cutting away at the constraints, thus prompting Harper to do the same, all the while the Sergeant and Conroy keeping a fastidiously watchful eye out for the larcenist's precipitous approach. "Listen to me very carefully," I whispered to the tribe as I continued to cut their fetters, "when we get you loose of these, I want you to *quietly* make your way out of the house… do you understand? *Quickly* and *quietly*. Your daughter is okay and across the street at the neighbor's house; she's the one that called. Do *not* come back in here until a Cop tells you to." They all nodded, through a deluge of tears embedded upon their faces, to indicate their understanding of the injunction given, making haste the second they were liberated, thankfully unmolested.

Now, the capture of the marauders remained, who were believed to be – seeing as how all the rooms on the first floor were secured - somewhere upstairs, either unaware of our presence (that being a singularly more suitable diegesis and highly preferable orientation in the Sun Tzu playbook, giving us the much coveted *element of surprise*) or extremely aware of the goings on with our whereabouts (giving them the conversely unpalatable upper hand… the *high ground*, as it were).

Taking out my firearm from its holster once more, we four creeped on tip toes, making our ascent up the aged, rickety, stairs to the unknown, hoping like hell there wasn't some sort of an ambush, planned by our friends on the second floor, awaiting us upon our reaching the summit. Four calamitous heartbeats raged beneath the vests of my comrades and I, each nanoscopic step bringing forth macrocosmic, resounding, creeks and cracks of the old hardwood, competing, and losing, the battle with the stillness that engulfed and eclipsed us. Sergeant Walsh, who lead the pack, turned his head, glancing down at us, I suppose, to assure himself that he was not alone, displaying, at the onset, a doubtful leer, shortly thereafter – once his eyes fixed upon ours - transmogrifying into a timorous, yet contented countenance of one who has not been forsaken; and, having this somewhat reassured look upon his mien, swiveled his dome back around, continuing the climb, as did we all.

Finally reaching the ridge, unchallenged, using hand signals to convey his orders, Sergeant Walsh gesticulated for Harper and I to go left, whilst he and Conroy would proceed right. Returning a gesture of compliance, in the form of a good old fashioned thumbs up, my partner and I veered sinistral toward what appeared to be a long and narrow hallway containing a bedroom and a half bathroom. Slowly, inch by inch, step by step, we drew nearer to the bedroom, which was located to the right of our position, as well as – within equidistance across from one another – the half bath. Regrettably and quite doltishly, if you really want to know the truth, we decided – again, using makeshift sign language – to spilt up. I ended up advancing into the bedroom, seeing as how I was already walking on that side of the hallway (lucky me), which happened to be insanely Stygian, forsaken of any semblance of light; therefore, unable to see my *own* hand before my face, I very well could not see the oncoming hand of the bad guy, made into a hardened, wrecking ball-like fist, cutting through the darkness and connecting with my jaw, sending me, instantly, to my knees… half of my consciousness hurdling somewhere across the room along with the firearm that was in my grasp.

Unable to call out, due to the fact that I – at that moment – had no recollection of pretty much anything my brain had ever so carefully stored into its database, due to the vicious blow that I received and all, I instinctively began to fight back. Only my body's innate will to survive – whatever was preprogrammed into my goddamn matrix - saved me from, God knows, what the criminal had in store to finish me off. I lunged towards him, wrapping my arms around his waste and interlocking my fingers to prevent him from escaping my grasp, not calculating that the perpetrator's hands were currently free to do what he wished, instantaneously placing me in a deep headlock with his left arm, my face now buried between his armpit and chest, followed by a wailing upon my temple with a series of calculated blows, slowly sending me to the lap of Morpheus, the incessant barrage of his pendulum-like swings ferociously connecting at will. With what little ability that remained, I released my grip - seeing as how he was apparently in charge of keeping us bound together with his mixed martial arts-like choke hold upon me – and offered a few inconsequential strikes of my own, the culmination of which having absolutely no effect on the brute that encumbered my comparatively substandard physique.

As I began to feel the life force drain from my body, a flash of light appeared before my eyes; seemingly, at that very moment, the proverbial heavenly white light leading me to St. Peter at the Gate. It was, however, merely the ceiling light which had been switched on, followed by what looked to be the Archangel St. Michael himself; but, in actuality, was my partner and savior – one, Officer Kevin Harper - soaring through the air and descending upon us, immediately taking hold of my oppressor and delivering to him successive welts and punts all about his face and body; the commotion of which drawing the attention to our two *confreres* across the hall, who stormed into the room and began providing additional, much deserved, punishment of the corporal variety upon the perp, before placing him in handcuffs, dragging him down the stairs, subsequently tossing him into the Police Car. Unfortunately, after searching the entire house from attic to basement, and everything in between, we discovered it to be void of any other intruders; surmising that, at some point during the scuffle, the other two spawns of Molach had made their great escape, eluding capture; but, like my ol' pal, Brentwood, once said, 'Never fret too much if a *mutt* gets away; they're criminals, and they're gonna keep doing criminalistic things… you'll get 'em another time, sooner or later;' so we didn't worry about it too much.

It was a pretty neat thing to see the family embracing one another as we began wrapping everything up; it sort of gives you this tingling sensation inside of your chest. They were all still decently shaken up, but the dad made a point to swing on over to thank us and all of that. Extending his hand to me for a shake, I giving mine in return, he said, "You know something, I never cared for the Police before… I never had a great liking for them as a whole… but I want to tell you that, after tonight, there's no one that I respect more. Thank you… thank you so much… for saving my family. I wish there were better words to express the gratitude… I wish there was more I could convey…"

"There's no need, sir;" I replied, "this is what we do… it's our job."

Holding back tears in vain, whilst still grasping my hand, the patriarch stated, "And a fine job it is, my friend. A very fine job, indeed."

X

"Operation Impact's goal is to reduce crime throughout the city by deploying more officers to high-crime hot spots, known as "Impact Zones." The NYPD employs innovative mapping and statistical tools in order to identify these zones and, once identified, develops progressive policing methods that are appropriate to the nature and number of crimes in each Impact Zone. Operation Impact focuses its efforts on gangs and narcotics, high-crime public housing developments and ongoing crime trends."

- *New York City Global Partners*

Not long after our fifth year anniversary, Harper and I were approached by the Special Operations Lieutenant, the guy that's in charge of all the entities serving some unique purpose or another within a Precinct, about being part of his Conditions and Anti-Crime Teams, two highly prominent units deployed throughout all of the Commands in the city to combat quality of life issues and street crimes respectively, especially so in the era of *Operation Impact*, the Police Commissioner's baby, which consisted a bunch of snot-nosed, shiny new Graduates of the Academy who were told that they were the next coming of Christ, or some crazy thing like that. I mean it, these kids thought their shit smelled of a rose garden... they could do no wrong in the eyes of the entire Department, so long as they were arresting the entire population of New York City. There was no mercy with these sociopaths; they'd arrest their own great-grandmothers if it came down to it. Honestly. These androids would unplug from whatever docking bay in which they were receiving their charge, pre-programmed to collar and summons the hell out of all five boroughs. One time, when one of those cyborgs wasn't looking,

I nearly poured some water on it to see if I could espy a spark or some other indication of an electric current… just to see if it wasn't really some kind of a robot. Seriously. I never did get the evidence I needed to support that particular conspiracy theory, though; but, that being said, I'm still not convinced that these individuals were not cybernetic in nature. I still have my doubts about it, you know? Thankfully, I rarely had to deal with any of those gestapo mother fuckers, besides the one time, which I'll tell you about a bit later.

Anyway, back to the part about the Lieutenant talking to us… The thing of it was, he only had one spot on each of the Teams, one Conditions spot and one Anti-Crime spot, so we – my partner and I – couldn't continue working together, which really sucked; you sort of develop a bond with a person after sitting in a rolling sardine can for a slew of years. We agreed, though reluctantly, to part ways; he joining the coveted Anti-Crime unit – a plain clothed group of Cops who drove around in an unmarked Police Car, scouring the Precinct confines for the lowest variety of vermin, and me becoming a part of the slightly less appealing Conditions team – our sect wearing the traditional uniform of the day, riding around in marked cars, addressing issues that, essentially, annoyed the living shit out of neighborhoods, banging violators out with every summons known to man who committed these pesky, but highly irksome, quality of life infractions. We were the pain in the ass Cops that exchanged your open and publicly displayed bottle of Hennessy for an invitation to Criminal Court… the illustrious Conditions crew, that was us. That being uttered, there was a singularly hefty difference between us and Impact; they having absolutely no boundaries between just and unjust. Many people actually thanked us for keeping their communities pristine, they really did; there was simply just a fine, delicate line between doing what we did and what the fourth reich's objective was… that's all I'm saying.

One thing you had to admit, even if you found yourself the subject of our seemingly trivial enforcement, New York City was one hell of a clean place in those days; that's one thing you can't dispute. I mean, you couldn't so much as sneeze in the wrong direction without getting one of those *tags*… what I'm trying to say is, there was very little tolerance for things like launching your phlegm all over the public sidewalks; chucking your spent potato chip wrapper into the wind; letting your one hundred thirty pound Rottweiler roam the neighborhood off its leash; making excessive noise outside, blasting your favorite jams from the brand new sound system you recently purchased, at un-Godly hours of the night, and all of that craziness. These are the transgressions in which my new associates and I corrected, and let me tell you, it was tedious and especially unpopular work, the hooligans not especially as thankful as the hard working residents in the hood.

"Sir, let me see your I.D." one of my new cohorts, Delgado (15 years on the Job), requested after witnessing an upstanding gentleman (I'm sure) nestled in between two vehicles – none of which were his - reaching into his now opened zipper, pulling out his modestly sized reproductive organ, and emptying his inordinately full bladder of urine onto both bumpers of the aforementioned cars, apparently finding it amusing to oscillate his amber stream of excreta from side to side, as would a gardener to his petunias.

Stuffing his genitalia back inside of his blue Wrangler jeans (which was no great chore, his phallus being most unfortunate in terms of magnitude), the degenerate had the nerve to ask, "Why you gotta see my I.D.?”

With the utmost reserve, Delgado answered coolly, in monotone, “Well, sir, you were taking a leak in a public place, which is frowned upon in this great city of ours.”

“What? that ain’t true. I ain’t do that!” exclaimed the aforementioned degenerate, with the countenance akin to that of a Texas Hold ‘em player, raising the stakes whilst in possession of a singularly paltry set of *trouble hands*.

Still in monotone, Delgado returned, “Sir, I absolutely *did* see you. And, sir, just so you are aware, the remains of your quite unhealthy shade of piss is still dripping from the bumpers of those cars over there; and, if I may be so bold, your crotch area is also soaked with said piss.” The guilty party, taking a glance over at his forsaken discharge, then down to his sopping wet groin, before returning his attention back to us with a look of dejection, said nothing to rebuke this case in point; therefore, Delgado continued, “I.D., please, sir… or I’ll have to put you in cuffs and figure out who you are back at the Station House… and if I do that, sir… if you make me do that… it ain’t gonna be a ticket. I’ll run you through the System and you’ll end up spending the rest of the weekend in Central Booking… and, it’s Friday, so you wont see the judge ‘till Monday. Get me?”

Having been checkmated, the man complied, accepting his freshly issued pink counterfoil directing him to the local city court house to pay for his peccadillo, head hung low, another victim of what was commonly known as the Impact era of policing, causing a huge *impact* on the wallets of many an infractor of the now immaculate *City that Never Sleeps*.

"Can you believe that guy?" I commented, in amazement at the man's unwillingness to concede defeat. "His dick was literally hanging out in the wind, and yet he still stood right in front of us, looking us dead in the eye, and made you explain the damn thing to him."

"Oh yeah," said Ramirez, another member of the four-man team (11 years on), "I can believe it… you'll see how it is with these people. They'll stand there with the bloody knife in their hand, and have the balls to ask you what knife you're talking about. Unreal… hey, Delgado, how many does that make for you? I woulda sworn you got the last one before this."

"Yeah, right, you know damn well it was my turn." rebutted Delgado. "I got fifteen tags for the month, the rest of you got sixteen; except for the new guy."

"How many do we need to get in a month, again?" I inquired, not ever formally asking what the quota was for that particular Team.

"You gotta get twenty a month, bro." Smith, the fourth cog, and *lifer*, in the Conditions machine (Seventeen years on, ten of which were in this particular unit) answered. "But, the beauty of this unit is, you can come in at the end of the month with a combination of parking summonses, moving violation summonses, or criminal court summonses. That's what I love about this team… see, the Crime Team has no choice but to come in with criminal court summonses, *plus* two felony arrests a month; fuck that! too much work for me. Here, you just wait around and watch as these savages desecrate their own neighborhoods, and then you slap 'em with the pink paper. Like shooting a ducks in a pond, my brotha'!"

"Used to be a lot less... a *helluva* lot less... but ever since those Impact scumbags came about, we sort of had to raise the bar, you know what I mean? Otherwise, they'd pretty much vanquish us and all of that shit." inserted Delgado.

"The groovy thing is, our Boss is great... Sergeant Warren." Ramirez added. "Man, he's aces, I tell ya. Dude don't give a fuck about nothin', and you'll never so much as even *see* him, so long as you *'pay the minimum rent'* at the end of the month. Now, if you come up short... well, let's just say I like it here and don't wanna go back to Patrol, chasin' the goddamn radio all day long. You know what I mean?"

"Listen, kid, you'll do alright. Just don't be trying any funny business and sneak yourself more tags than the rest of us. We run a well oiled machine here, you get me? We ain't nothin' like those Impact brats. We just do what we gotta do to live comfortably. If we find out you're padding your numbers and outshining us and shit, your locker's gonna end up on a subway car in Brooklyn, catch my drift?" Smith scolded.

Being that I was new *to them*, and – lest we forget the hierarchy that we discussed in the beginning of this story... in case you forgot – I only had a smidgen over six years, plus the fact that I was riding around with Cops who possessed an average of fourteen years when you added and divided their time up together, I allowed the threat to go unanswered. I had no wish to rock the proverbial boat with my new collaborators, if you get *my* drift.

About a month or two later, we were riding around the

Precinct looking for the usual low level offenders of peace, tranquility and cleanliness, when we happened to observe a commotion – a large group of people, to be more precise - in the middle of the street and thought, very seriously, about putting on the ol' blinders and moseying on passed it all. Somebody, I'm certain, would call 911… eventually. I mean, it wasn't *our* problem… not *exactly*. What I'm saying is: yes, we *technically* should have dealt with what was referred to as a *roving band* of people creating a hazardous, disorderly condition; but with that amount of people, best let the lower portion of the ol' totem pole deal with it… that's what Patrol Sectors – the guys who chase the radio around for eight and a half hours of the day - are for; so, we were all set to veer in the opposite direction of the maelstrom when we noticed – that is, when *I* noticed (the aforementioned proverbial blinders already being wrapped securely around the eyes of my cohorts) that there were Police Officers in the epicenter of the brouhaha, the prodigious crowd of incandescent civilians surrounding them.

"Hey, guys, there are Cops in the middle of that mob." I said, as the Operator of our vehicle leered at me through the rear view mirror, the whites of his eyes turning a singularly bright carnation pink.

"What are you? a Doppler Radar? Didn't you happen to notice that we were trying to get away from that mess?" an especially vexed Smith said.

"Yeah, kid, what's wrong with you?" added Delgado, seemingly quite disappointed at my find.

"Bro, if there's a collar, I'm not taking it… I don't care if it's my turn or not, you spotted it; so, it's yours, fuck that." Ramirez chimed in.

"Guys, there are *Cops* in the middle of that thing." I repeated, assuming that this particular fact would be sufficient to sway the querulous feelings of my teammates.

"Jesus. We're gonna have to have a long talk after this, kid. Seriously." Smith exclaimed, making a u-turn, having already put the aforesaid throng about a block and a half behind us.

As the four of us *re*-approached the bedlam, we could see that there were, indeed, two *very* new Officers – Impact Cops - holding tightly to the arms of two elderly gentleman (whom I would venture to age at no less than seventy or so) secured by handcuffs, swarmed by a very put-out crowd of people who clearly disagreed with the detaining of the doddering, old chaps. Making our way through the crowd, we arrived at the midpoint, immediately putting some distance between us and the swarm, while Smith addressed the neophytes. "Please tell me you got these two old fogies for homicide or something serious like that. Please tell me that, willya?"

"Nah, bro…" Now, I would ask that you, the reader, at this very moment close your eyes and imagine the sound of tires screeching to an abrupt halt or, for my more mature, seasoned lovers of the written word, imagine the sound of the record player needle violently scraping across the vinyl of your favorite Frank Sinatra piece… these singularly disturbing sounds being most apropos at this very moment in time, when the Impact Rookie uttered the words, '*Nah, bro.*' Such a thing, before the implantation of the aforesaid age of Impact, simply did not occur. You didn't dare address your *better stationed* Senior Officers with the insolence displayed by this unruly child; not if you cherished your miserable life. Let's get something straight: this particular radicle grows rotten from the initial embryo... nay, the botanist that embeds this particular seed into the soil is the culpable party, the one whom the fault lies; if not for the improper nurturing by the Instructors of these putrefied seedlings, this particular moment, and many, many, like it, would not have transpired. The Academy, surely, was to blame for the slight of our poor Rookie and all like him. I mean, even if you're getting pressure from the *powers that* be, the brain trust, as it were, you still have a direct line responsibility to teach some goddamn reality to these younglings. I get that they have a ridiculous curriculum that must be adhered to, but for Christ's sake, there's a human element here... anyway, what do I know. Back to what I was saying: the new jack continued his explanation and verbal *faux pas* upon my partner, "these two old fucks are disturbing the peace -"

"Looks like *you and your partner* are the ones disturbing the peace, *BRO*." interjected Delgado, acknowledging the blunder in vernacular committed by the youngster.

The Rookie, probationary Police Officer Jacobs, paid no heed to Delgado's sarcastic return, continuing, "They're both *under* for disorderly conduct. We're bringing 'em in."

"Dude, you can totally give them summonses and cut them loose, if you *really* feel the need to harass the geriatric community... you don't have to bring 'em in for a *dis con*." I submitted, in the event - giving Jacobs the benefit of the doubt – that he was unaware of the discretionary ability he possessed.

"Nah, bro…" Again with the '*nah bro*.' This kid was really starting to earn an ass kicking. Seriously. "… fuck that, I need another pinch for the month, I only got ten collars, so far, and it's already half-way into the month. I needa play catch-up, you feel me, bro? These two will bring me to twelve. Gotta put 'em through the System."

"Uh, look here, *Rook*," Smith began, "I don't know what in the hell you new guys are being told, but, uh… *twelve* bodies? twelve *arrests* for the month? What in the holy fuck… who told you to get *twelve* bodies in *one* month?"

"Who said anything about telling us to get twelve?" Jacobs cockily corrected, "I said I *only* will have twelve – including these old farts. I gotta get *at least* eight more before the month is through."

"At least eigh-… listen," pronounced a flabbergasted Smith, "that's just not how things are done around here… you tools are outta your minds. No one on this job is collaring twenty bodies a month… no one! We especially don't go around locking up little old men who were already on this planet a century before your dad regrettably forgot to pull out of your mom!"

With this, Impact Officer Jacobs - with all of seven months on the job - released his prisoner and lunged towards Smith with bad intentions, sending both of them tumbling down to the ground, the stripling shouting, "What the fuck did you say to me? you fucking old ass dinosaur? What did you say about my mother?!"

Now laying on his back, straddled by the enraged Jacobs, his collar scrunched up inside the balled fists of his rider, Smith shouted at the top of his lungs, "Get the fuck off me you little punk! get the fuck off me!"

After standing frozen in disbelief for a second or two, watching as the two rolled around the ground like a couple of Greco-Roman wrestlers – with the crowd hollering and hooting in amazement at the spectacle transpiring before their eyes – Ramirez, Delgado and I dove in to abort the skirmish, whilst Jacobs' partner stood by with a stupefied look upon his countenance, now securing both of his hoary captives.

"Break it up! Hey! break it up, I said! Cut it out, now! come on! people are fucking watching!" I shouted, as we all attempted to separate the two, their vice-like grips practically infrangible.

After what amounted to one solid minute of – let us be brutally honest - a singularly deplorable hug-fest, essentially culminating into a draw, with no clear victor (except, perhaps, the once angry onlookers, their vexation quelled after being provided some captivating entertainment), the two gladiators were pulled apart and hoisted up from the floor.

"Nobody talks about my mother, bro… nobody!" cried Jacobs, panting in between each word.

"Nobody was talking about your fucking mother, dude, that was not the point of what I was trying to say… at all!" justified an equally out of breath Smith, also struggling to acquire massive amounts of oxygen as he spoke.

"You clearly said some shit about my mother! you clearly did!"

"Dude, the point – the *only* point – I'm getting at is that we can't be going around arresting little old men… that's it. That's the point."

"And I already *told* you, I *need* to. I *told* you that I'm short and I *need* to catch up… you know what? this is pointless; we were told about guys like you in the Academy. They told us about you."

"Oh *really*? What, exactly, did they tell you about me? I'd love to hear this."

"They said that you'd all give us a hard time… that you'd try to prevent us from making collars… try to threaten us if we stopped. Yeah, we know all about you old dinosaurs… they even gave us a direct line to the Chief of Department's Office to report all of you separatists, not going along with the program. You know, this ain't 1990, bro. We're fighting a war out here now. We ain't walking around a foot post twiddling our thumbs and twirling hickory night sticks anymore. We're cleaning this fucking city up, and if you don't like it, if you ain't a part of the solution, you're the fucking problem, bro. Why dontcha just fucking leave? old timer. Why dontcha just vest out and go sip your vanilla Ensure on a beach somewhere and leave taking back the city to the *real* cops?"

"Oh, yeah… and collaring old men is really making a difference. Some real fine Police work, there, kid!" said Smith, wiping the remnants of the street from his uniform.

"Hey, brother," I said to Smith, taking hold of him, "fuck this guy, man. These Impact kids are on another level, you'll never get through to him… they're all brainwashed, it's a losing battle talking to him." Tugging Smith's arm slightly to indicate my wish for him to follow me away from the fray, I continued, "Come one, let's bounce outta here… come on, bro, let's go." I urged until he acquiesced, finally – although continuing to keep an eye on Jacobs the entire time – walking backwards towards our car.

Once safely back in the vehicle, after some time of silent mental - and for Smith, physical - recuperation, Delgado, whilst aimlessly looking out of the front, passenger side window, broke the ol' ice by uttering, "I'll tell you what, this job has taken a definite turn for the absolute worse."

"That's the understatement of the century." answered Ramirez.

"Well, I can't talk," I joined in. "I'm still a Rookie with my little ass six years on."

"That's my point, even with your six *minutes* on the job, you have more sense than those goddamn Impact fucks." Delgado opined.

"Man, I think your group was the last ones to have been taught some respect. After your class, the job went to shit with those guys." added Ramirez.

"Twenty collars a month! sheesh… I wouldn't wanna be in *their* shoes." rejoined Delgado. "That's way too much hard labor. I actually don't even know how they do it."

"They're robots, bro… I mean it, their not human." said I, throwing my one and a half cents into the conversation. "They don't even have any feelings, so they don't realize how much work it is.

They just keep going, arresting the entire world."

"I'll tell you what… mark my words… the community, sooner or later - I'd say within the next ten years - is gonna turn against them." predicted Delgado, like a modern day Nostradamus. "And you wanna know another thing? we're all gonna get caught up in the middle of it. You just watch… well, maybe not *you*, Smith; you'll be long retired by the time that happens.

"I did plan on staying until I aged out at sixty-three, to be honest… I got a lot of debt and the kids are gonna be in college around then. I don't know how I'm gonna manage with the way things are going down… I can only imagine ten, fifteen, years from now. By that time, these Impact assholes'll be bosses – *big* bosses, some of them. I'm all kinds of screwed, bros."

"We're *all* screwed, my dude." agreed Ramirez, emphatically shaking his head.

For the remainder of that evening, we did absolutely nothing – as opposed to *somewhat* nothing, compared to the younger kids of that new generation, quite honestly. After what had just transpired with Smith and Jacobs, though, no one was in the mood to lift one single finger. I guess we all supposed that the Impact fuckers would work enough for all four of us at that point. One thing was quite certain, if I may be so forthright, the ushering in of the Impact era certainly altered the dynamic, especially the chemistry, of the Department; there was no denying it. The men and women, or – as is more befitting of these seemingly bionic beings – cybernetic apparatus - who emerged from the conveyor belt to disinfect our once crime ridden metropolis had infiltrated, and appropriated from the ancient dinosaurs of the 1980s and 1990s, the Big Apple. This would not change… this would not go away. Even if, for some unthinkable reason, the Program ever ceased to exist, this genera of Police Officer would (as Smith stated) eventually become Sergeants; then Lieutenants; then Captains; Deputy Inspectors; Inspectors, and finally Chiefs, one star to four… the monkey wrench had been tossed in, the old cogs and sprockets quashed, the entire circuit board replaced with a state-of-the art, shiny new model.

XI

I spent a grand total of one year with that team, the Conditions team, and I must tell you that it was a year too much. Don't get me wrong, I absolutely adored the guys, Delgado, Ramirez, and even grumpy ol' Smith; it had nothing whatsoever to do with them; it's just that I always had this kind of longing to be in the *big leagues* along with my old partner and his squad. Thankfully, the Special Operations Lieutenant, the one I told you about earlier, the one who gave *this* gig to me, approached once more, offering a spot on that coveted Anti-Crime Team, where I would, once again, be rejoined with Harper (well, Harper and one other guy, Quinn, plus the Anti-Crime Sergeant, McKinney, who – as opposed to the typical Conditions Sergeant – was an integral part of the Team, ninety-nine percent of the time riding around, and jumping out, with them when it was time to strike. If you happened not to be paying attention the first time I mentioned it, this unit – appropriately known as '*The Jump Out Boys*' throughout the entire Department for the simple fact that, when they spotted felonious or serious misdemeanor street crime afoot, they promptly, and quite literally, *jumped out* of their unmarked Police Car to apprehend the dastardly demons – took to the streets in regular civilian attire, tossing away the traditional blue uniform and its gargantuan gun-belt, along with it the thousands of accessories attached thereon, exchanging it for non-Department issue cargo pants (cargo shorts in the summer) or denim jeans; a baggy shirt representing some kind of sports team (baggy to allow for the bullet proof vest which rested underneath); a baseball cap; and, most importantly, a mere pancake holster for the firearm, lessening the load off of the ol' hips.

It was really good seeing Harper again; although, it's not

like we *never* crossed paths during the year's separation or anything crazy like that; it's just not the same thing as actually riding in the car for eight and a half hours a day, five days a week, you know what I mean? Anyway, on my first day as an Anti-Crime cop, I was ready to rock-and-roll, donning all of the appropriate attire – black, Reebok running shoes; beige, somewhat fitted, cargo pants; New York Yankees grey road uniform jersey with the number 51 on the back, representing my most adored player, Bernie Williams; and, a matching Yankees hat, which I ceremoniously wore backwards - anxiously awaiting the arrival of my new Teammates, none of whom were anywhere to be found, nearly two hours having passed since the commencement of our tour, prompting me to conjecture that I had been left behind… sort of an initiation for the new guy, perhaps? Well, I must have looked like a lost puppy tied to a pole outside of a grocery store, wondering where on Earth his owner had gone, because at some point I was approached by a Cop that happened to be loitering around the vestibule of the Command, a perplexed look painted upon his mien, who asked, "Hey, bro, you don't feel like workin' out?"

"Working out?" I inquired, quite confused by his query; wondering, perhaps, if he previously had invited me to an exercise session which happened to slip my mind.

"Yeah, with the rest of your Team." he informed. "You don't wanna join in on getting buffed? You *do* know that the Crime Team works out in the gym for the first two hours of their tour, *don't you*?"

"Su-re… sure, I do… yeah, I, uh… I just didn't feel like it today." I stammered, in all reality not knowing to what ritual he referred.

"Ah, yeah, I understand; I'm not much of a gym person, myself!" he commented, patting his paunchy belly. "It's a pretty religious thing with those guys, workin' out and all. I wouldn't miss out on too many of them if I was you… it's like some kind of a goddamn bonding moment or something like that, you know what I mean?"

I smiled and nodded, quite vexed at the snub from my new contingent, wondering why on God's green Earth they felt the need to exclude me from the past time of pumping iron. I feigned like I was wandering off in some unknown direction, so as not to arouse suspicion from the Officer - who may, or may not, have bought my lame excuse about not wanting to join the Team during their liturgy session; but, in reality, I made my way to the Command's gym where I did, in fact, see the misplaced members of my group – including the Sergeant - who were in the midst of a very intense weightlifting plenary, dripping in a deluge of sweat, each muscle group swollen and well represented in what the one and only Arnold Schwarzenegger adroitly dubbed, "the pump." Unaware as to my emergence, most likely due to the blaring sound of Metallica's 'Sandman' bellowing out from the sound system, they continued to lift at a degree ferocious in proportions, slamming the hardware down upon the ground, similar to that of a running back spiking the pigskin after penetrating the end zone for a touchdown. I traversed my way further into the room, making myself known to the crew, "Hey, fellas, I didn't know we were meeting in the gym."

"Yah, bro, we do this shit everyday before we hit the street…" disclosed Sergeant McKinney, rising from the ground, slapping his hands together to clear the dirt from the floor whereat he had just completed a perfect set of diamond push-ups. "…gotta get jacked because that's what *they're* doing out in the field. They ain't out there sitting around, eating jelly doughnuts like some of these fat fuckin' cops we got around here, you know what I'm saying? Anyway, I thought you knew."

How, exactly, in Satan's sweltering underworld, I was supposed to know that particular bit of information is beyond me because, apparently, I was left out of that particular group chat. "No, no one clued me in." I replied, shooting a brief, inquisitive look over to Harper, who, in response, turned his head in the opposite direction. Reverting my eyeballs back to McKinney, I said, "Won't our Lieutenant be upset if he finds us in here?" It was with great naïvety, evidently, that I asked this cretinous question, drawing, immediately, glares of wariness my way from the clan of sweaty Crime Cops.

Having worked with each other for a significant period of time, Harper – the only one who did not *completely* leer at me as though I were an informant for the enemy, and probably feeling shitty for not having made me aware of the preliminary activities – broke in to explain, "Not at all, brother… as a matter of fact, the Lieutenant joins in sometimes. And besides, what can anyone possibly say to us? We're building our bodies, getting stronger to handle our business in the streets… it's not like we're goofing off or any crazy shit like that. You know what I mean?"

"Yah, dude, we ain't goofin' off." parroted the Sergeant, before asking, "You ain't gonna go droppin' dimes on us… are you? new guy?"

"I don't know, Sarge," Quinn chimed in, "he kinda looks like a cheese eater to *me*.”

I hated to break it to them, but it seemed to be a pretty well exposed bit of, what they conjectured, esoteric information, seeing as how that random Cop from the vestibule appeared to be decidedly aware of these particular goings on. Before I could reply, my mouth slightly agape, Harper cut in, “Gentlemen! gentlemen! Of course he’s not gonna rat… I rode with this guy for five years, steady Sector Adam, where we waded through the shit every single day.” Noticing that the rest of the Team, whose looks of consternation sat heavily upon their mugs, appeared to be ill convinced, he declared, in a voice implying the utmost sincerity, “Guys, seriously, I *vouch* for this guy… he’s a friend of ours.” Then, subsequently traversing across the room to where I stood, he placed his arm around my shoulders, provided a slight squeeze of reassurance (for whom I hadn’t a clue… perhaps more himself than anyone else in occupancy), adding, “I trust this little fucker with my life… if you trust *me*, you gotta trust him… he’s one of us… he’s good.”

This pronouncement seemed to placate Quinn, as he returned to his decidedly intense set of *bench presses*; but, Sergeant McKinney, who appeared much less convinced, kept his crazed, apoplectic, eyes fixed upon me, as a lion would a spectator on the opposite end of the Zoological cage, whilst commencing his dumbbell shoulder shrugs, utilizing a ponderously barbaric amount of weight, being the cause to the effect of his insanely large and rounded out trapezius muscles, I’m sure.

“Don’t worry, brother, you’ll be fine…” Harper, arm still resting upon my shoulder, his face leaning into my ear, whispered. “They’ll come around. It was the same when I joined the team, you know? It takes awhile for them to warm up. This ain't the Conditions Team, you know? We're a very tight knit crew and we get into some pretty heavy shit… they gotta get to know you before you can be trusted. We think out of the box when we're doing our thing out there, you know what I mean? We don't exactly follow the goddamn Patrol Manual, if you get my drift; so, we all gotta be on the same page… we gotta be simpatico in the brain, you get me? But don't worry, me vouching for you is huge. I'm basically saying, if *you* fuck up, then *I* fuck up; which helps. Except… the thing of it is… now you *can't* fuck up… get me?" he finished by removing his arm from around my shoulders, placing a hand upon my chest, giving it a few questionable pats, before continuing to dab all around my upper body, all the while feigning as though he were providing a friendly gesture. Was I being checked for a wire? It certainly goddamn appeared to be the case.

I nodded to indicate my approval, wondering if I had made a mistake in joining this scaled down version of a mafia of sorts. Would I fit in with this *Parvus Cosa Nostra*? And, more importantly, would they accept me into their fold? or would they take me into the middle of the desert, whack me, and stuff me in a shallow grave? All of that remained to be seen. One thing was for certain, 'this is sure to be an interesting journey, for sure,' I thought to myself, as the Boss' beady peepers continued to gawp in my direction, he now midway through a set of bent-over dumbbell rows.

"Hey, new dude, come spot me with this set of bench presses." Quinn called out from across the room, directing his request to me.

Harper gave me another pat, this time on the back, to convey (I think) a feeling of, *'you see? everything will be alright,'* supplemented with – what I suppose he intended to be – a comforting smile, but was actually more akin to a timorous visage, imploring to me, '*please, for the love of God, do not get us whacked.*'

***

Later that evening, after the significantly cardinal visit to the protein shake spot – a most necessary comestible for those that choose to undergo the process of muscle destruction and regeneration - followed by a pitstop at the McDonald's drive-thru window, we finally set off to *make a difference* in the world. As we drove along, everyone still working on devouring their victuals, Quinn, from the driver's seat, lowered his window to launch the pickles from his burger out onto the street, to which Sergeant McKinney – seated at the front passenger side, where most Sergeants placed themselves when out with their Officers – responded, with much petulance, "Bro, you're throwing away the healthiest portion of that burger."

"I hate pickles; they're like soggy cucumbers… who in the hell wants to eat a soggy cucumber? Not me." he insisted, slinging the remaining three pickles like miniature frisbees across the now littered pavement; the sort of thing that my old Conditions Team spent the entire day addressing.

I offered a chuckle from the rear passenger side seat, not daring to utter a word, glancing over to my left where Harper sat finishing off his six piece nuggets, also flashing a grin across his mien. I have to admit, the group seemed pretty tight; which is to say that they seemed very close. I admired the way Harper fit in so comfortably and hoped that I, too, could soon possess the relaxed, care-free, attitude of my new little regiment. With a feeling of promising contentment, I turned to gander out at the now dark, late summer night sky, passing a variety of stores that were all currently closed for the day, when I noticed someone enter one of the establishments through what appeared to be a broken window of the entrance door, something that no one else in the conveyance seemed to have noticed, still polishing off their nosh. Uncertain if I should make mention of this nefarious deed transpiring before my very eyes, not knowing whether such an act would further the suspicion of my being the rodent they all suspected me to be, I took a deep breath and eructed, "Hey, I think a guy just broke into that store."

"What's that? new guy?" Quinn inquired, making eye contact with me through his rear view mirror.

"That… store… right there;" I stammered, "I think someone broke into it."

Sergeant McKinney, leaning forward, now fixing his eyes on the window as we drove by, agreed, "Yeah, somebody probably jacked that store, most likely gone by now."

"No, Sarge, I think I saw someone go in…" I timorously corrected.

"You *think*?"

"I *know*… for *sure*… I saw him." I affirmed, with a slightly more authoritative voice, practically holding my breath to control the trembling sound emanating from my vocal cords, as a result of my heart beating like the high tom of a drum set, fully expecting him to tear my head clean off my shoulders.

Instead – instead of him knocking my block off – he commanded, "Okay… here we go, boys! You two back there, quietly get out and make your way back to the storefront, but walk on the other side of the street and keep out of sight . These places are all one way in and one way out, so he's gotta come out of that same window; me and Quinn will spin around the block, quick, in case he gives you two the slip. Got it? Alright, let's go."

Harper and I glanced over at one another, nodding before jumping out of the car; subsequently heading back to the scene of the crime, crouched below the parked vehicles on the opposing side of the presently uninhabited street, all the while keeping a watchful eye on the broken window. As we crept ever closer to the landmark, my breathing becoming erratic, the burglar, as was predicted by McKinney, emerged from whence he entered, carrying in his hand what appeared to be a flat screen monitor of a computer. In a flash, I sprang up from in between two cars and dashed towards him, yelling to Harper, "Shit, bro, there he goes!" causing our good friend, the thief, to break into a full-on sprint down the block, forsaking his prize, throwing the monitor to the ground where it happened to break into a few million pieces.

I could hear, now in the near distance – having taken off after the bad guy - Harper screaming, "Bro, wait, wait…" but it was too late, I was already chugging full steam ahead at the heels of my prey, like a lion in pursuit of an antelope, having absolutely no regard or concern as to the whereabouts of my associates who were, incidentally, now several blocks to my stern.

Everything around me was a blur. I could, somewhat, see the passing objects around my peripheral, clearly indicating that I was advancing forward, but I'd be damned if I could tell you what exactly those objects were. My only quest was to keep pace with the target, a chase that lead the both of us down several city blocks, across numerous streets – nearly being flattened by a few oncoming cars – and finally into a wooded park, void of any other humans, which my fellow marathoner realized (I surmised by his decelerating to a walk, then a full stop, finally placing his hand in the vicinity of his waistband) was the end of the road, as it were. Seeing this, I pulled my nine millimeter Glock 19 from its holster and - still running at full force to catch up to his position, having been about fifty feet behind him the entire race - raised the weapons up to my eye level, taking aim at his center mass until I realized, now espying his empty paws balling into fists, that the burglar apparently held no deadly weapon of his own; therefore, I altered myself from a shooting position to raising the firearm up high above my head, subsequently striking downward, analogous to Thor and his illustrious hammer – still in full motion, mind you - connecting with his grill, sending him, at first, to his knees, then, seconds later, face down upon the earth to dream of whatever fantastical repressed thoughts lay dormant in the subconscious of a sleeping common criminal. He was knocked out, cold.

Harper, in the ensuing moments of my placing the handcuffs onto my prey, finally caught up to us and signaled, over the radio, our location, so that McKinney and Quinn could rendezvous with us near the park. As we peeled the bandit – who was now slowly waking from his forty winks - off of the floor, Harper exclaimed, with an amused countenance, "Bro, I almost couldn't find you! Once you cut across the street and went into the park, you were ghost! I'm lucky I turned left instead of right as soon as I entered this fucker."

"Dude, I didn't even know where I was, *myself*!" I replied, still sort of catching my breath from the run.

"Good shit, bro… real good! You're a fucking natural, my man."

Awaiting us at the entrance of the park, Sergeant McKinney and Quinn stood by the car with the rear door wide open tantamount to proverbial welcoming arms, clapping their hands in celebratory applause, as I tossed my very first Anti-Crime collar, a burglary, into the back seat. "Wow, popped your cherry on the first night, huh?" commented McKinney, with a sort of half smile, as though he were attempting to restrain his true emotions, that of a singularly pleased supervisor who now gets to tell his boss, and his boss' boss – the Commanding Officer – that *his* Team snagged a felony arrest.

"Beast!" Quinn added, giving me a congratulatory pat on the back of the head.

"I told you, Sarge… he's a natural… he's okay!" added Harper with a wink in my direction.

"Yeah, I suppose." the Sergeant rejoined, cool as all hell, before turning to me. "I'm still gonna keep my eye on you, Cardona… but good work tonight."

***

Eventually, after some time still dealing with the incessantly circumspect ganders from my partners here and there, things finally fell into place with the Crime Team. I think showing up to the gym and getting swollen with the guys most definitely aided in that outcome… not to mention the fact that, concomitantly, I got pretty darned jacked in the process; which is to say, I developed an exceptionally muscular physique, something that most definitely didn't hurt when, outside of work, I'd swing on over to the beach to strut my tanned and oily stuff all along the boardwalk and shit. Between working out with the fellas and spending five out of the seven days of the week in the car, we had, in practically no time at all, developed a pretty decent relationship with one another; and, at the same time, became one of the most valuable Teams in our Command. What I mean is, we were really doing well putting away some of New York City's *bad hombres*, who were perpetrating some extremely huge crimes like robberies; auto thefts and break-ins; burglaries &c. In addition to all of that, we were lifting some serious weapons off the streets, preventing innocent folks from getting shot, stabbed, and whatnot. We ended up getting ourselves printed in a few of the local papers who reported that we were practically heroes, on a remarkably consistent basis, which felt pretty damn good, to be completely honest. I mean, what *isn't* to enjoy about basically being on top of the proverbial world? I'm pretty goddamn sure that if *you* were, essentially, being hoisted upon the shoulders of your community, paraded around for all to relish like Super Bowl III Champion Joe Namath of the New York Jets at the Miami Orange Bowl, you'd get a little tickle under your jock strap, too. I'm positively sure you would.

Anyway, before I get lost in my own reverie – what with imagining that I was a Hall of Fame athlete and all of that shit - I shall return to the story at hand… every night, right after we tossed the iron around for a couple of hours, we would stop by the clerical room to check out the current crimes going on within our Precinct, while also looking to see if there were any outstanding criminals who needed capturing. We'd end up printing out the mug shots of these individuals to keep an ol' eye out for them while we were doing our rounds during the evening; which proved fruitful, catching a good amount of these scums of the Earth. One Saturday night, after doing all of the aforementioned administrative prerequisites (well, not *right* after… I mean, we still had to get our bacon double cheese burgers with cheesy fries; but definitely right after *that*), we had occasion to circle around the night clubs that were located in the area because of the crazy fights that sometimes occurred, involving some heavy duty armaments… that, and – to be blatantly transparent - also gaze at the hot chics, flashing their devilishly saucy outfits – when, suddenly, we spotted someone who we recognized from one of our printouts… one of the earlier mentioned scoundrels that roam the planet.

"Yo," started Quinn from the driver's seat, "isn't that Andrew Jones? right there in front of the club?"

"Where? which one?" McKinney answered, squinting his eyes and leaning forward to grasp a better look.

"Right there, in the middle of that little cluster of girls." Quinn frantically pointed. "The one wearing the gray Timberlands."

Sergeant McKinney reached up to his visor to pull out and unfold one the photos before examining it, comparing the picture to the young gentleman who Quinn had adeptly spotted, and finally exclaimed, "Yeah, dude, I think it *is*."

"What's he wanted for?" I inquired from the rear of the car.

"Says armed robbery and attempted murder… says he jacked an old lady of her purse, then shot her. Also says assault on a Police Officer. Apparently this mope fought and resisted whoever tried to collar him… ended up escaping." the Sergeant commented, whilst reading the synopsis from the printout.

"And is dumb enough to come out to the clubs." remarked Harper, emphatically shaking his head before finishing, "Well, better for us… stupidity like that keeps us in business."

"Here, here." signified Quinn.

"Okay, so what's the plan?" I asked, scoping out the scene in front of the club, keeping eyes on the subject.

"You guys get out here and standby while Me and Quinn head to the back of the club to cover the rear entrance, in case he dips inside when you approach."

"Here we go, boys." I exclaimed, as Harper and I exited the car.

We, as inconspicuously as two extremely light skin individuals could be at a predominantly African-American occupied night club, made our way slowly to the suspect's position, giving enough time for Quinn and the Sergeant to make their way around the block to the opposing end of the discotheque. Unfortunately, the best laid plans of mice and men *gang aft agley*, in the words so eloquently put forth by Robert Burns; and so it was… as one Mr. Andrew Jones spotted the very *out of their element* undercover Officers, that would be us, slithering in his direction, he took off like a chiropteran out of Hades, leaving the lovely ladies, with whom he had only moments ago made acquaintance, to choke on his dust. "Fuck! we got a runner!" shouted Harper, Andrew Jones immediately sending us off to the races in the middle of the street, which happened, incidentally, to be filled with seemingly every single car ever manufactured, causing us to dodge the automobiles, all the while keeping our eye on the absconder. A thought flashed through my mind, passing and crossing all of those vehicles, and that was to dive onto, and slide across, at least one or two of the hoods, the way I imagined it some eight years prior, just before good ol, Sam Herzog bursted my bubble about the damn thing that very first day in the auditorium; but I didn't do it, I didn't pull the Starsky and Hutch move of my dreams across any of the cars… I'll tell you what, though, I *seriously* thought about it, that much is for sure.

Keeping pace with the lead pony was no easy task and I wished, at that moment, to have given increased attention to a more cardiovascular based workout – making a mental note to fit that into the ol' agenda next time I was throwing the weights around in the gym – feeling myself losing some steam, falling slightly behind *Jesse freaking Owens* over here (although, I have to say, I was still slightly ahead of Harper, so that had to count for something; I'm sure you would agree). Thoughts of me having to withdraw from the relay entered my cranium, my legs beginning to feel like two steel beams, my chest tightening, preventing a full flow of oxygen to enter my lungs, until Mr. Jones suddenly came to an abrupt halt within twenty feet of us, deciding at that moment to pull out a black nine millimeter firearm from his waistband and point it directly at my face – the muzzle clearly aligned with my line of sight – simultaneously squeezing the trigger. With all of this transpiring in a matter of mere seconds, I had only enough time to try and come to an immediate stand still; however, my body's momentum caused me to enter into a skid for a few more inches, after my legs ceased to move, creating the sensation as though I were one of those cartoons characters who continue to slide forward long after they have stopped running, not having nearly enough of an opportunity to retrieve my Glock 19.

Upon his depressing the trigger… about three times, I might add… hearing only the hollow sound of, 'click, click, click,' I came to the realization that, fortunately for me (unfortunately, I am certain, for Andrew Jones), his hammer had malfunctioned, prompting him to hurl the weapon at me, instead; thereafter, resuming his flight. Stunted, as you can imagine, in my tracks – assuring myself that I had not been inundated with projectiles – I also recommenced the chase, Harper in tow after retrieving the forsaken gun, leading us up and down a plethora of blocks, through several alleys, and finally to an apartment building of which Jones entered, climbing several flights of stairs, seemingly having wings to aid his ascension, whilst, on the other hand, as it were, Harper and myself straggled behind; except, this time around, my partner outpacing me by a significant distance, the stairs proving a very cumbersome obstacle, and before I knew it, both of them were out of my site, they having exited the staircase out unto the roof landing.

Time ceased, as the remaining, torturous, climb to the roof seemed to me an eternity, not knowing the plight of my compeer; each and every step bringing with it a second more of helplessly agonizing anticipation. I'll tell you right now, there's no feeling quite like it, knowing that your partner is alone with someone that has no regard for human life, especially the life of a Police Officer. The thought of the unthinkable gave me a second wind that impelled me heavenwards to the apex where I erupted through the roof landing door; however, much to my perplexity and great consternation, what I witnessed was… nothing. Scanning the entirety of the roof, I had begun to imagine the worst; visions of their marred and bloodied bodies upon plummeting to the cement, eleven stories below, swirled around my mind like a cyclone upon a midwestern prairie. I slowly staggered toward the parapet, caring not to discover whatever grim truth existed on its opposite end; but, just before I could peek my now blurry and practically tearing eyes over the periphery, a hand appeared – the body to which it belonged remaining an enigma - followed by another, then the upper portion of a head, followed, finally, by the beleaguered voice of my partner, Harper, who precariously called out, "Help me up, bro… help me up."

"Fuck! are you okay?" I exclaimed, as I pulled him up to safety, witnessing that he was soaked in a crimson bath of life fluid.

"Yeah… yeah… I'm… I'm okay;" he panted, now laying supine on the ground, feeling all around his body with blood stained hands, apparently taking inventory of his essential parts, "but I think *he's* dead." Harper concluded, motioning with his thumb in the direction from whence he climbed.

I stepped over to the ledge and realized that there was, apparently and unbeknownst to me, a fire escape leading, from that uppermost point, down to street level; and, somewhere in between – about a flight or two below - lay our dear friend, Mr. Jones, also covered in a layer of sanguine solution. "Shit! you think he's really dead, bro?" I inquired, not truly anticipating a reply.

"I dunno, I didn't stop to ask." was my partner's sardonic repost.

I took another look, just to see if I could discern the perpetrator's membership status in the world of the living; but could see very little through the omnipotence of the dark. At some point, McKinney and Quinn - along with the entire Platoon of uniformed Cops - who, evidently, were all scouring the ends of the Earth looking for us, showed up in droves. We had, unintentionally, stopped transmitting the progress of our chase some time before entering the building; however, luckily for us, someone – a concerned tenant whose portion of the fire escape was now currently occupied by the tattered framework of Mr. Jones – called 911, alerting our comrades as to our particular bearings. "Holy fuck! there you guys go! We've been looking all over the damn place for you two!" exclaimed Quinn.

"Yeah, I was about to fucking call aviation over the radio if that 911 job hadn't have come over! Where's the perp? Did you lose 'em?"

"No, we didn't lose him… but he may have *lost* his life… he's sort of over the ledge there." Harper said, motioning again with his thumb, still laying flat on the ground.

"Over the ledge? Is he *dead?*" Quinn asked, heading over to the wall with the Sergeant, along with everyone else that showed up, to take a gander.

"I ought to get myself a medical degree… all this asking me if he's dead… I don't know, man! somebody should go down there and ask him." Harper commented, his sense of humor clearly not wanting for anything.

"Bro, I think he's moving." said one of the Cops, swinging one of his legs, then the other, over the wall to begin making the descent. "Yeah, man, he's definitely moving… he's actually trying to make his way down to the next level."

"Fuck! he's a perseverant one, huh?" McKinney said, joining in the declination from the brow of the roof.

Having absolutely negative amount of energy, still in recovery mode from the actual pursuit, Harper and I lay there, attempting to collect ourselves, intaking as much air as our lungs would allow. I turned my head towards him and asked, once again, "Hey, are you okay? I mean, are you *okay*?"

After taking a few deep breaths, he answered, "Yeah… I'm okay. Better, I guess, now that I know he's not dead and shit. That would've sucked, you know what I mean?"

Emitting a slight chortle, I answered, "Yeah, I suppose that would've sucked pretty bad, bro."

"Sucked as bad as a three dollar hooker." he added, sending us into a fit of chuckles.

Saying nothing else, we remained on the roof for a bit longer before heading down to the car; and, eventually, back to the Command where all of the fun administrative stuff, processing the arrest and all of that, awaited us. If you're wondering what ended up happening to good ol' Andrew Jones – especially if you're one of those jelly hearted types who want to join hands, sway back and forth, and sing along with every perpetrator of violence on the goddamn planet, the kind of person that shouts at the top of their lungs, "*so and so* didn't deserve to die," even though *so and so* just got through putting a gun to bunch of people's heads, whilst also pilfering their possessions –

you'll be happy to know that he, miraculously, survived the tumble with just a slight gash on his head… he ended up being just fine; so you all can put away your signs of protest; go on ahead and pick up the phone, give a call to whatever celebrity professional agitator was scheduled to spew his ornery rhetoric at the durable masses and tell him to save it until next time. Andrew Jones - the man wanted for attempting to take the life of Gloria Jackson, a seventy-five year old grandmother who, while on her way back from the market, crossed paths with our antagonist, before she was heinously shot and left for dead (her tiny, floral patterned coin purse, containing a whole thirteen dollars and eleven cents, the object of the schizoid's desire, and the price, it would seem, for her life) - was alive and well. I hope you're satisfied. Sheesh.

***

A couple of years later, my Team and I were all just driving around aimlessly, with the intentions of doing absolutely nothing at all. We had days like that, once a week if we were lucky, which were called 'down days.' On these down days, we'd go grab ourselves a couple of cigars each and puff away like a bunch of goddamn chimneys, while checking out the *smoke shows* in their minuscule outfits around the confines of the Precinct. If it was raining or some shit like that, instead of stalking the mademoiselles, we'd find a bridge to park under and just peacefully smoke, talk, and listen to music like gentlemen. It was nice. If you ask me, I liked those moments the best, sitting there under the bridge and just taking it easy. To tell you the truth, I'm not the kind of fella that goes around chasing skirts all over the damn place, it's just not my cup of Earl Grey, if you get my drift. I mean, sure I like to *gander* at the goddamn species… I *am* a fully functioning heterosexual male, after all; but, if you gave me the choice between a room full of women - who were sure to throw themselves all over you the entire night - and a nice quiet spot where I could just enjoy a Tatiana cigar (perhaps throw in four fingers of Screwball on the rocks), believe me, I'd pick the latter every day of the stinking week. Seriously.

Anyway, so we were just rolling around the Precinct, the cabin of the car engulfed in a delightful haze of tobacco smoke, just as one might see in a trendy downtown cigar lounge, and decided it would be a grand idea to park right in front of this bar that was filled to the brim with smoking hot college girls, students who attended this swanky university that was in the immediate vicinity, when someone - a civilian - runs right on up to the car like a madman and begins hysterically banging on the passenger side window, screaming for help. And if you're wondering how in the world this guy knew we were the Police, when we were supposed to be camouflaged in a goddamn unmarked car and not wearing regular uniforms, it's because, by this point, the entire city figured out the big ol' secret… pretty much any Ford Crown Victoria or Chevrolet Impala was sure to have a bunch of Law Enforcement personnel packed inside of it. Exclamations of, "Fuck;" and "You have got to be shitting me;" and "No fucking way, not tonight" undulated amongst the haze of the cigar exhaust inside the car before McKinney cracked the window, releasing said plume into the face of our complainant. "How can we help you, sir?"

"There's a… there's a man… a man… he's got some kind of sword… he… he cut some people… please… around the corner… please help!" the overwrought man exclaimed with a trembling voice.

"Fuck my life, bro." McKinney murmured in our direction, naturally out of the panicked gentleman's earshot; then, turning to the unhinged citizen once more, replied, "Okay, sir, we'll check it out." subsequently raising the window.

"We going? or we getting outta here? … I mean, it *is* our down day." Quinn commented, placing the gear shifter of the car in drive, slowly pulling the car forward.

McKinney, glancing at his side view mirror, replied, "Ahh, fuck, we gotta deal with it… he's lookin' at our license plate."

Quinn, glancing at his rear view mirror, Harper and I breaking our necks looking back through the rear windshield, confirmed that the man in peril was gawking at the one thing that could identify us in the event that we, perchance, decided to beat it the hell out of there. Listen, my most beloved reader, before you lose your mind (because I can see that look upon your face that says, 'what sort of monster *are* you for not responding to a request for help of that magnitude?'), I'll have you know that we actually *did* end up going; and, if you want to get all hyper-critical about the damned thing… remember, I only told you what we were *thinking* in the car, and you most certainly can't hang us for having private thoughts. No one ever went to the electric chair for what they were ruminating in their ol' frontal lobes, you know what I mean?

We pulled up to scene and, sure enough, there was the boor, wielding what looked like a pretty legitimate, exceptionally large, samurai-style sword, dripping from point to handle with spatters of claret sap, his victims at his feet appearing like slain, conquered, bevy. "Son of a bitch." uttered McKinney.

"We're gonna have to kill him." is what impetuously shot out of my mouth. I saw no other way. The crazed look in his eyes indicated, without question, his intention to eliminate whatever unfortunate creature happened to cross his path.

Exiting the safety of our vehicle, with complete disregard for our personal welfare – in the fashion of all keepers of the peace - we drew our guns and ordered, at the top of our lungs, for him to drop his weapon, to which he responded by conveying his intent to mince us into several itty bitty pieces, whirling the sword rapidly in a circular motion toward our direction like a goddamn ninja warrior or some craziness like that. How we did not simply fill this fine upstanding gentleman with all of our nine millimeter projectiles, to this day, I haven't a clue; instead, unbeknownst to the swordsman, Harper and I had swiftly taken a position behind him, the Sergeant and Quinn attracting his attention frontward. Shortly thereafter, my partner using the butt of his expandable baton to strike just above the nape of the offender's neck, the would-be martial artist was sent, quite instantaneously, into a squatting position, whereafter his central nervous system notified his manus to release the sword, the deadly weapon falling with a clang to the concrete. Quinn and McKinney completed the take down with a few lefts and rights to his temples, just to make certain that he was entirely incapacitated before placing onto him the metal bracelets.

When we arrived at the hospital, having to tend to the one or two scrapes and bruises acquired at the hands of his captors – in addition to, *peradventure*, a slight concussion – our lovely guest was *extremely* conscious and quite up in arms, so to say, about being in our custody. He was especially annoyed, incidentally, upon realizing he possessed the aforesaid impairments (said scrapes, bruises, and concussion), screaming at the very height of his lungs, "They tried to kill me! Police brutality! they tried to kill me! They hit me with they gun! they hit me in the back of my skull with they gun! I gots brain damage! I gots brain damage!" While that latter part of his declamation was true – his mention of 'brain damage' (a disability which, I am all too certain was prognosticated well before his encounter with the four of us… an absolute understatement even) - the former portion of his rant, the portion concerning the ferocity in which we conducted our business, captured the attention of everyone present in the emergency room, causing somewhat of a stir, drawing some pretty contemptible glances our way from the staff, as well as the glut of patients sitting with their thumbs up their asses, waiting to be seen by a doctor. It, on the face of things, never dawned on these nescient passerby's and onlookers that this cancer to society just hacked up a bunch of people for no reason other than it suited his fancy… of course, they had not a single goddamn clue as to *that* essential bit of information. It's just people's unvarying impulse to criticize and condemn the very Protectors whose presence allows these clueless denizens to enjoy the peace of mind they get when walking down the street, not having to concern themselves with getting sliced into a million pieces by ninja swords and shit like that. The thought of it all just drives me simply mad, if you really want to know the truth. I just don't understand the logic… I really don't. One day, someone is going to have to sit me down over some coffee and cucumber sandwiches and explain to me how, in the world, to deal with rogue members of humanity who only live and breathe to do harm to all the innocent biological organisms on this celestial body we call home. Seriously, how do we deal with them? Their sole purpose is to cause torment to us all; yet, when they commit, and are arrested for, the worst atrocities, we pacify and coddle them;

we give them clean and humane lodging – equipped with cable TV, air conditioning, three square meals a day and playground time on the yard - all the while, there are *peaceful* humans who wouldn't so much as squish a bug that landed on their godforsaken noses, with absolutely no home, no form of electronic communication, living in squalor on the streets, begging for currency to buy food (and maybe a bottle of Wild Turkey); yet, our tax dollars do practically nothing to care for these unfortunate souls… not compared to where the money goes to support the jails, that's for sure. The ghouls and goblins of the world… well, they get it all, don't they? They really do.

One of the people who bought into the whole production – the prisoner's tirade, that is - was his nurse, who made sure to give us the business when it was time to check his vitals and all of that crap. "You people need to un-shackle this poor man, so I can take his vitals." she demanded. Although he was, indeed, cuffed to the railing of his bed, his arms were otherwise wide open, definitely allowing for whatever needed to be done by way of health care; therefore, her request, honestly, was insanely superfluous.

"Ma'am, you *really* don't want this man un-cuffed… he's not a very friendly fellow." I advised. "Plus, it seems you have plenty of space to get the blood pressure band around his arm. Plenty of space."

"Well, I can't do my job if you insist on -"

"Excuse me, nurse, you can take his vitals just fine;" McKinney interjected, echoing my sentiments, "you don't need the cuffs to come off one bit."

Emitting a snort, she retorted, "Well, at *least* give the man some privacy!" yanking the shades closed.

The four of us exchanged silent gestures of grief, unsurprised by this act of malice for what she believed unfair treatment towards her patient; it was something we were all too familiar with, having dealt with similar fiascos on endless occasions prior. Suddenly, though, a scream was heard from the other side of the curtain; however, it was not the expected high-pitched female shriek of our nurse, but one of the male variety that filled the air. "Help! Help! she tryin' to smother me wit da pillow! she tryin' to kill me! help!"

We rushed over toward the sounds of the lamentation, pushed the divider aside, and espied the nurse standing, in a quite dumbfounded manner, by his side, a look of unquestionable perplexity upon her mien, one half of the vital conduits in her paws, the other half now all about the floor. "I... I... didn't even touch him! I... was... I was just about to take his blood pressure! Officer, I swear I didn't -"

"Lady, we tried to explain it to you... the guy is *not* playing with a full deck." Quinn lectured. "Why don't we just leave this nice little curtain wide open," he continued, while replacing the shades open to its furthest most point, "and you can go on ahead with taking Lucifer's temperature and all that good stuff, privacy not needed."

The nurse, wisely, obliged and *that* was – or so we thought – that. As the night went along, though, we ended up over by the CAT scan machine, where another lovely health care professional – Doctor *such-and-such*, God bless her soul (and I mean that... seriously, God bless the nurses and doctors of the world), pretty much commanded that we remove Mr. Mosley's bondage bracelets (that was his name, by the way… Winston Mosley). "Doc," I began, ready to divulge what I thought to be a singularly obvious injunction, "like we explained to the nurse back there, this guy… I don't think it's a very good idea… this guy is kind of a psycho."

"I really don't want to hear the song and dance, Officer;" The *song and dance*, she says… unbelievable. "I can't tell you how many countless times I have had this very discussion with your colleagues, and my stance on such a thing will never, ever, change. This man *can not* go into the CAT scan machine with those things on. Period." she concluded, referring to the handcuffs, absentmindedly rubbing her *very* pregnant belly… about seven or eight months with child, if I had to take a stab in the ol' dark to guess.

We all figured, since he was pretty much confined in that room – there being only one way in and out of the damned thing – and we could clearly see him from the glass window that separated us, what could possibly be the harm in complying with her order; so, I reached for my cuff key, removing the ringlet from his wrist, and as I did so, he sort of gave me this eminently creepy gaze, which I can't really describe… you kind of had to see it for yourself. All I can say is, it sent a shiver down my old veritable column, if you get my drift. Apparently, no one else caught the glare, and thought, perhaps, I was imagining the lecherous ogle in my noggin – seeing as how, on a pretty regular basis, I have this kind of propensity to embellish a thing or two (what I mean is, I *may* have this nasty little habit of adding some – shall we say – colorfully outlandish supplements to any given schema… hey, at least I can admit it. Some people go around bedecking their war stories to the point in which movie screen writers are lining up, duking it out for sole proprietary rights and shit. I'm not *that* bad); on that account, upon returning to the opposing side of glass, I kept my eyes peeled like a couple of spent bananas on Mr. Mosley. "Bros, I'm telling you," I exhorted, "there's something not right with this… I don't think it was such a hot idea to let him loose."

"Dude, we're right here… where is he gonna go?" exclaimed Quinn.

"Yeah, that fucker has gotta come through us if he's thinking of tryin' to break outta here." McKinney agreed.

"Exactly, fat chance of that… he doesn't have his death sword anymore, *and* he's balls-ass naked under that hospital gown. No chance he gets by us." Quinn appended.

I acquiesced to their logic, but carefully watched as the Doctor prepped him for the tube, all the while she placating him with words of gentle benevolence. "Are you comfortable, Mr. Mosley? Would you like some water before we begin? You'll be in the machine for some time, so why don't I pour you some refreshing water?" Thereafter dispensing the liquid into a plastic cup, handing it off to him with a warm, gingerly, smile upon her countenance, resting assured – I can only imagine – that Apollo the physician, Asclepius, Hygieia, Panacea, and all the Gods and Goddesses of medicine that bore witness during the swearing of her Oath as a professional healer were smiling down upon her from Olympus, giving the good doctor a big ol' thumbs up of approval. Winston Mosley, in turn, expressed his undying gratitude by throwing the water directly into her face, subsequently wrapping his rather large hands cleanly around her tiny neck, and squeezing it with all of his might; her entire face becoming a shade of midnight blue in mere seconds.

By the time we could barrel into the room, she was already in her third dream, having passed out, collapsed upon the floor. As for Mosley… well, let's just say it's fortunate for him that he was already located at a hospital whose focus dealt in serious trauma. That being said, I shall leave that particular gory description of events to my reader's imagination… but do, please, feel free to indulge your most vivid sense of cognitive inventiveness. One thing is for certain, wherever your most powerfully evocative thoughts lead you, it, when everything was all said and done, culminated into one big *magilla*, one big *jam sandwich*, speaking in the vernacular of my profession, wherein all of the internal investigative entities associated with the Police Department were activated. It's kind of expected when you put people into comas, I suppose. What I mean is, after you rattle someone's brain matter around their skull, you ought not be taken aback when high ranking officials, along with a couple of intimidating individuals in business suits, come looking for you with a few hundred questions in mind to ask. We got a visit from the Duty Captain, the guy that's in charge of the entire borough on any given day, who asked us, my Team and I, a bunch of questions about what happened, and also interviewed all of the doctors and nurses who happened to be around the pandemonium during the time of occurrence. He was pretty decent about it, the Duty Captain. He sort of sauntered into the Command (where we all were loitering around processing the collar at that particular time, except for Harper who had to stay with the incapacitated Mosley at the hospital), within one or two hours of the incident. He was an older gentleman who looked about fifty or sixty years of age, although he most likely was much younger, with hair that resembled untouched snow; chunky, bright red cheeks; an oversized nose of the same color; a rotund belly which protruded from his once gleaming white shirt, now a shade more akin to chartreuse; faded blue pants that had, long ago, lost their luster – most likely a decade or two prior to his visit that day; and, finally, a pair of old boots whose souls were long departed from this Earth, well into the afterlife, leaving behind the forsaken leather carcasses that enveloped his size ten feet.

"Alright, kid, tell me what happened tonight… you tuned up a mutt, huh?" the Captain inquired, picking the remnants of the chicken broccoli rabe, which was recently consumed, from his teeth with the elongated nail of his pinky finger, carefully inspecting the retrieved specimen as an entomologist would a new species of bug.

"Sir, I -"

"Easy, kid, easy… I been there a hundred times… and then some. Just tell me what happened… and be brief about it; I ain't tryin' to be here all night, get me?" he slurred, the odor of Jack Daniels and garlic emanating from his breath.

"Well, sir, this guy -"

"Mosley… Winston Mosley… that right?" he inquired, glancing at his little notepad, which looked as though it had seen its final days about a decade ago, all of the sheets having been filled to its entirety, forcing him to scribe upon the cardboard at the end portion of the decrepit thing.

"Yes, sir, Winston Mosley… he was wielding a sword, a samurai sword, around -"

"You got the sword?" His eyes lighting up like the Rockefeller Christmas tree at Christmastime.

"Yes, sir we have it… we're vouchering it for arrest evid -"

"Well, shit, kid, let's see it!" He was obviously more enchanted at the prospect of laying eyes on the weapon than hearing one single word I had to say.

"Yes, sir…" I replied, ready to continue my debriefing, until I realized – his facial expression displaying a singular disappointment having literally wanted to see the object in question that very instant – it was not my words that would quench his desires. "…oh, you mean right now, sir?"

"No, tomorrow!" he exclaimed, sardonically, before continuing, "of course right now! What in the hell, kid?! I wanna check that fucking thing out!"

I ran into the arrest processing room where Quinn was helping to log the cutting instrument into inventory, retrieving it for the Captain who, halfway coming back to present it to him, had already risen with a countenance akin to that of a birthday boy on the verge of receiving his bounty, arms extended outward to take hold of the sword. He struck me as one possessing the delight of a portly child within reach of a confectionary establishment, which was quite surprising for the simple fact that I just assumed all executive members of the service to be tight asses, having tremendous hard-ons for us sub-basement level peons, maintaining little interest in fraternizing with the likes of a lowly Cop such as myself. I suppose he was into that kind of thing… exotic weaponry and all… because he practically orgasmed upon taking hold of the phallic ornament. In all actuality, it was a really attractive looking piece, I must confess. The handle was black, intricately designed, depicting an assortment of ancient, Asian warriors striking various poses of combat, gold in color; and they, the warriors, were all donning these gorgeous as hell red and green kamishimos, accentuating the artfulness of the piece… the details of it were impeccably painted and probably belonged in some kind of a museum, amongst other rare treasures of the world. A real collector's dream, I'm sure. To tell the truth, I'm really into that kind of shit… art and all. I can head on over to any gallery, any day of the week, and be completely contented with doing absolutely nothing else but gazing at the artwork. Seriously. I love just going to those places and appreciating rare and valuable artifacts; it's peaceful as hell, you know? Anyway, the Captain, practically drooling all over the thing, said, "Okay, go on, you were saying?"

"Saying? Oh, yeah, um… yeah, so Mosley was swinging this thing around, and he ended up cuttin' up a bunch of people -"

"Anybody dead? victims, I mean?" he inquired, not at all looking at me; instead, fixing his unblinking eyes at the weapon, his grip of it suggesting that he fancied himself a bonafide ronin or something maddening like that.

"Dead? no, sir, no one died… just pretty badly hurt. About five people cut up pretty bad. They're all in the emergency room getting st -"

"So, he was swinging this around when you pulled up?" he interjected, making horrifically poor attempts at various samurai fighting stances. "When you arrived at the scene, he was holdin' it… and moving around… like this? Standing this way?"

"Yes, sir, well, something like that… he was holding it and swinging it around like some kind of a lunatic when we pulled up to the scene… so, all of us got out of the car and we -"

"Well Jesus, kid, why didn't you pop 'em?!" he yawped at the top of his lungs, now standing erect, his particularly sonorous voice drawing the attention of a few random Officers that happened to be passing by. "I mean, why didn't you just shoot the fucker? Seems like a good fucking shoot to *me*!"

"I… yes, sir, it would have been a good shoot. He was holding it, swinging it around like crazy and we clearly saw the victims on the fl -"

"Damn right it'd have been a good shoot… open and shut… done deal. Shit, now you're gonna have to deal with whatever Internal Affairs drudges up because of the whole hospital thing. That complicates things, you know. It complicates things. See, you light 'em up on the street, it ends there, get me? It ends there because you see a guy cuttin' up a bunch of people, still holdin' the damn thing when you get there… shit, it doesn't *get* any better than *that*. Instead, you end up going to the hospital - yada, yada, yada - then this guy gets his brains bashed in… now you gotta deal with *IA*. Fuck, kid. Fill 'em up with lead next time… empty the clips, you know?" he lectured, finally, and most reluctantly, handing back the sword, still making this sort of longing eye contact with it, as a lover would to his beau who has boarded a locomotive set to journey to a distant land, never to return, as I drew it away.

"Yes, sir, I'll try and remember that for next t-"

"Well, I gotta be going… I'm not tryin' to be here all night, you know. It's not like I got time to sit around here all day long, see?" he concluded, reaching into his pocket and pulling out a maduro colored cigar, taking the front tip to his nose, inhaling its fragrance with one hand, whilst simultaneously feeling around his body with the other for, what I assumed to be, something in which to set the finely rolled object ablaze; and, upon discovering it in his front pocket, he then offered an emphatic wave bidding his adieu, shortly after piling into his vehicle, and peeling off like a race car driver coming out of a gas pit in the middle of a nip and tuck race.

***

In addition to that interview with the Duty Captain - bless his heart - about a week or so later, we had all gotten *sent for* by our friends at Internal Affairs on account of the severity of the situation… which is, I will tell you without any shame, always an emotionally stressful time. I think it's meant to be that way. Emotionally stressful. I have it on good authority that they, IA, get a kick out of giving the business to Cops who get themselves jammed up; like, they know the power that they possess and are very well aware how mentally burdened the subjects of their investigations become; it's all one big game that leaves a lot of tormented human beings with – what the besieged souls believe – no choice but to *end* it all. Rather than endure all of the humiliation and anguish, Cops just wind up blowing their brains clear out of their skulls. A really crappy affair. We, my Crime partners and our union appointed attorney, walked into the office located all the way downtown at Hudson Street which, in and of itself, is a mind-fuck; I mean, the whole place was designed to make your insides churn… from the cold, sterile, walls bearing nothing but posted signs of all the things that one can do wrong to land oneself in this particular predicament, to the seating placement where they make the miscreants sit and cogitate about what horrid presentiment was to come, all the while the employees of the investigative unit are walking back and forth, leering at the subjects of misconduct as if they were the masterminds behind Auschwitz or some craziness like that… I half expected Adolf to walk into the room to answer for his atrocities. It's a quite unsettling feeling, if you have yet to grasp the idea. Quite unsettling, indeed.

"Officer Cardona?" a fine looking gentleman - with the most amazing hair, classically styled with a smart, flawless, part on the right side of his dome; wearing an extremely handsome dark blue suit jacket; draped over a button down shirt, the shade being of a lighter blue; well pressed pants, the crease of which seemingly could cut like a Ginsu knife; and very shiny, quite stylish, black leather shoes, most likely Kenneth Cole or some other high end, classy as hell, brand - called to me. "This way."

After throwing a glance – an almost final, '*it was nice knowing you guys,*' kind of glance toward my compatriots - I followed him into a conference room where I espied two people just about to take their seats: the first being a fairly attractive, but extraordinarily plain, female in her thirties wearing no make-up; blonde hair, pulled back and put up into a tight bun; lavender button down shirt – the top two buttons of which were left unlatched, revealing an especially delightful peek of her cleavage; topped with a gray business jacket; and, a matching pair of, from what I could see, form fitting slacks, also gray in color. The second individual happened to be a lanky gentleman, also of about thirty years of age; his thinning hair revealing the entirety of his skull, having been made worse by his applying water and hairspray to it – most likely moments before this interview; wearing an insipid brown suit jacket and pants, with an equally mundane white button down shirt; and, to seal the deal, this hideous tie encompassing some kind of abstract, Van Gogh-type, design plastered all over it, resembling a regurgitated meal of pizza having contained, before the purge, every single topping known to man, sitting behind a large, polished, conference table of mahogany wood and, resting atop of it, a small, silver recording device accompanied by a manilla file folder with an entire ream of papers stuffed inside, wherein the printed information, all having to do with my career with the Department, was stored. "Have a seat, Officer." said the female, motioning towards the unoccupied seat on the opposing side of she and her cronies.

My lawyer and I took our places at the catechization table, he shooting me a nod and wink as if to indicate all would be well; but, in all reality was more of a, '*you are totally screwed, kid*,' look. After reading to me the required liturgy of rights and regulations, basically letting me know that I was going to get the can and end up in the slammer if I lied about anything, the dreaded third degree had begun. It was all so very intense. You kind of get this especially distinct feeling that you're the very criminal you spend everyday of your life locking up. Boy, I'll tell you, a guy goes out and risks his hide all day long, looking for, and putting away, bad people, making the city a safer place to go out and enjoy your daily frolic, and the minute a fella like myself puts a bastard (who, essentially, made a human salad out of a bunch of innocent civilians with a blade) in the emergency room – the second you put that son of a bitch in intensive care – your life is over. Disheartening. After asking me a slew of questions about who I was, and where I worked, and all of that insanely redundant crap that they already knew (the reason for asking me, I guess, so that whomever was listening to the tape would know exactly who to fire and incarcerate when it was all said and done), *Van Gogh* began, "Officer Cardona, tell me, in sum and substance, exactly the way the events unfolded that night leading up to your arrival at the hospital."

'... in some and substance, *exactly*...' he says; this guy was either a moron or a genius by way of disconcertion. "Well," I began my soliloquy, "we were driving around the Command's high crime area, conducting some directed patrols to address street crimes therein, when we happened to get flagged down by a concerned, distraught, citizen who stated to us that there was a sword wielding gentleman causing injury to some individuals adjacent to our location. We then, expeditiously, made our way to said location and witnessed Mr. Mosley, the subject, indeed utilizing a samurai sword to inflict *very serious* injuries upon several victims. We then, utilizing the force necessary to put an end to the assault, brought Mosley down to the ground, thereupon securing handcuffs to his wrists, placing him under arrest." I, of course, left out the part about us having a down day and smoking a bunch of cigars. Only some sort of a goofball would have divulged that kind of thing at a hearing; I'm sure you can understand that... you'd probably do the exact same thing if you were running around in my good ol' size eights, even if you won't admit it.

"Nice verbatim quote from the Department manual, Officer; but, how about you tell me what you were *really* doing?" Now, let me just pause here for one brief moment, if I may... the thing you simply have to understand, what you have to get, is that whenever one of these scrutineers asks you a *specific* question about a certain thing, you can bet the last penny in your pocket – along with the lint that flies out when you go in to retrieve said coin – that they already know the answer. They already know *exactly* what happened... and the only reason that they're asking *you* about the damn thing is so that you can perjure the living hell out of yourself all over that shiny recording device, whose tiny flashing red light is judging your every stinking syllable with each illuminating pulse, as if opining to everyone in the room, 'liar... liar... liar...' The problem is, what my problem right then and there was, I didn't realize that bit of essential information. *I* didn't know it, although – apparently – my lawyer did, attempting, quite frantically, to get my attention by kicking the living hell out of my foot underneath the table... apparently his arcane attempt to grab my attention, an attempt that, I'm embarrassed to confess, escaped the purview of my understanding at that particular moment in time.

"I *am* telling you the truth..." I pleaded. "... that's what we were doing. As Anti-Crime Cops, it is our job to address -"

"Again, I'm not interested in the text book answer." he interposed. "Let me ask you *this*: were you at Umberto's Cigar Emporium earlier in the evening? and before you answer, let me offer you a little help." he said, pulling out a few eight and a half by eleven glossy prints of good ol' Umberto's surveillance footage.

Seeing that the proverbial jig was up, there being no apparent denial of the very clear fact of the matter at hand, I kept my answer curt, "Yes."

"I see... and after you purchased these cigars, you then smoked them in a Department vehicle." he continued, placing more evidence on the table, these being especially high quality photographs, graciously supplied by the cameras belonging to the watering hole that we parked in front of, cameras which are positioned to capture images at the ingress of the location, showing some especially embarrassing images of my Team and I blowing rings of smoke up in the air, smiles of joy and rapture plastered across our faces, the good Sergeant ogling a passing *belle fille*, biting down on his lower lip as if he wished nothing more than to have his way with her right then and there. How utterly humiliating.

Clearing my throat, I answered, "Yes."

"Right; which, as you are aware, Officer, is prohibited?"

"Yes."

"… and while you were smoking your cigars in the Department vehicle, which is unauthorized, you were not, in fact, in a high crime area; but, instead, as you can see here in these pictures, were parked in front of…" he paused to glance at one of the reams of paper in the folder before continuing, "McGillicuddy's Bar and Grill, which is, according to the crime stats I'm looking at here, not in an area that is experiencing any spikes in crime… unless, of course, you can enlighten us? Maybe you know something we're not seeing here in these intel reports? Although, I have to tell you, they are as recent as this morning, and we went as far back as last year; so…"

"No."

"No? No, what? Officer."

"No, there isn't a spike in crime in that area."

"I see… so, what precisely, were you doing there?"

"That's irrelevant," my lawyer adamantly broke in, pounding his fist down upon the table, "he's already admitted to being at the location; it's irrelevant to inquire as to why… that's a Command level inquiry and something his Commanding Officer can address… he was still within the confines of his Precinct; therefore, not an Internal Affairs matter."

"Yes, counselor, but he made a *statement* just a minute ago… a *recorded* statement… about being in a high crime area when, in fact, he wasn't; so, my question speaks to him giving us false information, which *is* relevant and something I *absolutely* can address."

"Perhaps my client misunderstood the question…" he delusively suggested; then, turning to me, for the sake of the recorder, he inquired, "Officer, when you gave your statement regarding the high crime area, were you providing us with a *general* description, as opposed to a literal account, of what your daily activities entail?"

I began, getting my attorney's drift, so I responded by saying, "Yes, it was a general description of -"

"You're totally leading him, counselor!" the interviewer interrupted. "… you're *leading* him." he repeated, with a derisive chortle.

"Guys, this isn't a court of law here; it's a investigative hearing." my attorney lectured. "… *'leading?'* give me a break, for crying out loud."

"Fine… do you understand the question *now*, Officer? Any '*misunderstanding*' as to what I am asking *now*? Do we need to read the Department procedure about false statements again?"

"No, I understand now." I glanced over to my representative, who offered a quick wink in my direction.

"Thank you, Sergeant Willard;" the attractive inquisitioner interposed after a deliberate clearing of her throat, "I have a few questions of my own."

"Yes, Lieutenant," the distraught interviewer, Sergeant Willard, replied, also clearing his throat, his more of the unsettled variety, synchronously adjusting his abhorrent tie, "absolutely."

"For the record," she said, leaning forward and addressing the recorder, "this is Lieutenant Delaney, Internal Affairs. My question to you, Officer, is why did you leave the CAT scan room while the doctor was prepping the patient?"

That absolutely blew my mind, the fact that she and *Vomit Tie* would, of all things, ask such bewildering, and severely pointless, questions; it almost made me believe that these guys had absolutely nothing on my Team and I. I mean, think about it: of all the shit they could've asked, their primary focus was on the cigars, the '*girl watching*,' and the reason I went into the other room while the doctor prepared Mosley for his exam. Not one mention of Mosley's bashed in face. "We exited the CAT scan room because the doctor directed us to do so."

"That's not entirely accurate, is it?" she replied, looking through that confounded file folder.

I offered a quick glance over to my lawyer, whose peepers indicated to me that he hadn't a clue as to where she was going with her bemusing, before responding, "It is accurate to my recollection, ma'am."

"Hmm, I see." she said, putting the folder down to place her eyes upon me. "Do you recollect her requesting for you to leave the room? or did she simply ask you to remove the cuffs?"

I finally realized where she was going with this... these fuckers were witch-hunting. They had nothing else, nothing of significance, in which to lay at our feet, seeing as how the reason we had to tune up Mosley was because he was choking the living shit out of the pregnant doctor, to the point that she lost consciousness, so his fate was to be expected; therefore, this menial crap was to be our downfall. They were going to stick us with something, anything, to make certain there would be some sort of consequence... the public - at that point in time beginning to acquire certain rights and privileges to our internal files - would see that our investigative units were hard at work, cracking down upon the undesirable, heavy handed, storm troopers; tightening up the ship, screwing in the proverbial loose nuts and bolts. "I believe she asked us to remove the cuffs," I began to reply. "and it was my assumption... it was inferred... for us to exit the -"

"Thank you, Officer..." she interjected, "... you've answered my question; so, basically, you left the prisoner unattended, a clear violation of Department policy. This could have all been avoided had you done your job correctly, it would seem." she concluded, the look of a strangely subdued, but ultimately satisfied, smirk smearing across her countenance - similar to that of a malevolent queen who has learned of the 'unfortunate' equestrian accident suffered by her estranged husband, attempting to withhold the true feelings of joy within her heart - having to feign professionalism for the sake of all around her.

The rest of the interview was pretty much routine and isn't worth regurgitating in this chronicle. The only thing that you need to know, the only thing that is worth mentioning, is that we lost our Anti-Crime gig and got thrown to back Patrol… back in our regular uniforms, back in our regular cars, working different hours from one another. Pretty shitty, if you ask me. That's the thanks you get after all the hard work you do. The funny thing is, we didn't get canned because we beat good ol' Mosley senseless… not at all; we got the axe because we were smoking it up in front of that bar when we were supposed to be doing laps around the Precinct, looking for bad guys; and, the nail on the ol' coffin: not staying in the room while Mosley's brain was about to get scanned, leading to the *rear naked choke* the poor doctor received and shit. And before you go agreeing with that tidbit of information, satisfied of the verdict we were handed, just try and remember that, if it were not for the likes of us, the *mad ninja* would probably have sliced up a few dozen more people – maybe even someone you know and love - prior to anyone getting a chance to call 911… just try and remember *that* before you go siding with the enemy in this particular case.

XII

I spent the next year on the midnight tour - what most civilians might refer to as the *graveyard shift* - and it was brutal. The worst part of it was, you begin the tour on one day, at about eleven o'clock at night, and end on a completely different day, seven-fifty in the morning. Most of the people working that tour ended up, after a few years, looking like cast members of the Adams Family, baring a striking resemblance to one who has had occasion to making nightly rendezvous with ol' Vlad the Impaler, allowing him to suck the life out of their bodies… nothing but pale, cadaverous faces was what one would find on this shift, complete with these sort of deep, dark circles under their eyes, as if they hadn't had the opportunity to catch even one wink of sleep in the last couple of centuries. And they all possessed these insanely eldritch habits, weird neurotic behaviors, such as Officer Wilson's incessant nail biting that ended up leaving him with practically no fingernails at all; Officer Rodriguez's eating disorder, causing him to gnaw upon as much of his provisions as humanly possible before spitting it out into the nearest garbage can; Officer Ramos' shoulder tick, *both* shoulders, that made everyone with whom the poor bastard encountered think he never knew the answers to their questions; and, Officer Cuesta's uncontrollable need to utter, "Yeah, yeah… yeah, yeah… yeah, yeah" before he addressed his interlocutor. A real bunch of characters, I'm telling you.

I decided I had to get the hell out of that situation… fast, so I spent every waking moment studying for the Sergeant's exam, which occupied pretty much the entirety of my conscious, and unconscious, hours. I had begun to develop a pretty good relationship with a few of my supervisors, so they sort of *hooked me up*, which is to say they did the right thing, by giving me assignments that wouldn't distract my insanely intense swotting sessions. On a midnight tour, one of the best assignments was the switchboard operator, which – in those days – should have been a cinch, the post charged with merely answering the phones (which I regularly placed off of its hook) and greeting the civilians who walked into the Command to make complaints and all of that crap (that task not being especially omnipresent during the un-Godly hours in which I worked); the real problem, the thing that proved to be the more pressing issue, were the Cops that - quite like the customers at Macy's on 34th Street, swirling in and out of the revolving door all day long - incessantly waltzed in and out of the Command… every minute of every hour. It was practically impossible to concentrate. They'd just march on in, in droves, and plant themselves right before me, in spite of my study material unquestionably splattered all about my workstation, a clear indication that I *just might* be attempting to concentrate on my work, and begin these terribly pestiferous conversations that would spark the interest of the other loitering Officers, igniting many confounded perpetual disputations above my head.

"Hey, you catch that MMA fight last night?" Officer Dempsey began, as I attempted, in vain, to retain the Duties and Responsibilities of a Patrol Sergeant into my brain.

"Yeah, man… that Anderson Silva is such an asshole. I can't believe he won!" answered Officer Diaz.

"What a blood bath, though…" replied Dempsey, "it looked like that crime scene we had a few weeks back; the one where that guy shanked his wife with a butcher knife all over the place... remember that? She dragged herself from the bedroom to the front door and died right there, leaving that huge trail of blood. That's what that fight reminded me of… the blood part, I mean."

"You ain't kidding… it really *was* a blood fest." Officer Bautista chimed in. "Chael Sonnen almost had him! I can't believe he tapped… in the last round with a minute and fifty seconds left in the fight."

"Bro, Sonnen didn't tap, the dude kept fighting!" broke in yet another dawdler, Officer Quigley.

"Are you insane, bro?!" shouted Dempsey, pounding his fists on the table, sending my papers off in different directions, the aftermath of which I most calmly retrieved. "… he clearly tapped! They showed it in the slow motion… he definitely did tap."

"What? are you an Anderson Silva fan or something?" Diaz passive-aggressively inquired of Quigley, in defense of Dempsey's rant.

"I'm a *fight* fan… I don't go pretending taps didn't occur just because I happen to like a particular fighter." Quigley justified, in a matter of fact tone of voice.

"Oh brother! look at you…" Dempsey, the epitome of a *true blue American* – the kind that made certain to fully represent the *red, white, and blue* in every which possible way - continued to lecture, "…what a righteous human being you are. A regular old Plato, aren't you? That sounds so very *just* and so very utopian. Jeez, you ever heard of loyalty? Chael Sonnen is an American, you fucking communist. What is wrong with you? How's about showing some goddamn loyalty!"

"Dude, what in the fuck are you even talking about… I'm talking about an MMA fight, not politics, you psychopath!" Quigley shot back.

"What do you think, Jimmy?" Diaz asked of me, thus drawing all attention in my direction. "… you saw the fight, didn't you? Did he tap or what?"

Lifting my face from my studying, a thing that was clearly, at this point, a lost cause, I replied, "I didn't see it… I've been *trying* to study, so I had no time to catch the fight."

"Bro, this was a mega fight… how could you possibly have missed it?!" Dempsey panted, as if I had missed the next coming of Christ.

"Yeah, dude, I wouldn't have missed it for anything… especially not for anything having to do with *this* job… fuck that!" agreed Quigley… I suppose, at the very least, I had to be thankful that he and Dempsey were no longer at each other's throats.

"Well, I really have to pass this test. I can't do this patrol crap anymore, I really can't; especially this freaking tour. I mean, don't get me wrong, you're all such a wonderful bunch, but I just can't work these hours… I'm not built for this kind of mental and physical anguish. I'm really not. And anyway," I continued, grabbing my papers; stacking them into a neat pile; and placing them off to the side, seeing as how there was not a chance in hell I was going to get any studying done, "I'm not too hot on mixed martial arts. I mean, what's with the super tight and super microscopic spandex shorts? And the bare feet… jeez, that's just intolerable. Then they always end up on the floor, locked up in these really latently homosexual positions… I just can't get into it."

"Weeeellll… would ya get a load of *this* fag…" Dempsey declared, providing some of that good old, all American, hardcore, sentiment. "… he don't like the short shorts and the grappling holds. What's the matter? ya gettin' feelings you can't quite describe when you see that kinda stuff? you fucking homo."

"Yeah, that's exactly right… you hit the ol' nail on the head. As a matter of goddamn fact, I'm getting those tingly kind of feelings right now, Dempsey." I asseverated, sardonically. "Why don't you come a little closer so I can show you what I mean?" I concluded, launching a bunch of kisses in the air, outstretching my arms.

"Oh my God! get away from me, you goddamn queer!" he exclaimed, jumping backward with his hands raised high in the air, as if I had a communicable disease he had no wish to contract, leaving me to wonder why I hadn't utilized that particular tactic sooner.

I thought better of it, though – and real quick; I mean, I didn't want these guys running around telling people that I batted from the opposite side of the plate, if you get my drift… not that I have anything – whatsoever – against that kind of thing. I happen to have many close friends, and a couple of family members, who subscribe to that way of life, and I sort of love them a lot, so there's not a prejudice bone in my entire body about the thing; it's just that I wouldn't want anything said about me that wasn't true. It's as simple as that. It's not a factual statement about me and that's all there is to it; like, I don't enjoy eating oatmeal, so I wouldn't want anyone running around telling everyone how much I loved it, because then, before you know it, the entire universe will end up brining me endless bowls of the stuff, then I'll have to make all kinds of excuses as to why I'm not shoving it down my throat. People, everyday, will come from all over the place with tons and tons of goddamn oatmeal, trying to get me to taste *their* recipe, and pretty soon I'll have no space in the refrigerator because of it all. No thanks. "I'd much rather watch boxing…" I commented. "…but the old matches though; not the new stuff. Like, Mike Tyson, Evander Holyfield… even Mohammed Ali, Joe Louis, Sonny Liston… that's the stuff I like."

"Jeez, bro, that crap was like a million years ago. MMA is where it's at today… boxing is garbage now. You can't even pronounce the Heavyweight champ's names anymore, it's always some communist Russian or Ukrainian guy with a bunch of consonants and no vowels. Fuck that." said a more subdued and reassured Dempsey, creeping back towards my direction, comforted, I'm certain, at the fact that I was not the homosexual he believed me to be just moments ago.

"Yeah." was my curt reply. I only threw that opinion about boxing in as a segue, a distraction of sorts, to get him to stop thinking I was a goddamn *friend of Dorothy*; so, there was no need to dispute the differences in our opinions about the sport any further. Luckily, a job came over in his Sector, so he had to beat it the hell out of there anyway, which was just fine with me, going right back to my studying as soon as he and the rest of the cohort skedaddled.

I began, again, to bury my face in the material, attempting to retain the ridiculousness of the Department manual. It really was obnoxiously insane. The biggest problem with that thing was its unfathomably infinite volume; it was - no lie - about fifteen hundred pages. Really… I shit you not. What's worse, its millions of pages were inundated with conflicting and redundant crap that made absolutely zero sense when reading it from beginning to end. It was divided into these crazy sections that were supposed to sort the whole mess out; but, in actuality, made no difference whatsoever because the confounded thing was written and amended at different time periods, commencing way back in the Industrial era and concluding in the present. For instance, one section could have been written a hundred years ago, and another section a month ago; now, the problem with that is: the fella who went and did the more recent entry didn't bother to cross reference his part with the existing stuff, so he typed a bunch of shit that severely contradicted everything else. If a regular person, with a normally functioning brain, were to read that damned book from cover to cover, he'd come out of it stark raving mad, in need of some serious psychoanalysis, that much I fully guarantee you.

I'll tell you what, they even had this part in the book where it tells you all of the ranks and positions within the Department and exactly what in the hell they do all day long… in this brilliant Manual, the had some administrative house mouse, the *plant manager* for Christ's sake, a guy or gal who never leaves the command, engaged in all kinds of hard labor like mopping, sweeping, and hiding in the basement for half their tour – affectionately (or perhaps not) nicknamed *the broom* – responsible for placing fresh coal in the furnace that provided heat within the building; which, naturally, hadn't been an expected task for that poor schmuck since about the early 1930s; yet, it was still listed as a duty of said *broom* according to the book… and, herein lies the rub: anything that made an appearance in that deplorable excuse for a guide book was a testable fact on exam day. Insanity. Oh, and don't for a second think that it, the question on the test, was as simplistic as, *'who puts fresh coal in the furnace.'* Not a chance. The queries on the exam were the equivalent of someone bringing you on over to a minefield, where all that could be seen was flattened dirt, no sign of any explosive devices anywhere, and saying, 'Okay, pal, move it… and don't go stepping on any mines.' That's pretty much the best way to explain a typical Sergeant's exam. You can imagine, now – maybe – what it was like for me to retain any of that information, especially having to do it whilst working on that carnival of a midnight tour.

One night, when I thought for sure I'd have some God forsaken serenity – perhaps due to the fact that it was torrentially raining outside, the Station House being in a sort of zen-like state of tranquility, there even being a goddamn chamomile scented candle burning at the desk - the front door flies open, and from it a human being comes soaring through the air, literally airborne, subsequently descending, and sliding like a baseball player whose objective it was to reach second base without being tagged by the opposing player, directly in front of the Desk Sergeant who, incidentally, didn't so much as move a muscle in response to the spectacle before her. As for myself, I simply could not resist standing and glancing over the desk out of sheer disbelief… the precision of the toss alone was mind boggling. A few seconds later, the Arresting Officers, Dempsey and Quigley – the apparent caber tossers - entered the building, sauntering over to where their prisoner still remained, prostrate and unmoved. "We got this guy for bein' a mope, Sarge."

"That's fine, boys," answered the Sergeant, seemingly unmoved by the Scottish Highland-esque performance of the

Officers, "but what's the real charge? so I can enter the thing in the Command Book." she concluded, finally standing up, leaning over his desk to take a peek at the unfortunate soul, who had yet to move a muscle. "Say, this guy isn't gonna be a problem, is he? He's not dead or anything is he?"

"Nah, he'll be okay." answered Dempsey, bending down and inquiring of the perp, "You're gonna be okay, ain't you, Mope?" afterwards lifting him completely off of the ground with brute-like strength, standing him upright, revealing his bloodied, but conscious, mien.

At this point, the perp, in a bold and unexpected move, swiveled around and ejected from his mouth a very thick, brownish-yellowish loogie, commixed with the sanguine fluid currently gushing from his nose, that landed flush upon the face of Officer Dempsey. In what appeared, at least to me, to be slow motion - subsequent to Dempsey's internal, cognitive, processing of what exactly just happened to him – the fifteen inch hand belonging to the eighteen year Police Department veteran made its way above his head, then came barreling down onto the face of our guest with the might of a JB Hunt eighteen wheeler, creating a hauntingly vicious sound upon making the barbarous connection, sending the prisoner's entire body back to its original position on the floor, where he remained until his intake at the desk was complete; thereafter, brought into the arrest processing room to complete his booking. These sort of fascinating encounters is what I experienced all the live long day during that year on the anathematized midnight platoon, so you can surmise for yourself how any hope for my receiving a passing grade on the test was doubtful at best.

***

I did end up taking the test, not sure one way or another as to the outcome, having absolutely zero presentiment about the confounded thing; after six months of brain melting studying, I was just glad it was all over with, honestly. What I did, what I decided to do, now that I had some free time on my hands, I figured I'd go to visit my dad, because I hadn't seen him in awhile with all the cramming and shit. As I headed toward his building, I happened to spot a familiar face… it was Rose, who had already espied me from the opposite side of the street, now waving frantically like a mad woman, screaming, "James! Jimmy! Hey!"

I waved back and shouted in return, "Rosie! Hey, how are you?" nearly getting mowed down by a few dozen cars in the process of crossing the street.

After a singularly pleasant exchange of warming embrace, she asked, "How have you been? beautiful stranger. I haven't spoken to you in, what? like, a year?" It had been about that long on account of the fact that I was working those ghastly midnight shifts, plus the whole matter of me preparing for the test and all; and, as for actually *seeing* her in the flesh, it had been about ten years, on account of us having our lives to live and shit.

"Yeah, I have these really un-Holy hours… midnights… plus, I was studying for the Sergeant's exam for like… ever."

"Sergeant's exam? Oh, my goodness, how perfectly amazing! James Cardona, Sergeant of Police! I am very impressed, sir!" she exclaimed, with that perfectly flawless smile of hers, the kind of smile that contorts the eyes in such a way as to resemble the twinkling of a star on a clear, summer evening.

"Aw, thanks… I appreciate it; although, I probably failed miserably."

"No way, I'm sure you did great! I'm sure of it. You're a smart cookie… you always have been… so I have no doubt, whatsoever, that you absolutely aced it with flying colors!" she said, in such a lovingly upbeat manner that anyone, but myself, would have instantly found themselves sliding down rainbows and petting goddamn unicorns all over the place; not me, though. I have a sort of impenetrable force field around my happy place… not much can get through. It's made of the very same material as whatever the hell can destroy Superman… the Kryptonite. It seriously is.

"From your lips to God's ears." I responded, in my best gloomy tone of voice. "The thing, the test, was meant to completely sabotage us. Like, it's not even about what you know, but more about finding the traps they set for you. It's out of control, trust me on that."

"Well, let's just give it some positive energy… put the positive vibes out there and let the universe do the rest."

"Wow, so spiritual! I didn't know you were so zen!"

"Oh, I'm all about positive energy and putting good vibes out. You can't let the negative overwhelm and consume you… you have to take the reigns and make things happen, you know? You should get into meditation! It really has helped me so very much. I've actually been doing it for quite some time now and I can't even begin to describe how much it has made a difference. It's like a personal secretary for your mind, putting all of the chaos in your head into neat little file folders. You actually end up *feeling* lighter. Seriously, I walk around feeling as though I have wings… almost like I'm gliding through the air."

I thought, at that point, she should – instead of wasting time talking to the likes of me - go straight home and write a book about pure happiness; either that, or maybe sign-up, forthwith, to become some sort of a motivational speaker… there are thousands upon thousands of people about to pull the ol' trigger, about to leap off of the ledge, that could use her spiritually uplifting comportment… I not especially being one of them, negativity sort of being my preferred dish. "I shall remember that."

"Serious! try it… try to find a nice, quiet place – maybe throw on some soothing music and light a candle – and just sit with your eyes closed and quiet your mind… let the bad thoughts just drift off and out of your mind. But you have to be serious about it! You really have to believe that all will be well. I mean it!"

"Okay, okay, I will definitely believe!" I exclaimed; afterwards, throwing in, "I swear!" because her countenance revealed a look of doubt as to my sincerity.

"Good! Where are you headed? To your dad's?"

"Yeah, it's been awhile, and I need to check in… he starts thinking I don't care anymore and all of that craziness."

"Okay, just promise that you'll hang out with me before you get completely lost again… before another ten years pass!"

"Yeah, that sounds like a plan." said I, quite unconvincingly, I suppose, receiving the forthcoming tongue lashing:

"You're so full of shit! You know damn well you're not gonna come see me… why not just tell me so?!" she began… her *meditative high* clearly crashing down like timber in a forest upon being struck by lightning. Don't stand there and placate me, as if I were some kind of dumbass who can't tell when I'm being jerked-off… jeez, James… give me a little more credit… show some damn respect for my level of intelligence!" Outside of her nuclear power plant-like meltdown, she was on the money, as it were; I mean, she was pretty perceptive. I wasn't entirely truthful in my covenant with my old friend, I must admit. It's not that I didn't want to spend time with Rosie, that's not it at all. She was a beautiful person, inside and out, and I always enjoyed our moments together; it's just that I know myself… I know that, since coming onto this job, I had developed an extremely low tolerance for the civilians of the world; therefore, once I'm out of sight of a person that's not a member of the Police Department, I pretty much forget that they exist. I know that sounds harsh; but you have to understand, the life of a Cop is pretty goddamn demanding. Between the incessant shift changes; grueling tours on the street; and mentally draining experiences answering jobs, it's not that easy to mosey on over to your friend's house for a get together; someone that has absolutely no clue what in the living hell you are ever talking about. They just don't get it. These creatures, the inhabitants of the normal world, really can't begin to fathom the things you share with them… trust me, I have tried. They sit with these sort of flabbergasted looks on their faces, as you spend half your time explaining, translating, every bit of jargon that glides fluidly out of your mouth - as an adult explains life to a five year old, needing to pause when coming across a certain word or phrase in which the child has never heard - that you go through in a day… and that's just not something I want to do. I'd honestly rather be all alone with my stresses and strifes than to stop every five seconds to delineate the vernacular and such to someone who just does not comprehend what it is to be on my Job.

"No, I really will!" I dissimulated. "As a matter of fact, I'll call you later tonight, and we can set something up. How's that?"

"Do you *promise*? I don't want to make you do something that you don't want to do. I don't want to twist your arm or anything… I feel like I'm twisting your arm, for Christ's sake."

"No, Rosie, you are not twisting my arm… not at all. I said I'd call you and I meant it! You're very important to me and I *want* to call you… *and* see you. Listen, I'll call you later; I have to get to my dad. It's been ages since I've seen him and I want to make sure to spend some time."

"Yes, good… call me later… don't forget! And tell your dad and Gracie I said hello!"

I promised her I wouldn't forget about a thousand more times – minus the second half of the latter request which I knew I would, most likely, be forgoing… sending my sister Rosie's regards… for the simple fact that I hadn't spoken to Gracie in a few spins around the Sun, and most likely wouldn't any time soon – subsequent to us giving each other a farewell hug and kiss; afterwards, crossing the street again, giving her a final wave goodbye, she returning the gesticulation, all before heading into my dad's apartment building. It would be the last time I would ever see or speak to Rose for the remainder of my days as a living, breathing organism on this planet. I never kept the promise of reaching out to her, and I suppose she had no interest in pursuing a hopeless case. I'm not too worried about it, though; I mean, I know that she will be okay and that she'll meet someone who can really appreciate the wonderful person that she is, as well as give her the normal life that she deserves. I just know it.

***

My father's house always had a certain fragrance, like his own comforting brand of *parfum* that could only be conjured up utilizing his personal essence. It was the smell of my home. If you blindfolded me, took me on a long drive, brought me to a location unbeknownst to me, spun me around five times after we arrived, and told me to breathe in, I would know the undisclosed location to be my dad's based solely on his scent. "Jimmy Time!" he shouted upon opening the door, "Where you been? I been looking all over for you!" This was his playful salutation whenever you went to visit him; it didn't matter if your last rendezvous was a day ago or a year prior, that was the typical, frolicsome, greeting given. Notwithstanding this constant variable, I noticed that Mr. James Cardona, the elder, had developed some indications of physical maturity; his once blooming and vibrant brown hair was now thinning, the color fading a bit, giving way to intermittent grays here and there; under his eyes there existed signs of fatigue, crows feet now making their unsolicited appearance.

"Yo, Pop, what's up?" I answered, as we offered one another an embrace before I headed, subsequently, straight into the kitchen to raid the refrigerator; I was pretty hungry and needed a quick fix of nosh, and he always had pretty decent stuff.

"You hungry, kid? I got some cold cuts and some Wonder Bread. You want that? Or I also got some whitey fish with boiled potatoes I was gonna snack on later." he offered, already taking out the meal from the toaster oven, where it was currently keeping warm.

"No, I don't want to take your snack for later… I'll make a sandwich… and I think it's pronounced *whiting.*"

"Say what?"

"The fish… you said, '*whitey*;' but, I'm pretty sure it's '*whiting.*"

"Jesus… excuse me: white-*ing*! white-*ing*! Do you want the damn fish or not?"

"Hey, I'm just trying to help you out over here… you don't wanna go into the fish market full of a bunch of Caucasians and say you want 'whitey,' do you?"

Completely disregarding my civics lesson at that point, he answered, "You're sure you don't want the fish? I already ate it for lunch… it was just some leftovers I didn't wanna waste. You can have it, if you want." he insisted, still holding onto the meal.

"No, the sandwich is perfect." I said, commencing to take out the necessary items for sandwich building.

"Well, don't mind if *I* actually eat it, then! Just don't be lookin' at it and licking your lips while I eat! I gave you your chance to have it!" he jested.

"I'll try my best to resist the temptation!" I replied with a chuckle. "So, how's things? Anything new?"

"With me?" he asked, placing the fish filet and potatoes onto a plate for his consumption. "What could be new? The newest thing in my life is the latest episode of Blue Bloods on TV tonight. That's the highlight of my life, Jimmy."

"Aw, come on, Pop; you're always doing something out of this world every time we talk. How are those dance classes going?"

"My salsa classes? they're going good. I'll tell you what, you should look into doing it, you'd meet a lot of smokin' hot females there, my friend."

"I know, you've mentioned… eh, it's just not my thing. I'm no John Travolta."

"John Travolta… that's funny." he snickered. "*John Travolta* isn't even John Travolta anymore! Anyway, that's the beauty of these classes, you don't have to be… John Travolta… that's why it's called dance *class*. You spend the whole day learning how to do the steps in the arms of beautiful women all day long. That's what I do. I fake like I don't know what I'm doing, so these dames can hold me even closer to them… to, you know, help me mimic the moves and all. Works like a charm, my boy… like a charm." he concluded by performing a little salsa jig, swinging his hips and spinning around the kitchen, all the while his eyes shut, biting down on his bottom lip.

"You dirty, dirty, old man." I giggled, shaking my head whilst he continued his award winning performance. "I don't know, we'll see… I'll look into it." I added, with apathetic enthusiasm.

He chuckled before replying, "Yeah, right. I know my son better than he knows himself… '*I'll look into it*' means you won't. You have to be more like your sister: when she says she's gonna do something, doggonit, she does it… and with enthusiasm, too! Speaking of which, have you spoken to her, lately?"

"Uh, well -"

"Let me stop you right there, son. I *know* you haven't spoken to each other because I just got through talking to her about an hour before you arrived. Jimmy, how many times have I told you, you guys have to -"

"I know, I know!" I interjected. "We have to keep it touch with each other because we're all that we have."

"That's right, and after I'm gone, after the good Lordy Lord takes me Upstairs with Him, you two are all that's left. You gotta stay tight, you understand?"

"I understand."

Verbalizing nothing, but offering a look, a deathly stare, that could melt all of the ice in Antarctica, his point of failing to be placated with my averment was made abundantly clear.

"I mean it! I truly, truly, mean it. I will call her… I will!"

"We shall see… anyway, how are you doing? How'd that

test go? Am I looking at Mr. Sergeant Jimmy Cardona? or what?"

"God only knows… the whole thing is meant to drive a person insane, with all of the trick questions that are about a mile long. After reading an entire page of some crazy ass, convoluted question, they ask you these bizarre, indirect questions that you never expect they'd come up with." I responded, placing the finishing touches on my ham, cheese, tomato, and mayo sandwich.

"I'm sure you did well, kiddo, you're a smart cookie."

I swiveled my head around toward him with a countenance of bewilderment. "*Smart cookie*? Funny… that's *exactly* what Rose said… she said that *very exact* thing… literally, those words."

We moved into the dining area and placed our comestibles onto the table before he said, "Oh, you spoke to Rose? how is she? I see her mom from time to time at the market and she always tells me what Rosie is up to. She's a principal of a school now, you know… not just a teacher anymore."

"I know, Pop, it hasn't been *that* long since you and I have talked! You *do* know that you and I have spoken, like, a hundred times this past year on the phone since she was promoted, and you tell me about it practically every time."

"I don't know, your calls are super-duper sporadic, I can't keep track of everything we speak about! Maybe if you called on a more *consistent* basis…" he teased, digging into his whiting fish and boiled potato, and I into my singularly delightful refection.

"Yeah, yeah, yeah… come on, Pop, you know I was busting my butt with this damn test… you know that very well."

"I know, I know… I'm just pulling your leg, don't get all sensitive on me. So, yeah, she's doing super well, a principal now. You know, I'm surprised you and her never hit it off and became a thing."

"*Rosie*? nah, she's more like a kissing cousin than a regular girl… we grew up together and -"

"I *know* you grew up together;" he interrupted. "you little rascals were always running in and out of this apartment to get your snacks before scampering back outside for hours and hours. You two guys were attached at the hip when you were kids… at the hip, I tell you. That's why I always figured the both of you would end up hitched. She is a beautiful girl… and still single, you know."

"She *is* beautiful, and I *know* she's single. I just… I don't know… I just… I don't even know who *I* am, yet. Like, I haven't truly figured out who exactly I am and what my purpose in this world is, you know? Let alone bringing another person into my freakin' life, now having to figure out me *and* somebody else. It's just too much, you know? It's *way* too much for me to deal with right now."

"Jesus H. Christ, Jimmy," he lamented, putting his fork down, which meant that things were about to get serious. Whenever my father was in the middle of eating, followed, abruptly, by his placing down the utensils onto his plate, best believe that you were in for a town hall lecture. I quickly ingurgitated a piece of sandwich into my mouth; because, if his digesting were paused to deliver a sermon, you had better believe yours was, too. "I just don't understand you sometimes. I really don't. Let me ask you something… seriously. I'd love to know: do you think you're the only one in the world who feels that way? That you're the sole person in this universe trying to figure out who you are and what *it* is all about? Don't you realize that *everybody* is trying to deal with that very same issue? And I got news for you, my son: you never *stop* trying to conquer that problem, either." He paused to give me one of those brain penetrating stares, the sort that parents give to let you know that there is nothing in the world more serious than what they're about to say at that very moment in time. The one that's supposed to drive the ol' point home, so you'd better be listening because there just might be a question that, if you're not paying full attention, you might get wrong… then you'd have to listen to the entire disquisition all over again. I widened my eyes to focus on *the rub*, as he continued, "Don't you get it, Jimmy? That's the whole point of life itself. You try your best to figure it out, and while you're doing all of that figuring, you do the little things, here and there, to make you happy; you don't *deprive* yourself of happiness. That's what life is all about: life is about incorporating the beautiful and shedding the unsavory, that's the cycle; and, in the end – when it's all said and done - you just pray that you've tacked on enough of the pleasant and shook off as much bitterness as you could. That's life."

"Wow, Pop, that's pretty deep… you should've been a philosopher… Ralph Waldo Emerson has nothing on *you*."

"Well, I don't know about any Waldo, but I *do* know that you have to allow yourself to be happy… *that* I do know. And if it's not with Rosie, then so be it… but don't sell yourself short by denying happiness if you have an opportunity to grab it by the horns."

"I know, Pop… I understand." I really did understand. I mean, I'm not some kind of ignoramus who can't discern the particulars of a life-educating homily from a wise old man. It's just not as simple to apply it practically, you know what I mean? It all sounds spectacularly luminous spewing out of the pie holes of Plato, Nietzsche, Confucius, and my dad; it's another thing entirely for the rest of us simpletons to actually *do* something about. It's not as easy – while these theoreticians effortlessly and eloquently hurl it at us - to put it all into action. It's not. I kept that little tidbit to myself, though. Anything other than the response I provided would've set the old-timer off again, and I most definitely did not wish for that. Besides, there aren't enough words in the linguistic vault that which could do battle with the contemptibly negative thoughts existing in one's mind. A war within one's own conscience supersedes any syllable spoken… you, first, must change your mode of self, your soul, before anything else in this world has a shot in hell of getting through the ol' cerebral matter, and right now my soul was unwilling. I had already begun to develop some pretty flavorless feelings towards the Department, what with everything transpiring before the test and all… feelings that I hoped would dissipate with the recent promotion to Sergeant, a fact which remained to be discovered.

"Good." he replied, satisfied, I suppose, that I acquiesced. "Whew! all this talking made me even more hungry… I think I'm gonna have me a sandwich to go with this whitey… oh, sorry… white-*ing*!"

I'll have you know, I did think really long and hard about what my father said that day, and I suppose, as I said, he had a pretty good point and all… just in case you're sitting there thinking about how much of an ass I am for not taking his advice. I, incidentally, must disclose that I don't do a very good job at latching onto the good things in life. I'm somewhat of a pessimistic, cynical, kind of a fellow, if you haven't picked up on that by now. Positivity rolls off of me like pelts of rain from the feathers of a goose. I need to work on that particular aspect of my life; like my father articulated: I need to hold fast to the things that are most meaningful, and dump the garbage that weighs me down.

XIII

I'm going to fast forward us, if you are indeed still with me, a few months – about seven to be precise – into the future, where the story finds yours truly at his new Command, performing the newly assigned duties as a Sergeant of Police. It turns out the eight to ten hours a day, seven days a week, for six grueling months, actually did pay off, receiving a score of ninety-seven on the ol' exam. Not bad. The only issue with getting promoted, any time you move up another rank, is that you have to leave your old Command; they don't want you working in a place where you've developed any kind of relationships… good or bad. The thing of it is, they figure if you made a few friends, you're likely to bend over backwards for those folks, giving them whatever their little hearts desire, and not reprimanding them when they are caught goofing off, not conducting themselves appropriately and shit like that; and, conversely, if a bunch of people got on your last nerve while you were there, people whose faces you wanted very much to put your fist through, you'd probably look to give them all kinds of hell now that you're a supervisor. It's a valid argument, I have to say; there were a few sons of bitches that I'd like to have gotten my hands on over at my old stomping grounds, that's for damn sure.

My new geographical area of employment left much to be desired, being located in one of the most horrendous areas of the City; every despicable act of humanity that one could conjecture occurring on these particular streets. Needless to say, I was less than pleased to receive this assignment, an understatement of epic proportions, rest assured. To be unswervingly forthcoming, I sort of wished I could relinquish my promotion and just go back from whence I came… I really did. I pondered a great deal about it, let me tell you. A *great* deal. Even the countenances of the new Officers left me with the bitter taste of regret in my mouth, with ogles that insinuated a kind of territorial warning, the way in which a dog glares at an intruder who has entered its domain. It didn't matter at all that I was a ranking officer, either… not one bit. It was still their dominion, a place in which they had been appointed long before my arrival; therefore, it was completely understandable as to their misgiving of my advent; I, too, before being promoted, provided to freshly promoted Supervisors the stare of death upon their entrant from time to time. In any event, I got to my new digs before the crack of dawn (so the midnight shift was still on duty) and stood in front of the large desk for a bit, where the Desk Sergeant held her post, she not knowing who I was, suspecting, I can only surmise, that I was merely a new or visiting Officer, seeing as how I was attired in my regular street clothes and everting like that, addressing me in an especially audacious manner, as was customary for that particular charge. "Yeah? what is it?" she barked, without lifting her eyes from whatever the hell she was doing (most likely an intense game of solitaire on her mobile device).

"Hey, I'm a newly promoted Sergeant assigned here… Cardona."

"Oh," she replied, her tone lightening, her green eyes perched above a deep, dark, pair of circular contusions, due to the grueling midnight hours, now meeting with mine, "why didn't you just come straight around behind the desk? You're a Sergeant now, you don't have to stand in front of the damned thing like a Cop… Jesus, making me go through a whole production over here. What in the hell do they teach you at Leadership Training, anyway?" she concluded, throwing a bunch of papers around to, I suppose, provide a particular emphasis to her chagrin.

I apologized profusely for the oversight, and pretty much got reamed out for that, too. No one wants a bunch of jeremiads poured all atop them like syrup on a stack of pancakes, as much as they *think* they would. First of all, there are no *real* apologies other than actually altering one's actions. The mere utterance of the word, "sorry" is, for all intents and purposes, akin to the numerical value of zero… it just doesn't exist; except, of course, to indicate as a symbol that it does not exist… to express that there is no such thing. Look, I can't explain the enigma any better than that; it's just a cumbersome as hell thing to deal with, that's all. Anyway, let me tell you, it's not easy transitioning from a subordinate rank into one of the loftier variety, especially if you've been that certain former rank for ten years, like myself at this particular point in the story. I espy those bright blue chevrons on the sleeves of a New York Sergeant and I instantly get the ol' pucker effect. I really do. And for those of you not well versed in that particular idiolect, *the pucker effect*, that's when your *sphincter ani* bolts its doors shut, preventing any and all egress and ingress beyond its borders. That's pretty much how I respond to *any* presence of authoritative figures, truthfully speaking; and, I've been that way for my entire life, so it's not something that's likely to change. I'd like to think it's because I have a certain level of respect for anyone in the position of ascendancy; and, truthfully, that's the way it ought to be. People who go around saying whatever they want, doing whatever they want, and acting however they want, just create anarchy… one big old Wild West is what it ends up being; where bandits just roam around lighting fire to whatever they desire, no one following any goddamn rules, and that's not good for anyone at all. It's just not a savory set of circumstances, you know? That's just my opinion on the matter, but who am I? No one.

"Stop apologizing all over the place, will ya? Jeez! What? your mama didn't cuddle you enough when you were shittin' in your diapers or something?" she ululated. "Come over here so I can show you a few things you'll need to learn. Name's Filipa, by the way." After I practically begged forgiveness for apologizing in the first place, ad nauseam, I moseyed on around the desk area so Filipa could teach me the ins and the outs of the operation. In the middle of the tutorial, she turned to me and said, "Cardona… hmm. You know, I heard about you… heard all about you." concluding with a stare that imbued no specific emotion, leaving me to wonder what in the hell that statement was supposed to mean.

"Heard about me? Like, in a good way or a bad way?"

"How do you think? I'm sure you know what you've done… I'm sure you know *very* well!" she stated, one eyebrow raised high, like the goddamn Gateway Arch in St. Louis, Missouri.

"Uh… I… don't… know…" I stammered, honestly having no clue as to what she could possibly be referring, although quite concerned about its allusion to some insane thing I may have partaken; something that, I'm certain, would be immensely frowned upon by my employers.

"You don't know, huh? Why do I find that hard to believe?" she replied, still doing the Gateway Arch thing. I was honestly becoming extremely put out by this woman's enigmatic implications. If there's one thing I simply can not tolerate, it is someone who, having something of apparent significance to say, ends up beating around the proverbial goddamn bush all the live long day, instead of just spitting it out of their stupid mouth. That kind of a thing can really test my last nerve, is the very simple point I'm driving home.

"Well, I'm sure whatever it is, it was well deserved." I finally conceded, no longer caring about the ramifications of a clean admission to whatever infraction I may or may not have committed. "I don't usually do things that I don't mean to do; and, if I did, if I *did* do something that I didn't intend to be hurtful in any kind of way… well, then the person ought to come straight out and say how they feel about it. This way, I can get the damned apology over with and we can all move on, you know?" I ejaculated, the pounding of my heart causing my voice to shake and crack like a California fault-line after an earthquake.

"Holy shit, new guy, take it easy… what? you got some kind of anxiety disorder or something?!" she exclaimed. Boy, oh boy, do I hate that. I absolutely hate it with an indescribable passion. Here you have someone who just spent the last ten minutes riling me up – really twisting my bloomers in a goddamn knot - and the very second I get testy about it, she goes and accuses *me* of having a couple of hemorrhages. "I was just saying," she continued, "that I heard you were the heavy handed type… that you got a couple of cinderblocks for hands with the bad guys… putting them in hospitals, then tuning them up once they're in the emergency room and everything. That's all I was trying to say. Jesus." Love that one, too… the person puts you through the ringer, breaking your stones by beating around the ol' bush for a few hours, then has the absolute unmitigated impudence to utter, '… *that's all I was trying to say.*' Madness. Borderline sociopathic behavior, without a doubt.

"Well," I replied with a violent change of demeanor, calm as all hell, now fully confident of my footing with this mind fucking cacodaemon, "I was an active cop, and I was in a couple of aggressive Units; so, I suppose that's to be expected, isn't it?"

"I guess… I was never into any of that stuff, to be honest - Special Units and all of that shit. I mean, I get it; you need 'em to clean up the streets and all of that crap… but it was never for me. Give me good old fashioned Patrol any day of the week. No muss, no fuss." Waiting, I suppose, for some rejoinder from me, and there being none, she proceeded with her gratuitous gabbing, "It's the backbone of the Department, you see? Patrol. Without it, what else have you got? I mean, who else is gonna answer all the 911 calls and do all of the reports? you know what I mean? And as a Sergeant? well, you just can't beat it. You really can't. We're the ones that run the whole show out on the street."

"What about the Lieutenant? and the Captain?" I naively inquired. "Aren't *they* the ones that run the show?"

"The Lieutenant and the Captain?" she repeated with a cackle that sent her head reeling backwards, as if someone had grabbed hold of her ponytail from behind; a laugh similar to that of certain questionably satanic colleen residents of Salem, circa 1623 AD, missing only a cauldron of boiling water filled with wing-of-bat and eye-of-newt, before concluding, "New guy, you better get one thing terribly straight right now: if you know what's good for you… if you value your rotten life, you had better *never* bother Lieutenant O'Hara for anything in this entire world, except if someone is filled with puncture wounds and is likely to die. That man, bless his soul, doesn't leave the basement lounge until it's time to either go home or time to go the pub, you get me? You don't ever go bothering him. And the Captain? ha! well, you just try and walk into his office without being sent for… you just go try it and see what happens to your sorry ass!" she frantically concluded. This was the same woman, by the way, that just moments ago accused me of having an anxiety disorder.

"Got it;" I placatingly answered, "no Lieutenant and no Captain."

"Goddamn right. This here is *my* Command. Get me?"

"No, Lieutenant, no Captain, your Command…" The lady definitely had some sort of narcissistic, Doctor Jekyll and Mr. Hyde issue going on, so I figured the best thing was not to rock that boat. When you find yourself face to face with a living, breathing, Penny Dreadful, you should definitely not go around poking sticks at the wretched thing; whatever madness is laying dormant inside may just end up ejaculating, splattering its vile and putrid matter all over your sticking face.

***

It turns out, a week or so into my new assignment, that my new Captain, Anderson, *did*, in fact, send for me. No sooner had I walked in through the doors of the Command for my tour of duty, than the Desk Sergeant on duty, Jameson, practically throw himself at me with the countenance of someone who was charged with a life and death task of the utmost import; the failure of which bringing forth death to he and his heirs. "Hey, bro, the Captain wants to see you in his office… like, *forthwith*!"

'Really?" I asked, my core instantly growing cold, the guts

within tightening into several hundred knots. "He wants to see *me*? Are you sure it's *me*? James Cardona?"

"Yeah, I know who the hell you are, bro! What in the fuck did you do? You just *got* to this Command!"

"Hell if *I* know… I guess I'm gonna find out soon enough." I said, making my way into the Commanding Officer's office, expecting – for reasons associated with my natural born luck, which wasn't the greatest, let me tell you – a complete shit show.

The office space was cold and sterile, void of any human life; that is, outside of the human being that sat, stoically, behind the old wooden desk, riddled with countless, deeply imbedded scratch marks, making it appear as though a master chef had been utilizing it as a cutting board, slicing and dicing his pork shoulder all day long. One would liken the entire room, as a whole, to, perhaps, a vacant and forsaken storage unit, or maybe a place to put an unruly adolescent with the intentions of scaring the living hell out of them via sheer nothingness, instructing the scoundrel that *this* is what would happed if they continued down their mutinous course of action. There were no family portraits of any kind, nor any personal effects that would give some indication as to who in the world this person actually was, and what he was all about. As for the Captain himself, only the blinking of his eyelids - although smeared with darkened circles, similar to a woman whose mascara has run amok from a deluge of fallen tear drops, the cause of which, I could only assume, was sheer exhaustion – disputed the fact, providing, barely, portents of a living organism before me. His gray, wiry and disheveled hair; gaunt, sunken in facial features, as if something from within himself were pulling his countenance inward towards the center of his brain;

dried out, blanched, skin tone; almost translucent, colorless, irides; and cracked, severely dehydrated lips greeted me in a somewhat listless voice, as he muttered, "Sergeant Cardona, I presume? Sit down." to which I complied, prompting him to continue, "Getting settled in fine? at least I hope."

"Yes, sir… just fine. Getting to know the men and women real w-"

"Good, good… that's grand. Listen, I got a folder in front of me here," he interrupted, pulling out a folder the size of *'War and Peace'* from beneath an insane pile of papers encompassing most of his work space, having absolutely no discernible order to them, several of the sheets possibly serving as makeshift handkerchiefs and paper airplanes at some point during the filing process, "and it seems to me you've got some much needed experience. What I mean is, I've got a spot to fill… an Anti-Crime Sergeant spot to fill… and it appears as though you are the very man I need to fill it. Get me?"

Now, here I must pause and make something painstakingly clear to you, my dear bibliophile: I, in no way, shape, or form wanted anything to do with any kind of Special Operation, especially of the Anti-Crime variety. I mean, come on… after everything that transpired – all of the crap that went on – in my old Command with Internal Affairs, and our Team getting obliterated and all of that jazz, there was no way I wanted any single thing to do with the likes of that kind of horse manure ever again. Shifting back and forth in my seat, kind of like there was a sudden infestation of microbes crawling uninhibitedly inside of my pants, I answered, "Oh, sir… well, I… thank you, but -"

Staring into my soul with those lifeless peepers, he cut in, "I'm not sure I'm enjoying the reaction I'm receiving here, I gotta be honest with you, Sergeant."

"I'm sorry, sir, I really am… it's just that I had no idea… I didn't expect…"

"Look now, if there was some kind of misunderstanding here, let me take this opportunity to clarify… I'm not *asking* you, Sergeant. This here is an order, get me? I'm down an Anti-Crime Sergeant, and I'll be damned if I put anybody in that kind of a spot who didn't have some experience doing the damned thing, see what I'm saying? It's just not an option… not a choice, bud. I need someone that knows the ins and outs of the goddamn spot… you get me?"

"I understand, sir." I acquiesced, with flatline exuberance, my vital organs feeling the sensation akin to one's final moments on Earth.

"Good… good. Now that *that's* straightened out, you'll want to see the Special Operations Lieutenant, Lieutenant Christianson; she's expecting you in her office. She'll fill you in on all of the specifics of the thing, you get me, Sergeant?"

"Yes, sir. Thank you, sir." is what I managed to extract from my languished constitution, my weakened knees barely supporting my body's wish to make an expeditious exeunt from this bastard's office. The last thing I desired in this entire crummy world was to be a part of some goddamn Team; it was all kinds of trouble that I was hoping never to have to deal with for the remainder of my career. I had different plans now, and none of them included running around like a maniac looking for the worst scum in New York City. My goals were centered on taking more tests, climbing the promotional latter and all of that kind of nonsense, and this assignment was going to take a giant shit on those objectives. Now, instead of studying my ass off, to get the coveted white shirt position of Lieutenant, Captain, Inspector, and above, I was going to become a *Jump Out Boy* once again, only *this* time I'd be leading them. The very thought of it practically made my lunch of boneless ribs and fried scallops leap from the pit of my stomach onto the tip of my tongue; which, if you haven't the ability to visualize, is an especially distasteful feeling. Especially.

***

The Special Operations Lieutenant's office was the antithesis of the Captain's. I could see, as I arrived at the threshold, that there were a plethora of wonderfully framed portraits of different shapes and sizes, proudly displaying her family all about her bookshelf and desk. Hanging on the wall just beside her was this singularly beautiful abstract painting consisting of the most brilliant colors, the artist seemingly having used such delicate strokes as to instantly make one feel at peace, a sensation of warmth and tranquility overcame me, all of my pent up frustration and negative energy from my encounter downstairs simply cascaded out of my pores and onto the linoleum floor, subsequently oozing out into the hall where it would, I'm sure, most patiently await my return upon the conclusion of this meeting with my new boss. Very allaying. Although her door was wide open, I knocked to announce my presence.

"Oh, hey, my new Anti-Crime Sergeant, right? Come on in." the Lieutenant said, welcoming me with one of the brightest smiles

I had ever laid my eyes upon. She was a real looker, let me tell you. She had these eyes, sort of a crystallized blue, that instantaneously sent my heart shooting straight up on into my throat; I almost had this impulse to look away due to their sheer ability to seemingly read my every thought and emotion… I actually had to force myself to keep them locked in her direction. Very powerful stuff, her gaze. Her long, blonde, hair was loose, cascading over the front and back of shoulders like a golden waterfall. As she stood up from behind her desk, leaning over and extending her hand for a shake, I could see that she was a tiny little thing, standing about five foot, five inches – if I had to guess; but her *prodigious gravitas* appeared larger than life and I was instantly not only impressed, but intrigued, wanting nothing more than to genuinely make more of her acquaintance.

"Yes, Lieutenant Christianson, apparently this is true; that is, according to the Commanding Officer, ma'am."

"Oh, please, dispense with the formalities and call me Selena." she insisted, returning to her chair, motioning, by way of gesticulating her extended arm in front of her, in addition to a slight nod of her head, for me to take a seat as well - to which I obliged - all before she continued, "I'm sure you know how intimate Special Ops is, seeing as how you were a Conditions and Anti-Crime Cop before you got promoted..." she paused here to take a quick peek at a single sheet of paper on her desk containing, what I conjectured to be a synopsis of my profile, "… and I'm assuming by your negative rejoinder that you weren't a willing participant in the matter? Drafted, were you? for this particular position?" she inquired with a half smirk and raising of one eyebrow, which I thought terribly attractive, quickly developing a schoolboy crush on my new supervisor.

"Volun*told* I believe the expression is." I said, with a slight chuckle, referring to the conjoining of the two words 'volunteered' and 'told,' which – in our thing – occurs quite frequently, not exactly possessing the ability to tell Supervisors to shove their assignments up their asses, us schmucks, thereby, accepting any terribly unwanted gigs.

"Well, I can certainly understand that feeling." she responded, quickly making me feel at ease by explaining, "It wasn't too long ago that I was sort of in your shoes… I was the Anti-Crime Sergeant at my old command, before I got promoted, and let me tell you, I went into it kicking and screaming; I wanted nothing to do with it."

"Drafted?"

"Basically! The thing of it is, at the time, I just thought it was too soon for me to be a Crime supervisor. Like you, I had just been promoted to Sergeant. I thought it'd be a better idea if I had gotten some experience in the rank before going to Special Ops; but my Commanding Officer at the time, Captain Shannon… well, he thought otherwise; so that, as they say, was that."

"How did it work out? I mean, did things turn out okay back then?" I was genuinely interested in that particular fact because it really was a kind of mirror image to my situation. I honestly wanted to know what she had to endure… what she did to help herself get through it all… to cope; because, at this point in time, I seriously and truly felt as though I did not possess the dexterity required to complete this task… not one single bit.

"I ended up really falling in love with my Team…" she replied, "…DiCarlo, Morales, and Jackson - crazy fuckers; so, yeah, things turned out pretty okay. I got launched from the gig down the line because of this douche bag Lieutenant… it's a whole thing, don't ask; but up until that moment, I was really happy that I had been given the opportunity. We did some really great things – did a lot of good work out there. And you know something? I really learned a thing or two about myself leading that Team; I learned that if you give something your all – if you really apply yourself to a thing, work hard, and be good to your guys, then you can hold your head high with pride. It's all anyone can ever expect, your very best. And if they don't appreciate that, well then fuck 'em. You know what I mean?"

"Wow… now you're a Special Operations Lieutenant. Pretty neat."

"Yes, it has its good days and its horrendous ones; but overall I have to say it's been a good spot. It's not the same as exclusively working with the Crime guys, though, you know… I'm responsible for every single Special Ops gig in this joint: the Domestic Violence Unit, the Warrants Team, my summons guys and gals… it's a lot of work. Thankfully, though, I am almost at the proverbial end of the tunnel. I can see the light, as they say. Just three more months."

"You're retiring? You look like you're in your twenties, Lieutenant!" I exclaimed, immediately wondering if I had crossed the line with the slight hint of coquetry.

"Ah! bless your heart… you've already won some brownie points! Good work, James! And, again, please call me Selena… we're all friends in this Unit." she replied, instantly quelling the concern for my display of familiarity.

"Thank you, Lieutenant… I mean, Selena." I said with a chuckle. "I'm sure your loved ones are looking forward to that momentous day… your retirement. You have a beautiful family, by the way. Three kids? I see."

"Yes, my sweethearts! Joseph, Joshua, and Josie." she said, taking up the picture frame, gandering at it with a countenance of indescribable tenderness that only one's maternal endearment could imbue.

"Gorgeous. Is your husband on the job? Is he a Cop, too?" I asked, fishing for an answer to the *real* question: *are you available for me to work my charm upon*? Yes, yes, I'm a bastard… we already covered that a few chapters ago, remember?

"My Justin? dear Lord, no! My lovely husband is a stay at home dad right now. He used to teach English for the Board of Education, but now holds down the fort! We wanted the babies to have a certain stability at home, you know? We thought it best to have at least one of us there at all times, and he agreed for it to be him, God bless his heart. He's actually a writer now. He writes works of fiction about life, love, and all of that shit… he's published, too. Really good stuff."

The harangue about her lovely husband, Justin, doused the embers of passion that were running rampant inside my core, and – lets be completely outright about the thing – my trousers, for her. She belonged to someone else, heart, mind, and soul; so, I curtly answered whilst rising from the chair, "That's so cool… I'll have to read some of his stuff! Well, I appreciate the time, Lieutenant… I mean, Selena. And I'm gonna give this a legitimate shot. Like, I give you my word that you'll receive my all." I concluded, motioning toward the door with intentions of making a rapid departure.

"Listen, don't kill yourself out there on the streets. I only ask one thing," she said, stopping me in my proverbial tracks, "and that is to look out for your Team; this is the most important thing of all. You have an awesome group… hard workers… they'll take care of the *numbers*, you just take care of *them*. Their last Sergeant went and got himself picked up by Internal Affairs because he was dumb enough to put in for an outside Unit while still on probation. I told the fucker over and over: wait until your two years are up, then you can put in for a million outside gigs if you like. IA is just waiting to snag people with less than two years in rank, like pointy toothed sharks wading patiently in the waters for unsuspecting surfers. Oh well." she shrugged her shoulders before concluding, "Anyway, James, it was a pleasure to meet you; if you need anything at all, my door is always open. And if it isn't, it's only because I'm pulling on one of these bad boys!" she concluded, retrieving a cigar from the cedar wood humidor on her desk, lighting it and emitting into the air a plume of vanilla rum scented smoke… quite a pleasant aroma, I must say; and a distinctly sexy sight, watching those remarkably devilish, plump lips wrap themselves around the cigar… just being honest. I'm certain that you wouldn't want me omitting a thing like that, would you?

"Ten-four, ma'am;" I said with an inadvertent smile, my internal, coitally deviant thoughts betraying me. "and thank you, again." I said, shutting the door to her office. That Justin was certainly a lucky fellow; hopefully she was appreciated by him at home.

***

Later that day, I met my Team of three Cops, a motley crew, as it were, of sorts: Morena, the most senior of the three, with salt and pepper hair, giving him the countenance indicative of the proverbial wise old man in any given village, the one whom all the tribesmen turned to solve the most peculiar of problems, warding away any quandary with sage and black magic; Guzman, a very gung-ho Army veteran – the type who sleeps with his rifle, not just to provide him with immediate access in the event of an unexpected home invasion, but also as a thing in which to canoodle, as one would affectionately spoon their significant other on a rainy Sunday morning - with only a handful of years on the job, but whose good instincts and sharp wit more than made up for whatever nescience he possessed; and, last, but certainly not the least in any fashion, Calderon – affectionately known as 'Whip,' not at all due to any sort of unparalleled skill set behind the wheel of a Police Car, as was my initial thinking upon hearing the flashy moniker, but, instead, referring, quite comically, to his contumacious need to deposit tons of whip cream onto his extremely intricate caffeine beverages – who held the distinction of having the very least amount of time on the job amongst the Teammates.

I traversed down to the basement where, incidentally, most Anti-Crime offices are located, knocked on the door (which was bolted shut), and, after a loud unlatching sound on the other side of the solid metal door, was warmly greeted, albeit through a half inch crack, "Hey! what's up, Sarge!" exclaimed Guzman, peeking, initially, from behind the aforementioned door, now swinging it wide open, revealing the zealous Officer with his rifle at the low ready position, as if he were defending a bunker in the middle of a war zone and could possibly have encountered the enemy attempting to infiltrate the encampment at any moment. "Welcome to the Wolf's Den! Enter, sir… enter!"

"The Wolf's Den… wow, I like it." I replied upon entering, whilst looking around at the quaint little nook, which appeared more like a college dorm room than an office in a Police Department facility: complete with a regulation sized, distressed American Flag; two desks, each with their own computer terminals; white deck lights, which were strung up along the four walls of the room; a large, flat screen TV, equipped with cable and a gaming system; a fully stocked refrigerator containing a variety of tasty little tidbits and liquid refreshments; the essence of frankincense and myrrh filling the room from an incense stick burning somewhere within; and a futon bed with a Mojave throw blanket, accompanied by matching pillows where, as it happens, Calderon was sprawled out, sipping upon an especially frothy Dunkin Donuts potation, topped with extra whipped cream, most of which was resting upon his upper lip, curved upward at the edges into what I discerned to be a welcoming smile, as he wriggled his fingers 'hello' in my direction, signaling to me his salutation.

"Yeah, bro," said Morena, who was planted at one of the two desks in the office, studiously examining crime stats on the computer, "we're the Wolf Pack, that's our spirit animal… we're very zen in here, Boss… if you didn't already notice." he said, referring to the aforesaid interior design and essence of a Buddhist temple undulating through the air.

"Yes, I see… very nice. Very cozy."

"Sit, sit, Sarge… this desk over here is yours!" exclaimed

Guzman. "Us three share the one Morena is sitting at. Just make yourself comfortable. You want coffee? there's fresh coffee brewing right now because Whip over here decided to show up with Dunkin only for himself."

"Dude, I asked you if you wanted Dunkin!" shouted Calderon, exceedingly crestfallen that he was called out for the error of omission.

"When? mother fucker! when did you ask if we wanted Dunkin?!" hollered Morena, violently swiveling his seat in Whip's direction, ready to do battle in the name of the slight from his partner.

"Remember that time, it was during the snow storm – the big one – and I was like, "Hey, do you guys want Dunkin? but you two were like, 'nah bro, we don't want any Dunkin,' so I was like, 'okay, fine.' Remember?"

"My man," Morena broke in, slapping the back of his right hand with his left, creating a powerfully emphatic sound effect after every spoken word, to accentuate his point, "what are you even talking about? That was like, seven months ago."

"I know, but I figured you just didn't like Dunkin or something… you *really, really,* sounded like you hated it."

Morena, displaying a countenance of sheer disgust at this exceptionally unsatisfactory justification, and without providing any further retort, simply stated, "I can't." before turning himself back toward the computer.

"Sarge, you have to excuse this brute… you can see what

pounced on a gentleman who attracted their fancy for a stop, due to the fact that he was ingesting a narcotic substance from a makeshift crack pipe – which, upon espying us, he launched from his grasp - whilst a gravity knife lay visibly clipped upon the front of his pants pocket.

"Hello, sir, and what a pleasant evening it is tonight." said Guzman, swiping the knife from its resting place and handing it to Morena, subsequently beginning to frisk the man from head to toe for any further objects of which could most unpleasantly impale us.

"Very nice piece of contraband you got here." Morena said, flicking the blade open and shut with ease.

"Yo, man! whatchu doin in my pockets, yo?!" the denizen yelled to Guzman, quite dismayed at the shake-down.

"Well," answered Guzman, "I'm frisking you for any further weapons and -"

"*Further* weapons?" the gentleman interjected, "My man, whatchu talkin' about? *further* weapons."

"Well, fine sir, this…" Morena held up the knife, "is called a weapon -"

"Man, that ain't no weapon… that there is just my gravity knife."

"Y-e-s, that would constitute a weapon according to New York State Penal Code 265.01, sir." instructed Guzman. "And then there's the matter of the crack stem - Penal Code 220.50 - you so swiftly chucked onto the public sidewalk right over there… that, by the by, a violation of health code 16-118 -"

"That shit ain't mine."

"R-i-ght… and then there's this bag of crack latched onto, uh, this…" Guzman paused to inspect the hard, rusty object now being removed from the person of the detainee, a small glassine envelope containing the aforesaid narcotic hooked thereon, "… this… tiny screwdriver? you have in your pocket, which is most likely not yours, either."

"Damn, bro… jackpot!" exclaimed Morena.

"*You*, sir, are what's called, in our thing, a *whale*!" remarked Calderon, subsequently mimicking the sound of a whale horn; the reference alluding to any individual who had committed multiple violations at one time, the delivery of his comment being pretty humorous, I have to say.

Nights such as that were plentiful, the guys having a certain fire about them when it came down to working; which, in turn, made me look like some kind of a superstar in the eyes of Lieutenant Christianson and other such executives who concerned themselves with our productivity. And the best part of it was, I literally had almost zero *real* responsibility. I mean, as a Sergeant, I didn't make arrests (as it goes for any Supervisor); but with Cops like this, I didn't even have to bust any balls, speaking in the evocatively eloquent vernacular of our subculture. Now, you'll note I said *almost* zero responsibility… there were plenty of times when I had a thing or two to do. For instance, there was this one time, a few months later, on a night wherein we were driving around, doing what we usually do, when suddenly this known gang banger, Ronald Hutchinson, walks

260

passed the unmarked car and, with his hand, gestures as though he had a gun. He thereafter takes this imaginary gun comprised of his fingers, points it at us, then closes one eye as though he's aiming, feigns to shoot, then mouths the word, "bang!" Well, let me tell you, if you didn't already envision our reflexive response concerning the matter, this activated the ol' emergency alert system within our car, causing the *Jump Out Boys* to jump out… causing the *Wolf Pack* to pounce.

"What's good, Ronnie? haven't seen you in a minute!" said Morena, as we all surrounded the individual, the boys immediately frisking the perp from head to toe.

"My name ain't *Ronnie*, it's *Ronald*. Get it right." he snapped confidently, although his facial expression betrayed him, lacking the conviction put forth by his spoken words.

"You like mimicking as though you got a gun, huh? You get off on that kind of shit?" inquired Guzman rhetorically, not actually expecting Mr. Hutchinson to provide an earnest response.

"Man what are you even talking about? I ain't mimic nothin', dog… you just out here harassing innocent people tryin' to go about their day. If I wanted to shoot ya'll, I wouldn't do it with a pretend finger, how you like that?"

"Ooo, I like that *a lot*! That sounds like a threat. Hands behind your back, tough guy." Calderon said, grabbing Mr. Hutchinson by the collar of his shirt, bringing him over to the hood of the car to be cuffed.

"Police brutality!" Ronald began to scream. "Police

brutality! They about to lump me up! Somebody get this on camera!” prompting, instantaneously, an agglomeration of his associates to come out of the cracks and crevices of the city sidewalk from all different directions.

“Here we go…” exclaimed Whip, rolling his eyes in disgust at the prospect of the coming mob, “… put your hands behind your back, Ronnie. Don’t make me have to break your arms.”

“Oh shit! you heard that? Did ya’ll hear that? He just said he was gonna break my arms! Look! look! he’s breakin’ my arms! ouch oww! help!” Ronnie screamed at the top of his lungs, hoping that this would incite the crowd in becoming angered enough to intervene, a tactic often used to provoke all hell to break loose, more times than not ending with jammed up Cops, a cell full of prisoners, and frivolous law suits, where the payouts of hundreds of thousands of dollars awaited the crafty street thugs.

Shouts of, “Let him go!” and “dirty fucking Cops!” and “fuck the Police!” rang out from the horde of people now surrounding us, creating an extremely disagreeable scene to say the very least, all the while Ronald continued to prevent Whip from placing his hands behind his back, causing the Officer to take hold of the perpetrator’s forearms from the rear, pressing them inward in an attempt to bring the arms closer together, the ultimate goal being to attach the cuffs to the bandit’s wrists; Guzman, in the meanwhile, doing his very best to assist on the opposite end of his partner. Morena and I tried – in the midst of that *mishanter* – whatever we could to keep the crowd at bay, the sum total of that equating to practically nothing at all, we being heavily outnumbered and everything. To make matters a million and three times worse, over the top of the masses, during the uproar, came hurtling a glass bottle down upon the head of your chronicler, me, instantly splitting my forehead open, releasing a deluge of crimson colored ichor, which cascaded down into my eyes, immediately robbing me of my sight and, incidentally, my ataraxia. I lost my mind, so to speak. "Fuck! I can't see, bro, I think I got hit with something! I can't see!" were the frantic shouts ejaculating out of my mouth.

"Shit! You got hit with a bottle, Boss…" Morena shouted, now unholstering his Smith and Wesson, wildly waving it at the crowd, whilst crying out, "Get the fuck back! get the fuck back! right now!"

The angry mob responded by collectively taking a few steps back while ducking from the firearm's line of sight, with shouts of, "You gonna shoot us all, Cop?" and "You can't hit us all, pig!"

The next sound I heard – and, again, there is no way to express the elation… the sheer euphoric jubilation… of this particular resonation heard in the distance whilst an inpouring group of remarkably angry people enwreathe your bloodied mien – was the sound of a multitude of Police sirens, causing many participants totaling the swarm to vamoose in various directions, equivalent to the reaction sudden bright lights have on nighttime roaches; those choosing to stick around being met with the full impetus of the Platoon consisting of a great many flummoxed uniformed men and women, all of whom were now sending bodies flying to and fro in order to break up the encircled angry throng. Anyone who did not comply with the stentorian orders given by the incoming gendarmes were face-planted onto the concrete and placed into metal bracelets, afterwards becoming guests of *L'otel les Policiers*. In times such as these, resistance is futile and inadvisable; the sole objective for the men and women in blue during these calamitous moments is to put an immediate end to the chaos, and this is not done through peaceable or pleasurable means. What I mean to say is, there is no true thought process involved in this task; the crime stoppers, during times such as these, are absolutely not experiencing rational and logical thought… instead, a kind of robotic, autopilot, kicks in… self preservation mode takes over. It's either kill or be killed (figuratively, but sometimes literally), and the human being's *will* to survive, to resist its demise, overthrows compassion and mercy… Charles Darwin would surely not be disappointed at this presentation of his theory in perfect living action, in spite of the displeasure felt by the receivers of this renowned principle.

At some point throughout this pandemonium, Mr. Ronald "Ronnie" Hutchinson was secured into a marked Police Car with a couple of Uniformed Officers, our unmarked being reserved for my expeditious flight to the nearest emergency room. "Hang on, Boss, we're gonna get you to the hospital!" exclaimed Guzman, as he began dipping and dodging vehicles at an insanely exorbitant rate of speed, in an effort to transport me to someone who could restore my sight and keep me from bleeding out all over the goddamn place.

"Fuck! is it bad? is it real bad?" I frantically inquired, attempting to espy my reflection from the sun visor mirror (I had been thrown into the front passenger seat); however, I was unable to determine the severity of the injury due to the overwhelming amount of blood erupting from the wound, my entire face blanketed in life fluid.

"You're good, Sarge! you're good!" began Morena from the

back seat, in an attempt to mollify me, "just sit back… tilt your head back. You gotta keep the blood from pouring out of your skull, bro… anybody got a tissue or rag or anything?"

"No, bro…" Calderon answered, also from the rear, "all I have is this handkerchief my grandma knitted for me. It's such a beautiful little hanky that I keep for good lu -"

"Give me that shit, bro!" Morena interrupted, snatching the precious keepsake, immediately placing it upon my gash and applying pressure.

"Dude! grandma's hanky!" exclaimed Calderon with much anguish, reaching out at the now sanguine soaked cloth.

"Don't worry about it, bro, granny will be fine." answered Morena. "She'll make you a new one… this time with frills and valentine's. Sarge, keep this on the wound and apply pressure."

I held onto grandma's snot rag, placing pressure as Morena directed, thinking all the while that this was *it*. That was the way I was going out of the picture and into the afterlife… death by Pepsi bottle. The distinct feeling of my life-force making its grand exeunt was irrefutably prevalent as shock had begun to set in, sending me off into a deep siesta. The last sounds I heard were the now muffled voices of my pups, who watched as their alpha slipped out of consciousness; my last words being something to effect of, "Say, I don't feel too sexy."

"He's passing out, guys!" yelled Guzman, taking a quick glance at me, while unremittingly whipping through the lanes of traffic.

"You think he's gonna die? ugh, that's so sad, we just *got* this one." commented Calderon, wishing, I'm almost positive, to have rather been half-way into a nice, large, cup of extra creamy iced latte.

"Shut the fuck up, bro, nobody's dying. What in the fuck is wrong with you?" scolded Morena; which was the last thing, incidentally, registered by my good ol' hippocampus before going *night-night*.

***

I woke up a bunch of hours later not knowing, initially, where in the name of all that's holy and pure I was. Everything was pretty foggy for a little bit as my eyes attempted their very best to focus; just the bleeps and blips of the vital machine could be discerned at the onset of my awakening; that is, until I heard the sound of a familiarly comforting voice ask, "Hey kiddo, how's my boy?" It was my dad, who had apparently, at some point, been notified of the incident.

"Hospital?" is all I managed to emit on account of my weakened state, still not able to fully focus my eyes or move one single muscle in my body.

"Yeah, kid, you're in the hospital… you managed to split your head open while you were out there messing around in the streets." Funny, but as he uttered these words, I imagined myself, right then and there, as a youngster of seven years old. Inside my head, I was this little boy who fell off a bicycle and bumped his head, my father there to comfort and console me. Maybe it was some kind of a subconscious, repressed, wish of mine… even before the cataclysmic incident. There were many times, since becoming an adult, that I wished for nothing more than the ability to return to those innocent years of childhood, bearing no other responsibility than to play with my friends, go on adventures, explore the new and exciting world around me, and other such things that I missed so very dearly; or, even, complaining about school and homework, not being able to go out with my girlfriend due to the fact that I was grounded for some odd thing or another, as if that were the worst thing that could ever happen to me. The best part of it all, my youth, was at the end of every day, I'd come home to my old man who always had a deep as hell lesson in life for everything, which he'd share with me and Gracie over a nice plate of fish sticks, macaroni and cheese, and some iceberg lettuce with vinegar and oil. We'd sit there stuffing our faces, misappropriating each other's fish sticks, intently listening to his sagacious orations, not realizing, at the time, the importance of it all, we being punk kids and all. I'll tell you what, I sure as hell realize the significance to it all now. I really do. Anyway, the point is, that's probably why I imagined I was that young child on the hospital bed... I mean, I'm no goddamn Sigmund Freud or anything insane like that, but that'd be my educated guess and all.

"Jesus. It hurts." I said, finally able to slowly move my hand up toward my head, feeling nothing but a bunch of bandages.

"I'm sure, I'm sure... that's no little scratch on your skull." he commented.

"Gonna be okay? I'll live?"

"Live? yes, you'll live." he said with a chuckle. "The cut was pretty deep; they gave you about ten staples. Those are bandages that you're feeling. It's wrapped up pretty good."

"Staples? damn it! looks bad?"

"Nah, not at all… you just look kind of like Frankenstein, that's all." he joked, sending him reeling from his quip, my father typically being a huge fan of his own humor.

"Frankenstein was the doctor's name, Pop… the actual monster that he built from different body parts didn't have a name; he was just, *the monster*." I corrected, with a strained voice.

"Oh! well, in *that* case, I guess you look like the *monster*!" he replied, in what – I assume – he thought was light-hearted jest, as his additional subsequent chortles insinuated.

I managed to look around the room and noticed that there were a plethora of floral arrangements and other little *get well* nicknacks surrounding my hospital bed. "Wow, pretty flowers."

"Oh, yeah, beautiful. Gracie had the orange ones delivered… she called a few times to check on you, but you were still knocked out."

"Mm… that was nice of her. I'm surprised she cared enough."

"Ah, come on now, kiddo… you know she loves you. You know that. You two just have to get your shit together and stop the petty nonsense. When I'm gone, you two are all you've -"

"Yes, Pop, we're all we've got when you're gone… I know, I know."

Not wanting, I surmised, to get into a squabble, what with my head having been freshly melded back together, he changed the subject and said, "Anyway, I thought it was *on-time* that all your buddies came by to see you… one gorgeous one, too; she said her name was Selena… a real looker! What's her story? Single?"

"Selena?" I repeated, having to think for a few seconds, my brain still not fully functional. "Oh, my Lieutenant… Selena Christianson."

"Yeah, yeah, that's it; she *did* say she was your Lieutenant, but you know all that Cop stuff means nothing to me. Man, she's a real dime-piece! Why don't you look into *that* for yourself? If not, send her my way, why don't you? She's right up my alley, you know what I'm saying?"

"Pop! what the… first of all, she's married with three kids; second, she's, like, *way* older than me -"

"Age, my son, is but the number of times the Earth spins 'round the moon, you know what I'm sayin'?"

"The *Sun*, Pop… the *Earth* spins around the *Sun*, not the moon… and the moon spins around the Earth." I corrected, shaking my head and rolling my eyes.

"Well, well, well… look who's feeling better!"

"Anyway, she's married… that's the point. And I'm not looking to get with anyone; it's not what I want. I *told* you that."

"Yeah, well, I need some grandkids to hang out with. I'm a lonely old man and somehow, someway, you need to get me a couple of those."

"Pop -" I began with intentions to lecture, but was cut off by the knocking, and simultaneous opening, of the room door.

"Knock-knock! anybody home?" said a familiar voice. It was Calderon and, behind him, Guzman and Morena, all bearing with them flowers and trinkets.

"Hey, fellas… your gang is here, Jimmy." said my dad, standing and welcoming them into the room.

"Hello, Mr. Cardona, good to see you again, sir." said Morena. "I see that our patient is finally awake! that's great news!"

"Yes, he woke up not too long ago. He's already well enough to tell me all about how the *Earth* spins around the *Sun*, and all of that shit."

Having *absolutely* no idea to what my father was referring, the guys provided a polite chuckle and placed their items amongst the rest, except for Calderon, who brought his offering directly to me, laying the thing upon my lap. "What is *this*?" I enquired of the egg shaped plushy doll that he presented to me.

"It's Humpty Dumpty!" he informed, as if I should have known very well the identity of the oblong shaped character whose fractured shell mocked my present laceration. "See the crack across his head? It's *you* Sarge!" he concluded with a colossal smile across his face.

"That's cute, that's cute." my father commented, along with a titter, appreciating the effort of Calderon's wit.

270

"We tried to stop this atrocity, *Sargento*, just so you know;" commented Morena, "but, Whip Cream insisted, so there you go." This eliciting a collection of chuckles from the audience in the room.

"Don't make me laugh, guys, it hurts like hell when I laugh!" I cried, once again reaching for my dome.

As the laughter subsided, the room door flew open once again, this time revealing my old Teammates, Harper, Quinn, and Sergeant McKinney, all possessing flowers and bibelots of their own. "Hey, what's all the racket? this is a place of healing, not a comedy club!" Harper bantered with a monumental smile across his face, he and my old cohorts entering and shaking hands with everyone present.

"Holy crap, brother, you look like Frankenstein meets the Mummy… in that old Abbot and Costello movie!" commented McKinney.

"Hey, it's actually just *the monster*." corrected my dad, "Frankenstein was just the guy who built the creature!" he concluded, shooting a look over to me with a wink, prompting me to roll my eyes once again.

"Is that right? I'll be damned!" replied McKinney, seemingly quite intrigued at this revelation of epic proportions.

"Somehow I seem to have a memory of that fact;" added Quinn, "something my English professor was babbling about during our reading of Mary Shelly's novel… who knew it'd be a topic of conversation so many years later in a hospital room!"

"So how you holding up, champ? That's some lump on your head! Just can't seem to stay out of trouble, can you?" remarked Harper, coming over to me, leaning in for what is most masculinely referred to as a *bro hug*, which entails just a smidgen of affection, just enough to allow the receiver of this gesture to know you care, whilst not inadvertently setting off any alarms as to question its sexual motives, that being, as I have already expressed, an especially prodigious concern within our *thing*.

"I'm holding up. You should see the other guy – that damned Pepsi bottle got the worst of it… shattered into a million pieces." I quipped, the room appreciating the dry bit of humor, emitting a chorus of chuckles.

"He gave us a good scare, I'll admit it." Morena asserted. "For a minute there I thought it was a lot worse. I didn't know what to do but to grab you and throw you into our car… fuck that ambulance shit."

"Fuck, yeah;" supplemented Guzman, "who knows how much worse it would've been had we waited… it was a good call, Morena."

"Yeah, except the part where you soiled my grandma's hanky… you have no clue how hard it was for me to expl -"

"What he *means* to say," interjected Guzman, "is that it was his absolute pleasure to aid you in whatever menial way he was capable." he concluded with a reprimanding look upon his countenance.

"Yeah… *that*." Calderon consented, shrugging his shoulders, placing his eyes upon the floor, like a scolded toddler who had been *timed out*.

I will say, that particular moment… the *entire* moment, including the whole mess with Mr. Hutchinson; the crowd; the race to the hospital; and now - especially now – the hospital room… was a true turning point for me. It was then that I felt a kind of connection, a bond – if you will - between myself and these men… this pack of wolves (I, indeed, include my former Teammates as members of this guild… even ol' Brentwood, as a matter of fact, rest his soul). For, as spirit animals go, this bunch was about as good as it gets. There was established, in those turbulent and tumultuous years leading to that frame of time, the truest sense of strength and loyalty, the deepest of connections for one another, something I would not ever again, for the remainder of my time with the Police Department, experience to any degree. Take it from me, for whatever in the hell *that's* worth, relationships like the ones I developed with Brentwood, Harper, McKinney, Quinn, and now this litter of Pups, are rarely ever forged in a lifetime… it's like finding microscopic shards of sapphires in the rubble, deep in the mines of Madagascar whose incalculable value defines the very essence of life itself, the positivity of the beautiful, precious, stones in life amongst the negative muck all around them. As a wise old man, *my* wise old man, once said, "…hold fast to the things that are most meaningful…" and I most certainly would hold on to this feeling until my last living day. One thing is eminently undeniable: these alliances are a rare jewel and should be cherished always and forever, if you ask me.

***

Something should be divulged to the ones whose optic globes

continue to gaze upon this particular opus, something about the dear old Department in which I was employed at the time of this chronicle that I think ought to be shared; and that is: the Organization which polices the great metropolis that never snoozes is such an insanely elephantine factory-like conglomerate, as I alluded to earlier, that it – as an Entity – ironically has absolutely no idea how *efficiently* each and every one of its many sprockets are doing, how *well* said sprocket is functioning; it only knows if the pinion has ceased to fire, thereby rendering it obsolete and useless, ready to remove the thing and replace it with another. For instance, let us just surmise for a moment, if you will, that you are a hard working drone – someone who *pays their rent*, as it were, meeting (sometimes even superseding) whatever expectations are given – but all of a sudden, for whatever reason, fall into hard times with, perhaps, some kind of… oh, let's say a disciplinary situation for ol' shits and giggles. Well, let me tell you, good luck with *that*; the Job will chew you up into cud and spit you out onto the floor, where you will sit and rot under the baking Sun, along with all of the other useless waste that exists in this world, for as long as the unforgiving Entity sees fit. And that is a bonafide guarantee.

What brought on this particular rant? you ask? What could possibly have set this historian's mood askew? Fear not… I shall, indeed, share these morbidly disheartening circumstances with you, post haste. After about five years of roaming the plains with my Pack, successfully affecting an infinite amount of arrests and addressing some serious quality of life issues that infested the Precinct, which lead to many a bad guy being put away – the Wolves feasting upon the Sheep - we ended up being hunted by an even deadlier prey than any mighty canine could fend off… you guessed it: our good friends at Internal Affairs. It would seem that my Team was, in essence, *too* good at their job, grabbing the attention of IA, causing them to follow us around all over the goddamn place while we were conducting our business of crime fighting. I say, '*too* good,' due to the fact that we were not merely doing all of the good work that I just described, but actually leading the *entire* Command in the realm of aforesaid arrests and summonses (legitimate ones of the felonious and serious misdemeanor variety), and this kind of thing raises all sorts of proverbial red flags with the unit whose primary function, as you all have already been made fully aware, is to quell any unsavory activity going on within the Department. This, friends, is why I was – and, to this day, still am - perplexingly discomposed with the Organization. On the one hand, you have your Commanding Officer, Lieutenants, and every other Boss you work under, telling you to "*go out and get 'em,*" giving you all kinds of hell when you don't perform to their standards; and, on the other hand, you have the rest of the Department, including the relics that work at Headquarters, that will hang you by your goddamn pinky toenails when you go off the beaten path to actually get things done. Bananas.

No one, not them and not the public, wants to actually admit to the fact that the only way to catch a criminal is to take on the persona of the beast. Simply put, good guys can't catch bad guys with good guy rules. It simply will not ever happen. Not consistently. I mean, sure, you'll get a few whippersnappers here and there by playing nice, enough to even appease your masters, as well as John Q. Citizen… conduct a few community meetings and show them the smoke and mirror stats, have them thinking all is well in the world, when all the while anyone who is actually out there *really* trying to put the monsters away gets *sent for* and dealt with. Guys and gals in

Blue will bring in a plethora of bullshit arrests just to get on board and meet their unwritten objectives, maybe some poor bastard with a suspended license or perhaps some homeless bum who decided to make camp in a Housing stairwell, and all will be well, their careers safe and sound, not having to worry about the bogey man calling them downtown for a nice Department investigation. But you just go on ahead and try to tackle the *real* criminality afoot in the city, the real evil mother fuckers who bring about the last chapter in the Bible… kiss your job goodbye and say hello to your new roommates in C-Block, at some goddamn state penitentiary, if you punch the wrong beater and abuser of women in the face or shoot an unarmed rapist in the middle of his escape, fresh from a sexual assault. A sad, sad, truth.

Anyhow, the way we found out about the tail from our *pals* was I got *sent for* by my Special Ops Lieutenant – my *new* Special Ops Lieutenant, Davidson - and he was *no* Selena Christianson, let me tell you right now… the *exact* opposite, if you care to know; and I'm not just speaking on her physical, outwardly beauty, either. I'm talking about something that is worth a million times more, and that was her loyalty; something that this new bastard just did not evince, I'm sorry to say. His door was open and I could see that he was sitting behind the desk, his face buried in a ream of papers. I knocked to make myself known, and entered upon espying his wave for me to come in. Looking around, I could see that much had changed since its former tenant departed, having reached her twentieth year, heading off into the sunset of retirement with Justin… lucky guy. The feeling of *Mahayana*, of total serenity – what with her colorful paintings and generally soothing aura – was long gone, replaced with nothingness. Where her frames once hung, now remained only the outlines of portraits once prominently displayed, along with the screws embedded into the sheet rock that held these treasures in place, exchanged for dozens of binders containing endless crime stats.

"Cardona," he began, "take a seat… we need to talk, bud," he barked; which, mind you, is never a good presage of things to come.

"Yes, sir? is everything alright?"

"I wouldn't say that… no." he stoically replied. His brows scrunching inward toward the bridge of his nose. He was a younger man, born approximately five years after my induction into the planet, and had about that much less time on the job than myself; which, by the way, hurts like hell, me being a pretty proud kind of guy. What I mean is, it's not easy taking orders from someone who wasn't even out of high school when I was hired. Just putting things into perspective, imagine this young buck at the age of sixteen, telling me what to do at twenty-one. A horrifically insane thought, isn't it?

"Oh." I replied, feeling the sensation of a thousand and one butterflies fluttering about the epicenter of my core. I mean, he may have been younger in life and on the job, but he still wore the bars of a Lieutenant on his collar, so I sort of had to respect and fear the potential of his wrath.

"Yeah… seems you've had company for some time now. Just got word from the powers that be, and it ain't good." he commented, looking through some papers that appeared pretty official, what with the words, 'Internal Affairs Case File' on them.

"Who? what company, sir?" I inquired, not letting on that I espied the forenamed Case File in his hands.

"Seems IAB has had some kind of a hard-on for you and your Team… looks like they wanna fry your eggs on a skillet for some questionable arrests your boys been making." he stated, his light brown eyes finally meeting my own, staring at me with a countenance that suggested his unmitigated discontent.

"Sir, I'm sure I don't understand… what exactly is it that they find questionable?" I asked, having a few damning ideas in mind, knowing very well, indeed, *exactly* what we were doing out there. I wasn't going to sit around and volunteer the goddamn thing to the man, though. I had absolutely zero faith in his ability to keep such a thing between the two of us, something that was truly missed in Selena. What I mean is, when I divulged the intimate details of our goings-on, our contentious escapades out in the field, to her, I knew for certain that the information remained secure; and, whatever convoluted mess needed smoothing out, she was the first to make sure it got done, no harm befalling anyone under her angelic wings. The very antithesis of my new overseer.

"Well, from what I've been told - and that's not much, seeing as how it's kind of an active investigation – you guys have been stopping people outside the Precinct borders. You've been poachin' in other Command's confines, you know? But look here, that ain't the real problem. The *real problem* is, while you been doing all that poachin', your guys have been puttin' *this* Command's confine's addresses on the paperwork. That's kind of falsifying documents, you know what I mean, big guy? Like, that's a crime and shit, you know?" He continued to leer at me, possibly attempting to read my facial expression like some intense CIA interview of a terrorist cell about to blow a bridge to smithereens. I tried not to give away any *tells*; however, I have this insanely bad habit of gulping down a few gallons of saliva when face to face with these kinds of intense situations, you know? It sort of causes my confounded Adam's apple to ping pong up and down in plain goddamn sight; which, in turn, makes me the most horrific liar in the entire miserable world.

"Lieutenant," I began, the whole Adam's apple thing happening in the process of the statement, "I'm sure, if that were indeed the case, it's because my guys couldn't get a clear address at the time of arrest… you know, maybe they had to get the collar in the car in a hurry or something."

"Don't you ride around with them, *Sergeant*." he remarked, enunciating my rank in the most condescending of tones. "I mean, you're *supposed* to be riding around with them. Wouldn't you *know* if that were actually the case? And secondly, the information I'm gettin' is that there's *multiple* occurrences of this kind of thing goin' on with your guys. Are you telling me that this report is completely inaccurate? Is that what you're saying to me, *Sergeant*? That this whole investigation is some kind of *oopsy daisy*?" he concluded, clearly butchering the expression, '*upsy-daisy*,' which is something a parent might utter to a child who has fallen on its face.

"Yes, sir… I mean, no, sir. I'm saying… I'm saying…" I actually didn't know *what* I was saying. The fact of the matter is that it was all true: we were making arrests in one location – a location not within our geographical area of assignment - yet putting addresses associated with our Precinct boundaries on the reports. Why? do you ask, would we commit such a brazen, *non licet* act as this? To understand the reasoning behind it all, one would have to empathize with the plight of someone in a Special Operations Unit, wherein the weight of crime stats come tumbling down upon you with the force of the Huascarán avalanche; bearing the responsibility of keeping the Commanding Officer clear from the proverbial crosshairs of the aforementioned mighty big wigs at Headquarters (who, incidentally, for the most part, as I touched on earlier, have not seen a city street since the days of Fort Apache in the Bronx). "I'm saying," I continued, "that I take full responsibility for my Team's actions… they only did what I asked them to do."

"I see. So you're willing to fall on the sword for this? You're gonna take the brunt of the whack?" That's all this man was concerned with… it was what he was waiting to hear. He only wanted to know that his position was secure, that he was not in any kind of jeopardy of losing his gig and possibly being launched to another Command. That's what it all boils down to with these new types of Supervisors. Fealty? fidelity? brotherhood? these are words no longer associated with the Department of now. Those precious, salient, sentiments having long ago retired with the dinosaurs many, many, pension checks ago, all who are now currently enjoying their mojitos on a white sandy beach somewhere, God bless them.

"Yes, sir, I am."

"Alright, well, I've been told that if you took it on the chin… if you didn't fight them on this… that, instead of the full force of IA comin' down on ya, they'll accept a transfer outta this Command."

"Out of this Command?" I parroted. "I thought the worst thing they could do to me was kick me out of my gig for something like this. I didn't think they could launch me to another building!"

"I mean look, Cardona, would you rather I just press the big red button and take this thing to the top? Would you rather that? I'll tell you right now, that won't be a simple launch; that'll be some serious consequences… we're talking suspension, vacation days lost, you name it. They'll throw the book at ya. And just because you made 'em do all that leg work, they'll probably think of a few more choice things to throw in there. I wouldn't recommend it, if you asked me. Not at all." Why on Earth would I ask *him*? And what would possess him to think that he knew better about anything at all? The nerve of this guy. Let's be clear, I am of the old school and respect the rank, any rank, above me because that's how I was taught so many years ago, but for this little rascal to think that, just because he wore the white shirt of an executive, he could lecture me like I was his goddamn little brother… it just kills me; just give me an order and I'll follow it, this is what I am obligated to do; but, the sermon? for Christ's sake, give me a break. On top of it all, the kid was of the Impact era when he was hired onto *my* job; he was one of the brats I told you about earlier – the ones that went to that blasted Impact program and never learned the true essence of this Department. He never learned to be a true Brother. This fucker was just one of those sons of bitches arresting the entire City of New York, just to pad their numbers… just another machine on the assembly line. A contributor to the destruction of the coveted Blue Fraternity.

The very thought – the whole thing – sickened me. Throughout my entire career, all I had ever done was give every bit of myself to the Job: as an Officer, I worked the tempestuous storm that was the four to twelve tour, and toiled on the Conditions and

Anti-Crime Teams, doing every single thing that was ever asked of me – no questions; and when I got promoted, it was the very same thing… against my will I was given the post of Crime Sergeant. And although it all turned out to be a pretty darn good thing, having developed such a beautiful relationship with my partners and all, the expectations were, let's be honest, insanely astronomical… nevertheless these commissions were always met with no resistance. Yet, here I am, sitting in front of this person who honestly couldn't care less about any of that; because all that matters now, apparently, is that I am that small, broken cog in the bigger mechanism that requires removal and replacement. I am no longer needed, therefore I have become an expendable, useless, prong that will be tossed into some bucket containing other useless parts like myself.

This is the way of the institution that proclaims itself to be the largest and best Police Department in the entire world… 'bigger than some country's armies!' as I propounded in the beginning of this tale. Sometimes, I think, a certain thing can grow *so* large that it no longer has the ability to sustain itself; much like the great Roman Empire – whose might was felt throughout Western Europe, Greece, the Balkans, the Middle East, and North Africa - meeting her demise by becoming so colossally overgrown that one territory knew not what the other was doing until it was too late… such was the case with the Department, it having not a single clue as to what one lowly Sergeant accomplished on any given day of the week in his insignificant role as an Anti-Crime Boss, only that he ceased to function in conformity with the greater apparatus. Such a thing was of no import to pretty much anyone outside the walls of the Command… or, to be extremely honest, even to anyone outside of myself and the boys on the Team. Let's be real, do you actually think regular Patrol Cops, ones who work in the very same building as the Conditions Cop or the Anti-Crime Cop, give two shits about each other? Let me enlighten you: they don't. Not one little bit. I mean, look, sure some Cops get along with others… I'm not saying that everyone wishes death upon each other or any crazy thing like that… it's just, on the whole, there aren't a lot of Officers who really care one way or the other about what the Special Operations guys are up to; it's not at the ol' forefront of a fella's concerns, is what I'm trying to get at. And when one of us fall from our pedestals, for whatever reason, it's not a thing that causes any sleepless nights for anyone. Not one iota.

I left the Lieutenant's office with instructions for my new assignment, which was located in an entirely different borough of the City, mind you; so, you can imagine the bitterness, the ball of hot liquid magma that was swimming around in my chest, as I went down to the office to break it to the guys. I opened the door to the office – with Morena at his usual place in front of the computer, looking at crime stats; Guzman meticulously shining his rifle with a cigar dangling from his mouth; and Calderon sipping his iced coffee drink (extra whip cream on top and around, as was customary, his upper lip) – and I almost felt the incredible urge to start bawling all over the place. I mean it, I almost began crying right then and there. I think they knew something terrible was afoot because each one of them stopped what they were doing, staring at me with harrowing countenances.

"Hey, boys," I began, "I… uh… there's something I need to tell you." I stammered, not really having the will to continue.

"Fuck! it didn't go well, did it? We're all getting kicked out of the gig, aren't we?" said Guzman.

'Oh no! We're getting kicked out of the gig?" cried Calderon, shooting straight up from the futon bed. "But I don't want to go to patrol! I forgot all of the codes to mark the jobs! And I'll have to work with someone I don't know! And I wouldn't even know what to do at a fire job! And my uniform… I don't think my uniform fits anymore! And I -"

"Relax, numb-nuts! Why not let the man speak?" scolded Morena, nearly ready to slap the hysteria out of Whip Cream.

"No," I reluctantly continued, "not all of us… just me."

"Oh, thank God!" Calderon uttered in relief, laying back to continue his frosty beverage, not one of us acknowledging his inopportune sense of solace.

"What?! are you serious? That's insane!" lamented Morena.

"That is just some serious nonsense!" added Guzman, placing his rifle into its case. "What tour are they sending you to? days? midnights?"

"They're launching me out of the entire Command… to another borough."

The Team, collectively, let out a hapless groan followed by open handed slaps to the their own foreheads and general looks of disbelief across their faces. "Bro," Morena began, "this isn't right; all we do is bust our asses, day in and day out… what did Lieutenant Davidson have to say about it? Did he even try and fight for you?"

"Nah," I responded, "at least, it didn't seem like it… he didn't give me that impression. In all actuality, he kind of sounded like he was urging me not to even fight about it. In so many words, he basically just told me to eat it. He said I'd be better off that way."

"Fucking coward!" shouted Guzman before continuing, "I'll tell you what, he's no Lieutenant Christianson, that's for damn certain. She would've fought for you for sure. These fucking new jack Bosses are for shit, bro. They have no clue what it is to be a leader."

"He's right, my dude;" Morena agreed, "she would've stuck her neck out for you. She would definitely have made her voice heard… she played no games."

"Well, none of that matters now." I began. "The only thing that matters, my only reality, is that I'm getting transferred… by this time tomorrow, I'm going to be assigned to a different Command; and I'll tell you what: I feel like resigning. Seriously, I feel like putting in my papers and vesting out. I don't wanna do this anymore. I don't wanna be a part of this fucked up system any longer. I mean it… I'm done."

"Nah, don't say that, bro." Morena consoled. "Never let this job defeat you. If you leave, do it because you found something better in life… leave on *your* terms. Don't do it while you're down and out; do it while your up and coming."

The logic was sound, but I wasn't really in the mood to be lifted up; to be very honest, I just wanted to continue wallowing in my own misery. Sometimes, even though the chips aren't *completely* down, you still need to go through a mourning process; otherwise, your brain may not properly categorize the damned thing, leaving you with all kinds of confounded unresolved issues later on in life. I'd much rather go through the proverbial motions of grief... for good ol' overall mental health's sake, you know what I mean? Anyway, I spent the rest of the time packing up my stuff in these duffel bags that we had laying around the office and said my fairly wells - which were pretty somber as you can pretty well imagine, complete with a deluge of tears and several warm embraces – and then took off for my new abode.

XIV

I swore to the good Lord above that I would never lift one single, solitary, finger during the two remaining years of my ferociously rumbustious career. Not one. As I've already mentioned, ad nauseam, too much of my soul had been given to this thankless job, so there was no way in hell I was going to hand over any more of myself to these swindlers of the human spirit. Word of my transgressions spread throughout my new working place like the Black Death Plague of 1346, what with the nickname *Bait and Switch* being bestowed upon me. I was known as the guy who had his team *cook the books* for the sake of ameliorating our statistical superiority over all else in my old Command. When assigned to my new Squad, whispers of, 'watch out for *ol' Bait and Switch* over here, he's a regular *wolf of Wall Street*!' jocularly swirled around from the other Sergeant's mouths. This, friends, is the reason why I was filled with great astonishment when called into the office of my new Commanding Officer, being sent for by Captain Yates, and offered — you guessed it – the Anti-Crime Sergeant's position. Outrageous, I know. "Ah, Sergeant Cardona, come on in… shut the door behind you, please." said my new C.O., a very spritely young man of about, no more than, thirty years old or so (which meant that he passed every single test with the minimum amount of time necessary to do so… in essence: got onto the Job at twenty-one years old; Sergeant within five years, that's twenty-six years around the Sun; Lieutenant within two, twenty-eight; and Captain at thirty). He was a handsome man, his overall appearance being that of what one might equate to a typical businessman, maybe a CEO in some high powered company; he was pretty tall, about six foot three; dark brown hair pushed all the way back and gelled to perfection, like the way a slick mafioso boss might style his locks; steel grey eyes that were pretty entrancing if you happened to have occasion to lock yours with his; and a handshake that could break a couple of your finger bones if you weren't careful with your hand placement within his grip.

"Thank you, Captain. I'm sorry to meet you under these circumstances. I'm sure you heard all about me and my troubles." I said, just getting my hand into the appropriate groove during the shake, right before he applied the squeeze, so as not to require an x-ray and physical therapy down the road.

"Not at all, not at all!" he yawped in a resoundingly stentorian voice, whose strident reverberations could be heard dying down somewhere up in the northern Pocono Mountains. "Listen, I called you in because I have a spot that you may be interested in, the Anti-Crime spot. The Sergeant I have there now would much rather be a part of the Neighborhood Coordination Officer Program, the Department's newest baby... which I'm sure you've heard all about... very exciting new program."

"Yes, sir," I answered, "the Cops in the Program are all assigned to specific areas everyday to connect with the community... kind of like the old 'C-Pop' program back in the day."

"I'm sorry... the *what* Pop?"

"C-Pop. Community Patrol Officer Program? That's what they called it when *I* got on the Job, almost twenty years ago. It's literally the same thing with a brand new name. The Department does that, it sort of regurgitates old strategies with new labels." I lectured. I don't think he liked that too hot. He seemed to be a true believer in the Department, and didn't take kindly to my belittling the precious new and improved version of the old C-Pop program, especially since he had absolutely zero clue that his generation's version *was*, essentially, a '*2.0*' of the older one. And he especially didn't appreciate, I can pretty much bet all my marbles, that I sort of threw my time on the Job in his mug; however, nothing was going to ruffle this young little chic's feathers more than what I had to say next: "Anyway, Captain, about the whole Anti-Crime Sergeant's spot… the thing of it is – and I say this with all due respect – I'm not interested." I waited just a brief moment for a response, but receiving nothing more than a tilting back of his head, a widening of his eyeballs, mouth slightly agape, I continued, "I mean, hopefully you won't take this as insubordination towards you or anything like that… like I'm refusing an assignment or something… but I just can't do it. After everything I've been through… all the crap I've done and what I've given to this job… the only thing I ever got from being part of Special Operations, when all is said and done, was bounced and launched. As I mentioned, I'm sure you've read all about it in that gargantuan sized personnel folder on your desk there… about what happened to me when I was an Anti-Crime Cop and an Anti-Crime Sergeant. Quite honestly, all I've gotten for it all was one big middle finger at the end of the day, so that's gonna be a hard pass, Captain."

"I see. Well -"

"And, sir – I'm sorry to cut you off; but, if you're gonna tell me I have no choice, well, you had better suspend me now, because my choice is I won't do it. I'm really sorry to sound like I'm being disrespectful… I don't mean to be; I've always shown great deference to my superiors, just call any one of my Bosses and they'll tell you that it's one hundred percent true. It's just that I can't do it anymore. For my own well being… I just can't." Still awaiting a reaction of some kind, I paused yet again; still getting none, I really pressed my ol' luck and hit him with the rub: "Oh, and sir, if it's at all possible, I'd love an inside assignment… something with an office, behind a desk… maybe the Training Sergeant's spot? where I can be '*Far From the Maddening Crowd*,' as Thomas Hardy so eloquently titled his literary work. I think I deserve it… after all that I've given of myself, my bit for king and country and all of that… I think I deserve it."

***

Needless to say, he absolutely did *not* give me that inside assignment; instead, placing me on the *graveyard* shift, with the aforesaid ghouls and goblins of the Department I told you about earlier on in the story, as a regular ol' Patrol Supervisor. Well, I suppose I ought to be thankful that he didn't take away my gun and shield for that stunt I pulled in his office; it's pretty serious business speaking to a Supervising Officer that way, you know… a person could get the goddamn electric chair for that kind of thing. Thinking about it now, I guess I really should be obliged for his mercy. I showed up to my newly assigned tour with a countenance that exuded sheer deprivation; which, in all reality, was to be expected, if you ask me… the Job had deprived me of my will, my drive, my spirit, to push forward – and my face was a chalkboard for that indisputable, disrelishing fact, causing most of the men and woman of my new Platoon to avoid me like one would a person with a scratchy throat at the height of the Covid-19 pandemic, which is to say I was circumvented at all costs.

The only human being I really had anything to do with was my driver, Officer Jenko, a wily veteran of the Department with over twenty years on the Job, which I greatly appreciated to no ends. His experience, not only with being an Officer, but life in general – he being my elder by about five years - made riding around in the Police Car extremely, refreshingly, tranquil, I must say. The only downside of the wretched thing was having to respond to the asinine jobs that accompany routine Patrol; such as, if you were wondering: noise complaints regarding neighbors talking too loudly in the adjacent apartments; allegations of animal abuse due to the incessant meowing of cats; morons disputing over parking spots; mother's inability to make their children go to school in the morning; and thousands more protestations such as these in which a Law Enforcement Officer must endure in the Big ol' Apple, because there is no filter in the 911 system; you can literally pick up the phone and lodge a grievance about anything in this city, and the Police are charged with responding to deal with it all. I'll tell you something, if I were in charge of it all, the first thing… the *very* first thing… I'd do is revamp the entire emergency calling process. I mean it. If someone dared to call in a complaint for some horrifically cretinous reason, I'd have them banned from having the ability to call again. At first, they'd get a time-out or something like that, I'd be reasonable for first-time offenders; but if they had the balls to do it again, they'd be barred for eternity. Seriously.

After roll call, where I handed out the assignments to my Platoon, I made a beeline from the inside of the Command to the car, offering curt responses to the hellos and other salutations from people I did not know, people I did not *want* to know. I opened the door and was greeted by Jenko who, like a true man of seniority, had the vehicle pulled up to the front, ready to go; which, let me tell you, is an invaluable quality… the ability to have the Supervisor's chariot ready to rock and roll, as it were, is a lost art. Nowadays, these Rookies will have you waiting around while they chit chat or flirt with the newest graduates; they'll actually have you standing by the *locked* passenger side door, with your goddamn hot coffee in your hands, until they finish trying to be the one hundred and third guy to flirt with the same new girl – who, by the way, now thinks she's the goddess Aphrodite after having been drooled over by the entire Command, when in all reality she wouldn't be a blip on the ol' radar in the land of the real. Seriously, there's actually a conversion chart to compare the hotness of Cops to civilians outside of our thing. In the Cop world, you'll have this particular Officer that everyone falls flat on their stupid faces for… she or he will register as a *10* in Police Land; conversely, though, you take that *very same* person and toss them out into the civilian world, where normal people live and breathe, that poor sap will end up losing a good four or five of those points. That's the God honest truth, too... no exaggeration.

Anyway, I got into the car with old man Jenko and, once I closed the door, it immediately felt to me like a protective cocoon. Everything was right with the world at that point. "Ah! hello Jenko, always a pleasure to see you, my friend." I said, taking a sip of my freshly brewed Bustello coffee.

"Hello there, Sarge. How goes it this evening?" he replied, with a most radiant aura, it truly was a pleasure to be in his company.

"It goes about the same as it did yesterday… and for the remainder of my miserable time left on this God forsaken job." I responded, shaking my head at the thought of the mere months remaining on my contract of spiritual death. I swore, with my right hand, to twenty years, and twenty years they shall have… not a half-second more.

"Ha! you said it, Boss… where to? anywhere special? Are you hungry?"

"Yeah, some Spanish bread with butter from that bakery we always hit up sounds real sexy, it will go swimmingly with this Bustello I have in this here cup." I said, lifting my travel mug of joe.

"You got it." he said, placing the car in drive.

"How do you do it?" I inquired, after a few moments of silent thought. "…stay on this Job over twenty? knowing all the crap that goes on… with the way things have changed."

"Well, Boss," he reposted, "I try not to think about it, to the honest with you. If I give it too much attention, I'd drive myself insane. Besides, I'm not staying *too* much longer… I figure maybe another couple of years or so… to pad the ol' pension, you know?"

"Yeah… I just don't see myself staying one singular second after twenty years. Not a one. Fuck that. I'd leave now if I could." I opined, wishing I could close my eyes and wake up on retirement day. Having to finish off these final grueling months was cruel and unusual punishment, in my humble opinion.

"I hear you, Sarge… I don't blame you; things definitely ain't the way they used to be. There's no place for old timers like us anymore. These kids nowadays don't have any respect; but you know, I suspect that every generation ends up saying that about the next set of new jacks that come on the Job. I'm pretty darn sure that the Cops from the 1970s, 80s and even early 90s looked at us like we were a bunch of aliens from outer space. It's just the way it is. Just be glad that you and I are almost done with it all. Soon, we'll be relaxing on a beach somewhere in the Keys of Florida… a white sandy beach, sippin' on some goddamn fruity drink, just watching the waves of the ocean crash onto the shore. Until then, we just have to be contented by the thought of it. Just keep breathing in and out until we get there."

"Yeah, I suppose you have a valid point, my brother… white sandy beach with a fruity drink. That does sound delightful, doesn't it?" I pondered, at that moment, of good ol' Brentwood and how he didn't utter more than two words to me for weeks before finally accepting me into the fold, about how he'd make me walk a mile to the car, put the car in drive and roll out with me barely in the goddamn seat. It was a pledge process that, at the time, I didn't understand or like; but a necessary rite of passage that made me appreciate the value of being a member of the, once, greatest fraternity in the world. The memory brought on a little smile, thinking of how that sort of thing just didn't take place anymore. The Officers today would never stand for it, quick to call Internal Affairs or contact their local news station to report what hardships they've endured upon arriving at their Command… if they didn't happen to *fall in line*. These hellions of today come in with a sort of expectation that simply did not exist once upon a time. They would not, I'm very certain, survive one day in a car with Officer Brentwood… not one; and they most certainly would've had an aneurysm or two had they experienced one of old McMahon's roll calls, or my Academy Instructor's gym blocks. "It's just the way it is." I muttered, repeating the sentiment of Jenko.

"Yes, sir-eee." he replied, with a slight chuckle.

We sat quietly - after grabbing some of that bread from the bakery that still did the *right thing* by the Police, granting us the very taboo *on the arm* comestible (some places still valuing the time honored tradition, although most would have the nerve to put a price on such a thing) - when our tranquility was most rudely interrupted by Central, who very tempestuously shouted, "Be advised, I'm now receiving a family dispute with a firearm at 7373 Victory Street, apartment 3C... child caller states that his mother and father are arguing, father pulled out a gun and is holding it to his mother's head, child says to 'please hurry, he's going to kill my mom.' I tried the call back number, but it goes to voicemail. Sergeant, you read on this dispute with a firearm?"

Grabbing my radio, I replied, "Sergeant read, show me responding." Subsequently glancing over to Jenko and uttering, "there goes our *warm* bread and butter."

"Yes, sir-eee." he replied, offering his signature chuckle, whilst shaking his head and placing the car in motion.

Upon arriving at the location, the immediate area inundated with the Police Cars that had already arrived, Jenko and I stepped out of the car, realizing that all the Officers were gazing upward, prompting us to follow suit. What we witnessed through the third story apartment window was the singularly horrific sight of the aforesaid child caller in the arms of his father, both looking down upon us, the patriarch clenching tight to a weapon, the silver revolver mentioned in Central's broadcast, the muzzle of which now currently resting on the right temple of his son.

"We gotta get in through the rear of the building… I don't want this guy to snap, seeing us all bum-rush this place at the same time." I announced aloud. "Hey, Jenko, me and you will go through the back and see if the landlord has a spare key or something." Then, turning to the rest of the Cops, I added, "Torres and Barry, you guys come with us, but head straight up to the third floor in case this guy makes a break for it; meanwhile, me and Jenko will work on getting the key; Henriquez, Suarez, Brandon, and Chan, you four stay right here and keep an eye on that window... throw some crime tape around the area to block off pedestrian traffic… make sure no one comes in or goes out until I say otherwise."

Torres, Barry, Jenko and myself headed towards the rear of the building, where we split up according to the plan: Torres and Barry to the third floor, while Jenko and I checked for the spare key with the landlord in the basement, where a rather nettled gentleman responded to the undoubtedly puissant pounding upon his door, swinging it wide open whilst shouting, "What?! motha fucka!"

"Sir," began I, "I'm terribly sorry to disturb you, but one of your tenants is holding a gun to his kid's head and we need the spare key – if you have one – to get into his apartment. Do you happen to have one? a spare key."

"Ugh, here we go again! It's apartment 3C, isn't it? I bet it is." he exclaimed, reaching behind his door and retrieving a ring of keys.

"Yes, sir, it is… do you know them well?"

"Well, I don't know them *very* well. I only know that they're always fighting and shit… day in and day out… always shouting and banging. Every day I get all kind of complaints about this from the other tenants. Dude has got to go… you fucking people should do something about his ass." he exclaimed, handing me the key.

"Thanks." I said, providing no response to his lamenting on the matter, seeing as how the Police have not a single thing to do with removing anyone from their domicile… something you'd think a landlord knows a little something about. "We'll get this back to you when we're done."

We left the cellar and headed up the stairs to the third floor, where Torres and Barry could be seen at the foot of the staircase landing, holding a position of cover behind the wall, sidelong of the dreaded apartment. "Any movement?" I inquired of the two.

"Nothing, Sarge. We can hear the kid crying inside once in awhile, but no one tried coming out of the apartment; also, we just called Chan and he said the father and son aren't at the window anymore… they lost eyes on them."

"Okay." I said, whilst grabbing my radio to raise Central over the air. "Central, can you do me a favor and give me the call back number to this gun run?" A 'gun run,' once again, being any job which deals in the existence of said weapon in any capacity. Then, turning to the guys, I explained, "I want to see if this guy will pick up the phone and talk to us before we go in and make it ugly… and even if he *doesn't* pick up, it'll give us an idea as to where he is in the apartment based on the ring of the phone; once we know *that*, we can try to make our way inside with the key."

I called the number that Central provided and, surprisingly, the maniac picked up the phone (and, more importantly, I could hear the ring, along with his voice, seemingly some distance away from the front door), "Who the fuck is *this?*" he cried.

"Good evening, sir, this is the Police Department… we got a call about a dispute at your location. Is everything alright?"

"Fuck you! we good! we don't need no Police!" was his laconic reply, before disconnecting the call.

"Alright, boys," I said, addressing the men, "seems as though our friend has no wish for our services. We shall, therefore, use the key to get in… it sounds like he isn't anywhere near the entrance, which is a good thing." With that, I gingerly crept toward the door and – as quietly as I humanly could – placed the key into the hole, turning it ever so slightly until it unlatched. Fortunately, as I slowly pushed open the door, the sounds of a child's cry drowned out the creeks of the rusty old hinges, allowing my Cops and I to make our ingress into the apartment silently and unmolested. As we traversed the foyer into the small hallway that lead to the living room, we detected an amalgamation of the metallic miasma of blood mixed with the potent emanation that gun power produces undulating through the air, leaving us to surmise that the poor matriarch had been extirpated, her carcass most likely somewhere slumped over in a nearby room. This conjecture was soon after verified by the spatters of rufescent liquid upon the walls and floor, followed shortly thereafter by the grim discovery of the lifeless body that formerly housed the aqueous solution, slumped over on one of the couches, a portion of her skull removed by the projectile emitted from the perpetrator's pistol.

With our firearms drawn from our holsters, we crept as

quietly as the creaky floors allowed, holding our breath with each advancing step. No longer could we hear the cries of the little boy who had adroitly made the call to 911, bringing us to this very point and time; so there was no way of discerning where exactly the threat lay. There were two bedrooms at the end of the hallway, and I immediately was inundated with flashbacks of the home invasion in which I had responded, so many years prior… nearly twenty years prior. Memories of entering that dark room and being trounced by the bandit who would have, doubtless, taken my life had Harper not discovered us to foil the baneful act ran rampant in my mind; this, causing an indescribable numbness to overcome by entire body. My heart thrashed inside my chest as I turned to make the silent signal to my three subordinates indicating my order to cover the door behind me, afterwards working my way into the first room, slowly turning the door knob, hoping to God that it didn't give rise to my presence.

The very next sensation I recall, upon cracking that door open and taking a step into the room, was a bright flash of light followed by a thunderous boom. That's it. There were no ensuing memories for the days to come, just bits and pieces, really; there existed some groggy, obscure, images – silhouettes of people here and there, coming and going; the sounds of monitors beeping and voices uttering things I could not understand. At some point, though, I realized I had been inside of a hospital room, it being pitch black, as it were, the only form of illumination coming from the hallway, leaving me to conjecture that it was well into the depths of the witching hours, when I caught sight of a pretty decent looking nurse who was taking my vitals in the said darkened room, "Ah, look who's up?" she, the nurse, said with a most melodic voice, like that of an angel's harp playing its harmonious chords at the Pearly Gates above… was I dead? Had my soul been transported up the rungs of Jacob's Ladder? "I'm Mia and I'll be your nurse until the morning shift arrives… and how is the patient feeling?"

With somewhat labored effort, I managed to squeeze out, "Thirsty."

"Thirsty?" she repeated, reaching for the container that housed the hydrating fluid. "Are you in any pain? Can you take a few breaths for me?" I did as she asked, subsequently watching as she scribed her findings on a clipboard before continuing, "You're very lucky, Mr. Cardona; not many people come back from this kind of thing."

"What happened? why am I here?" I inquired.

She looked up from the aforesaid clipboard, briefly staring down at me with a dour look upon her face, before saying, "You received multiple gunshot wounds, Mr. Cardona; two bullet wounds to your chest, which were stunted – thank God - by your vest, and one to your right thigh, which caused a vascular injury. Someone in the field placed this tourniquet on you successfully… it's the only reason you're alive, my dear."

She proceeded to lift up a clear bag to show me the tool used to save my life, and - wouldn't you know it – it was the very one purchased by Ms. Gracie Cardona… my big sis; the second time the thing saved a life, this time my own. 'I *really* ought to get around to thanking her for that goddamn thing.' I thought to myself.

The sudden influx of that especially shocking information, the entire event, was too overwhelming to process straight away.

I lay there with a dumbfounded look upon my countenance until something occurred to me… "Excuse me," I began, "can you tell me what happened to the other Officers that were there? I was with three of my Cops when… when it happened. Do you know if they're okay?"

With an expression of hesitation, she replied, "I'm not authorized to… they don't let us discuss that kind of thing… I'll page the social worker on call and have them talk to you about everything."

I presumed the worst at that point. I mean, she wouldn't go and call the head shrinker if everything was copacetic, you know what I mean? I'm sure she'd be willing to deliver an agreeable bit of news with absolutely no problem, whatsoever; therefore, I surmised that things were most likely at their absolute rock bottom. A million and one visions bombarded my mind, none of which were pleasant in nature, and all I wanted to do at that point was rip off all of the wires that attached themselves to my body, every single one, and beat it the hell out of that place. I almost did, too… I unplugged almost every one of those damn ports, not caring one single bit about the consequences of such an action. The only thing that mattered to me, right then and there, was to know the plight of my Officers. The thing of it is, they sort of drill that kind of thing into you at BMOC; which, by the by, stands for Basic Management Orientation Course (the classes you take after you pass the Sergeant's exam). They drill it into you to 'take care of your Cops;' over and over again; and any good Sergeant will always do whatever they can to look after and protect whomever is within their purview… only the douche bag ones don't, you know what I mean? So I needed, desperately, to figure out how in the hell my guys were doing.

Just as I attempted to detach myself from every one of the tentacles – fused, moored, and taped to the entirety of my fuselage (all the while screaming something to the effect of, 'get me the mother fuck out of here!') – an Officer, whose identity was unknown to me, being that he was a *fresh off of the assembly line* new guy whom I had formerly never been acquainted, and social worker, an older, but also quite attractive woman of about fifty years of age entered the room, she nearly reading me the *riot act* for making all the ruckus. "Mr. Cardona, what on Earth? you can't just go unplugging yourself! These are your antibiotics and your blood pressure and… *honestly*, Mr. Cardona! what were you thinking?" she lectured, grasping the now tangled bundle of wires, attempting to decipher where and how to return it all to their appropriate spigot ports. "My word, we'll need the nurse to come in and redo all of this insanity!" she concluded, lifting up her head to see if she could catch sight of Nurse Mia.

The unknown Officer, apparently not knowing what in the world to do, stared at me in utter shock, grasping with both hands onto his gun belt (a thing Cops do when they don't know what else to do), and saying not a word. I took a few deep breaths to calm the ol' nerves and apologized. "I'm sorry… I *really* am… I just need to know what happened to my men… I went into that apartment with three Cops: Jenko, Torres, and Barry… would you happen to know… are they… is everyone okay?"

I inferred, based upon the inauspicious countenance of my fellow colleague, who was still cluelessly latching onto his gun belt, that the presentiment was nothing good, breaking his eye contact with me and placing his glance, first, upon the floor, followed by the walls, and, finally, the ceiling… everything and anything, but me; after which, he slowly and quietly backed out of the room. The social worker, meanwhile, took a deep breath before saying, "You have a lot of visitors in the waiting area… many of them have been here since the day you came in. It's been three days since then… since you were rushed into the emergency room. Would you like me to get one of them? Maybe it would be best to hear it fr -"

"I just want to know what happened to them… I don't care who is the one that tells -"

Just then, seconds before I reached the point of a mental breakdown, the Rookie returned, this time with another Service Member whom I *did* have acquaintance… it was Officer Barry. "Hey, Sarge, Sarker over here said you were finally awake… man, you had everyone worried."

"Barry! thank God… where's everyone else? How's Jenko and Torres? Are they okay? No one seems to want -"

"Torres is good, Sarge… Torres is good…" he replied; however the caesura between his words gave rise to my suspicions about Jenko's prognosis, and I feared the worst.

"Jenko?" I inquired again.

Barry removed his glance from mine, lowering his chin into his chest, and said, "Jenko… he's gone Sarge… he… he didn't make it. They worked on him… they worked on him for a bunch of hours – right downstairs in the emergency room."

"He was shot?" I asked; but, between you and I, the question was more rhetorical in nature, the answer having already been intimated via Barry's locution. I mean, it was also safe to assume that was the case, seeing as how I was strapped down to the damned hospital bed for that very reason.

"The fucking savage! he just let go a bunch of rounds when you two entered the room, Sarge. He didn't even say anything… he just kept shooting. You guys didn't have a chance; there was no warning. Me and Torres… we just dove onto the floor outside the threshold of the door and waited for a break in between the shooting. Once we realized that he might be reloading his ammo, we exhausted every round in our magazines on 'em, Sarge… we filled that mother fucker up. I kept depressing my trigger long after it was empty… my slide was locked to the rear and my muzzle was smoking like a chimney, but I kept on pulling at that trigger. I just couldn't believe what was happening… I *still* can't… I still can't." His voice trailed off at the end of his last few words, seemingly entering a deep rumination.

Having temporarily lost the ability to function on any level, I continued to sit there on that bed, saying nothing and barely able to move one single muscle… sort of like I was stuck in a coffin or some craziness with no ability to budge in any direction. I remained in that frozen state for some time, I'm not sure how long – it felt like an eternity - but after awhile, the social worker, who had never left the room, said, "Mr. Cardona, would you like some privacy now? I think, perhaps, you should get some rest. This is a lot to swallow."

"The boy." I said, still gazing straight ahead, addressing no one in particular.

"What's that? Mr. Cardona?" she asked.

At that point, I looked over to Barry and repeated, "The boy… the one who called 911… the one who had the gun held to his head? How is he? Did he make it?"

"The boy? yes, Sarge, the boy somehow managed to get away from his father sometime after we got into the apartment… that's why we didn't hear him crying or screaming after we entered. He got away and hid in his room; we found him in a closet underneath a pile of clothes. He's fine, Sarge. He's with his grandparents."

"Okay," I said, with an exhale of relief, "good… good." It gave me some bit of solace to know that the kid made it out okay – well, physically okay anyway. I'm sure he will, for the remainder of his days in this lifetime, be haunted by his father's handiwork; something I truly hope he works out in his ol' brain, lest we have another homicidal maniac on our hands in a few years, you know what I mean?

"Alright everyone, let's give him some rest." said the social worker, leading Barry and the Rookie out of the room, before turning to me and saying, "Mr. Cardona, you get some rest… I'm just a page away if you need me for anything."

I thanked her, and also apologized to Nurse Mia, who was plugging all of my severed lines and tubes back into the matrix. She, Nurse Mia, didn't get sore about it, though… she just quietly went about the whole thing, adding a sympathetic smile here and there. The lovely nurse was present, having returned to the room during the revelation of my late driver, and I'm sure, in her line of work, she had occasion to witness some pretty intense things over the course of time there at the hospital; therefore, I'm guessing she possessed an idea as to what was swirling around in my noodle that night, as her soothing ganders implied. You don't always require the spoken word to get a sentiment through; sometimes a caring glance or a slight touch to the shoulder can carry the weight of a mountain… or, more importantly, *lift* that burdensome weight from off of your shoulders.

XV

The rest of my time with the Department was pretty uneventful; just a bunch of physical and mental therapy sessions for the injuries I received when I was shot and all. The bastards actually put me back to full duty somewhere down the line – if you can believe that - although, I have to say, most of the time I sat behind that colossal wooden desk that one sees when one has occasion to visit a Police Station, writing in an even bigger log book (basically a journal on steroids) that Sergeants and Lieutenants write in all day long, consisting of every single thing that happens in the Precinct throughout the day, giving us all kinds of finger and wrist ailments by the time we're through. The worst thing about it all, I ended up getting chewed out a few times by my supervisors… all of whom had countless years less on the job than I had (mostly those confounded Impact kids that grew up and became Supervisors, just like my old Conditions partners – the ones I told you about awhile ago - predicted). A few of them, the higher muckamucks, having the unmitigated gall to expatiate about this or that if I happened to mess up on something. I guess in their warped minds, they felt as though they owned the right to lay down the law to a fella who got on the job way before the hairs on their unmentionables were fully bloomed. In my day, you left the dinosaurs alone; you didn't go calling them up to the office to lay it on thick with the poor old bastards when they happened to spill some proverbial milk. The thing of it is, they, the old timers, did their bid; they should be left completely alone and sheltered… cared for like the elderly at an old folks home, until their final days on this God forsaken Job are concluded; you need only change my soiled diaper and retrieve my pudding, that's it… no homilies necessary. That's just the way I see it… it was *the way*, once upon a time in a world long forgotten.

I ended my *illustrious* career hardly knowing anyone; all the faces around me practically being foreign. The thing of it is, no one stays around anymore long enough to be remembered. In my day, a guy hung around for awhile, you know? They really did. Guys would retire with twenty-five to thirty years on… sometimes even more! You literally had to tap a guy on his ol' shoulders and say, "Hey, pal, you just turned sixty-three years old, you sort of have to leave now." Nowadays, the Job has become a nursery school playground, filled with little tikes running around all over the damned place, emulating what they *believe* to be experienced Officers of a bygone era; except, they don't do a very good job of it at all. The truth is, there aren't any more of those old guys around to teach the youngsters of today, as I stated; so, now that I think about it, you sort of *can't* blame the kids. I mean, if you left a slew of ten year olds in a room with no supervision, do you honestly think you'd come back to anything less than all be damned? Doubtful.

Many more changes contaminated and polluted the job, all – in my humble and gratuitous opinion - having to do with the zeitgeist of everyone's societal attachment to recording devices and the wicked advent of social media. We live in an age where everything in the entire world is not only recorded, but also launched out into the cyber world where anyone living in a cave, in the remotest little corner of the world, with decent Wi-Fi, could receive such transmissions, allowing them to join in on the banter. This is a powerful enemy of the Police, let me tell you. As I have already beat into your head, in order for there to be law and order – to seriously root out the evil doers of the world, who, again, do not play by our utopian rules of justice - you must become the wolf.

There is no other way. It is naïve to believe that you can reason with the nefarious and evil-hearted monsters of this world; these individuals only use this display of weakness (it is a weakness in the scoundrel's eyes) to their advantage. I will never forget the words of a criminal, one of the ranking members of some local gang, that we happened to pick up for a slew of violent crimes, who very plainly said to me, "You know what, Officer? I'm gonna be out before the ink dries on your paperwork… and you wanna know why? Because this beautiful system – the American Justice System – makes it so fucking easy for me, that's why. And you wanna know another thing, Officer? there's more of a chance to get *you* off the street than it is me!" Here he provided the most sinister laugh I had ever heard, before continuing, "All I gotta do is make some kind of shit up about you… maybe you punched me in my stomach a few times, maybe you spit in my face… hell, maybe you even tried to fuck me in the back room of the Police Station! All I gotta do is say something like that, and boom! there goes your gun and shiny little badge. As for me? well, I'll be right back on the street by tomorrow, not missin' a beat." he concluded, sitting back with this repulsively sardonic grin that made my insides churn. I'll tell you what, though, his rant isn't too far off the beaten path; it certainly does happen, as you may have read about in your local newspaper or seen and heard on some television or radio program spewing hate about the Police. All I'm saying is, just think about what I have asseverated. Just *think* about it. Soon, I'll be long gone - hopefully by the time anyone gets their hands on my particular tale - so all of these problems won't really affect me too much… I just feel bad for the new jacks coming up on the Job. These kids have no chance; and, what's worse, they won't even know any better because there's no one left around to tell them any different. Sad.

The day finally came when I had to swing on over to Police Headquarters to make things official… the end of things. You can't just fly off into the wild blue yonder when your retirement day comes, like in one of those God-awful movies they make about the Department. They really are horrendous, some of them. I mean, just a bit of research would make all of the difference, you know what I mean? A bunch of these flicks don't even *try*; what with the substandard vernacular and insanely poor portrayal of what they *believe* the Police do all day long… it's as if they think all we do is chase bad guys in the police car at insane speeds down the highway; get into shoot-outs with bank robbers, bullets flying all over the place; diving and sliding over the hoods of cars. Sure, like, *that's* what we do all day long. Anyway, I stopped by the Command before going to HQ to pack a few things from my locker, seeing as how I wasn't going to be using it anymore; and plus, I'm certain, some insanely thoughtless fuck was most assuredly awaiting my departure to commandeer the damned thing as a *tertiary* coffer, knowing full well that some poor sap didn't even possess *one*, having to share a half-locker with a buddy. Selfish pricks, I swear.

I reached into all of the pockets of my uniform pants, shirts, and jacket, to make sure there weren't any valuables or perhaps a few bucks laying dormant therein, which was sort of a habit I developed growing up with my dad, who always struck gold when doing my laundry, taking what treasures I forsook, thereafter claiming the ancient and most sacred law of *finders, keepers* (that guy, my Pop, was always a helluva hustler, that's for darn certain); what I found inside of my duty jacket's inner pocket, to my pleasant surprise, was a note written by good ol' Brentwood that I had failed to notice all the years since his passing the thing down to me. I have to admit, my heart raced just a tad upon espying the correspondence, nearly tearing the decades old letter into pieces trying to unfold it. The contents of the epistle are as follows:

Hey kiddo, your old pal Brentwood here. Just want to let you know that it was a pleasure working together with you for the short time that we did, and that I think you're a good egg. Say, I hope there are no hard feelings about the way that things started out. I mean, you were rookie scum, what in the hell was I supposed to do, treat you like a goddamn king or something? Anyway, before I hot tail it out of this Goddamn city, I just want to leave you with a few of pieces of advice, if that's okay with you... always trust your gut, if it stinks like rotten fish, it's probably rotten fish. Also, always have your partner's back. I mean that literally and figuratively. Like, always watch over each other at a scene, but also – maybe just as important – don't let him fry on a hot pan alone, you know? Don't let the cheese eaters divide and conquer the two of you. And lastly, don't give up. There'll be days when you think maybe you can't handle it, like the weight of the job is too much for you to deal with, like maybe you want to say fuck it and "end it all." Well, don't. You keep fighting, kid! Don't let them defeat you, don't let them win. Those fuckers would love nothing more than to not have to pay out a damned pension, you know what I'm saying? Alright, kiddo, it's time for me to skedaddle, I'm off to greener pastures. Who knows, maybe we'll see each other some day... on the other side of the rainbow! Until then, so long, and stay safe.

Your friend, NTB

***

As I signed my name on the dotted line of my retirement paperwork at Police Headquarters, I overheard some of the big wigs passing by, going on about the spike in crime and what they were planning on doing about it all. I thought to myself, 'These are not the problems of mine any longer. Put me out to pasture and let me graze under the setting sun!' before grabbing my complimentary coffee mug with the Department's logo plastered upon it (a parting gift for all my blood, sweat, and tears), afterwards heading out of the building. As I walked down the busied street, people hustling and bustling, going about their daily grind, I turned around to take one last look at the Headquarters building; which, for some strange reason, hadn't the colossally omnipotent impression as it once did. There was within me, I have to confess, a doting feeling… a sort of nostalgic sentiment… for the damned place. I guess when you do something for such an extended period of time – ions it seemed – you're going to get a little misty-eyed when it's all said and done… there's pretty much no avoiding that. A mind's natural inclination (for most of us) is to cling to what we know… creatures of habit and all… so it stands to reason that a stupid tear would cascade down my miserable face before turning back around and heading home.

***

After the twenty-one hour and one minute drive - a good one thousand four hundred and thirty miles – we finally reached the Overseas Highway, the conduit connecting Miami to the magical Florida Keys, which would, eventually, deliver us to our final destination… Key West. The sight was right out of a spectacular painting: the pristine, clear waters overlapping the rich lands of the

Lower Keys, inundated with beautiful palm trees; the pale blue, cloudless sky overhead… one felt as though they were traveling through the heavenly Caribbean islands. With the windows rolled down, the essence of this feeling could be drawn in and savored, sort of like bringing a tropical libation to your nose and inhaling the wonderfully aromatic decoction before allowing the velvety liquid to drizzle onto the tongue.

"Man, Jimmy! this is really on-time… just gorgeous." my father said, from the passenger side, looking out onto the vastness of the waters in sheer awe.

"It *is* beautiful, Pop. They say this is one of the longest bridges ever to be built. It spans all of the Keys right up to Key West. It'll take us a little over an hour to travel this road; so if you want, we can stop off at Key Largo or some place and grab a snack… maybe some fresh fish tacos and a pina colada?"

"Lord, yes… a pina colada sounds lovely right about now… extra rum in mine, please!" commented Gracie, catapulting from her seat in the rear, her face now in betwixt my father and I.

"Yeah, that sounds real good, Jimmy… let's do that." he began, never taking his eyes off the majestic sea. "I want you to know something, my son. I know I gave you a hard time about the *Po*lice thing… I know I gave you a lot of shit about that. I just wanted you to know… well… that I'm proud of you and everything you've accomplished. You did a great thing and I'm… like I said, I'm just real proud. That's all."

I took a quick peek at him (quick on account of the fact that I was driving and kind of didn't want to send us plummeting into the

Straits of Florida and all) and could have sworn he was shedding a tear or two; although I couldn't be entirely certain because he was sort of still looking out of his window. I didn't ask him about it or even let on that I suspected he may have been; instead, I just reached out and placed my hand on his shoulder, gave a little squeeze, and replied, "Thanks, Pop… that means a lot."

After a brief moment of silence, Gracie said, "Hey, you know whose house still stands over in Key West… Ernest Hemingway! We should go over and check it out at some point. You still like him, don't you? Hemingway? You used to love reading all of his books when you were taking those literature classes in college… you could pick it up again, reading his stuff, now that you're retired."

"Hemingway? yeah he's good." I replied. "I *did* enjoy reading his stuff. I don't think I'll be messing with that kind of thing for awhile, though. I mean, to tell you the truth, at this point, the only thing that I'm interested in is reality, you know? After twenty long and calamitous years of the bizarre and unreal, I think I've had my fill of the world of make-believe."

"It is a far, far better thing that I do, than I have ever done; it is a far, far better rest that I go to than I have ever known."

- A Tale of Two Cities, Charles Dickens

End

A COLLECTION OF VIGNETTES

Vignette I

Obsessions and Crossroads

Jasper sat up restlessly in his bed - the way one does when one is riddled with haunting memories of liable deeds, or the inquietude of events to come - thoughts of *her* running rampant through his head, like a stock car rounding the Indy Race Track at two hundred miles per hour – the operator of such a rocket on wheels in a desperate tantivy towards the finish line, the incessancy of the introspection being too much for his weakened constitution to bear, leaving him to feel as though the prospect of ever consuming victuals - or ever having the ability to enter into rapid eye movement sleep, to dream as a child of innocence… dreams of confectionaries and gimcracks under a Christmas Tree – was an entirely implausible and quixotic notion. The translucency of her brown, almond shaped eyes were presently affixed - like a bottle of libation to a merchant marine who has recently reached his port after a long voyage - to his brain, burned into the retina of his innermost self, although she was a continent away… they bedeviled him the way in which a widow woefully and heart wrenchingly becomes beleaguered by her dearly departed, leaving her to manage the pilgrimage of life remaining – the twists and turns of every lonely path now before her – destitute and forsaken. He closed his light brown eyes to allow hers to appear more clearly in his mind… the memory of them implanted permanently upon his heart, causing said vital organ to skip a proverbial beat; in turn, precipitating the entirety of his body to feel as though it could no longer perform any and all necessary functions, culminating to an imminent shut down of epic proportions… the end of all things, as it were. The last time he had actually seen her… had actually kissed her silken cheek with his lips, leaving on them the flavor of cotton candy, fresh from a carnival… had placed one hand on the small of her back and the other hand across her shoulder blades, creating an electric current which surged throughout his entire body… had heard the sound of her voice, mesmerizing and heavenly, her French accent undulating through his ears like a celestial song written for the cherubs who fly as high as the whitest, puffiest clouds that hover over the Earth on the warmest of spring days, gazed upon by lovers as they lay side by side upon the verdant grasses of an open field, surrounded by sunflowers at full bloom… had studied, up close, her Mona Lisa-type smile, just the slightest simper (a seemingly inconspicuous venereal bidding) that sent his insides into summersaults… the last time indulging in any of it was about six months, or so, ago… much, too much, time elapsed for him to endure such suffering. He could still remember that day, like a permanent tattoo etched not into his epidermis, but into the young man's amygdala, hippocampus, and the cerebellum equally. The foreboding fear of possibly never beholding her beauty again sent his muscles into atrophy; unable to move – or breathe – or think – or live. His vivid recollection of the way she smelled… such a clean and natural scent, as if she spent the entirety of her day wading in lavender, vanilla, and eucalyptus… served as a healing elixir for his soul; no medicine-man could ever concoct a more effective love potion. He wished that he possessed something, anything, of hers to bring to his proboscis, to inhale her quintessence into his lungs, to attain the high that one might receive when intaking the pleasantly euphoric fumes of sage or charas; colors would be brighter, he would laugh again, time would mean nothing… he could live on her essence and her essence alone, like two celestial beings traversing the infinite cosmos together as one form of interminable energy.

Ms. Juteuse Capucine made her living as a singer of jazz, an internationally renowned creator of music who enjoyed much success all around the globe that we call the planet Earth, what with successfully performing in Europe as well as in all of the major cities in the United States of America. She was an internet sensation, having basically developed a following that, if commanded, could very well invade a small country, or whatever else she enjoined, once her sect was sent reeling into a somnambulistic state from her bewitching melodies. Initially, before their first *close encounter of the third kind* – because she was, essentially, from some other world - Jasper, quite honestly, was merely one of these aforementioned disciples, one of Juteuse's followers; that is, until his manuscript, a novel written by he about a series of failed relationships and what one should never, ever, do when interested in having affairs with the opposite sex, was published, making him somewhat of a local celebrity in his own right; although, in all reality, it paled in comparison to the éclat currently being enjoyed by the mademoiselle with whom he held a *beguin serieux*. That being said, however, she was, in fact, extremely enamored with his work, and was always intrigued by his conversation; albeit, of the texting variety… they had not, at the onset, actually had a verbal conversation; instead, their 'talks' were limited to whatever social media outlets, in which they both subscribed, existed… beginning at first with depressing the *'like'* or *'thumbs up'* option, slowly progressing into selecting emojis of affection, then leaving comments (initially, innocent and extremely general little quips regarding their respective posts); until, finally, Jasper's confidence allowed him to begin personal dialogue, to which she responded, much to his stupefaction and great pleasure, favorably.

***

The preamble, the preface, to the aforementioned ramblings in regards to the inaugural getting together, if you will, lead to the last time she stood before him… the moment in which she smiled her smile, rivaling that of Theo Van Wijngaarden's, 'Smiling Girl,' which beamed at him like the Sun's rays on a clear spring day at Battery Park, within the vicinity of Battery Place on the north side, State Street to the east, and the Hudson River to the west, flaunting a clear view of the majestic Statue of Liberty in all its glory, where it was decided that they meet briefly (the brevity not being his choice; for, if left to him, he'd have spent the entirety of his day at her side). He received a text message while working on the manuscript for his next book in his studio apartment, at Mulberry and Grand Streets, wherein he domiciled; the aforementioned manuscript, ironically, being a story about an unattainable female and the man who obsessed over her. Upon hearing the alert from his cell phone, he half glanced over at the device to espy the name of the caller. When he realized it was his beloved Juteuse, the girl in which his soul belonged, he sprang up from his wooden writing table, practically knocking it over, sending some of the pens, and other random stationary articles, spilling all about the floor. She, as per the text message, suggested that they meet at the park within the next ten minutes, if that – incidentally - weren't a problem for him, she inquired; to which he impulsively replied, "Of course! Please tell me where in the park you would care to meet! give me a location… what street?" This message to her taking several attempts to complete, as his fingers competed with the throbbing of his wildly pulsating heartbeat, resulting in a jumble of incoherent words being transcribed onto the screen, before finally – after a long, deep, breath – he was, in the fullness of time, able to send. As he awaited her response, he frantically grabbed anything he could find to accouter himself; donning a pair of blue, 'skinny' GAP jeans; a white, 'fitted,' American Eagle T-shirt – both of which, incidentally, accentuated his incredibly toned physique – that which somewhat, according to himself alone, resembled the Statue of David; and, a pair of black Doc Martins, faded and scuffed, with the classic yellow stitching above the soul of the shoes. Finally, about three minutes later (although, in his mind, days had elapsed), she responded, "State Street and Pearl Street… I'm out for a nice walk along the park... is that a good location? Can you make it?"

"Can I make it?!" he lamented to himself, as if to indicate, 'Are you *kidding*?' before actually typing, "Yes, of course! I'm on my way… I'll be there in ten minutes," looking at his chronometer and realizing that this was practically impossible, as it was nearly five in the afternoon; therefore, he would be competing with the confoundedly chaotic malady of rush hour traffic.

Subsequent to essentially flying down five flights of stairs, incidentally skipping three to four steps at once, racing across the street to his grey Honda Accord, zipping manically through lane after lane at exorbitant rates of speed in the fashion of the late Dale Earnhardt, unceremoniously and frantically cutting off his fellow drivers like a man gone mad, running a red light here and there, he received another text from her, "I'm walking into the park to get a better look at the Statue of Liberty, is that ok?"

He glanced at the clock on the dashboard of the car and realized that twelve minutes had elapsed since initially agreeing to meet her, thereby putting him two minutes *in the red*, as it were. With his left hand on the steering wheel, he grabbed the phone with his right and responded, "Yes! that's fine… I'm almost there! See you soon!" followed by a gratuitous smiley face and pink double heart emoji; afterwards, tossing the phone back onto the passenger side seat, pressing down upon the accelerator with his right foot, nearly hitting an elderly man who, incidentally, in a trice, found a youthful spring in his step - a step that he conjectured was long since surrendered to his twilight years - having to now broad-jump out of the way of the moving vehicle recklessly operated by our dear protagonist. Finally, after a few additional near brushes with death, Jasper arrived at his destination, in front of the iconic landmark that Juteuse's fellow countryman, one Frederic Augusta Bartholdi, so graciously created and gifted to a young United States of America some one hundred and forty five years ago. He jumped out of his vehicle… legal parking spot be damned… and scampered through the park, riffling through the crowd like a Bedlamite, attempting to espy her through the endless masses of human beings going to and fro in every direction imaginable.

"Hello! Juteuse! hello!" Jasper said, frantically waving his hands in the air, as he caught sight of the five foot three frame making her way toward him. As she drew closer, he could see that her brown, wavy hair was brushed back into a ponytail; she was wearing a small, black, jean jacket, wrapped around a short, yellow, v-neck t-shirt that was cut off just below the bottom of her modestly sized breasts, exposing her belly button piercing; a red fanny pack that she sported across her chest; tiny blue jean shorts, whose hemline nearly allowed for the revealing of her especially toned nates; and, open toe sandals, exhibiting her unpainted, but well manicured, toes. His heart nearly stopped at the sight of what he thought to be the singularly most beautiful thing that his eyes had ever gazed upon.

Juteuse returned the wave to Jasper… slightly less maniacal, but no less meaningful, along with an infectious smile that spread across her angelic face. She did have somewhat of an intrigue for the young man of thirty-something. Having published his aforesaid novel with successful results was something that gave rise to her interest in him, she possessing a love and passion for the literary arts, wanting one day to scribe a chronicle of her own. "Hello, hello! Jasper!" She replied, still waving and flashing her gleeful countenance.

He rushed toward Juteuse to meet her halfway, immediately taking her into his arms for an embrace along, simultaneously, with a kiss to her cheek, one in which she happily returned; however, again, not one which was given with quite as much vigor as the infatuated young man's. "How are you? How is your day? Are you enjoying the city? How much longer are you staying? Will you be returning to France very soon?" Jasper asked the barrage of questions in between the thumps of his heart; which was, incidentally, beating at such burgeoning rates as to activate his Apple Watch, now frantically buzzing around his wrist, warning its owner of an impending case of cardiac arrest.

"Oh, my! So many questions!" she replied with a slight chuckle, a laugh which was not in any way meant to slight her interlocutor, being done with such graceful, delicate femininity – akin to a Lady in a king's court - that he, too, giggled before looking away as she began her response to his inquiries. "I'm very well and my day is going wonderfully; yes, the city is very lovely! It's so beautiful… so very much to do. I think I will not be returning to

France just yet, as I have some… how do you say? gigs?… lined up in Los Angeles in the coming week; so, I will be postponing my flight back home… such a headache *that* will be, I have to say!"

Jasper - listening as intently as one would when one is being addressed by that of an authoritarian professor, with the prospect of a pop quiz at the end of the lecture - received the last portion of her dialogue with some trepidation; he had hoped she would be staying in New York a bit longer, perchance obtain an auspicious opportunity to sit down to a quiet lunch and drink with her. He kept his disappointment within himself, not desiring to effuse even the slightest vibes of repelling, negative, energy towards her work, something he knew was extremely important to the young singer. Instead, he replied, with feigned excitement, "Los Angeles! that is so exciting! I bet you can't wait to get out there… I hear the weather is amazing and the people are so friendly and laid back."

"Yes, I've been there, for my shows, so many times and I always love it. I mean, I love New York; but it's such a different atmosphere… as you say, it is very laid back. Here, it is always rush, rush, rush; but there," she paused to emit a sigh of relief, "it is more of a… '*I will get to that when I can!*'… sort of mentality. I must say, it is very relaxing." she concluded with another giggle.

"Ah! Yes, I have heard. I've yet to experience it for myself, as I have only gone west as far as Louisiana… New Orleans."

"Ah! Marti Gras. I know this place! It was once a French colony, no?" she commented, with an air of pride gleaming across her countenance, melting Justin's heart with her ingenuous innocence.

"Yes, Marti Gras… and that's right, Louisiana was,

indeed, French territory before the Louisiana Purchase… *tres bien, madamoiselle!*" the smitten young man responded. "Well, you will surely be missed, I must admit.; and, I'm certain that you will *kill it* out there. I'm sure they absolutely adore you and your music… make sure to send me pictures!"

"Of course! Of course! I want to thank you so much for giving me my book… your book. It's so wonderful. I think it's so amazing that you wrote a book… an author! my goodness! It's actually something that I would love to do one day, to be able to write a book. I have so many thoughts in my head, so many things that I've experienced… I would love nothing more than to be able to put them all on paper; but, where to begin? That's the problem. I'm sure you know exactly what I mean. Was it difficult? How did you develop your characters? Do you write it all down somewhere? like an outline?" Juteuse was genuinely interested in Jasper's work, probably as interested as *he* was in *her* – amongst other feelings; however, neither of the two possessed the courage to admit such a thing to one another.

He fought back the excitement of her interest in his writing; although, deep within his chest, the sensation equivalent to that of a fantastical orgasm engulfed him. "Half of the time I don't know what's going to fly out of my character's mouths. They sort of have a mind of their own, you know? It's like they're really alive… like they're real people. Honestly, I'm just sort of a schizophrenic with an outlet… the characters are all in my head, always talking or doing something… I just write it all down and then, before I know it, the book is done! Does that sound crazy? I'm sure I sound like a raving lunatic." Jasper replied, his countenance beginning to blush.

"No, no, no, not at all… not in the least!" she denounced, reaching out to touch Jasper's arm, the action, incidentally, sending waves of inexplicable energy throughout his entire body, before continuing, "I find that so fascinating. I really do. I can't even imagine being able to sit down and create such a thing. It's honestly so very amazing. Are you working on anything now? on a new project?"

"Oh," he hesitated, knowing full well that he could not tell her the truth; he couldn't possibly tell her that he was, in fact, working on another book – a love story of sorts – about her… about a woman that he desperately wanted, but knew he could not have. "I'm working on a few things… nothing crazy, just a few things. I'm kind of piecing it all together, you know what I mean? It's all in shambles right now… like a big jigsaw puzzle, you know?" He stammered over his words, wishing he could tell her how he truly felt, but it was impossible; their worlds were light years apart. The very fact that he was standing before her had now become one of the newest wonders of the world; therefore, to imagine anything else… anything more… was surely a most sinful act of rapacity, and very much a delusion of grandeur.

"I see. Well, whatever it is, I'm sure it will be a success… you are a wonderful writer. So, what will you do today? with the rest of your day? Will you work on your novel?"

What he wanted to say… what he desperately *wished* he could say… was how much he'd love to have spent the rest of his day with her; perhaps some lunch, followed by a long walk in Central Park? And this was only a hard second to what he *actually* was thinking; that is to say, what he *truly* wanted was to express how he'd love to have spent the rest of his life with the girl whose face was the alpha and omega of his day. He stared deeply into her dark brown eyes for a brief moment, hoping that they'd confess his desires; maybe she would receive the message on some type of subliminal, sixth sense, sort of level. She, regrettably for him, did not; consequently, he dryly replied, "Well, I suppose I'll go home and figure something out. I don't know… yeah, maybe I'll do some writing, I'm not sure. That kind of thing just sort of comes to you at all crazy hours; I can't really control it, you know what I mean? I can't just sit there and write on command, is what I'm saying. What about you? Got a hot date or anything?" He was half sorry he had uttered the last part of his locution, fearing that the worst-case-scenario answer would be something he absolutely had no desire, or ability, to receive.

"Me? Oh, nothing special. I've actually got dinner plans with some friends at a wonderful little place called… how is it? RH Rooftop Restaurant? I've been working so hard… all the time working, working, working; I never take time to reset. This is something I plan to change about myself. I'm always afraid that if I don't work, I'll become irrelevant, like I won't matter anymore… and this is very bad. I mean, it's okay to step back and recharge, you know what I mean? It's okay… like, everything will be okay. I know this is easier said than done… this is why I must practice. Like my yoga… I love my yoga because I can really let go…let go of everything… mind, body, and spirit." she concluded, removing her jean jacket, as the sun poked its searing rays over one of the buildings, beating directly onto her face, transforming the color of her eyes into a kind of translucent shade of caramel; an effect, incidentally, that utterly made his heart leap into his throat.

As she spoke, he could hear her, he understood and processed

every word; but, his eyes couldn't help but wander about her body…
all of it… becoming bewitched with her aura, her prepossessing
quiddity, which gave off a glow that, had anyone in this world – or
any other world for that matter – gazed upon her, they would have
no reservations in claiming they had espied something sent from the
heavenly clouds above. As he did so, as these thoughts traversed
through his mind, a smile, unbeknownst to him, spread across his
countenance; he enjoyed Juteuse from head to toe, especially the
quirky things encompassing her… things such as the black, hooped,
nose ring that wrapped around her left nostril, as well as her body ink
of an intricate design that ran sporadically down her left arm, which
was now visible upon disrobing from her jacket. Jasper, still deep
in contemplation, wondered if there were more tattoos in places he
could not see… places he *longed* to see. "Yes, most definitely!" he
uttered, after some hesitation, finally snapping out of his reverie, not
realizing that his focus had become preoccupied with the soaking
in of her body, devouring every bit of her like a refreshing libation.
"I completely understand. It's sort of the same with my writing…
it pretty much takes me to a place far away from reality, like some
kind of a high; it makes me feel lighter, somehow… like I can float
or something crazy like that. The problem is, if I don't write, I feel
as though I've failed myself somehow, like you say, I no longer feel
relevant… like, I no longer matter; so, I suppose it's a kind of double
edged sword, as they say. I mean, I'm sure it's a thousand times
more intense with what *you* do… the music industry is certainly a
way more fast paced thing… I'm sure. Well, listen, I don't want to
keep you any longer… what I mean is, I'm sure you have a lot to
do… to prepare for your plans tonight."

"Yes." Juteuse looked into his eyes, as if to urge him to

impose himself. She, deep down, wished for him to be more aggressive; it was not her way to be so forward as to ask a man to join her for dinner plans – especially coming from a country wherein, compared with that of their more dynamically assertive American counterparts, women did not display such aggressive freedom of expression; however, if Jasper were to suggest that he attend, she would gladly have accepted. "I suppose." She concluded, with much despondency, not receiving the response that she had hoped.

He leaned towards her for a hug, wrapping his arms around her waste as tightly as one could without dislocating a rib bone, she returning the embrace, both closing their eyes and wishing for more; however, neither pursuing their inner desire. "Well, it was so… it was lovely to see you." he said, slightly leaning back from the hug, but continuing to grasp onto her shoulders, not willing to completely disjoin from her body. "Maybe when you get back from L.A., perhaps maybe we could have lunch or something? That is, if you're not terribly busy."

"Yes, that would be nice… I'd like that."

Jasper watched as she began to walk back in the direction from whence she came, slowly being swallowed by the swarm of people going in every which direction in the park, regretting, with every parting step that she took, that he had not told her precisely how he felt. This, herein, concludes the lasting memory ingrained into his mind and heart; the time when he last beheld his *plus belle fille du monde* before him. I kindly thank you for tolerating the nostalgic flashback, as I understand them to be a tedious burden upon an audience wanting only for the chronicler to get on with the narrative.

Later that night, during the proverbial witching hours, Jasper sat staring through his laptop monitor, with a blank look upon his countenance, not having the wherewithal to focus on anything but the woman who occupied every portion of his brain. Unable to sleep, he decided to do a bit of scribing; however, the faculty to perform such an action was rendered somewhat inert… all he could ponder were incessant and haunting images of his sweet, French peony. He began perusing his social media, scrolling through endless memes posted by scorned inamoratas whose boyfriends had apparently reached deep into their chests and destroyed their souls, leaving them no choice but to log on to their Facebook and Instagram accounts, launching a barrage of virtual anguish… messages such as, 'People fuck with your feelings until you have no more feelings;' 'May you be brave enough to choose yourself even when he doesn't;' 'Three lies I'm tired of hearing: I promise, I love you, I'm sorry;' &c., until he stumbled across something posted by Juteuse Capucine; it was a promotion for an event in which she would be performing in Brooklyn, New York. She was to appear at a nightclub called 'the Blue Room' - a trendy, but intimate, little establishment that featured artists of the jazz variety - that was to take place in a few days. His heart skipped a million beats, as he could hardly contain his emotions, involuntarily standing up from his writing table having absolutely no purpose in doing so. Instantly realizing this fact, he sat back down onto his chair, staring intently and pensively at the post, clicking – impulsively – the 'message' icon with intentions of sending to her a communique, watching as the cursor blinked at him mockingly upon the screen, as if to say, 'What now… what now… what now…'

The promotional post included some short videos in which one could see her at work, as it were, creating the most awe inspiring music that could ever enter one's external auditory canal, captivating one's most inner workings and such. In one of the videos, she could be seen, in all of her splendor, outdoors in front of a pond, nestled under and in between what looked like a dome made of trees with lush, green leaves sprouting from its branches, surrounded by wild flowers of the most vibrant yellows, pinks, oranges, and purples. In the center of it all was Juteuse, the conductor of the melodic and seductive music which emanated from the speakers; instantaneously diving deep into Jasper's spiritual essence… sending him to a place where he wished to remain forever and a day, if such a thing were a possibility. Jasper watched her sway back and forth to the music, as a patient would a hand held time piece in which a hypnotist rocks before their eyes, in a trance-like mental state. Her brown hair - loose, wavy, parted to the side and barely touching her shoulders - could be espied being gently kissed by the rays of sun that peeked through the trees, with one of the wild flowers, yellow and white in color, attached toward the helix of her ear. Juteuse's exotic features, the high cheek bones and sultry eyes, were charmingly accentuated by the natural beauty that surrounded her; she wore a black bikini top that covered her firm breasts, exposing her tight core; blue jean shorts that lovingly caressed her posterior and upper thighs; around her neck hung a gold, looped chain; and, around her arm, she wore a bracelet of some kind that wrapped around her forearm like a miniature snake. Nothing in this world, nothing in which he had ever bore witness, was as captivating as this picture of perfection; his heart continued to race, wishing, with everything making up his being, that she were his to do with as he pleased. Jasper realized, at this very moment in time, the sensation in his chest was more than love… it was an obsession.

An epiphany struck, at that precise moment, like lightning during a tempestuous storm… there was no choice in the matter; he would make an appearance at this 'Blue Room' and, once and for all, profess his undying love for the harbinger of nirvana that enchanted his stolen, aching, heart. He could no longer contain the uncontrollable energy that surged inside of his enflamed core, making him feel as though he could spontaneously combust at any moment; therefore, the matter was settled. Just then, his cell phone rang; 'Careless Whisper,' the epic 1980s tune by George Michael, being the ring tone, alerting him to the fact that it was his brother, Ian, on the other end of the line… this ringtone being chosen in jest as a retaliatory act for his sibling assigning the song, 'Push it,' by Salt N Peppa, accompanied by a picture of Jasper dressed in drag (a Halloween costume worn at a recent masquerade soirée) plastered upon the screen. He answered the call, "Hey little bro, what's happening?"

"Yo, yo, yo! How goes it? Whatcha doin'? playin' with your pee-pee?" This inquiry sending Ian into an uncontrollable fit of an unadulterated and convulsive guffawing at his own *buffola*, he being the greatest fan of his own humor.

"Yeah, that's what I do all night long. I just wreak havoc on my dick and wait for your phone call. Life stands still in between our conversations, didn't you know that?" Jasper responded, rolling his eyes, half insulted at this perverted, but – on any other given day – alarmingly accurate inquest.

"Yes!" Ian said, in between another boutade of laughter. "I

certainly *did* know that… remember, we grew up together; so, I know all of your dirty little secrets.”

“How can I forget? You remind of it at every possible opportunity. What are you doing up so late? Isn’t it passed your bedtime?” Jasper teased.

“It is *absolutely* passed my bedtime; but, I can’t sleep. I could ask you the same question, though; I expected to get your voicemail… what are you doing up? obsessing about Juteuse Capucine?” Ian asked with a sardonic giggle.

Jasper half looked over his shoulders before answering, “How in the hell did you know that? Are there spy cameras set up in my apartment?” His countenance turning crimson at essentially being caught red-handed, the winsome image of the subject at hand encompassing the entirety of the computer monitor, as the video of her performance continued to play on.

“Yes! in every room! I can even see the color of your panties!” He laughed once more before continuing. “I hear her music clearly playing in the background, you stalker. What are you doing? gazing in ecstasy at her pictures in your photo album to the music? you psychopath?”

“As a matter of fact, for your information, I’m not *gazing* at my photo album. I’m looking at a promotional video she just put out on social media; she’s gonna be in New York City in a few days… at a place called ‘The Blue Room,’ in Brooklyn.

“Oh, wow, are you gonna go see her?”

"I don't know… I haven't decided."

"What? What kind of stalker *are* you? Of course you *have* to go! What do you mean *you don't know*?! Stalkers stalk, you crazy boy! As a matter of fact, not only do you absolutely have to make an appearance, you also have to somehow manage to show up at the airport as she deplanes. Like, you have to stand there at the gate with a sign that says her name… and you have to *bedazzle* it with glitter and neon ink! That's what you have to do. That's *exactly* what you have to do."

"You're ridiculous, you really are. I think *you* are the *real* psychopath, you just live vicariously through me; but the psychotic thoughts are there, baby brother, they really are. Anyway, I don't know… I mean, I'm sure she doesn't want to see my face at her event. I'm sure there are a thousand and three other faces she'd rather see than mine. This girl has her pick of the litter… all over the world. Have you *seen* some of these European guys? They're fucking flawless… straight out of a Vogue magazine, perfect hair, black suits and ties, and those goddamn banana hammock speedos at the beach… I can't compete with that."

"That's true… and there *you* are, sitting around in your *wife beater* T-shirt, the one with extra virgin olive oil and Cheetos stains, with all the holes… and three day old *scumdies* with pee and shitty skid-marks on 'em. I get it… I'd be apprehensive, too; but, bro, you can't skip this thing… I mean, when's the next time you'll be able to stand in front of her again? Probably never… or a damn long time from now, that's for sure." Ian implored.

Jasper mulled over the latter portion of his brother's words for a moment, ignoring his gibing, focusing on the more salient point of possibly never having another opportunity to meet with Juteuse, before responding, "Maybe you're right… I don't know… maybe."

"There is no maybe… there is only '*do*.'" Ian said, providing his best *Mr. Miyagi* impression – the old sensei from the 1980s movie, *Karate Kid.*

Jasper chuckled at the reference, as Ian had a certain adroitness for mimicking movie stars, before replying, "Listen, I'm gonna get some sleep… all this excitement has my body ready to go into shut down mode."

"Yeah, get some rest… I'm about to hit the hay myself." Replied Ian. "And don't think about that too much; it's an easy decision… you have to go… there's no choice in the matter. Once in a lifetime kind of thing going on here. You hear me? Are you listening to me? Are you?"

"Alright, alright, little brother… good night, rest well." Jasper exclaimed before ending the call. He continued to stare into the monitor for a bit longer before finally heading to bed, still not certain as to what conclusion in which he would come. On the one hand, there was this feeling… a feeling comparable to that of impending doom, as a death-row inmate awaits the pull of the lever, or being swallowed up by the ocean, his lungs brimming with water, no longer able to complete their task of intaking oxygen… it was as if he were losing control of every single emotion that a human being possessed, the only cure for this uncontrollable affliction being the sight and sound of Juteuse, the angel that rescued his spirit from this unrelenting torment; therefore, it stood to reason that he must follow the counsel of his sibling. On the other hand, he realized that – apart from what this chronicler has exposed of our protagonist, cognizing, incidentally, that he was not *actually* out of touch with reality – this notion of the two being an item, as it were, was a far fetched, absolutely unrealistic, fantasy… a figment of his imagination; ergo, he could not very well attempt a tryst of any kind. Such an assignation would surely prove to be an error of sound judgment; but, if one were playing the tantalizing game of *devil's advocate*, one could make the argument that some of the worst mistakes in human history were, in the end, the catalysts of the best and most significant happenings on the face of the Earth. These opposing thoughts wrestled around in his mind like two Roman gladiators whose only impetus was ending the life of their co-combatant.

Her music continued to undulate from the speaker that rested on a night table at his bedside, the room being lit by the low lighted glow of a salt rock that also sat by his bed, something that provided to him an inner warmth and comfort, very much like a child's nightlight, warding off evil beings such as thc boogie man and other creatures from the worst parts of a youngster's imagination. He lay there, attempting, quite fruitlessly, to quiet his racing heart, wishing to have never met her, wishing never to have looked into those damning eyes… those coffee colored windows to her soul; desiderating to never have smelled the tincture of her perfume, that lethal, noxious, fume having the ability to alter one's sanity, like the fatally potent kiss of Hawthorne's '*Rappaccini's Daugher*;' craving never to have allowed the cosmic energy of their two spirits to intertwine and knot like a confounded over-tied shoelace, when placing his hands upon her during their embrace. No… wait… on second thought, he didn't regret one thing about any of it; he cherished it, every moment. To consider anything else would be a bold faced lie; and, with no one else in the room, the person whom he would be deceiving was himself, so why fight the truth? He gave in… he surrendered to his reality and closed his eyes, concentrating on his breathing to quell the somersaults in his core – breathe in, hold, breathe out – until his mind fell numb, entering into a deep, meditatively induced sleep.

The dreams, hauntingly vivid in every way – every taste, sound, feeling – tormented him throughout his sleep; some about *her*, some not. The ones that included Juteuse were of the singularly agonizing sort, manifesting itself in the form of her engaging in the most intimate of activities… sexually deviant activities… with *other* men, whilst she and her apparent lover pointed and laughed at Jasper, he standing before them completely naked (minus the existence of his manhood). He tried desperately to run far away from the two – inamorato and inamorata - but, to no avail; he could neither move nor speak, but only stand there and absorb the incessantly painful and brutally mocking berating of him. From this nightmare he awoke in a proverbial pool of sweat, his heart beating against his chest like a war drum, his entire body trembling as if stranded in the middle of the Arctic with no tarpaulin, no form of covering, to warm his frigid carcass-like body. He sat up in the bed, looking around the darkened room – with only the glow from the aforementioned salt rock providing illumination - not exactly certain where he was at first glance. It was about five in the morning and the Sun had yet to make its appearance, Jasper having only been asleep for a grand sum of three hours. In spite of this fact, he could no longer remain in the bed; so, peeling himself from the comfort of the sheets, stumbling like a drunken wino whose entire night consisted of binging on liquefied companionship, he sauntered to the bathroom to brush his teeth and wash his haggardly face.

As he conducted his toilet, staring at himself in the mirror, his mouth filled with frothy suds from the toothpaste, he questioned his life, wondering as to the purpose of his existence. Jasper often deliberated about this, never truly understanding the significance of his being a member of the human race, always feeling a kind of disconnection from every single person he had ever known in his entire life. This being a sentiment that always possessed his thoughts, commencing as early as his ability to have conscious, introspective cogitation; his childhood invariably riddled with doubt and lack of confidence in himself. The fact of the matter is that Jasper Loring, throughout his boyhood and adolescence, was the smallest of the children within his age group; and, in turn, felt as though he were the least capable of any task being performed by his peers… the former being an indisputable fact, the latter being a figment of his overactive imagination. Growing up, he had not the fortune of owning wardrobes of the latest fashion or the gaming systems in which the other adolescents of his zeitgeist possessed; therefore, as an effect to this cause, his self-esteem was embedded somewhere deep in the sub-basement of his Qi… a feeling that traversed within his nucleus for all the days leading up to this very moment, as the aforementioned toothpaste residue continued to ejaculate out of his mouth, down his chin, and into the sink.

He washed his mouth of the forsaken foam and headed to the kitchen for some coffee, Bustello brand, which just so happened to be his absolute favorite, the simple reasoning being that it made him feel, immediately upon consumption, as though he'd been electrocuted by a source of immeasurable energy. He decided he'd take his java to Central Park and watch the sunrise; something that he did quite often to calm his beleaguered quintessence… it helped him to sort out all of the random, messy, thoughts running amok inside of his brain. As he walked along the trails of the park, which was, for the most part, desolate – apart from the random jogger passing by here and there – Jasper began to feel a sense of calmness come over him, like a warm throw blanket on a chilly autumn day. The smells of the park - scents of pine; fresh, moist soil; and the waters of the distant pond - served as succor to the weight he felt upon his heavy shoulders, now seemingly hundreds of pounds lighter. The brilliant light from the rising Sun was triumphant to him, imagining that he had such majestic eloquence, such incontestable ascendancy, as the brightest star in our sky, Jasper's chest inflated with vigor.

As he continued to traverse the wondrousness of Central Park, passing, now, the renowned and quite acclaimed Tavern on the Green, he considered entering the establishment for some comestible. Gandering at the menu just outside the front door of the restaurant, Jasper felt the vibration of his phone, which rested in the rear pocket of his blue, faded, GAP skinny jeans; his favorite pair, incidentally, wearing them so often that the indentation of his male member protruded prominently for all who had the fortune or misfortune – dependent upon what floats one's boat, if the reader will - to bear witness. The aforementioned detail, concerning the impact his protuberance made upon the dungarees, was a fact in which he was very well aware and, parenthetically, being – in his own words, if the topic were ever inquired upon – extremely *un-endowed* (such as Jasper thought he happened to be), was not entirely proud of the confounded little thing. He reached for the phone and witnessed the name 'Greta' across the screen, along with the profile picture of a strikingly beautiful young woman of twenty-three, with jet black hair; dark brown eyes; a small, dark beauty mark that sat alongside her nose, on the left side of her face; and a strong, pronounced chin; altogether, making up a face that resembled someone of, perhaps, middle eastern heritage. He decided, reluctantly, to pick up the call; for, the last time they had spoken, it amounted to a less than pleasant conversation.

In an attempt to catch you, the reader, up to speed, as it were, this chronicler will provide a brief synopsis, if you will, on their tumultuous relationship – that of Jasper and Greta. The two made their inaugural rendezvous at a local pub in which Jasper was the consumer of libation for sale, and Greta the servant of said source of tipple. At the outset, their meeting was similar to that of every cliché romance story known to man, filled with long goggles into each other's eyes; tingling sensations traveling throughout the body when either of their hands made contact with the other, &c, &c., &c. As the relationship developed, nevertheless, it matured into a consistency equivalent to that of aged milk; which is to say, it did not prosper into the coveted degree of star crossed lover status that one reads about in the most romantic of novels. They did, incidentally, remain exceptionally good friends, keeping in touch via communications devices and meeting for a brunch here and there; such was the case with the aforementioned phone call in which Jasper now received.

"Hello?" he said, answering the call in melancholic fashion.

"Hello, gorgeous!" she replied, quite obversely in comparison with his salutation. "How's tricks?" The word 'tricks' emanating from the informal vernacular of the early twentieth century (the phrase appearing in many a classic silver screen film, starring

Humphrey Bogart, or perhaps even an episode or two of Abbot and Costello); translating to: 'how are things.' It was a thing they both uttered to each other upon commencement of their conversations… a form of intimacy, if you will. These things between lovers (even though former in status) cannot, and must not, be questioned; for, it serves – for many a twosome – as a source of comfort and security; a tale to have told the future children and grandchildren; or, perhaps, to serve as a tidbit at a cocktail party, to entertain people surrounded by the vast assortment of hors d'oeuvres… who are we to judge?

"Hey, Greta… *tricks* are well. And yourself? what's the good word?"

"Nothing much, just thinking of you and your beautiful face."

"Really? My beautiful face? I'm an absolute mess… I haven't slept in over a million and three hours." Jasper replied, looking at his face in a window's reflection of the restaurant, poking at the bags which rested below his eyes, now resembling two high end, soft leather hand bags.

"I'm sure you're as stunning as ever!" Greta rebutted.

"Lord… no. What are you up to today? Anything special?" Jasper countered, greatly wishing for the interlocution to shift in any direction but his own; but, by the same token, not entirely interested in the reply.

"Nothing at all… and you?"

"Not much. Nothing at all, really. Just taking a walk in the park now, but nothing special on the agenda."

"Perfect! Then you can meet me for lunch and some drinks later on! And don't try and wiggle your way out of it, mister! You just admitted to me that you have not a thing going on!"

"I guess you got me there." he uttered, cursing himself for not thinking of some excuse to avoid such an undesirable invitation. "Alright," he continued, "where were you thinking? Do you have something in mind? because I wouldn't have the slightest idea where to go… I've got a thousand and three things on my mind so I -"

"Ooo," she interrupted, "I know this cute little place, Pier 66 Maritime… you'd love it! They have the most amazing clams there… and a bunch of other really yummy things to nosh… Let's do that! Oh, I can just taste the freshness of their seafood, honestly to die for… really."

"Yeah, I suppose." Jasper replied with vapid enthusiasm. The thought of meeting with her drained him; a day spent with Greta never without utilizing the fullest extent of his energy reserves.

"Great! Let's say in a couple of hours? We'll meet at the place! I'll see you there, love."

He ended the call not entirely understanding why he had agreed to this meeting, knowing full well that all he could think about, all that was on his mind, was Juteuse; however, Greta had a way, a charm, about her that could not be resisted – a master of malediction was she. For as long as they were an item, she managed to manipulate her partner into staying long past the recommended expiration date of their propinquity, the way in which one might hold fast to a provision that has gone stale in a cupboard. The fact of the matter is, the decision to part ways from one another did not lay – in any way, shape, or form - with the young woman; but with our very own protagonist. By his own admission, on many occasions, he made it abundantly clear that he was, by far, the worst at maintaining relationships… it was a curse of sorts. It was why his novella, 'What Not to Do in a Relationship,' was a huge success; it was written – although a work of fiction – based on his many failed attempts at participating in romantic affairs. Greta, as a matter of fact, was well aware of his disability – his romantic ineptitude - upon their initial meeting. It wasn't too long ago, inside of the aforesaid bar in which she was employed, when they two sat together for the first time, he confessing to this particular deficiency. Truth be told, it was *her* idea to write the account that bore the name of his misfortune; so, in all fairness, there was some foreshadowing in the matter, and one oughtn't have been startled by the revelations that eventually unfolded in their lives… certainly not Lady Greta.

Jasper made his way home from the Park, forsaking his original plan to dine at Tavern on the Green – his smoked bacon, scrambled eggs, on flatbread would simply have to wait - and jumped into the shower to prepare for the engagement with his former belle, taking with him all of his toiletries, consisting of every exorbitant, name brand shampoo, conditioner, facial scrub, body scrub, foot scrub, pumice stone, and all other things that could possibly either slow the aging process or make his skin appear similar to that of a younger… much younger… man. Jasper loathed growing older; he cursed every culprit that could have had a hand in its conception… Pandora and her pestilential Box, Eve with her anathematized apple… he cursed them all. He especially wanted nothing to do with being above the age of twenty-nine, a thing that had become an inevitable reality approximately three years ago; therefore, he did whatever it took to thwart its detection. As the steaming hot beads of water ejaculated down upon his face from the shower head, he imagined he and Juteuse under a rainstorm in France, with the Eiffel Tower soaring above them in Paris, or better yet, the verdant gardens of the Chateau de Versailles, walking along its architectural opulence amongst the vibrant and aromatic wild flowers of all different shapes, sizes, and colors, like King Louis XIV and his *amant silencieux*, Francoise d'Aubigne, hands interlocked, saying nothing as the waters of heaven descended upon their soaking wet bodies, not a care in the world, just the two of them lost in their own universe, happy… complete.

After his shower, Jasper donned himself with another pair of blue, American Eagle, skinny jeans; an olive colored, fitted, v-neck t-shirt; camouflage converse sneakers, matching the shade of said shirt; and, a spritz or two of his preferred fragrance, Sauvage… a scent he thoroughly enjoyed, not so much because of the particular product itself; but, more for its poster boy, as it were, Johnny Depp, a celebrity whom he admired immensely; although, in all probability, was being paid handsomely for his image in association with the aforementioned *parfume*, most likely never so much as placing one drop of the stuff upon his epidermis. In spite of this dispiriting thought, Jasper still considered Mr. Depp a modern day James Dean and always imagined that the resemblance between the 'A lister' and himself was striking… an opinion not always readily shared with those that he made this comparison of grandeur. That being said, this author would readily confirm, if called upon to provide a testimonial in a court of law, with the *Good Book* below his left hand, that the two had *some* very distinct similarities… the seemingly permanent low brow giving the impression that everything in the entire world was a matter of great importance; the dark brown eyes that shielded any interlocutor from ever really knowing precisely what they were thinking at any given moment; the slight, subtle, smile whilst everyone else was regurgitating their lungs, laughing at something, at best, questionably funny; and, the overall mysteriousness of their demeanor, making any one who *believe*d to know the two conjecture as to who they really were, not knowing for certain what was going on in their craniums.

The restaurant was filled to capacity. Libations of all colors and sizes were well represented on the tables and in the hands of the patrons who filled the establishment. Through the sea of spirited people, Jasper espied Greta – she waving to him with, he had to admit, a most alluringly magnetic smile – who had already secured a table for the two, overlooking the waters of the Hudson River with the shores of New Jersey's Fort Lee prominently displayed on the opposing side, providing a warm, and quite cozy, atmosphere, as a pleasantly delicious breeze gently swayed from right to left, causing just a bit of Greta's hair to fall over eyes. "Hello, gorgeous!" she exclaimed, standing up from her chair, removing the rouge strands, placing them behind her ear, then greeting him with a warm embrace and kiss to the corner of his lip, feeling as though the authority of placing her lips entirely on his was no longer a viable option. "Isn't this place lovely? Don't you love it so much? Ugh, magnificent."

"It's pretty amazing, yes. Great seats." he responded, truly appreciating the ambiance of the place, he thoroughly enjoying that kind of thing… places that overlooked water, majestic scenery; it made him feel at ease, as if the world were a beautiful place after all, as opposed to the absolute train wreck it appeared to be most of the time.

"I love it… how are you, my prince?" she inquired, gazing into his eyes as though they were a pair of rare jewels, with the power to mesmerize the beholder, instantly transporting them out of the corporeal and into the astral.

"I'm… I'm good… hanging in there… can't complain." Jasper said, with much reluctance, he being the furthest from '*good*,' with nothing but Juteuse besieging his thoughts, the image of her face running rampant, on a sort of loop, inside of his brain.

Greta knew something was off, but – for the moment – chose not to press; she was well aware of his temperament and didn't want to push him away prematurely… there was the rest of the night for all of that. "Well, let's get some drinks in us, shall we? We need to loosen up those brow lines of yours! They look like a bunch of darned speed bumps going across the top of your head… excuse me, waiter…" she cried out, holding up her index finger, calling out to a server that was passing by their table. "Could we have a couple of Maker's, on the rocks, please… and the clams to start?" She ordered for the both of them, that being her way… a shining example of the *strong, independent, woman* type that never waited for a man to hold a door, push in a chair, or order her libation and comestibles.

"Of course." The waiter, eyes darting back and forth between the couple, replied. "Can I get you anything else?" His countenance implying that, perhaps, the gentleman would like to add his two cents to the order.

Jasper began, ever so slightly opening his lips, to supplement a basket of onion rings; however, Greta, not realizing his desire to augment her request, stated in a very matter of fact tone, "No, that will be all for now, thank you." To which the waiter nodded, shooting one last glance at Jasper before heading toward the bar.

"I kind of wanted onion rings." Jasper uttered, displaying an air of disgust across his mien, having, many a time, been a victim of Greta's aggressively authoritarian behavior whenever the two patronized any and every establishment together.

"Why didn't you say anything? And since when did you start liking *onion rings*? You *never* liked onion rings before… they'll make your breath stink, you know…. you don't want your *breath* to stink, *do* you? Onion rings? *really*, Jasper? Could you *be* more passive-aggressive toward me?"

"Passive-Aggress -" he started, before deciding not to complete the response to that *particular* jab, knowing full well that it would lead to conversations regarding their defunct relationship… the idea that he ordered onion rings to avoid being intimate with her was what she intended to convey, and this was an entrapment of sorts, leading down a dark, morbid, rabbit hole, as it were; so, he avoided it, addressing, instead, her immediate inquiries. "I don't even know which one of your seven hundred and three questions to answer first, jeez… for your information, I've *always* liked onion rings… you've only told me over a billion times that they make my breath stink; so, I don't understand how you could *possibly* forget that I like the deuced things. Secondly, if you'd have let me order my own damned stuff, I wouldn't have *had* to *say* anything to you about it at all… and, incidentally, I *did* try to say something… I *tried* to order them; you're just so goddamn aggressive that you didn't even realize it… just so you know."

"Well, *excuse* me for being thoughtful… I was only trying to be nice." Greta lamented, her countenance now dropping like a ton of cinderblocks.

"See, that's your problem… that was *always* your problem; you *try* too goddamn hard. You're always trying to do this, that, or the other; but, you never really know or care what the other person *actually* wants… you just do whatever *you* think everyone wants; but, you don't actually *know.*" Jasper concluded with a deep inhale and exhale before looking away from her, focusing, instead, out at the water. He felt awful, not intending for her to be hurt in any way; but, he thought, 'she forces my hand; she makes it so that I have no choice but to lash out at her.'

"I'm sorry… I didn't –"

"Just forget it, it's fine." he interrupted, still not looking in her direction, half wanting to get up and walk out. This scenario was all too familiar; it was a thing that had been played and replayed during their courtship, and he had very little desire to relive the drama that was their amorous entanglement.

"I didn't realize –"

"Greta, I said forget it… just drop the damn thing, please." Jasper insisted, breathing heavily, continuing to look out onto the water for solace, watching as the sailboats glided by, leaving behind ripples of water that gently landed upon the shore.

"It's dropped, gosh." she responded, feeling perplexed at his vexation. "What's wrong with you? You're super tense… this isn't like you."

"Nothing… nothing is wrong with me. Why does something have to be wrong with *me* just because I'd like some goddamn onion rings? Is that some sort of horrible thing? A capital crime now… to want onion rings… eh?"

"Hun, this is about more than just some stupid onion rings… I'm not dumb, you know. I know there's *something* going on with you, whether you want to tell me about it or not. I'd rather you be honest and tell me you don't want to discuss it; I'd rather that, than you sit there and think I'm a fool." Greta began to feel her emotions get the better of her, so she reflexively grabbed a glass of water, holding it up to her mouth longer than she actually needed to complete the sip, using it more so as a shield to disguise her trembling lips.

"Who said anything about you being a fool? I never –"

"Well, if you're gonna sit there and act like nothing is wrong, as if I don't know any better… as if you and I were not in a relationship for almost two years… then, yeah, you're kinda treating me like a fool. Just tell me to mind my own business… I'd honestly prefer that, Jasper, I really would." Greta affirmed, finally placing the glass of water down upon the table with just a tinge of pugnacity.

"I don't know why you feel the need to make everything such a big deal. I really don't. Everything is like a major case with you." Jasper countered, even now making no eye contact with Greta.

"Why *I* feel the need… everything a major case with *me*…

Okay, listen, this is spiraling out of control here; why don't we just start over… let's forget whatever we were just arguing about and have a nice lunch. Can we do that? Can we at least *try* to do that?"

Just then, the waiter returned with two glasses of Maker's Mark with ice. "There you are, two Maker's, on the rocks, and your clams are on the way. Would you like to order your main course now? or are you still thinking it over?" Directing his question to the young lady, having become fully aware that she was the governing body at the table.

"Actually," she began, "can you throw in an order of the onion rings, please? And, no, we're –" Greta stopped herself from declaring themselves unready to order, to check with Jasper, not willing to commit an identical *faux pas*, thereby leading to complete and utter entropy: "Are we ready to order the main course, hun?" asking with a half-smile and tilting of her head… clearly a thespian's attempt at playacting before the steward.

He leered at her, half shaking his head; but, surrendering to her charm, her witty implication, and correction of her initial oversight, replied – directing his response more to her, rather than the waiter, "No, we're not ready, yet."

"No worries, I'll just get that order of onion rings in and grab your clams." said the waiter as he, once again, scampered away.

"You didn't have to get the onion rings… that wasn't necessary." Jasper lectured, half rolling his eyes.

Greta chuckled, before responding, "Hey, you want to walk around with dragon breath, that's all you, hun… just make sure you gargle for an entire hour before you even think of putting your mouth next to me!" she chortled whilst taking a sip of her libation, intaking a piece of ice to chew upon it, leaning in to her former lover and feigning as though she were taking bites – love bites - from him.

"Oh, did you have plans on my mouth being next to yours?" he rejoined, in jest, letting out a tiny chuckle of his own, yet slightly leaning back and away from her nibbles at him, subsequently grabbing his glass to sip his whisky.

"Well, you never know… I'm kinda spontaneous like that, something that you are well aware of," was her reply, flashing a coquettish smile, offering conversation similar to that of the flirtatious interlocution they both, once upon a time, volleyed between one other.

"Yes, I'm well aware; although, I'd call it insanely aggressive, not so much spontaneity."

"Some pleasantly aggressive things could be considered a type of spontaneity, wouldn't you say?"

Perplexed at her connection between the two violently antithetical notions, Jasper ululated, "How in the hell are aggressiveness and spontaneity intertwined? In what world?"

"Well, you never know what chord it will strike. We've already witnessed that me taking the liberty of ordering our main course without consulting *Your Eminence* apparently puts you out; however, some things done spontaneously-aggressive might turn a person on… such as if I scooted on over to you right now and placed my tongue onto the back of your ear, and maybe swirled it around a little - how I know you like it - that would be the other side of the ol' coin."

"I suppose, I mean, when you put it *that* way." he replied dryly, not allowing himself to be baited by Greta's dalliance, now averting his glance away from her eyes and down at his drink; Greta, catching hold of this frigid break in eye contact, felt the disconnect within her chest, like a lamp being unplugged from an outlet. She knew something dark loomed in Jasper's heart, she suspected it to be another woman, but held no evidence to support that fact; therefore, remained mute, keeping her harrowing speculation buried, adjacent to where her heart lay enshrouded, buried under a thicket like a corpse whose soul had long departed this world.

The waiter returned with the victuals, placing them onto the table and saying, "Here are your clams and onion rings… still mulling over the main course?" he inquired, with a smile typical to that of a server when *working* their customers in the hopes of obtaining a lucrative gratuity.

Greta, turning to Jasper, answered, "Are we ready?"

"Umm, no, not yet… we'll think it over as we work on this stuff, thank you."

"Not a problem! Give me a holler when you're ready!" he said, before whisking off to tend to his other patrons.

"You knew very well we weren't ready… you didn't need to ask me. You made your point the first time, no need to create a spectacle of it, jeez." Jasper scolded, shaking his head, while sipping his drink.

"I wouldn't want to inadvertently piss you off again."

"There you go –"

"I'm kidding! Relax!" she asseverated, grabbing a fork, plucking out one of the clams, dunking it in the dipping sauce and placing it into her mouth, thereafter closing her eyes as though having reached unqualified, venereal, ecstasy. "Yum, ugh! you simply must have some of these clams, they're heavenly!"

Jasper complied, taking a one, dipping it in the aforementioned sauce, and placing it into his mouth. "It is pretty good."

"*Pretty good*? You, my darling, would walk through the Garden of Eden and have the unmitigated gall to say, 'Pretty cool flowers.' You really would. How are you even a writer… that absolutely tears me up."

"Yeah, let's compare these Long Island Sound clams to one of the most biblically sacred places in the history of the world. Let's do that… what a great idea. Jeez."

"Oh my goodness, would you lighten up? for crying out loud! Take a gulp of your Makers… take a *few* gulps, please!" she exclaimed, discharging a snicker, he responding with one of his own, realizing the preposterousness of his previous statement.

They sat in silence for a bit, eating, drinking, and enjoying the sights and sounds around them, until Greta, in a subdued tone of voice, broke in, "Jasper, can I ask you something? In all seriousness, can I ask you a question?"

"Do I have a choice? Can I say no?" he inquired, his voice

possessing a tinge of hesitation, before grabbing an onion ring, dipping it into the clam sauce, and taking a bite.

"Very funny… no, you can't… this is serious. Remember what we used to say? when we were an actual item? We'd get a *'serious'* pass… whenever we had something we really wanted to get off of our chest, something we felt was super serious, we'd allow the *'serious'* pass. It's the rules. Remember?"

"Yeah, the *serious* pass… I remember you utilizing that option incessantly; but, that was when we were together… does that apply now? Like, is that still a legally binding agreement, now that we're not a couple?"

"Yes, absolutely… that was a law that was put into effect; it supersedes and transcends titles… and very spiritual in nature… everlasting." Greta replied, in extreme earnest, wanting the jesting to cease, her eyes focused onto his in such a way as to indicate to her dialogist that this was to be received as a matter of the utmost import.

Jasper, recognizing the look, having encountered this particular scenario many times prior to this moment, acquiesced. "Jeez… fine. What is it?"

"Did you ever love me? Seriously, did you ever truly love me? If you didn't, it's okay… I just wanna know the truth. Don't be afraid to hit me with the reality of it all; I mean, if you never *truly* loved me, just say so. I can take it. I'm a big girl. And don't lie to me, you *know* I can tell when you're lying." she groaned, her eyes becoming watery at the conclusion of the inquiry.

"Is this why you dragged me out here? to ask me this crazy question? Honestly, you could've saved us the two hundred and fifty dollar restaurant bill and just asked me this crap over the phone."

"*Really*, Jasp?"

"I mean, come on… is this why you dragged me out here? You know, I actually have things I need to do. I'm not just sitting around doing nothing, you know. I'm not."

"Are you seriously so heartless? What is so wrong with me wanting to know if you ever loved me? Is that such an outrageous question to ask my once boyfriend? *Is* it? If you ever loved me… if there was ever any feelings for me inside that cold heart of yours… would it be so fucking… ugh, you made me curse… so… *freaking* difficult to tell me?"

"I don't understand why you need to know that… how does it benefit you? We've been over for ages. Why do you care to know that?"

"Ages, huh? Are you seeing somebody new? Is that it? *Are* you?"

"I don't see how —"

"You are! I knew… you couldn't even wait for… you know what? It doesn't even matter. I don't even know why I'm stressing about this. You clearly *don't* love me, you clearly *never* loved me… I have my answer." she uttered, a single tear finally cascading down her cheek.

"Oh, come on… are you serious right now? Just tell me

one thing… I'll answer your freakin' question after you tell me one thing." Jasper waited for acknowledgment to his counteroffer; but, receiving none, he continued, "Tell me why you *need* to know that. Why do you *need* to know if I ever loved you? I mean, we aren't together anymore; so, what in the hell does it matter? Does it change anything between us in any way? I personally don't think so; but, I mean, does it?"

"It *does* matter… to *me*. It matters to me because I need to know what to do with my life. I'm hanging on to… to… to I don't know what. I just want to know if I should let you go, once and for all." Greta replied, taking her cloth napkin and placing it onto the corner of her eyes to dab the subsequent tears that escaped from her ducts.

"Where is all of this coming from? What's gotten into you? We've been apart for –"

"I *know* how long we've been apart, Jasper; I certainly don't require a reminder from *you* about that. I really don't… you needn't continue repeating yourself. I sit at home like some kind of lonely old lady, counting all of the days that go by without you in my life, so I know *very* well how long we have been apart… trust me."

"Okay, so what's with all of this? Why all of a sudden, after all this time?"

"I just finished telling you why… is it too difficult for you to comprehend?"

"Yeah… actually, it is."

"You know what, Jasper? maybe this wasn't such a good idea after all. I think I should just go." Greta avowed, retrieving her purse from the back of the chair, placing the strap over head and onto her shoulders, commencing to ascend from her seat.

"Are you serious right now? You're gonna leave?" Jasper uttered, glancing around at the onlookers, who had now become aware of the tiff between the two.

"I have no reason to stay… you've made that abundantly clear."

"You're being ridiculous. You know that, don't you? You're making a whole big thing out of absolutely nothing. You realize that, right?" he remarked, continuing to scan the fellow patrons.

"And that, my love, is *your* problem. It's kind of always been your problem. You think only from your perspective. Not once do you ever see things from someone else's. You say this is 'absolutely nothing?' but to me it's everything… and you can't see that. You really can't… and, so, I'm going to make the decision, once and for all, to walk away from… from *this*; whatever *this* is. Goodbye, Jasper. I truly *do* love you; but, I have to love and respect myself a just a little more." she concluded, wiping away the trail of tears from her mien, subsequently walking away from the table toward the exit.

"Oh, come on… Greta, come on… come back… Greta –" He called out to no avail. Greta had made her exeunt from the establishment, leaving Jasper in solitude, only the peering eyes from the tables surrounding him as his companions.

The waiter, who at some point appeared from the midst of

the crowd of onlookers, placed the check onto the table, and stated, "I'm assuming you're ready for this… no rush of course."

****

The city lights shone brightly like a picture of perfection, as he crossed the Brooklyn Bridge into the boro that bore the conduit's name, on that crystalline summer evening. His heart beat relentlessly through his chest and he was singularly conscious of his breathing, which was rapid and erratic with anticipation, negative or positive - wanted or unwanted - anticipation he could not decipher. Every traffic light – as usual, according to the incessant misalignment of astrological stars and planetary systems – seemed to conspire against him; for, when he approached the confounded things, they all, instantaneously, commutated from green to red, as if to say - in scorned fashion, with arms folded across the chest, eyes closed, and looking upward like a spoiled child who refuses to do the bidding of his birth giver - 'No! I shall not allow you to proceed unmolested… you shall sit here and suffer in your deluge of sweat, in your amalgamation of anxiety and doubt.' Each red light brought forth more doubt, more angst, more heart wrenching clarity of juxtaposition; he knew exactly what needed to be done… he had not a clue what to do.

Upon exiting his car, he could hear the strumming of the bass, the pulsating drum beats of the percussionist, and the scales of a clarinet from the inside of the nightclub, across the street from where he parked his car. Drawing nearer, the azure neon sign which illuminated the name of the establishment, The Blue Room, could be seen in a brilliant blue hue, causing not only the building to glow, but the entire surrounding area to shine brightly, inviting anyone who had absolutely no interest in attending to drop whatever it was they were doing to stumble in, as it were, and take part. Jasper, stealing a quick peek at a mirror which hung just before the threshold leading into the club, conducted a quick inventory of himself to make certain he looked *the part*: his hair perfectly gelled and parted; his dark grey suit jacket free and clear of any lint, the collars of his white, button down shirt - the first three buttons of which were open, exposing his finely toned and tanned upper pectorals - were appropriately placed outside of the lapels of his jacket; his GAP skinny jeans accentuating his muscular quadriceps and hamstrings; and his black, Kenneth Cole shoes shined to perfection, the scent of Sauvage emanating from his body, the potency of which was increased by the rising of his internal temperature.

As he made his way through the enraptured crowd, he now possessed a clear view of Juteuse, she wearing a most elegant red dress which, from the rear, fell down to her ankles, and from the front a flirtatious slit – the lining of which was black in color - exposing her crème colored legs as far up as her thighs; long, black satin gloves that covered most of her arm, only her shoulders being exposed; and, black high heel shoes revealing just a hint of her toes, the nails painted in black; her wavy hair worn loose, parted in the center, streaming down upon her shoulders, accented with a red wildflower; microphone in hand, eyes closed in melodic rapture on stage, elevated above the crowd of people who swayed back and forth to the undulations of her music, some lifting their hands out to her as if she were a sort of Goddess - and they her disciples - a larger than life figure, engulfed by smoke of all different colors discharging from the fog machines surrounding the stage and swirling around her body, creating a resplendent, surreal, aura; her magnificently toned body oscillating to and fro in unison with the rhythm. He drew closer to her, the vibrations of the music sending chills throughout his body. As if driven by a kind of sixth sense, she lifted her eyes to meet his. She smiled. He smiled. Together their bodies synced as one, like a *pungi* to a snake charmer. Spellbound they two were, locked within one another's pneumatic force. Suddenly, as if abruptly awoken from a frabjous dream, he could feel, from his rear jean pocket, the buzzing of his cell phone; reaching back to retrieve it, reluctantly pulling it from its nesting place, he espied the name across the screen which read, 'Greta.'

Vignette II

It All Happens Below Heaven

(As the curtain is lifted, the only thing that can be espied by the audience is a bright, almost blinding, light. Nothing more. There are no chairs, tables, or other furniture of any kind; nor are there any windows... merely a whitewashed brightness. There is, however, a human male body, unconscious and naked, laying supine on the floor. Sonorous voices above the man begin to speak, none of whom can be seen, only heard)

Voice 1:

"This is his seventh life."

Voice 2:

"We are aware."

Voice 3:

"Do you conjecture he'll survive to completion this time?"

Voice 2:

"It is not for us to speculate on the matter, only to prepare and deliver him back *there*, that is our only task."

Voice 1:

"He won't survive to completion. He has shown an inability

to do so thus far; there is nothing to suggest that he will break his pattern."

Voice 2:

"As I indicated, such a thing is not for us to question; and, besides, we have been given instructions to allow his friend, Simon, to intervene… it may serve as the difference this time. Either way, it is not in our purview to debate the issue."

Voice 3:

"Are you not the least bit curious? I am especially riveted about this one. I have never seen such a thing as he… we have all dealt with the business of these beings and their rebirths – the evildoers who are returned as their worst nightmares, the philosophers whose souls transmigrate to the well disciplined bodies of newborn bees, ants, and such; but this one always seems hellbent on arriving at the same conclusion; whereas, the others end their paths in a variety of ways, this one is drawn to the same exact outcome all of the time, committing the final act in the very same fashion. Does that not astound you?"

Voice 2:

"He is a unique creature."

Voice 3:

"He appears determined to bring himself to termination. I wonder if we ought not just forgo the final transfer. It feels to be a wasted effort."

Voice 1:

"Perhaps he is flawed?"

Voice 2

(in a hushed and apprehensive manner)

"Are you mad?! Mind what you say! You know *He* may be listening."

Voice 1:

"What other explanation can there be? I only speak the truth."

Voice 2:

"The "*truth*" is whatever He wishes it to be… it is never for us to question. We've wasted enough time as it is, let us return to our work. Now, you two shall prepare to transfer Jonathan back down there. I will conduct the evocation reset of all those that are known to him, erasing the particulars of his demise from their memories… all will be as it was before his untimely exeunt, some of his cronies will merely think they've not spoken to him in a time, and vice-versa.

Voice 1 & 3

(Together):

"As you command."

(The lights are dimmed, the curtain closes)

***

(The curtain is lifted. The scene, now, is that of a living room, modestly sized, furnished with a singular love sofa, taupe in color, with a multicolored throw blanket draped across the top; a medium sized flat screen television (which is currently on, but muted, and displaying a random infomercial type program, resting atop a rustic, wooden tv stand; and several house plants of all shapes, colors, and sizes. Music is emanating from a small speaker that is resting on a coffee table which is placed in front of the protagonist, along with a bottle of red wine, some of it poured into a coffee cup. The character, Jonathan Cole, wearing a white, v-neck T-shirt; blue jeans; white Converse sneakers; and a black, leather jacket, sits somnambulistically on the aforementioned love sofa, gazing off into space, until the ringing of his phone breaks his trance; he picks it up. It is his life long friend, Simon)

Jonathan:

"Hello?"

Simon:

"Holy shit, you're alive! Where in the hell have you been? I tried calling you a million and thirty-seven times!"

Jonathan:

"Have you? I don't see any missed calls on my phone."

(He scrolls through his phone)

Simon:

"Yeah, I have… where ya been? Galavanting?"

Jonathan:

"I… I've been… I've been here, where else would I be?"

Simon:

"Anywhere else! God forbid, huh? I mean, you just sit there all day, doing… whatever it is you do."

Jonathan:

"I do plenty." **(He pauses)** "What in God's name am I supposed to do, anyway? What is there to do?"

Simon:

"Anything! Something! You can't just sit around all over the goddamn place, Jon, you really can't. You have to stimulate the ol' mind and spirit… you'll waste away just sitting and doing nothing with your life."

Jonathan:

"Very easy for *you* to say. You have got absolutely zero clue what it feels like."

Simon:

(Pauses)

"You're right, Jon, I don't *exactly* know what it feels like;

but I can imagine that it's a terrible… look, I'm not gonna sit here and act like I can even remotely know what you're going through. I just know you can't sit *there* all day and sulk! That's just a –"

Jonathan:

(Interrupts)

"Sulk? *Sulk?*" **(He emits a sardonic chuckle)** "As if I'm some kind of child who can't get the toy he wants at a toy store… *sulk*… ha!"

Simon:

"Come on now, Jon, you know that's not what I meant."

Jonathan:

"Oh, no? really? Tell me, Simon, what *did* you mean? Because the word 'sulk' is pretty fucking specific… it sounds pretty fucking specific to me, Simon."

Simon:

"Listen, would you *listen* to me for a second? for Christ's sake? I was just saying, for the love of God, that you need to get out more… to enjoy life and not let all of this negativity get you down. You can't let it consume you, is what I'm trying to get at. That's the point, you know?"

Jonathan:

"Yeah, yeah, yeah… I know what you mean. It's not easy, just so you are aware. It's not an easy thing for me to just go skipping through the woods, smelling the goddamn roses when I'm dealing with all of this shit, you know what I'm saying? It's really not."

(Jonathan rises and heads to the kitchen - a compact sized room which is separated from the living room only by a small island with a long, thin countertop - now standing before the refrigerator. He opens it and gazes inside, there is nothing but a half eaten apple; a tuna fish sandwich in a clear, plastic, bag; and, a can of soda. He takes the tuna fish sandwich, holds it up towards the light, as if conducting an inspection, but tosses it back into the refrigerator before returning to the sofa)

Simon:

"I know that, Jonathan. I know. I'm not saying it's an easy thing… I'm not saying that one bit. What I *am* saying… what I'm *trying* to say is, you just have to occupy your mind. You have to occupy it… to sort of *distract* it. Do things to make your brain think about any goddamn thing else other than the negative crap that it's mulling over." **(After a brief moment of silence, Jonathan not replying, Simon speaks again)** "Jonathan? you still there? Hello?"

Jonathan:

(Sips his wine before responding)

"Yeah, I'm here… for Christ's sake, I'm here."

Simon:

"Well, you didn't answer, so -"

Jonathan:

"I was drinking some wine, for the love of all that's holy and pure… can't a fella take a drink of wine? Is that some kinda violation of the rules or some crazy thing?"

Simon:

"Alright, alright, settle down… just settle down, will ya? I just want to know if you get me? *Do* you? Do you *get* me?"

Jonathan:

(After another brief hesitation)

"Have you heard from her? Has she said anything to you?"

Simon:

"To me? Why would she say anything to me?"

Jonathan:

(Reaches into his jacket pocket to pull out a pack of cigarettes, removes one, lights it, takes a long pull, holds the smoke briefly in his lungs, and slowly exhales before answering)

"I don't know… maybe because she's your goddamn sister? There's a wild idea as to why she'd say something to you. Whattaya say?"

Simon:

"Exactly *my* point. She's my sister, so she wouldn't say a freakin' thing to me… she knows very well that anything she says to me would be immediately relayed to you, my best friend, without hesitation. She wouldn't utter one single syllable to me about you or anything having to remotely do with you."

Jonathan:

(Takes another drag of his cigarette, a plume of smoke beginning to form around him)

"Do you think she'll forgive me? Do you think there's a chance?"

Simon:

"What I think… if you *really* want to know what I think… is that you should forget about that kind of stuff right now. I mean, right now – to be honest – you should be concentrating on getting yourself together… putting your pieces back."

Jonathan:

"Jesus… I knew you were gonna say that. You know that? I knew you were gonna say those *exact* fucking words. The *exact* ones!

(Takes another pull of the cigarette; flicks the ash into a makeshift ashtray - formerly a Chinese food container which, at one time, housed an order of egg foo young - on the table; rises from the sofa, walks over to the window, and peers out aimlessly)

Simon:

"Well… whattaya expect. I mean, it's the truth. It's the God honest truth. You can't be sitting around wondering about a million and thirteen other people."

Jonathan:

"I'm not worried about a million and thirteen people… I'm worried about one person. The most important person in my miserable, worthless, life."

Simon:

"You know what I meant… you know very well what in the hell I meant."

Jonathan:

(Takes one last drag of the cigarette before walking away from the window, extinguishing the butt into the makeshift ashtray, subsequently consuming the last bit of the wine)

"Yeah, I know what you meant. **(Walks over to the kitchen area, grabs another opened bottle of wine, this one white, from the corner of the countertop, removes the cork and pours the libation into the coffee mug)** "So have you seen her? Can you at least tell me that much? Have you seen her at all?"

Simon:

(Pauses in apprehension)

"I've seen her… yeah."

Jonathan:

"And?"

Simon:

"And? and what?"

Jonathan:

(Takes a gulp of the wine)

"Simon, for fuck's sake… you know exactly *what*!"

Simon:

"Jonathan -"

Jonathan:

"Simon! At least tell me how she's doing! Does she look well? Is she angry? Sad?… what? You can give me that… at *least*!"

Simon:

"Is she… Jesus, Jonathan… is she *sad*? Is she *angry*? Are you *really* asking me that? Do you actually *need* me to answer that question? I mean, are you *hoping* for an answer to that question other than the one you *know*? You *cheated* on her for the love of God… and with her best friend, of all people. The girl who she's known since she was six years old… since they were *both* six years old! I mean, honestly… you single handedly destroyed two relationships in one fell swoop! Do you *realize* that? Do you *realize* what you've done? Do you get the severity of the situation here?

Jonathan:

"I know… goddamn it… I know. I was just wondering…

I was just hoping… maybe there was a chance… maybe there was hope, you know?" (**Silence over the phone. Jonathan lights another cigarette in the interim, now pacing back and forth. He gulps the remaining contents of wine from the coffee cup and gets another serving from the bottle on the counter**) "Hello? are you still there? Is there something wrong with the line? did we get cut off?

Simon:

"I'm here… I'm here. I don't know what to say, Jonathan… what do you want me to say?"

Jonathan:

"I don't know… I don't know, either. I guess I want you to say everything is gonna be okay."

Simon:

"Jonathan -"

Jonathan:

(Interrupts)

"Relax, I know it's not. It's not gonna be okay. I know." **(Drinks more wine, takes another pull of the cigarette)** "So what do *you* think about me? Wait, let me guess… it's not important what you think. It doesn't matter what *you* think of me. Am I right? is that what you were gonna say? I'm sure it's *exactly* what you were about to say… I'm sure."

(Walks over to the sofa and takes a seat)

Simon:

"Well, it *doesn't* matter. What do you care what others think of you? What does *anyone* care about anything anyone thinks of them? People's attention spans are the worst of any creature on the face of this planet… I mean, not *literally*; but, when it comes down to it, for a so-called intelligent species, we really don't retain a whole hell of a lot of information pertaining to anyone, but ourselves… I'm mean, think about it; can you truthfully say that *you* remember – on average, in general, on a daily basis - what in the hell someone did or said? I'm talking about on any given day, when you're going about your daily routine; do you go around thinking of other people's mistakes or successes? I doubt it. I know *I* don't, that's for goddamn sure. Well? do you?

Jonathan:

"No, not really."

(At this point, Jonathan's voice is indicating signs of inebriation)

Simon:

"Exactly. So who gives a hot fuck what anyone thinks of you… *including* me.

Jonathan:

(Gets up from the sofa and heads to the wine bottle, walking unsteady, and pours)

"Damn it, fuck."

Simon:

"What is it? what?"

Jonathan:

"The wine is finished… wait, I think there's a bottle of whisky here."

(Begins to look through multiple kitchen cabinets)

Simon:

"Jesus H. Christ, I thought it was something important!"

Jonathan:

"It is! It is *extremely* important! It's all I've got to keep me sane, goddamn you." **(Continues scouring the cabinets, noisily knocking items over and is making a mess, finally espying the aforementioned half empty bottle of whisky)** "Ah! Here you are! I was beginning to panic, but, alas, here you are my sweet, my pet, my love!"

(He ends with a drunken snicker, removing the cork and taking a large quaff directly from the bottle)

Simon:

"Should you be drinking that way, Jon? Don't you think you should lay off it? whattaya say? ol' friend?

Jonathan:

"Oh you think I should lay off of it? do you?" **(Takes another huge chug of the whisky, the liquid spilling from the sides of his mouth)** "Well, I don't think I should… I don't think I should lay off at all. Whattaya think about *that*?"

(Begins to laugh uncontrollably, then transitions into a weep; at first a gentle cry, then a followed by heavier sob. He places his hands over his face, which is now filled with a deluge of tears)

Simon:

"Jon? Jon… are you… are you okay? Jon?"

Jonathan:

(Continues to cry and mumbles something indistinguishable, his hands remain over his entire face)

Simon:

"Jon… listen to me. Are you listening to me? Jon… Jon? Listen to me now, will you? Please."

Jonathan:

(Removes his hands from his face. His eyes are bloodshot and his face is completely smeared with his tears)

"I'm listening… I'm listening, for Christ's sake."

Simon:

"Just please stop drinking… please. Why don't you take a nice, hot, bath? How's about it, Jon? Take a nice, hot, bath and just soak for awhile. Can you do that for me? There's a good fella, now… just take a bath, soak, then climb into bed and sleep it off… there's an idea, huh? Whattaya say, bro? will ya do that for me? Will ya do that for your ol' pal?"

Jonathan:

"Bah! I don't wanna take a goddamn *bath*. Fuck a goddamn *bath*!"

Simon:

"Jon… Jon, where's… where's the *thing*?"

Jonathan:

"What *thing*?"

Simon:

"You know what *thing*. The *thing* you keep in your apartment… the *thing* I always tell you that I hate. Come on, Jon… where is it?"

Jonathan:

"Oh… *that* thing. You *know* where that *thing* is. It's in the same place that it always is; it's in the top drawer of my dresser… in my bedroom. Why?"

Simon:

"I wish you didn't have that thing in your apartment… especially in your condition. You shouldn't have it at all; but, especially now. I really wish -"

Jonathan:

(Interrupts)

"Maybe we'd all be better off if I just went ahead and actually used the goddamn *thing*… maybe every single person on this miserable planet would be way better off. That's what I think."

Simon:

"Don't talk like that… Jon, don't say things like that."

Jonathan:

"Well, it's true."

Simon:

"It *isn't*! It *isn't* true at all… not one single bit! Things always seem darkest before the dawn, Jon. Things always do. But it will get better. It will! I swear it will. You just have to let time heal the wounds. Give things time to settle down and you'll feel a helluva lot better. I know it doesn't seem that way; but, it's true. Time really does heal all wounds, bro… caterpillars turn into Butterflies, man… you gotta believe me. Do you trust me, Jon? If you trust me, then you gotta believe me.

Jonathan:

"Listen… I gotta go. I need to think. I need… I need… I just needa go. I needa just figure this out.”

Simon:

“Okay, Jon. Just promise me… promise me you won’t do anything stupid. I really wish you didn’t have that goddamn thing in the house. Promise me you’ll just take it easy. Just sleep it off, will ya? Promise me.”

Jonathan:

“I’ll talk to you later, Simon. We’ll talk later, okay? I gotta hang up… I don’t feel so hot right now… I’ll talk to you later.”

(Rubbing one of his temples and closing his eyes)

Simon:

“Okay, Jon, okay… we’ll talk later. I’ll call you later to check up on you, alright? Pick up the phone when I call, you hear me? Don’t make me have to go over there and knock down that door. You hear me? Say that you understand. Say it.”

Jonathan:

“Okay.”

Simon:

“No, say you understand. I want to hear the words. Say, ‘I understand.’ Say it now.”

Jonathan:

"For Christ's sake, I understand… I understand!"

Simon:

"There's a boy. Okay, get some rest. We'll talk soon, brother. Bye now."

Jonathan:

(Hangs up the phone and sits, motionless, for a moment. After some time, he begins to glance aimlessly around the room before rising to look out of the window again. He starts to whimper as he makes an about face to the counter to pour yet another drink, subsequently returning to the sofa, picking up the phone and dialing a number. Ringing can be heard before a female's voice answers)

Eleanor:

"Hello?"

Jonathan:

"It's me. Don't hang up… don't hang up. I won't keep you long. I just needed to tell you… to tell you… I just wanted to say I'm sorry."

Eleanor:

"Jonathan, I really don't -"

Jonathan:

(Interrupts)

Wait, let me just say this and I swear to you that I'll hang up and never bother you again… I swear to God, I won't. **(He waits briefly for an objection; there being none, he continues)** I realize that you will never forgive me… that what I did could never be forgiven; but you need to know… it's important for you to know… that this is the worst thing that I could have ever done. You need to know that I realize that. I'm not sitting around thinking that everything is okay… that I'm okay with it all and that I don't care what I've done to you. The fact is, I know what I've done is beyond any compassion or forgiveness of any kind, on any level. There's no excuse that could ever be given to explain my actions… none whatsoever. I just don't ever want you to think for one second that I'm sitting around, living comfortably with what I've done. **(He pauses. Eleanor does not speak. He begins again)** Listen, I know I'm the last person you want to hear from right now… ever… and I know you want nothing more than for me to disappear forever… and I get it… I completely get it. I just wanted to tell you that I am so very sorry for everything… so very sorry.

(He begins to sob uncontrollably)

Eleanor:

(Disregards Jonathan's crying)

"Jonathan, you can't call me anymore. What you did… it was disgusting. I could never have you around here. I could never have you even remotely in my life. You need to move along with your life and maybe next time – in your next relationship – you will remember what you've done and not repeat the same mistake. Remember all the chaos and destruction you've caused and don't ever do something so despicable again. **(Jonathan rises from the sofa as she continues to speak. He goes into the bedroom, opens and stares into the top drawer of his dresser. The object he is staring at cannot be seen. Eleanor continues)** Are you listening to me, Jonathan? I don't want you to call me… not one more time. Do you get that? Do you hear me? Not one more time. Do you understand me? Jonathan? Do you?"

Jonathan:

(Reaches into the drawer)

"Yes… I understand. I… I… Good bye, my love. I'm so sorry for… for everything. Thank you for being the best thing that's ever happened to me. You are an amazing person… you are so warm… so loving. I ruined it all. You gave me everything and I ruined it all. May I rot in hell for eternity. Good bye, sweet Eleanor… good bye."

Eleanor:

(The lights slowly begin to dim; Eleanor's voice can still be heard)

"Huh? what are you saying? Why are you speaking that way? What's wrong with you?" **(No answer from Jonathan. The set is almost completely black)** "Hello? Jonathan? are you still there? Hello? I'm going to hang up if you don't answer me. Hello? I mean it, I'm going to hang up the phone. Jonathan… you had better answer me."

Jonathan:

(The set is now black, nothing can be seen)

"Good bye."

(A bright flash of light and a loud, singular bang is all the audience can see and hear, followed by silence and darkness once more. The curtain closes)

Vignette III

The Librarian; from the Diary of Miss Leah Elisabeth

"We don't read and write poetry because it's cute. We read and write poetry because we are members of the human race, and the human race is filled with passion... medicine, law, business, engineering, these are noble pursuits and necessary to sustain life; but poetry, beauty, romance, love – these are what we stay alive for. To quote from Whitman: 'O me! O life!... of the questions of these recurring; of the endless trains of the faithless... of cities filled with the foolish; what good amid these, O me, O life?' Answer: that you are here – that life exists, and identity; that the powerful play goes on and you may contribute a verse."

> *-   Excerpt, Dead Poets Society*

My most cherished reader: this story is for all the young boys and girls who are in search of a role model... let it not be the one who merely scores the most points, the one whose ball gets hit the farthest, the singer whose jewelry and flashy outfit bedazzles the brightest; let it be, instead, the one who stimulates your mind, who challenges you to become a Hero in the Universe... someone who makes you better than you were yesterday, becoming another someone's shining star tomorrow.

> *-   J.L. Caban*

May —, 1964. I am twelve years old today, twelve rotations around the sun, and very sad... sad about what I am... sad about what I am not. I am too skinny. My nose has grown ahead of me like a forsaken blade of grass amongst a well manicured garden, and there are those who remind me of it. I don't like my name. I hate my name. I will not tell you my name. Please don't make me. No one ever asked me how I felt about it; I didn't choose it... I didn't give it to myself; 'tis merely a collection of letters, part the nomenclature which victimizes all that is living that which cannot name itself. Dost the butterfly wish to be a butterfly? the deer a deer? I can't talk to my mom about it, my name, because she is so happy that it was taken from the Bible. This impresses me not at all; for, the serpent also makes its appearance amongst these verses. Nay, nay, nay! I am another person; I am not the person that she thought I'd be... the person in the Book whose name that belongs, the person in her mind that she thinks is me. I am not what you see. I am another. I want to be another me... the other me... the one that I fashioned, the one that I made. I created her that day, the other day, in that magical place... all by myself. No, that's not true, that's not right. I didn't do it all by myself; I had some help. My new me, her story is thus: I found myself walking away from the playground where my siblings frolicked and played. I do not like the games that they are playing; I do not understand them... I do not wish to understand them. They are silly and don't make sense; they are a waste of time and there is not much time left; we are born, and then we die... fleeting is time, each second bringing us back from whence we came, back to where we belong. I walked and I walked, and then I walked a bit more, with no idea of where I was supposed to be; but, what does it matter to the likes of thee? Whether I am there or I am here, I am nowhere. Clearly it's somewhere. The Sun above bakes the Earth like a giant stew stove, and my long braids and bangs are sticking to me. I am not lost. I know this area like the back of my hand. I look at the stores, all so familiar. The one-eyed mongrel is resting by the door of the pet shop, I see him and he sees me; I smile. His growls don't frighten me, for they are but a metaphor that is my existence. At the corner is the sweet shoppe, I want some, but I have nothing in my pocket but nothingness. The Soundview train station is near and I can hear the incoming locomotive approaching, blowing its whistle. I look up those stairs that lead to the majestic iron horse and wish I could ascend and board that mystical conveyance. To where? Anywhere, everywhere, nowhere, where ever. My shorts are sticking to my skinny legs as I move again.

I am ready for something beautiful to happen to me. I am only twelve and have no idea how to live. I want to live because I am alive. I see and feel; but, I am filled with incessant fear and I am so confused. What is right? What is wrong? I do not know. I cross the street and see the building that houses the library. There is a bench outside and I think I might have a seat; but, I am sweating and want desperately to escape the sweltering rays of the sun. I enter the library and the coolness is embracing, inviting, and enchanting, is it this that which a departed, well attuned, Philosopher's soul feels upon its clamber toward nirvana? There is a lady I see that is approaching me. I have entered a place I shouldn't be, she will ask me to leave, assuredly. She is pretty, I think; I do not know what is pretty, only ugly. I am ugly, I know ugly very well, but I do not know pretty. She is wearing the clothes and the shoes of that era, most people who are happy wear these things… I do not. Her hair is dark and up in a bun. Her cat-eyed glasses are hanging on a silver chain around her neck. She smells of baby powder; this scent is pleasing to me… it relaxes me. Her name tag reads, 'Librarian.' I am so shy and my voice is too soft; another flaw, apparently; those who know me say I posses the vocal chords of a church mouse at silent prayer. I do not speak loudly. I tried to… *really* I did; but, it makes my brain feel drained. I do not like that.

The Librarian asks the typical question, "Can I help you find a book?" She looks at me with tender, caring eyes. I do not recognize this feeling, but my heart tells me that it is good, therefore I like it.

I am in awe of her. "I am not sure." says I. I gaze at her flawless countenance, then leer down at my scruffy, skid-mark ridden sneakers. I was afraid she would become impatient with me; Papi always does, and when this happens, the worst, most unbearable, pain soon follows, like a nightmare in which one cannot wake. I feel fear, my tiny body braces for impending agony, impending anguish, impending despair, impending desolation.

The Librarian has slender arms and painted nails in a shade of red that reminds me of a candy apple, the kind I see behind the window of the sweet shoppe. The kind I cannot have. Her demeanor is warm and inviting. 'I want to remember her,' I am thinking: this person is not wearing a scowl on her face; does not utter cruel and vile and derogatory and spiteful things to me; I do not see her silhouette through a deluge of tears; she does not have two faces. The woman reaches over and I flinch. She sees this and retracts as one would from a wounded stray ... does she recognize terror? Perhaps this sensation is known to her? Could it be that she too has wanted to sleep and never wake? She gently continues to guide me to a chair where a long, brown, table stands tall; on top of it, a plethora of colorful books of all shapes and sizes stacked together like a city skyline. I look, but do not touch; such things were surely not meant for me. She sits in another chair close to me. I shrink within myself. Am I in trouble? Will she reprimand me for ogling her literature? My gaze returns toward the floor. "What are your favorite topics to read about in a book?" she inquires, her head descending to rescue my downcast gaze, the warmth of her countenance capturing my attention, mine eyes grasp hold of hers as a dangling mountain climber in peril reaches for an extended hand, and together we ascend.

No one has ever asked me that question before; what thing do *I* like. I wonder: does she really care to know? I doubt this but, yes, I will answer her. "I love fairies and dragons, and wise and kind wizards." I am hoping she understands. '*It sounds childish,*' thinks I; but, she is smiling, my Librarian, and the entire room brightens like the rising of the Sun after the winter solstice.

Simple comfort, this smile; but, worth its weight in gold, and ever so joyous to one who is starved for understanding, to simply be a normal little girl – whatever this '*normal*' is - to enjoy her books, dolls, crayons, and coloring books, such trivial things to some, such treasures to me. Ever since I could remember, I would draw or write in my little black and white marble composition notebook, drawings and stories of far off places I wished to see, strange and interesting people with queer, fantastical faces. Strangers I wished to meet… and to become, instead of paying attention to my teachers hum drum, much to the chagrin of these educators of the mind! My Librarian tells me to wait by the table; she will bring a book and we can read it there… together. "Thank you." I said, as politely as I could, wanting very much not to turn her away.

The air in the Library was Devine. My body felt cool, I could breathe. My bangs were no longer sticking to my forehead. '*It is so delightful sitting here,*' I think. It smells of warm wood and old books and she. God surely cherished the writers and readers of the world to create such a wonderful place as this paradise, and here I sit, surrounded by this myriad of books written of far away lands and places I will never see; but, while I am reading the story, I am there… my imagination is unleashed and it is a wonderful thing, the songs of these lands that I now long to sing. It matters not whether the story is real or make believe: if it makes you contemplate the existence of life; makes you imagine the possibilities from the improbable; connects to you, mentally and spiritually, feeling - with all of your heart - the love and the warmth of the characters… then its worth is incalculable, invaluable. *'That is why God gave us a mind, to imagine';* I begin to say to myself, *'no one can stop me from envisioning, conceptualizing, dreaming, wishing, believing.'* I pondered not on Prince Charming and his gallant white steed… what dilly dallying, shilly-shallying notion, indeed. I charm myself. In my imagination I am running like a deer through the verdant lushness of the forest or up to the highest, most majestic Icelandic mountain tops… never losing my breath… then, once at the precipice, I spread my wings as wide as I can to soar through the sky like an eagle, looking down at the trifling Earth… nothing can reach me now. The foolhardy prince and his mare look up in amazement at *me*! I am so close to the Sun, Icarus waves and offers to me an exultant wink whilst wearing a simper upon his mien. I dive into an ocean to cool my skin from the center of the Solar System, the waters so clean and clear I could espy the tiny fish nibbling at my toes, the great white shark makes way for the likes of me, the dolphins lovingly embrace their queen. The feeling, all so free. God is here… I often don't believe in Him, but surely He created this place in my mind, and so I know He dwells here.

I watch My Librarian make her way back towards me. I want

to remember her face. Her light blue eyes like the clearest of skies, not a cloud in sight… they mesmerize me, they capture me, they own me, my goes heart thump, thump, thump against my chest; the shape of her aquiline nose, strong and pronounced; the lines of her jaw are like a shield maiden's from a Viking country, as if she hailed from the ancient northern regions of the Danes, where the proud Germanic peoples made their homes. A warrior princess, she is, taking up the sword to defend her territory, warding off invading tribes of men from entering what was hers, something that was not theirs to possess; her lips are full and of the color pink, like a bag of cotton candy from a circus filled with wondrous splendor; '*Don't forget her… please, don't ever forget her.*' I implore myself. She then places a book in front of me… such vivid images, so beautiful to see; it makes my soul feel like the hue of a rainbow, bursting with every pigment known to man, thereafter diving into a cauldron of the most precious of jewels; a story of fantasy, of long, long ago. "I think you will enjoy this book very much… it is one of my favorites!" reveals she, with an immaculate smile, displaying a singularly perfect set of teeth, more radiant than a shining light beaming through a diamond… such a rare jewel is my Librarian. She takes a seat beside me, leaning in, so that I may see the pictures in the book; she clears her throat, fixing her eyes upon me once more, together we prepare to transcend the world of the real. She begins to read to me, the *real* me… Miss Leah Elisabeth.

Vignette IV

An Excerpt from an Untitled Work; The Woodlawn Incident Chapter

Goddamn air smells like a million rubber tires on fire; from sunrise to sunset, it's this

incessant odor that makes your nostrils, your lungs, and your brain feel like they're going to explode. Most people walk around with masks over their faces; but, unless you got yourself one of them industrial types of masks, like the ones that have the dual filters in them, you're just wasting your damn time… pointless; all the bad air just goes right through those cloth ones. At the end of the day, I cough up about a few pounds of a kind of black soot, like if I gargled a pint of charcoal or some crazy thing like that. It ain't pretty, I'll tell you that much for sure. You'd think they'd supply us with something better; I mean, we *are* out here helping people and all… at least, that's what I think we're doing. I'm not really too sure about it, if you want to know the absolute truth. I'm not certain at all what we're really doing out here. We get to wear these pretty cool uniform shirts, though… like the ones they used to wear when there was still countries and cities and towns and crap - before everything went to shit, that is – but it ain't exactly the same as in those days… from what I remember of it, anyways. You see, I was only about ten years old when it all went south, when the world turned upside down; I remember little bits and pieces of precisely the way it all happened; although, the senior guys could probably give you a much better account of the thing. Since you're asking me, seeing as how I'm the only damned person awake right now, I guess you'll just have to be satisfied with what I can recall. We'll have to keep it down, though, because these grunts are pretty damned cranky if they don't get their fucking beauty sleep, you know what I mean?

Anyway, like I said, I was about ten when the world fell completely to pieces; so we're talking about some twenty years ago, definitely way before *your* time, rookie. It didn't all happen at once, either; not like some nuclear bomb, life-ending asteroid, or space-alien invasion – the way the movies all predicted the end of days to be. No, it wasn't anything like that at all. It was some crazy-ass virus that did the trick to wipe most of us off this crazy planet, if you can believe that. At first, they called it COVID-19; but that was only the beginning, at a time when things seemed pretty bad; but, in all actuality, it was only the start. Somewhere around the year 2021, a little over five million people dropped dead – and that absolutely made everyone go bat-shit crazy… like, everyone lost their goddamn minds and all of that crap, thinking that was the worst of it. Shit! little did they know… little did they know. I don't have to tell you, seeing as how you've traveled a pretty far distance to get here, that a helluva lot more people bit the bullet than that. Fuck, five million? Jesus, that's chump change compared to what we eventually lost. Five million… ha! What would they have felt? what would they have done? had they known what the *real* total would eventually be. Five million? Man, I don't even *know* the goddamn real total… gots to be around at least five billion. At *least* five billion.

Well, once things leveled out, people started trying to build society back up and all of that good stuff; but, it didn't go too well. By that time you already had the psychos running around, rapin', stealin', robbin' and what have you. Just a vicious bunch of degenerates, those *Brigands*; they'd cut their own mama's organs to barter at the market places, without so much as a second thought, mind you; not at all a second fuckin' thought. Gives me the chills just thinking about it… makes my damn ball hairs stand up, for cryin' out loud. Then you got those ridiculous villages or '*settlements*' – as they like to be called; man, there ain't nobody stupider than that lot, I'll tell you what. Thinking they can go about normal life, like a society or some dumb shit like that. Fucking wakadoodles. They think just because they build themselves a wall, plant themselves some vegetables, and post those useless *Sheriffs* inside of the joints, that they're safe from any of the shit out here. What a joke, honestly. They're living in a dream world, if you ask me. A goddamn fantasy land. It's only a matter of time before their little worlds come crumbling down. No, sir, it just won't do. Best fucking gig going is this one right here… being a *cop*. Nothing safer… nothing safer.

Like I said, they gave me this neat uniform shirt from the department that used to handle the old New York City area… you like it? I got a sergeant's shirt, because, well, I'm a sergeant and all. You can tell it's a sergeant's shirt because of the blue chevrons right here under the patches; you see that? I don't know about you, but there's something about this here particular uniform that does it for me; not just me, but a bunch of folks. I'll just have you know that this police uniform I'm sporting was really popular once upon a time… well, I mean, not always in a *good* way. I guess you could say they were *infamous*, the police from New York City back then. They had all kinds of shows and movies about them – that was when there *were* shows and movies. People hated them, the cops; but, they couldn't get enough of watching them on those television shows and movies and stuff. Anyway, we all wear different uniforms, us cops… you don't have to choose this one; that is, *if* you make the cut. Some of us wear uniforms from the guys and gals that patrolled the cities they used to call Los Angeles, Chicago, Miami, Boston… you name it, we got it all. The original *real* cops managed to get their hands on a whole load of the uniforms years and years ago, and we still wear them today… ain't that something?

Anyhow, I'm only telling you all of this because it seems like they're gonna let you come along with us to the home of the Brigands… in the middle of the Wasteland… today; so, I suppose you need to know a thing or two beforehand. Apparently – if they didn't already tell you – these particular bunch at the Woodlawn Settlement were being raided by those savages more than usual in the past months. They paid us, pretty handsomely I must say, to conduct some extra patrols in their area to address the situation. Seems as though just only a few days ago, a couple of the local females over there was taken – one of pretty grand import - and they blame *us*, of course, for what went down. Ain't that a goddamn hoot? They can't stand us farther than they can throw us; but, they always want our help. The more things change, the more they damn well stay the exact same; that's the very way it was before the apocalypse… the mob hated the ground the police walked upon while they're precious little worlds were unaffected; but, when all hell broke loose, sure as shit they picked up the phone (the device they used to communicate with) and screamed for help. We always find ourselves goin' over there and savin' their asses; although, a lot of those asses are attached to some pretty little bodies, I must confess! Take real good care of themselves, those dames at Woodlawn Settlement do. Well, they better! Otherwise, I don't think we'd put so much of our concern in racing over there as much, and as fast, as we always end up doing. That's for hot damn sure. At any event, I'll tell you what, I sure am glad that now, in *our* day, we get what's coming to us for our service, for our protection. Nowadays, we get what we're owed… what we *deserve*. Jeez, I'm getting ahead of myself over here, ain't I? Let me tell you about that day; the day a couple of my pinhead officers ran into some trouble with those cavemen, the Brigands, and their leader, Umberto Salazar, over at Woodlawn. The whole reason we're even dealing with the mess later on today.

It was a day like any other day; not a damned thing special about it. Sun was just as hot, the air was just as filthy… nothing out of the ordinary or unique about any of it. I was sitting right here in this very seat where I'm sitting now, shining my rifle or something like that (you gotta keep your guns clean… remember that, it's pretty goddamn important, what with all of this God forsaken dirt, dust, and soot flying all over the place and all), when Lucas comes stormin' through the gate, hollerin' and hootin' about a job he just come from with Amos. Said he was doing his patrols when some insane shit went down at Woodlawn Settlement… was hard to understand him at first, seeing as how he was out of breath and all; and I could see that his uniform shirt, the old Chicago police department shirt, was torn and burnt a little here and there, his usually tanned and quite handsome face – no homosexual innuendos intended - now pale and haggard looking, his normally well groomed hair lookin' like a tornado passed through it; so, I knew something pretty intense must've ensued and shit. "We… got… problems! Real… problems…" Lucas said, out of breath, gasping for each word, like a fish when taken out of the water. I can see by the look on your face that you're wondering what a fish is… well, I either sit here all day explaining the way things was, or I get on with my story about that day; so, you better decide which… I ain't hangin' here all day givin' you lessons about the way the world was *and* catching you up about this here story before we get movin'. Let's just stick with the shit that happened to Lucas and Amos, shall we?

"Slow down, slow down, Lucas... can't understand a lick of what you just said. Take a goddamn breath why don't ya. Take a seat, here, you two." I said, getting up from my chair and leading them both to sit down.

He took a few breaths, collected himself as much as he could, then started again, "We was over by the Woodlawn Settlements... just doing our patrols, you know? Checking out the chics coming in and out of the gates and all... we was only doing that, nothing else, just about to head back here, when all of a sudden shots rang out... about four or five... we took cover behind the car, behind the engine block like we's supposed to and all, and tried to get a look at who was doin' the shooting..."

"Who?" I interrupted. "Who was doing the shootin'?"

"I'm gettin' to that!" he replied, still somewhat out of breath. "Well, they stopped shootin' at some point and sort of called out to us.

"Hey pigs!" shouted one of the Brigands. "Little pigs? oh, little pigs? Where for art thou, little pigs?"

"We stayed behind that cover and answered back, 'that you? Umberto? You got some goddamn set of balls takin' shots at the cops... a real set.' That's what we said."

"Aww, I wasn't trying to kill ya'll..." Umberto answered in that raspy voice of his, just picturing the brown teeth and garlicky odor comin' out his mouth. "… you *know* if I wanted to kill you porkers, you'd a been bacon by now!" he heckled, followed by the mating sounds of the aforementioned animal.

**

… plenty of those little beasts (pigs) around, so I don't have to explain to you what *that* is! I shall continue with Lucas' account of things …

**

"What do you want? Umberto!" we asked, our guns ready to return fire at the slightest sign of aggression, even though, like I told you, Boss, from what I could get sight of – and from what I confirmed later on - we was outnumbered by about a dozen of them greasy, dirty, bastards.

"Nothin' from *you*, copper!" Umberto yelled back. "We just want what's ours from inside those pretty little walls in there… a certain little maiden who belongs to us! Seems she escaped our confines and found occasion to bring herself to Woodlawn over here and marry the Governor. So she'll be comin' back with us!" he concluded, violently clearing his throat, reaching deep within his chest, thereafter regurgitating all of the phlegm and mucus stored within, finally heaving the tawny colored liquid from his mouth, launching it about a couple of feet in front of him.

"Me and Amos gave each other a look, like we knew we was no match for the amount of Brigands there, so nothing was really stopping them from moseying on out of the settlement, simply takin' what they came for and all… and we figured we'd just pick up the pieces later… I just hate knowin' that that son of a bitch thinks he got the better of us and shit, you know?"

"What'd ya do, Lucas?" I asked, my heart sort of dropping, kind of already knowing the answer to my question.

"Well, we… we sort of… well, we took a few shots at those mother fuckers. You know?" Lucas replied apprehensively, before finding a sort of courage, confidently affirming, "I mean, we can't go lettin' these bastards take shots at us now, can we? I mean, word gets out that you can go shootin' cops again, without death bein' a retaliatory option… well, imagine that!"

His mouth was moving, but I barely heard a thing; I was too damn busy thinking about the retribution coming our way. It was only after some brief hesitation that it dawned on me to ask, "And the car? Where is the car?"

"The car?" he responded, with great reluctance in his voice, as if only asking the question to bide his time in having to providing an actual answer. "Well, like I said, I didn't want them thinking we was gonna stand for getting' shot at -"

"Yeah, I got that little tidbit;" I interjected. "… what happened to the car?"

His eyes darted over to Amos, who had, up until now, been quiet as a field mouse that has had its feet cut off and vocal cords removed. Amos, the smaller of the two, usually deferred to his partner in moments such as these. He was about three or four inches minus the height of Lucas, with a balding head and full beard, some muscle tone; but not quite as stout as Lucas. His uniform shirt flaunted the remnants of the Los Angeles police department, also possessing markings of some sort of bout with an inferno. He cleared his throat a few times before answering, "It sort of got blowed up."

From sheer bewilderment, I remained mute for a few seconds, my eyes unable to even so much as manage a singular wink. "How exactly…" I finally uttered, "did it get, '*sort of blowed up*?' Can you please explain that to me?"

Amos' eyes, now in turn, fell upon those of Lucas, pleading for succor, not wanting to bear the responsibility for explaining their dereliction, to which Lucas obliged, "Boss, it seems they went and got themselves a couple of rocket launchers since our last soirée over at the Mount Pleasant Settlement."

"Rocket launchers?" I exclaimed in disbelief. "Where in the hell did the devil-loving Brigands get rocket launchers? and without us hearing a syllable about it from anywhere?"

"Boss, I don't know;" began Amos, "no one at Woodlawn seems to know anything about -"

"No one at *Woodlawn* seems to know? What in the fuck do I care about what *Woodlawn* knows or not knows?! The whole purpose of us doing patrols around these settlements is to know what we need to know, *before* anyone else does, Amos! Woodlawn, Mount Pleasant, Valhalla… none of them ain't supposed to know anything that *we* don't already know, get me?!"

"Yes, sir… I know sir…" Amos stammered, offering yet another visual cry for help by leering at Lucas for relief.

Seeing this inaudible plea for assistance, Lucas cut in, "Boss, we do our patrols everyday, like we're supposed to -"

"Oh, like you're supposed to, eh?" I interrupted again. "So being inside of the gates of Woodlawn is part of *'like you're supposed to?'*

The pair looked at one another as if to say, 'how in the world did he know that we were *inside* of the gates of Woodlawn?' Before it was concluded that I, their boss, Sergeant Jackson Coleman, was some kind of all knowing, all seeing, sorcerer, I quelled their outlandish conjectures, putting an end to their stupefied facial expressions, and revealed, "those handmade goddamn bracelets around your fucking wrists, you nitwits… the green, white and gold braided bracelets, the colors of that settlement… you didn't leave wearing them this morning; so, you clearly paid a visit inside while you were out there, *'doing your patrols like you're supposed to.'*

Satisfied that I wasn't some kind of warlock, who'd end up hurling a goddamn spell at them, transforming their dumb asses into something more useful, like a couple of bottles of gasoline or maybe even two raccoon sandwiches, Amos decided to provide me with just a little more fuel for the fire… no pun intended, "Er, uh, and Boss?"

"Dear Lord, what? What else could you *possibly* have to tell me?"

"They sort of took someone from Woodlawn;" he continued with a look on his face that made my insides ball up into knots, "someone kind of important. And the settlement says they already paid us for the patrol, so they kind of expect us to deal with her kidnapping and stuff."

"Sort of *took* someone?" I asked, "*Kidnapping*, for Christ's sake?

"Y-ye-yes…" spluttered Amos, "… the truth is… the truth… well, when they launched that goddamn thing at us, we… I guess… we kind of high tailed it outta there, you know what I mean, Sarge? I mean, we had nothing to retaliate with, and all of that shit; so I guess we kinda left the settlement unmanned at that point. I'm guessin' that's when the Brigands went in there and took the governor's wife, Alicia Pennington, and a few of her handmaidens. They -"

"Christ o'mighty! Alicia Pennington? the Governor's wife?" I broke in. "Wait, wait, wait… just wait a minute!" I lamented, realizing a very vital piece of information being missing. "If you – as you so eloquently put it – '*high tailed it out of there,*' after the rocket launching thing, how in the hell do you know what happened afterwards? How do you know about this… this kidnapping business?" The eyes of the two met yet again, aware of the blunder just committed; they hadn't figured on how to explain knowing the happenings of what transpired *after* the attack on their police vehicle, seeing as how, before they admitted to having fled the scene of the crime, they previously bold face lied about that particular portion of the story. There being no response, I asked once again; giving them an opportunity to think on it a few seconds, to giving me a goddamn answer before I threw them in the hole… the 'hole' being our little holding cell for the cops when they commit minor infractions – death being reserved for the more serious of transgressions… you know, like, stealing funds from our vaults, or taking side gigs from settlements, fattening their own pockets, instead of submitting the appropriations to said vaults.

Lucas, finally finding a voice, stated, "Well, boss, we... I suppose, before we fled for our lives... before gettin' the hell outta there, we... we... we hid behind that big ol' oak tree that sits a few feet away from the entrance of the place. That gigantic one, you know? The one that's a couple of hundred years old... the pretty one with all of those -"

"Yeah, I know the goddamn tree, Lucas! Thanks for the descriptive insight! Jesus H."

"Right." he continued. "So, yeah, I guess we saw everything from there... from behind the oak."

"What *exactly* did you see?" I asked, losing my patience; talking to him at this point was like pulling teeth, for crying out loud.

"That's when we saw them dragging Mrs. Pennington out by that fiery red hair of hers." Lucas continued. "The governor and a few of his sheriffs tried to fight off Umberto and the rest of the Brigands, but they was no match, of course... I mean, that's what they give *us* money for... ain't that right, Sarge!" he finished with a bestial laugh, like the cackle of a hyena, at the irony of his statement.

"You are entirely too inept for words, Lucas." I said, not finding the humor in his satirical comment. I went ahead and sent both of them to the goddamn hole, afterwards swinging on over to the lieutenant's quarters to tell him *what was what* about all of this mess.

The Lieutenant, Bigamy Stokes, who you'll be seeing later

on, before we get on our way to the Wasteland, is of the insanely burly variety – every muscle in the entirety of his six foot one frame is exceptionally well represented. He chooses to don the shirt of the old Dallas police department, it being an extra, extra large in size, but ends up looking like a child's small, due to his barbarically chiseled physique. I entered his chambers and gave him the low down of what Lucas and Amos reported to me. Needless to say, he was a touch *put out* by the whole thing. "So let me get this straight…" he began, in his usual stentorian tone of voice, "… these two wastes of life, instead of doing their patrols – the patrols we were already paid in full for – they decide to go on in and make a day of it… they go strolling on in, inside of the walls, sampling the food, shopping for knickknacks, foolin' with the women… and in the meanwhile, the Brigands get close enough to the gates to pose a threat to the settlement, shoot at our cops, annihilate one of our vehicles, and run off with the governor's wife… also known as Umberto's former concubine… and a few of her aides. All the while, these two worthless bastards watch it all, somewhere behind the bushes."

"An oak tree… the big one… just outside the gates… that's what they hid behind." I begrudgingly corrected, wishing immediately that I hadn't, receiving the look of absolute death from Stokes.

"Listen, Sergeant, we can't let things like this go uncorrected, you get me? The whole idea of the police, the whole reason people give us shit loads of money, is that we provide a service. And this service can not ever be disrupted or put into question, because the minute our little flocks of sheep realize that we ain't worth puttin' out for, that's the day we stop eatin' and livin' in comfort; and, a topic which is slightly more of a pertinent matter, the goddamn Brigands just may get the idea that they can roll all over us whenever they want. That's kind of a huge problem, see what I'm gettin' at?

"Yes, sir… I totally get it, sir."

"Listen here, we're gonna round up all three of our platoons, forthwith… all hands on deck here, you get me?… and then we're gonna head into the Wasteland, get that pretty little Mrs. Alicia Pennington back to her husband, along with her little minions, and hand the governor the head of Umberto Salazar as an apology for our failure to provide appropriate security to that beautiful little oasis of his, the Woodlawn Settlement. That's what we're gonna do. Am I clear on that, Sergeant Coleman?"

"Crystal, Lieutenant."

"Good." he said, followed by a brief pause, looking down at some sheets of paper, before glancing back up at me, and finishing, "That is all."

Well, that's pretty much the whole of it… that's pretty much everything that happened right before you arrived. I guess it's just your luck that all of this is going down on your first day on the job and all. Anyway, I can hear stirring in the barracks, the men will be up and about soon enough, and you'll get to meet them all before we get on our way. We had better start heading on over to the mess hall to grab some chow… there's no tellin' when we're gonna have another chance for a sit down meal. If the shit hits the fan out there in the Wasteland, food is gonna be the last thing on our minds, you know what I mean?

J.L. Caban, born Jose Luis Caban IV, is a Puerto Rican American writer who was born at Mount Sinai Hospital in Manhattan, New York, on October 18, 1972 to his father, Jose 'Joe' Luis Caban III, and mother, Lisa Calladine, raised in the borough of the Bronx. In his youth, J.L. Caban attended public schools in the Bronx, New York, which included the Walt Disney School (P.S. 160), Dr. Daniel Hale Williams School (I.S. 180), and Harry S. Truman High School, where he became an honor's English student, in addition to joining the Roman-Greco wrestling team, as well as the baseball team; both of which saw much success during the years of his participation. J.L. then enrolled at Lehman College, where he not only became a peer counselor, but also a disc jockey for his college radio station (not to mention successfully DJ'ing at various trendy nightclubs throughout New York City on the weekends), in addition to becoming a Brother of Kappa Alpha Psi Fraternity, Incorporated, all before earning both a Bachelor of Arts Degree in Psychology, as well as a Master of Science in Education. Shortly thereafter, he enrolled in an English course at Columbia University, wherein he earned a creative writing certificate; something he is proud to say that is shared in common with his literary icon, J.D. Salinger. He subsequently went on to teach English at an inner city school in the South Bronx before joining the New York City Police Department, ultimately achieving the rank of Sergeant. From a very young age, Caban has always had an interest in writing, having penned a multitude of stories; several of which appearing in his previous novellas, entitled 'Moving On' and 'Butterflies in Production; Five Short Stories,' both publications, incidentally, going on to achieve Best Seller status. J.L. Caban has four children whose names are Ashley Angelique, Jesiah Manuel, Jose 'Joey' Luis (V), and Julian Lincoln; and, is married to the love of his life, Cecilia.

Mr. Caban would, once again, like to pay tribute to the team at Atlas Elite Publishing Partners/ebook Marketing Solutions for all that they painstakingly do.

Michael Beas, Publisher

Dar Dowling, CMO

Tom Colleran, Formatter